THE POLITICIZED MUSE

THE POLITICIZED MUSE

MUSIC FOR MEDICI FESTIVALS, 1512–1537

Anthony M. Cummings

PRINCETON UNIVERSITY PRESS

PRINCETON, NEW JERSEY

Library of Congress Cataloging-in-Publication Data
Cummings, Anthony M.
The politicized muse : Music for Medici festivals, 1512–1537 /
Anthony M. Cummings.
p.   cm. — (Princeton essays on the arts)
Includes bibliographical references and index.
ISBN 0-691-09142-0
1. Music—Italy—Florence—16th century—History and
criticism.   2. Music and state—Italy—Florence.
3. Festivals—Italy—Florence—History—16th entury.
4. Florence (Italy)—History—1421–1737.   5. Arts,
Italian—Italy—Florence.   6. Arts, Renaissance—Italy—
Florence.   7. Art and state—Italy—Florence.
8. Medici, House of.   I. Title.   II. Series.
ML290.8.F6C85   1992
780'.945'5109031—dc20   91-35069

This book has been composed in Linotron Galliard

Princeton University Press books are printed on
acid-free paper, and meet the guidelines for permanence
and durability of the Committee on Production
Guidelines for Book Longevity of the
Council on Library Resources

Printed in the United States of America

2   4   6   8   10   9   7   5   3   1

For my parents

CONTENTS

CONTENTS

ILLUSTRATIONS

❀

SOURCES

Figure 24. Reproduced from AnnaMaria Testaverde Matteini, "La decorazione festiva e l'itinerario di 'rifondazione' della città negli ingressi trionfali a Firenze tra XV e XVI secoli," in *Mitteilungen des Kunsthistorischen Institutes in Florenz* 32 (1988): 324–52, especially p. 340. Copy in the Princeton University Libraries

Figure 27. Victoria and Albert Museum, London

Figure 29. Photographie Giraudon, Paris, and Bibliothèque Méjanes, Aix-en-Provence

Figure 41. By Permission of the British Library, London

Figure 42. Bibliothèque nationale, Paris

THIS BOOK concerns the use of works of art, literature, and music for political purposes in Florence and other Italian cities in the years between the restoration of the Medici to Florence in 1512 and the election of Cosimo I de' Medici in 1537. When I began the research on which it is based, however, I was not intending to write a book. Rather, the research was to be part of a larger project in which I have been engaged for some time, a study of the Medici as music patrons in the late fifteenth and early sixteenth centuries. My intention was to read systematically through the principal contemporary Florentine "narratives," published and unpublished, in an effort to uncover references that might illuminate the musical patronage practices and experiences of the Medici. I found that the narrative accounts—histories, chronicles, family memoirs, and diaries—were unexpectedly rich sources of information about the musical life of the period; I found further—and this finding I might have anticipated—that the references were almost all of a particular type, that they were to the use of music on festive civic occasions. The narratives' authors would have been less likely for two reasons to record musical performances of other types that took place in Medici circles: many of the authors were private citizens who enjoyed no particular relationship to the Medici and would not have been witness, therefore, to performances that occurred in the privacy of Palazzo Medici; moreover, performances that were not out of ordinary, that formed part of the rituals and ceremonies, religious or secular, that were familiar to the authors, would have been less likely to occasion comment. The events they record, therefore, were in some sense exceptional.

I found, accordingly, that the narratives afforded a reconstruction of a series of splendid public festivals that occurred during the period in question, a period that witnessed the end of the Florentine republic and the beginnings of the Medici principate. The transition from republic to duchy, the acceptance of aristocratic rule by the Florentines, who were proud of their republican tradition and considered themselves the successors of the ancient Athenians and republican Romans, are the subjects of J. R. Hale's excellent book *Florence and the Medici: The Pattern of Control* (London, 1977). The potential interest of these festivals to political historians is that they are an expression of the political transformation that Florence was undergoing and of the changing status of the Medici family, since the texts of the explanatory songs that are preserved employ conceits and images documenting that transformation; indeed, the festivals were perhaps as much agents of the transformation as reflections of it, coded artistic expressions of a program of political consolidation. The potential interest to music historians is that they furnish evidence about some of the contexts in which performances of music figured in early modern Europe—a subject about which we are still surprisingly ill-informed.

As I continued to gather references from the narratives, however, I discovered that many of the texts were known, if not to music historians especially (for I know of little evidence that this material is very well known among my fellow musicologists), at least to those in other disciplines, especially art historians. It seemed to me, therefore, that the time was right for an attempt at a synthesis that assembled the known primary references (those drawn not only from contemporary narratives but also from primary materials of other types), incorporated the results of scholarship, and endeavored to fashion a coherent whole out of the material currently available. It is to that attempt at a synthesis that the following pages are devoted.

I WELCOME the opportunity to acknowledge the many debts incurred during the research for and writing of this book. I am grateful, first of all, to the Commissione per gli Scambi Culturali fra l'Italia e gli Stati Uniti for naming me a Fulbright Scholar at the University of Florence for the academic year 1988–89, and especially to Dott. Carlo Chiarenza, Executive Director of the Commissione, and Dott. Luigi Filadoro, a member of its staff, for many kindnesses extended during that year. I am also grateful to the Academic Advisory Committee at Villa I Tatti, the Harvard University Center for Italian Renaissance Studies in Florence, for naming me National Endowment for the Humanities and Robert Lehman Foundation Fellow at I Tatti for the academic year 1989–90. I am especially grateful to I Tatti's Director, Professor Walter Kaiser, and to the members of his excellent staff, for reasons others who have had the privilege of being associated with I Tatti will understand readily. I am grateful to the staff of the Kunsthistorisches Institut in Florence for permitting me to use their excellent collections, and, for the same reason, to the staffs of the Archivio di Stato and Biblioteche Medicea-Laurenziana, Nazionale Centrale, and Riccardiana. For many acts of kindness and friendship that made my two years in Florence so very fulfilling personally as well as profitably professionally, I am very grateful to Amedeo and Mary Ann Pinto, Sabine Eiche, Dott. Renato Pasta of the Department of History at the University of Florence, Dott.ssa Orsola Gori of the Archivio di Stato, Dott. Valerio Pacini of I Tatti, and Dott.ssa Roberta d'Avenia. Dr. Eiche offered invaluable assistance in obtaining the photographic material; without her help, the book's illustration program would simply not be what it is. (For assistance with the photographic material, I am grateful as well to John Blazejewski of the Index of Christian Art at Princeton University.) Dott. Pacini and Dott. Maurizio Gavioli, also of I Tatti, discussed my work with me on several occasions and offered helpful suggestions, as did Professors Janet Cox-Rearick of the Department of Art History at Hunter College of the City University of New York, Patricia Rubin of the Courtauld Institute of Art at the University of London, Christine Sperling of the Department of Art History at Bloomsburg University of Pennsylvania, Daniel Bornstein of the Department of History at Texas A&M University, Julian Kliemann of I Tatti, and Wolfger Bulst of the Kunsthistorisches Institut. Dott.ssa Stefania Goni and Dott.ssa Elisa Terrazzi, similarly, offered useful suggestions, especially concerning my transcriptions and translations of the Italian texts. Stephen Wheeler, formerly of the Department of Classics at Princeton, and Keith Falconer, formerly of the Department of Music at Princeton, assisted with the translations of the Latin texts; I am grateful to them both. My good friend Paolo Cucchi, Dean of the College and Professor of French and Italian at Drew University, was so very gracious as to read the entire manuscript with particular attention to my translations of the Italian texts and suggest several improvements. With characteristic generosity and interest, Margaret Haines, Editor of *Rivista d'Arte* and Research Associate at I Tatti, reviewed my transcription of Bartolomeo Cerretani's "Sommario e ristretto cavato dalla historia . . . in dialogo delle cose di Firenze" and offered a number of improvements. I am grateful to Dott. Gino Corti, for reasons that many, many others will understand immediately. Eve Borsook, Research Associate at I Tatti, offered valuable advice concerning my research when the project was in its beginning stages, as did Professor Felix Gilbert of the Institute for Advanced Study in Princeton; I regret that he did not live to see this book. Christine Smith, then Visiting Scholar at I Tatti, read a preliminary draft of the manuscript and offered a number of stimulating observations. Similarly, Kenneth Levy, Professor of Music at Princeton, read a preliminary version of the manuscript and discussed the material with me; but my debt to him is greater than my reference here would suggest: he was helpful and encouraging in many ways, and I am very glad indeed to have this opportunity to express my gratitude to him. Theodore Ziolkowski, Professor of Germanic Languages and Literatures and Dean of the Graduate School at Princeton, suggested the title of the book, for which I am grateful to him. J. R. Hale, Professor Emeritus of Italian History at University College of the University of London, and Dott. Nino Pirrotta, Professor Emeritus of Music at Harvard University and the University of Rome, read the final manuscript and offered many, many useful suggestions. I cannot imagine having had more helpful readers, and I am most appreciative of their assistance; indeed, anyone familiar with their distinguished scholarship will recognize instantly the indebtedness of my work to theirs. Sheryl Reiss, the author of a Princeton Ph.D. dissertation on Giulio de' Medici's art patronage ("Cardinal Giulio de' Medici as a Patron of Art, 1515–1523"), was always willing to discuss Medici patronage of the arts and was unfailingly generous with her material; I am very grateful to her. None of those who read drafts of the manuscript or discussed my research with me is in any way to be held responsible for errors of fact or interpretation that remain; they are solely my own responsibility. I am grateful to Lauren Oppenheim and Elizabeth Powers of Princeton University Press for their interest in my manuscript and for seeing it through to publication. William G. Bowen and Neil L. Rudenstine, who have twice been my colleagues and supervisors, first as President and Provost of Princeton, then as President and Executive Vice President of the Andrew W. Mellon Foundation, have always been understanding and helpful, in all ways; I welcome the opportunity to acknowledge how very grateful I am to them both.

MY DEDICATION acknowledges in a small way a debt that can never be paid in full; it is offered as a token of my affection.

PARTIAL GENEALOGY OF THE
MEDICI FAMILY

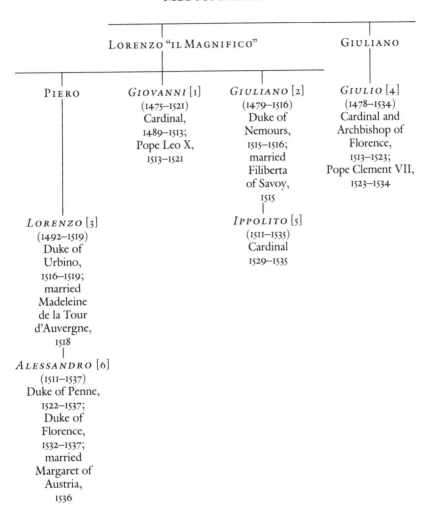

LORENZO "IL MAGNIFICO" GIULIANO

PIERO

GIOVANNI [1]
(1475–1521)
Cardinal,
1489–1513;
Pope Leo X,
1513–1521

GIULIANO [2]
(1479–1516)
Duke of
Nemours,
1515–1516;
married
Filiberta
of Savoy,
1515

GIULIO [4]
(1478–1534)
Cardinal and
Archbishop of
Florence,
1513–1523;
Pope Clement VII,
1523–1534

LORENZO [3]
(1492–1519)
Duke of
Urbino,
1516–1519;
married
Madeleine
de la Tour
d'Auvergne,
1518

IPPOLITO [5]
(1511–1535)
Cardinal
1529–1535

ALESSANDRO [6]
(1511–1537)
Duke of Penne,
1522–1537;
Duke of
Florence,
1532–1537;
married
Margaret of
Austria,
1536

The bracketed numbers indicate the order in which the members of the Medici family succeeded one another as the family's principal representative in Florence in the years 1512–37.

TO THE READER

*Concerning the Translations and
Scholarly Apparatus*

MY OBJECTIVE in translating the texts of the documents and narrative accounts was to convey the meaning of the original in idiomatic English rather than produce an exact word-for-word rendering of the Italian or Latin. Some of the translations might therefore be thought to be rather free, and for that reason I have in all instances provided the texts in the original languages so that the relationship of the translation to the original can be determined immediately. Having said that, however, I would like to add that, although I cannot dictate to my readers how they read this book, I might express the hope that they do so once *without* referring to the notes, "usually considered . . . the sine qua non of historical scholarship," in Eric Cochrane's words. The notes were placed at the end of the book rather than at the foot of each page in order to facilitate the kind of reading I have suggested, in order that the flow of the narrative in the main text not be interrupted. Indeed, at one point I considered proposing to Princeton University Press that the notes be bound separately and made available only to those who specifically requested them. The main text, I hope, is self-contained and intelligible without reference to the scholarly apparatus, which is included here so that substantiation for any of the assertions I make in the text will be readily available to anyone who wishes to have it.

THE POLITICIZED MUSE

SOME ASPECTS OF
METHODOLOGY

ON WHAT kinds of civic occasions might Florentines of the early six-teenth century have heard music? And what kinds of music might they have heard? Some answers to such questions are to be found in a group of sources that Felix Gilbert called "narrative accounts," and in a concise and authoritative statement of the historiographic assumptions then un-derlying Florentine Renaissance studies, he wrote of them as follows: "The principle of modern historical scholarship—that insofar as possible history should be based on documentary sources rather than on narrative accounts—has been only slowly and gradually applied to the history of Florentine institutions. The reasons," he continued, "are manifold":

> Since the fifteenth century, . . . Florentine citizens with a literary bent have regarded the writing of the history of their city as a task of primary importance. . . . There are a number of histories written in the sixteenth century by men who were close to, or even contem-poraneous with, the events they described. Although the authors . . . held different political views . . . all of them had an intimate knowl-edge of events, institutions and personalities. Because these accounts contain so much detailed and authentic information, scholars felt it was unnecessary to turn to documentary sources as the basis for their work. Moreover, since the Italian Renaissance was usually treated as a cultural phenomenon rather than as a period of political change, scholars found the political documents in the archives of less interest than the various writings which revealed the personalities of Renais-sance figures. Writings of this sort had been preserved in Florence, and toward the end of the nineteenth century they were studied and published. Printed sources—the narrative accounts and the diaries of contemporaries—offered historians sufficient material for writing a full description of Florentine events.

"But these sources," Gilbert continued, "did not provide much infor-mation about political institutions and their development," for reasons he detailed: "Contemporary historians and diarists were inclined to assume that the reader would be familiar with the institutional framework; moreover, the authors themselves were less interested in institutions than in men and events. Since the Second World War, however, an increasing number of studies based on archival materials have appeared."[1]

The kinds of sources one utilizes correspond to the kinds of scholarly objectives one has, Gilbert has argued, and especially relevant to the history of Florentine institutions are the documentary materials he described. A different set of questions assumes that different types of sources will be utilized and perhaps that a different methodology will be adopted. Appropriate to historians' interest in recapturing the sentiments of historic men and women are the "narrative" materials that convey information of a different sort, and historians have turned (or returned) accordingly to the kinds of sources that Christiane Klapisch-Zuber, for example, has utilized so very effectively in such studies as "Childhood in Tuscany at the Beginning of the Fifteenth Century," "Holy Dolls: Play and Piety in Florence in the Quattrocento," "Kin, Friends, and Neighbors: The Urban Territory of a Merchant Family in 1400," and "Zacharias, or the Ousted Father: Nuptial Rites in Tuscany between Giotto and the Council of Trent." On the basis of the information yielded by such materials as the diaries and memoirs of contemporaries (what Italians call *ricordanze*), Klapisch-Zuber has advanced and enriched our understanding of the private lives of Italians of the early-modern period.[2]

One can chart a roughly similar progression in music historiography. Utilizing precisely the kinds of documentary sources Gilbert alluded to, musicologists, too, have produced a series of exceptional studies over the past quarter-century that have provided the indispensable basis for our understanding of fifteenth- and sixteenth-century musical life in various centers of patronage. Above all, they have provided answers to questions of the sort Gilbert described, questions of an institutional nature—about the composition of musical establishments, who their members were and how they were provided for, and the ways in which the composition of the establishments changed over time.

For music historians, the "narrative" sources, similarly, possess virtues and limitations and are accordingly more appropriate to some kinds of scholarly objectives than to others. In my view, their principal virtue is the fundamental one identified in my opening remarks: although the Florentine narratives of the sixteenth century rarely provide answers to questions of an institutional nature, they frequently provide answers to questions about the contexts in which musical performances figured in early modern Florence, questions of crucial importance on which the archival sources, ironically, are often silent.

It is not that archival sources never provide answers to such questions; one has only to cite the example of Anthony Newcomb's excellent book on the madrigal at Ferrara in the late sixteenth century (and there are other examples one could cite). In my view, the unusual success of New-comb's book is in part a function of its organization: Newcomb chose to relegate material pertaining to the Ferrarese musical establishment to a series of appendixes; he based his "narrative" instead on texts that refer to actual musical performances at the Ferrarese court, and although few if any of these references are so detailed that they permit us to associate a surviving work with one of the performances, the references are profiled so that a picture emerges of musical practices in Ferrara, which then serves Newcomb in classifying and analyzing pieces found in the musical sources.[3]

Nonetheless, documentary materials less often convey information about musical performances, at least relative to the preponderance of other kinds of information they contain. Of some fifty published archival references from the *fondo* Florence, Archivio di Stato, Mediceo avanti il principato, and related *fondi*, references that document the private patronage practices of the Medici in the years between 1512 and 1537, fewer than five record actual performances of music.[4]

The issue of partisanship that Gilbert identified—an apparent limitation of the narratives—may in fact be construed as yet another virtue. Although the early cinquecento historians wrote accurately enough, they were indeed partisan, "republican almost to a man," in J. R. Hale's words.[5] If a music historian's primary purpose in utilizing the narrative sources is simply to reconstruct events and not advance interpretations of them based on the sentiments expressed in the sources, the author's partisanship in that case diminishes in importance; and it is often enough the case that several narrative sources that record the same event report on it identically or similarly, so that one's confidence in the accuracy of the reports is increased. However, in my view, the narrative sources would be "underutilized" by music historians if read solely in this way. In this context their importance is precisely that they convey some sense of the sentiments of their authors. As we shall see, music was an important element of virtually all of the principal festive occasions in Florence between 1512 and 1537, and witnesses' responses to the music, as to the works of art and, indeed, to the very political events that occasioned the festivities in the first instance, communicate something of the "texture" of sentiment and of the aesthetic experiences, and aesthetic prejudices and preferences, of sixteenth-century Florentines.

Such information should be no less meaningful to historians of music than to other historians. "Historical interpretation," Benedetto Croce wrote, "labours to reintegrate in us the psychological conditions which have changed in the course of history."[6] The narratives, frequently more richly detailed and fuller than the documentary sources in material reflecting the sentiments and aesthetic responses of their authors, often afford a more successful "reintegration" than the sparer language of the documentary texts. The "reintegration" is more successful still when we can refer to surviving works of art created for, or depicting, the events described here, or to descriptions that are so full that the artistic elements can be reconstructed with confidence; many of the events described below are attested by such visual evidence, which serves us in our attempts to imagine them and completes our reading of the prose accounts.

The Florentine narratives' principal limitation is that they, like the Ferrarese documents of the late sixteenth century, rarely permit us to identify a surviving piece with one of the many performances described in the sources—though for different reasons. "Our harvest is one of empty husks," to borrow Nino Pirrotta's felicitous metaphor: "Would that it were possible to emulate those peasants . . . who, having sown their seed, gather in . . . a bountiful harvest and rejoice in its abundance. All these quotations merely serve to emphasize how little we know: the varied . . . music . . . has become little more than an empty string of words which fail to convey how the music really sounded."[7] And, indeed, in only three instances are there actual pieces of music remaining that were demonstrably performed on an occasion described below: the music for Antonio Alamanni's and Jacopo Nardi's *canti carnascialeschi* for the 1513 Carnival survives in manuscript Florence, Biblioteca nazionale centrale, Banco rari 230; Philippe Verdelot's *canzoni* for the 1525 performance of Machiavelli's *La Clizia* are preserved in a series of manuscripts and prints from the 1520s and later; and the musical setting for the *lauda Laudate el sommo Dio*, which forms part of the text of Feo Belcari's *sacra rappresentazione* "della Annunziazione," performed on the occasion of Margaret of Austria's visit to Florence in 1533, is preserved in Serafino Razzi's famous *lauda* collection of 1563.

As Pirrotta himself has argued in a series of brilliant essays, however, the very act of preservation is itself a function of the nature of the musical tradition represented by pieces that are notated.[8] Coexisting with that tradition, to some extent competing with it, were other musical traditions that are undocumented by the written sources precisely because they were based on different aesthetic principles. Yet these other musical traditions formed an important part of the "life of sounds"[9] that was experienced by Europeans of the fifteenth and sixteenth centuries, an important part of the "acoustical landscape."[10] If we were to draw conclusions about the musical culture of early modern Europe based exclusively on the works remaining in manuscripts and prints (Pirrotta has in effect argued), our understanding of that culture would be at best incomplete and at worst distorted. In reviewing the references to music in the Florentine narratives, one is struck by the relative infrequency of references to polyphony or to other kinds of music that would have required notation and by the broad context in which performances of music of such complexity figured—a context formed, for example, by the chanting of liturgical texts in ecclesiastical institutions, instrumental accompaniment to festive processions and the singing of participants in religious processions, trumpet fanfares on ceremonial occasions, the singing of explanatory or dedicatory verses in simple homophony on such occasions, instrumental music for dances, vocal or instrumental music for theatrical *intermedii*, and the extemporaneous singing of verses to the lute or viol in the intimacy of the home. The modes of musical expression, in short, were infinitely more varied than is suggested by the relatively few surviving examples of actual pieces of music.

In this connection, I would like to make one further observation concerning the narrative sources. The author of one of the Florentine diaries, Luca Landucci, was what would, in contemporary America, be called a pharmacist; another, Bartolomeo Masi, was a coppersmith. As such, they belonged to strata of society whose members' voices are not often heard, whose musical experiences are infrequently recorded in the sources we use. The narrative works thus afford insights into such experiences, which otherwise would be almost irretrievable. Given that many of the musical performances described here took place publicly, they formed a part of the experience of thousands of others who, unlike Landucci and Masi, left no record whatsoever of their responses. Here again, one is impressed by how varied those experiences must have been and how great the stylistic range exemplified by the pieces heard. As we shall see, Leo X's election was greeted in Rome with "suoni di varj instrumenti" and, depending upon the players' talents, in some instances those "suoni" must have been little more than cacophony, like the music for the rite of the charivari so masterfully described by Klapisch-Zuber.[11] However *we* may assess the artistic merits of such modest pieces, for many members of the Florentine and Roman *popolino*, they helped to shape notions of what constituted music, as much, perhaps, as the sophisticated art works preserved in manuscripts in Italian libraries, which rightly command our attention.

In an attempt, therefore, to reconstruct something of the Florentine "life of sounds" of the early cinquecento, to "reintegrate in us the psychological conditions which have changed in the course of history," I propose to examine some references in the principal Florentine narratives of the period to actual performances of music in Florence and other cities in the period between 1512 and 1537, performances occasioned by various civic and festive events associated with the Medici. Many of these references are known, to be sure, but they are scattered throughout many publications, and in assembling and reviewing them in so elliptically concentrated a form one gradually acquires thereby a more complete understanding of the place of music in the private experience of a particular family and in the public experience of a particular city.

PART I

THE FIRST YEARS OF THE MEDICI RESTORATION: THE UNION OF FLORENCE AND ROME

THE RESTORATION

THE REPUBLIC of Florence was renewed in 1494, at the time of the French invasion of Italy. A number of disaffected Florentine aristocrats, resentful of Piero di Lorenzo de' Medici's autocratic behavior and jealous of the diplomatic prerogatives he violated when he negotiated directly with King Charles VIII, succeeded in bringing the Medici regime to an end; Piero was exiled and his family's property confiscated and sold. He later died after several attempts to restore his family to Florence.[1]

Eighteen years later, the conditions of Italian political life had changed dramatically. Pope Julius II had expected that the renewed Florentine republic would be among the members of his "Holy League" (England, Spain, and Venice), but Florence, alone among the principal independent Italian states, instead entered into an alliance with France. The Medici negotiated an agreement with the League, which committed them to its financial support in return for their restoration to Florence. The military forces of the League easily overcame any resistance the Florentines could offer, and on September 1, 1512, Giuliano di Lorenzo entered Florence; he had last seen his native city as a boy of fifteen.[2]

In the ensuing discussions about the future of the government, one group argued for a set of moderate constitutional reforms that would have limited the authority of the Medici. Giuliano—introspective, by temperament inclined to be accommodating, to a considerable extent apolitical—conceded too easily to such arguments to satisfy the more ardent Mediceans, who appealed to his older brother, Cardinal Giovanni, and persuaded him to intervene.[3]

What might have been the first civic event of the restoration to involve the performance of music in fact never occurred. Cardinal Giovanni was papal legate to Tuscany and as such held a position of authority in Florence that was independent of his status as his family's senior member; although he was thus entitled to a formal *entrata*, he chose to forego the privilege:

> On the fourteenth of September, 1512, the day of Santa Croce, the Cardinal de' Medici entered Florence by the Porta a Faenza, and although he was papal legate to Tuscany, he did not want to enter by means of a procession, as was customary, and with a company of

citizens, but in their place armed men and a great many foot soldiers from the Romagna and Bologna, and he went to dismount at his house. The next day, he had to go to visit the Signoria after eating; and the Signoria asked many citizens to go to meet him, as a result of which he changed his plan and said that he would go there by night, in order to minimize ceremony, and thus he did; and the Signoria sent him the customary gifts of a papal legate, and he gave them fifty *fiorini larghi*; and afterward trumpeters and *pifferi* came to visit him, with great fanfare, and he tipped them well accordingly.[4]

On the following day, September 16, the citizenry was summoned to a *parlamento* in the Piazza della Signoria; in the presence of armed men in the employ of the Medici it had no choice but to authorize a *balìa*, a characteristically Florentine commission that was appointed when political circumstances dictated and was empowered to bypass established procedures for the governance of the city. The fifty-five members of the *balìa* were selected by Cardinal Giovanni, and the constitutional reforms they subsequently undertook served to restore the methods employed by the Medici regime in the fifteenth century.[5]

The Signoria had intended the entertainment that their instrumentalists had provided to serve as a gesture toward the city's new "first citizen," and they could not have chosen a more appropriate means to honor him. Giovanni de' Medici's musical interests are so well known and so amply documented that to describe them in great detail would be redundant; even a brief review of some evidence that pertains specifically to his interest in instrumental music, however, reveals a great deal about that interest.

Two instrumentalists (Galeatio Baldo and Gian Maria Giudeo) are known to have been in Giovanni's service even before his election to the papacy, and after his election instrumentalists were employed in apparently unprecedented numbers and occupied an important place within his musical establishment.[6]

Of the reports of performances of music in Rome during Leo's papacy, a number refer specifically to instrumental performances and serve to substantiate the claim made in an anonymous biography of Leo about the frequency of such performances in the Vatican palace.[7] In 1513, for example, Alessandro Gabbioneta wrote to Francesco Gonzaga that "yesterday I went to his Holiness, whom I found at the Belvedere with the archbishop of Florence, Giulio de' Medici. In the antechamber was the Most Reverend Cardinal Ippolito d'Este of Ferrara and the cardinal of Ancona. I visited his Holiness, and then Gian Maria Giudeo made music with viols."[8] In June of 1514, Baldassare Turini da Pescia wrote to Lorenzo II de' Medici, the pope's nephew, in a way that reveals something about the variety of circumstances that occasioned instrumental performances: "His Holiness is spending the better part of the day in his room playing chess and listening to instrumental music."[9] And in June of 1516, the bishop of Adria, Beltrando Costabili, reported to Ippolito d'Este that "Adriano, Auns, Sauli, Cornaro, and Medici ate there [on the site of the future Villa Madama] with his Holiness, and Signor Antonio Maria and Frate Mariano and 'il Protho,' with his musicians, attended." Indeed, the pleasure Leo derived from listening to instrumental music may have been equaled only by the pleasure he derived from hunting, as is suggested by a 1518 letter of Antonio de Beatis, Cardinal Luigi d'Aragona's chaplain and amanuensis: "The pope takes great pleasure in the entertainment provided at the expense of Cardinal d'Aragona and of the music of flutes, *piferi*, and so on, and of the hunt, and every day our house rejoices in the sound of *piferi*, flutes, crumhorns, *cornetti*, and every kind of music."[10] That there were many, many other instrumental performances about which we know comparatively less is suggested by the ad hoc payments sparely recorded in the papal accounts; many of the entries are written in a way that makes one wish for considerably more detail: in September of 1518, two ducats were paid to an unidentified musician who "played the lyre at the Rocca of Viterbo"; a month later a ducat was paid to a musician who "was playing the *cithara*"; and in June of 1521, five ducats were paid to "three *sonatori* of the harp, tambourine, and *violetta*, who played on the day of San Giovanni."[11]

Leo, moreover, was himself a lutenist ("he values nothing except to sound the lute," it was said of him),[12] and a passage in the diary of Paris de Grassis, the papal master of ceremonies, reveals that he was a harpsichordist as well: "Today the pope gave me, as a gift, the most beautiful *clavicembalo*—a most excellent monochord—valued at one hundred ducats, which he was accustomed to keeping in his room [quod ipsemet in sua camera tenere solatus (*sic*) est]; moreover, he said that he had gladly provided this because he understood that I delighted greatly in such sound, as indeed I do."[13] Nor was Leo's *clavicembalo* the only keyboard instrument in his personal possession; he may have owned as many as three organs, if the various references allude, as they appear to, to separate instruments: a letter of Castiglione's of 1521 to the marquis of Mantua documents a famous alabaster organ;[14] Cardinal Luigi d'Aragona honored the pope with the gift of an instrument that had belonged to the cardinal and that was featured in a performance of Ariosto's *I suppositi* in the Vatican Palace in 1519, its sets designed by Raphael;[15] and in 1517 and 1518 "Ubaldino dant.° Ubaldini *pictore fiorentino*" was paid sums of twenty and fifty ducats "for his work on an organ" and "for completing the painting of the organ in the *guardaroba*"—that is, the so-called Torre Borgia in the Vatican apartments, which served as Leo's secret treasury.[16] We should surely interpret the privilege Leo granted to Antico for the print entitled *Frottole intabulate da sonare organi* (Rome, 1517) in light of these references (although its appearance predates some of them), since it is evidence of another kind of interest in keyboard music.[17]

Leo also purchased gold and silver instruments imported from Nuremberg for the extraordinary sum of one thousand ducats: "domino Corrado Trompa de Nolirbergo for a clock and certain musical instruments made both of gold and of silver, given by him to his Holiness."[18]

On the basis of these and other references, it has been argued that the old Julian library in the Vatican apartments (what is now called the Stanza della Segnatura) may have been converted under Leo to serve as the pope's music room: its doors are decorated by Fra Giovanni da Verona with *intarsie* of musical instruments. According to this interpretation, "sua camera" in the text quoted from Paris's diary would thus refer to the Stanza della Segnatura.[19]

Finally, and perhaps most strikingly, on at least two occasions during Leo's papacy instrumentalists accompanied the singing of the papal choir in the *Cappella Sistina*, the very institution whose musical practices gave rise to the term used to this day to describe unaccompanied singing.[20]

One cannot argue, even on the basis of these many references, that Giovanni de' Medici favored instrumental music above other forms of musical expression or that in his interests in such music he was unusual among patrons of his time; the comparative material that would substantiate the second of these propositions is simply not available. At the very least, they do suggest that the Signoria's gesture of September 1512 was appropriate indeed.

But if the instrumentalists who performed for Cardinal Giovanni in 1512 were confident that they had succeeded in ingratiating themselves with the Medici, that confidence was in one instance misplaced. Cardinal Giovanni and his relatives moved quickly to reestablish themselves, and Michele di Bastiano *detto* Talina *sonatore*, who had entered the service of the Signoria in 1509, was among those turned out of office by the Medici in 1512,[21] notwithstanding his personal relationship to Giuliano de' Medici, his colleague in the *Compagnia della Cazzuola*.[22] Had there been any doubt as to the Medici's reemergent authority in all matters pertaining to the governance of Florence, large and small, Talina's experience would have served to resolve it.

THE 1513 CARNIVAL

THE FIRST important festive occasion that the restored regime organized and that involved musical performances was the 1513 Carnival. "A year that brought a change of government or a new Pope was a good one for . . . young artists," John Shearman has written;[1] in 1513, the Medici were anxious to demonstrate that their restoration promised considerable benefits, and in an attempt to ensure the Carnival's artistic success they solicited the participation of some of the city's most prominent artists and literati. Two companies assumed responsibility for organizing the Carnival activities; Jacopo Guicciardini's letter of January 8, 1513, to his brother Francesco suggests that the companies were founded toward the end of November 1512. Bartolomeo Cerretani, who was the author of one of the most important contemporary accounts of the events of the first months of the Medici restoration and a witness to them, reported:

> Pope Julius instructed Cardinal Giovanni to attend to the Ferrarese undertaking, and so he did, recommending his brother Giuliano to all his relatives and friends. At our behest, Giuliano formed a company like that of Lorenzo "il Magnifico," and it was called the *Diamante* [Diamond] because it was an old device among the Medici. It had its beginning in this way: we made a list of thirty-six, almost all sons of men who were colleagues of Lorenzo "il Magnifico" in the company of the *Zampillo* (or Magi). And having had them summoned for an evening at Palazzo Medici, where they dined, Giuliano spoke, calling to mind how his family and the others who were there had happily possessed the city, and because that had to continue, he encouraged and proposed *feste* for the coming carnival, and they were planned; Giuliano was thinking of giving the order that this company govern the city, and already there wasn't a magistracy formed where there wasn't one of our number. Since no one of us prevailed because of the expectations of each, Giuliano began, in his kindly way, to suggest that each succeed in such a way that that close group of young men (who were his contemporaries) cohere, as had happened with their fathers. It transpired that Lorenzo came to their meeting, the son of Piero and Alfonsina Orsini, about eighteen years old, raised in Rome, without advantages but freely. There were those who persuaded him that the city, having been his father's, belonged

to him, which induced him to want to form a company, and he did and called it the *Broncone* [Laurel Branch], all of its members his contemporaries from the leading families, and they also ordered a pantomime, as we had previously done.[2]

Already the different political sensibilities of various members of the family begin to reveal themselves in the contemporary sources: Cerretani's description of Giuliano's measured response to the claims of his colleagues in the *Diamante* is consistent with what one knows of his personal characteristics from other accounts; on the other hand, the portrait of an indulged, ambitious, and competitive Lorenzo does not flatter its subject. Accounts of the Carnival festivities themselves serve to substantiate some details of the profiles that emerge from Cerretani's narrative.

Lorenzo's *Compagnia del Broncone* performed on February 6;[3] the famous Florentine historian Jacopo Nardi, who was responsible for its elaborate program, was also the author of the text of the *canto Colui che dà le leggi alla natura*, whose music is preserved.[4] The procession was formed of four hundred torchbearers and seven floats (see figure 4).[5] (Vasari recorded that Lorenzo, having seen the three *Diamante carri*, desired "that they should be surpassed," and that Nardi's program called for seven *carri* expressly in order to exceed the number executed for the *Diamante*.)[6] As Janet Cox-Rearick suggested, Nardi's program was an elaborate allegory whose various elements represented the effects of *buon governo*: religion, *virtù* and prosperity, victory, poetry, and law.[7] The first float, drawn by a pair of oxen, represented the Age of Saturn and Janus (called the Age of Gold) and was accompanied by six pairs of mounted shepherds, clothed in skins, their shoes fashioned in imitation of ancient footwear, and each pair attended by four grooms attired as shepherd boys who carried torches in the form of dry trunks and branches of pine; seated on the second *carro* was Numa Pompilius, the second king of Rome and the originator of religion and sacrifices among the Romans, who was accompanied by six priests, richly attired in classical dress and on muleback, attended by Levites whose torches resembled ancient candelabra; the third, which symbolized the consulate of Titus Manlius Torquatus, consul after the first Carthaginian war, was drawn by eight horses and preceded by six pairs of mounted senators, attired in togas and accompanied by grooms who carried fasces and axes, symbols of the administration of justice; the fourth, drawn by buffaloes disguised as elephants, represented the victory of Julius Caesar over Cleopatra and was accompanied by six pairs of men in armor; the fifth, drawn by winged horses, carried Caesar Augustus, attended by six pairs of Poets on horseback, crowned with laurel (as was Caesar himself) and attired in distinctive costumes that varied according to their provinces; the sixth carried Trajan and was preceded by six pairs of Doctors of Laws attended by

Figure 1. Raphael, portrait of Pope Leo X (Giovanni di Lorenzo de' Medici) and Cardinals Giulio di Giuliano de' Medici (left) and Luigi de' Rossi

Figure 2. Workshop of Raphael (attributed to Francesco Penni), portrait of Giuliano di Lorenzo de' Medici

grooms who represented copyists and notaries and carried torches and books. After the six floats came the triumphal chariot representing the Age of Gold. On it lay a man dressed in rusted armor, as if dead, and from the armor there emerged a young boy, naked and gilded, who represented

Figure 3. Raphael, portrait of Lorenzo di Piero di Lorenzo de' Medici

the birth of the Age of Gold and the end of the Age of Iron. Also featured was a dry branch, symbolic of the House of Medici, which was seen to put forth new leaves,[8] its imagery anticipated by the torches carried by the grooms who attended the first float.[9]

Figure 4. Representation of the *carro*
"della Zecca" or "di San Giovanni"

Giuliano's *Compagnia del Diamante*, whose members included his cousin Giulio,[10] the future cardinal and archbishop of Florence who in 1523 became Pope Clement VII, performed two days later. Cambi reported that "the *trionfo* of Giuliano and of his company was presented on the day of Carnival, the eighth of February, 1513, from two hours after sunset until eight hours after sunset."[11] The author of the *Diamante*'s more modest program was the humanist Andrea Dazzi (1473–1548), who since 1502 had been lecturer in Greek letters at the Florentine *studio* and the university in Pisa;[12] the text of its *canto, Volon gli anni e' mesi e l'ore*, whose music is also preserved, was written by Antonio Alamanni. That Dazzi was an intimate of the Medici is suggested not only by his involvement in the preparations for the Carnival but by a sonnet of Machiavelli's, who in 1512 had been turned out of office by the Medici, imprisoned and tortured. In an attempt to ingratiate himself with the family and secure his release, Machiavelli, while still in prison, addressed several poems to Giuliano. Among them is one that ridicules Dazzi and provides an illuminating glimpse into Florentine cultural life and the rivalries that characterized it in the first months of the restoration as its potential beneficiaries—members of the city's cultural elite—moved to align themselves with the city's newly restored principal citizens.[13]

Three floats—constructed of wood and richly decorated—formed the *Diamante*'s procession: the first symbolized Boyhood, the second Manhood, and the third Old Age, and in each were appropriately costumed individuals who represented the particular age of man that the float symbolized (Piero da Vinci, Leonardo's father, is said to have been involved in preparing the elaborate costumes).[14] The floats' inscriptions—"Erimus," "Sumus," and "Fuimus"—suggest that several lines in Ovid's *Metamorphoses* (15.214–16) may have served as one of the sources for Dazzi's program: "Nostra quoque ipsorum semper requieque sine ulla / corpora vertuntur, nec, quod fuimusve, sumusve, / cras erimus."[15] Cerretani's account contains the further details that "a company of masqueraders had been formed for the *Diamante*" and that "there were more than five hundred torches."[16]

Five of the *Broncone carri*—the first, third, fourth, sixth, and seventh—were painted by Jacopo Pontormo, to one of which—the seventh—Baccio Bandinelli contributed figures in relief, among them the four cardinal virtues; Pontormo was also responsible for the painting of the three *Diamante carri* (he is said to have executed scenes in chiaroscuro of the transformations of the gods into different forms), and Andrea di Cosimo Feltrini and Andrea del Sarto, among others, were involved in their design.[17] Giuliano de' Medici would have known Sarto since late 1512: both were members of the *Compagnia della Cazzuola*.[18] Thus, presumably for the first time since their restoration, the Medici had enlisted the services of an important group of artists associated with the Church of the Santissima Annunziata;[19] Feltrini, Pontormo, and Sarto (and Franciabigio as well) were later to receive the commission for one of the most important artistic projects of the entire period, the painting of the salone at the Medici villa at Poggio a Caiano, and their selection has been interpreted as a kind of acknowledgment of the artistic supremacy of the "school" of the Annunziata.[20]

On the basis of Vasari's description of the artistic element, various surviving decorative panels—obviously *ephemerae*—have been associated with the 1513 Carnival.[21] Their thematic content, which clearly prefigures that of the decoration of the villa at Poggio, is unequivocally Medicean. Figures wear laurel wreaths in two panels attributed to Sarto and his colleague Feltrini (see figures 6 and 7), and in one of them a figure holds a laurel branch (see figure 6).

Pontormo, similarly, depicted a legend of Apollo and Daphne that traces the origins of the laurel to an episode Ovid described (see figure 9): after Daphne's transformation, Apollo adopted the laurel as his device

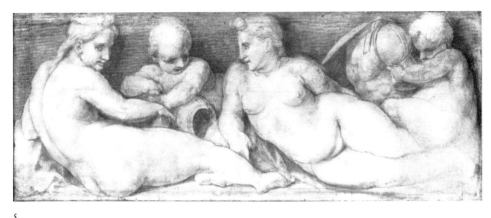

5

6

Figures 5 and 6. Decorative panels, attributed to Andrea del Sarto. Possibly executed for a *carro* for the 1513 Carnival

and predicted its role in Roman triumphs. The panels painted by Pontormo are thus the earliest extant works of the young artist, who was employed painting candles only a week before the Carnival festivities.[22]

Cambi's account clarifies the music's role: "each of the two *trionfi* had a song [appropriate to] the program of the *trionfi* [un chanto della finzione de' trionfi]; they went singing to the homes of those who had had

Figure 7. Decorative panel, attributed to Andrea di Cosimo Feltrini. Possibly executed for a *carro* for the 1513 Carnival

the *trionfi* made, or their friends."[23] The text of Nardi's poem *Colui che dà le leggi alla natura* is reproduced below from one of its principal sources, where it is entitled "Seven Triumphs of the Age of Gold made by the Company of the *Broncone*, 1512 [Septe TriomPhi del secolo Doro Facti dalla co[m]pagnia del Bro[n]chone Lanno. M.D.XII.]." Interestingly, at the conclusion of the text of the *canto* is a description of the *Broncone* floats that corresponds very closely to Vasari's. The print may therefore have served as one of his sources; at minimum, the fact that the description it contains corresponds to his suggests that his detailed account may be accurate even in its particulars.[24]

In the *canto*'s references to the ages succeeding one another (line 8), to the phoenix (line 16), a traditional symbol of return and regeneration, to the branch of the green laurel (line 17) and to the birth of the Age of Gold from the Age of Iron (line 18), among others one could cite, one sees immediately the close correspondence of Nardi's text to the "finzione" of the *Broncone trionfo*:

> Colui che dà le leggi alla natura   [1]
> In vari stati & secoli dispone;
> ma del bene è chagione,
> e'l mal, quant'e' p[er]mette, al mo[n]do dura:
> onde in questa figura
> contemplando, si vede

Figures 8 and 9. Decorative panels,
attributed to Jacopo Pontormo.
Possibly executed for a *carro* for
the 1513 Carnival

Figures 10 and 11. Decorative
panels, attributed to Jacopo
Pontormo. Possibly executed for
a *carro* for the 1513 Carnival

come con lento piede
l'un secol doppo l'altro al mo[n]do viene,
& muta il bene i[n] male, & il male i[n] bene.

Dell'oro el primo stato & più giocondo,   [10]
nelle seconde età men ben si mostra;
& poi nella età vostra
al ferro alla ruggin viene il mondo:
ma hora, essendo in fondo,
torna il secol felice;
& come la Fenice,
rinasce dal bronchon del verde alloro:
così nasce del ferro un secol d'oro.

Perchè natura el cielo hoggi rinnuova   [19]
e'l secol vecchio in puerile etade,
& quello del ferro chade,
che rugginoso, inutile si truova
a queste virtù giova,
a noi & a costoro
che furno al secol d'oro,
tornando quel, tornare a star co[n] voi
per farvi diventare simile a noi.

Dopo la pioggia torna il ciel sereno: [28]
godi, Fiorenza: & fàtti lieta hormai,
però che tu vedrai
fiorir queste virtù de[n]tro al tuo seno,
che dal sito terreno
havien fatto partita:
la verità smarrita,
la Pace: & la iustitia, hor q[ue]lla hor q[ue]sta,
t'inuiton liete insieme & ti fan festa.

Trio[m]pha, poichè 'l cielo ta[n]to ti honora   [37]
sotto il favore di più benignia stella.
Ciptà felice & bella,
più ch[e] tu, fussi mai al mondo anchora:
eccho che vien quel'hora
che ti farà beata
& infra l'altre honorata,
sì, che alla gloria tua p[er] excellenza
basterà il nome solo, alma Fiorenza.

What were the music's stylistic properties? As one sees, Nardi's text consists of five nine-line strophes, each of which alternates seven- and eleven-syllable lines (in this respect, interestingly, it employs a freer metrical scheme than most *canti carnascialeschi*, which are in *ballata* form);[25] the rhyme scheme is *ABbAaccDD* (here and elsewhere, seven-syllable lines are distinguished by means of lowercase letters, eleven-syllable lines by means of uppercase letters). The musical design was in part dictated by the poetic structure, certainly, but the fact that these pieces served a particular function and were performed under particular conditions exercised an even greater influence. The composer's objective was to balance two somewhat inconsistent aims: to invest these essentially modest works with features that would serve to sustain interest and simultaneously to fashion a work that would permit the explanatory function to be fulfilled. The second of these demanded that the text be fully intelligible, and the rhythmic design, accordingly, is predominantly but by no means exclusively homorhythmic (see example 1); what instances there are of independent rhythms in the different vocal lines occur almost without exception at the cadences that mark the conclusion of text phrases, and they begin on the penultimate syllable of the phrase. Variety in the rhythmic design is achieved instead through shifts in meter, from duple to triple at line 8 and back to duple at line 9. The sonorities are an inevitable consequence of the work's rhythmic characteristics; homorhythms invite full harmonies, and ordinarily all four voices participate, though there is an instance of variety achieved through a reduced vocal complement: line 6 of each stanza is set for two voices only (tenor and bassus) and only here is imitation employed, as if it were assumed that the sparer texture would have permitted the text to be understood, despite the use of the contrapuntal device of imitation.

We are thus in a fortunate position with respect to the 1513 Carnival: we possess detailed descriptions of the festivities, and some of the ephemeral artistic elements created by Feltrini, Pontormo, and Sarto have apparently survived, as have the two *canti*. One can imagine the streets and *piazze* of Florence on a February evening, crowded with observers and illuminated by the hundreds of torches carried by the masked and costumed participants in the procession, the ox- and horse-drawn *carri*, their panels decorated with representations of allegorical and mythological figures executed by the city's leading artists, the singing by the *cantori* of strophe after strophe of Alamanni's and Nardi's *canti*, which served, like the works of art, to elucidate the themes of the *trionfi*. Many Florentines must have been favorably impressed by the performances of the *Compagnie*; indeed, the fact that so much of the ephemeral artistic and musical element has survived—to an almost unequaled extent among comparable festivals of the time—may be one measure of the response. And if the objective had been to create the illusion of the return of a Golden Age, Cerretani's account suggests that the Medici met with success: "to the people it seemed as though the age of Lorenzo 'il Vecchio' had returned,

Example 1. Anonymous setting of Jacopo Nardi's *canto carnascialesco* for the 1513
Carnival, *Colui che dà le leggi alla natura*, Florence, Biblioteca nazionale
centrale, MS Banco rari 230, fols. 88ᵛ–89ʳ

Example 1, continued

Example 1, continued

with respect to the *feste*."[26] Cambi's reaction, however, was different: "They spent seventeen hundred florins. And thus the people delighted in nonsense and foolishness and no one spoke of penitence. The second cost as much as the first and all because Giuliano and Lorenzo had returned to their homeland, like their fathers heads of the city, from which they had been exiled for eighteen years."[27] As for the unfortunate baker's son who represented the birth of the Age of Gold and was paid ten *scudi* of the thirty-four hundred florins expended, he died shortly after the performance of the *Broncone* company, presumably as a result of the effects both of the gilding of his skin and of exposure to the February air.[28]

Cambi's response notwithstanding, the Carnival festivities culminated in the performance of a comedy in the Palazzo Medici on February 17 (as we learn from a passage in Sanuto's diaries), a performance that afforded

Example 2. Anonymous setting of Antonio Alamanni's *canto carnascialesco* for the 1513 Carnival, *Volon gli anni e' mesi et l'ore*, Florence, Biblioteca nazionale centrale, MS Banco rari 230, fols. 135ᵛ–137ʳ

Example 2, continued

opportunity for still more explicit reference to the Medici restoration and to evocative and increasingly familiar Medicean literary topoi:

On the seventeenth Vittorio Lippomano arrived in Florence. And immediately he went to the home of the magnificent Giuliano, who was getting up and greeted him warmly and had his nephew Loren-

Example 2, continued

zino summoned, the son of Piero. Then he took Lippomano to see the Most Reverend Cardinal, who made many kind gestures toward him, coming to greet him at the door to his room, and he left all of those who were with him, and stayed to talk for about three-quarters of an hour, and in leaving he turned to those who were in his room, who were more than twenty-five of the leading citizens of Florence. That evening a comedy was performed for Lorenzino in an upstairs room. The cardinal sent for Lippomano and wanted him seated next to him; and there were a good many citizens among them, all of whom thanked him for what he had arranged at Palazzo Medici. The comedy having been performed, the cardinal took Lippomano by the hand and led him to dinner with him.[29]

The reference to the distinguished audience in the account of Lippomano's visit is not hyperbole; among its members may have been Francesco Vettori, Bernardo Michelozzi, and again, Andrea Dazzi. The comedy mentioned in the account has been identified as *I due felici rivali* of Jacopo Nardi,[30] who thus emerges as one of the restoration's earliest and most important literary figures; he was, as we shall see, to be the author of *canti* texts for several future Medici festivals. One of the play's manuscript sources contains a dedication in which the play is described as having been "performed under the auspices of Lorenzo de' Medici" and illuminations that depict Medici devices: sprouting laurel branches ("bronconi") alternate with rings ("diamanti") and feathers in apparent reference to Giuliano's and Lorenzo's "rivalità felice." Nardi's title, however, may have been unduly optimistic: to judge from the tone of Cerretani's and Vasari's accounts of the preparations for the Carnival festivities, the "rivalry" cannot have been altogether "happy."[31] The comedy itself was preceded by "stanzas . . . sung on the lyre by an actor representing the poet Orpheus, come from Elysian fields, when the aforementioned comedy was performed in the presence of the Most Reverend Cardinal and the magnificent Giuliano and Lorenzo de' Medici,"[32] stanzas that are replete with Medicean imagery and oblique and overt allusions to various members of the Medici family: the opening strophe contains references to "eterna primavera" (line 1) and "verdi . . . foglie" (line 6), the second of which has been interpreted, reasonably, as an allusion to the laurel;[33] the second strophe opens with the line "Dapoi che il mondo & i' secul si rennuova" (line 9), which recalls some lines in Nardi's *canto carnascialesco* of February 6: "Perche natura el cielo hoggi rinnuova / el secol vecchio" (see lines 19–20 in the text of the *canto*, above). Elsewhere in the second strophe (line 12), Nardi employed a flattering metaphor that compared Giovanni, Giuliano, and Lorenzo to Augusto, Pollione, and Mecenate and that echoed his own earlier similar reference in the prologue of *L'amicitia*, whose introductory stanzas also employ the topos of the return of a Golden Age ("Ma sia chi a me insegni / in questa nostra etate / Augusto o Mecenate / il qual conforti e sproni"; "mutato il cielo in lieto aspecto / renoverà nel mondo il secul d'auro"). Lines 22–24 contain still further references to the laurel, as well as to Daphne (the daughter of Peneo), who, as we have seen, was depicted in one of the ephemeral decorative panels attributed to Pontormo and perhaps executed for one of the Carnival floats of a week and a half earlier:[34]

Da loco della eterna primavera, [1]
che nel suo sen le felice alme accoglie:
Gode, tra l'altre, una honorata schiera,
libera hormai dalle terrestre spoglie,
Di sé co[n]tenta et di sue opre altera,
A l'ombra delle verdi & sacre foglie.
Qual m'ha commesso che io demo[n]stri et vuole
La me[n]te sua co[n] mie roze parole.

Dapoi che il mondo & i' secul si rennuova [9]
De' cultor di parnaso et d'helicone:
Et che ancor hogi in terra esser si truova
Augusto Mecenate & Pollione.
Et tu, fiorentia, hormai contendi a ppruova
Con Roma e Tuscia e Latio al paragone,
S'allegra teco (et benche absente) applaude
La docta scola & canta le tua laude.

Ma voi, a cui Apollo illustra il pecto: [17]
udite quel che dice il Thracio orpheo.
chi vuole al nostro coro essere accepto
Et farsi in terra più che semideo,
Celebri, come più nobil subiecto,
La stirpe della figlia di peneo.
Et il verde germe del più vechio ramo,
Delle cui fronde ornare le tempie bramo.

Et tu che doppia vice in terra tieni [25]
Del gran Monarca subcessor di piero,
Columna adamantina che sostieni
La maggior parte del sacrato impero,
Come vero patron lieto subvieni
Ai sacri vati del vostro hemisphero:
Maxime a quello a cui sol basta e vale,
Come Thelepho, usar l'hasta fatale.

35

Although the recent change in the Medici family's political circumstances certainly gave Nardi's literary conceits invoking topoi of return and renewal a new currency and urgency, they had a distinguished lineage; they echoed not only his own Carnival song of a week and a half earlier but considerably more venerable models as well. Lorenzo "il Magnifico" himself had invoked the themes in one of his poems, and Nardi's *canto* and stanzas, consciously or unconsciously, are reminiscent of Lorenzo's verses:

> Lasso a me! or nel loco alto e silvestre
> Ove dolente e triste lei si truova
> d'oro è l'età, paradiso terrestre,
> e quivi il primo secol si rinnuova.[35]

Lorenzo's verses themselves recall other, still more venerable instances of the use of the topos: in *La Giostra di Lorenzo de Medici messa in rima da Luigi Pulci l'anno MCCCCLXVIIII*, Pulci recorded that the standard carried by Lorenzo in the 1469 jousts bore Lorenzo's motto "Le tens revient: che puo interpretarsi / Tornare il tempo e'l secol rinnuovarsi,"[36] which in turn echoes Dante's formulation in the *Purgatorio* (22.67–72): "Secol si rinova; / torna giustizia e primo tempo umano, / e progenie scende da ciel nova."[37] For a Florentine humanist of the late fifteenth or early sixteenth century, the most distinguished of all literary sources for the conceit—indeed, the text where it seems to have received its principal classical formulation—was Vergil's *Eclogue* 4:

> Ultima Cumaei venit iam carminis aetas;
> magnus ab integro saeculorum nascitur ordo.
> iam redit et Virgo, redeunt Saturnia regna;
> iam nova progenies caelo demittitur alto.

Nor were Nardi's *canto* and introductory stanzas in *I due felici rivali* the only texts from the 1513 Carnival to employ traditional Medicean literary topoi; Professor Cox-Rearick remarked on the "Laurentian" qualities of the text of Alamanni's *canto Volon gl'anni e' mesi et l'ore*, which paraphrases Poliziano's *Stanze* (1.72):

> Né mai le chiome del giardino eterno
> tenera brina o fresca neve imbianca;
> ivi non osa entrar ghiacciato verno,
> non vento o l'erbe o li arbuscelli stanca;
> ivi non volgon gli anni il lor quaderno,
> ma lieta Primavera mai non manca,
> ch'e suoi crin biondi e crespi all'aura spiega,
> e mille fiori in ghirlandetta lega.[38]

So very resonant a complex of references as that evoked by Nardi's stanzas cannot have failed to elicit a response from the more learned members of the audience, Giuliano among them. The youngest son of "Il Magnifico," himself a poet, authored some seventy-five *canzoni, capitoli, sestine, sonetti*, and *stanze* during his lifetime.[39] As for Lorenzo II, although he may not have found the literary allusions so very meaningful, he presumably appreciated the stanzas' overt glorification of the House of Medici.

The stanzas were performed in a manner that exemplified a particular musical tradition, one with which the Medici were fully conversant, to be sure: no less than in other Italian humanist circles and centers of musical patronage, the practice of extemporaneous solo singing to the lute, lyre, or viol (see figure 12)[40] was absolutely central to the musical experience of fifteenth-century Florence, and several members of the Medici family were active as patrons and in some instances as practitioners of the art themselves. So abundant is the testimony to the practice—and so varied in nature—that here I can quote only a small portion that nonetheless constitutes impressive witness.

"We have sent you the *vihuola*," Luigi Pulci reported in 1468 to Lorenzo, then at Cafaggiolo;[41] later, in 1472, Lorenzo, again at Cafaggiolo, wrote to Niccolò Michelozzi to request his viola, and his letter conveys a note of urgency that suggests the importance of the practice to him: "I await the *viuola* and the other things, and at any cost see to it that you bring them with you."[42]

The correspondence of Poliziano, who himself was reported to have died while singing a lament for the death of Lorenzo to the accompaniment of a lute, contains references to Piero's improvisatory singing: in a letter to Pico della Mirandola, Poliziano wrote that "Piero also sings verse, both from musical notation and to the *cithara*,"[43] and in a letter of 1490 to Lorenzo, then at Bagno a Morbo, Poliziano reported that "not two evenings ago I heard Piero sing impromptu, for he came to assail me at home with all these improvisors."[44]

Several of the most renowned lutenist-singers of the late quattrocento were intimates of Lorenzo's. Baccio Ugolini, who played the title role in Poliziano's *Orfeo* in Mantua in 1480, was a member of Lorenzo's chancery,[45] and his extemporaneous singing was said to have elicited Lorenzo's approval.[46] Documentary and literary evidence testify to the extraordinary artistic success of Antonio di Guido, one of the famous *cantimpanche* (strolling players) of San Martino.[47] Antonio's reputation was already established as early as 1459: in April of that year, Galeazzo Maria Sforza was received by the Medici at their villa at Careggi on the occasion of his visit to Florence, and Antonio's singing so impressed Sforza that he was prompted to write to his father and report on his impressions;[48] later, in August of 1473, Lorenzo, then in Vallombrosa,

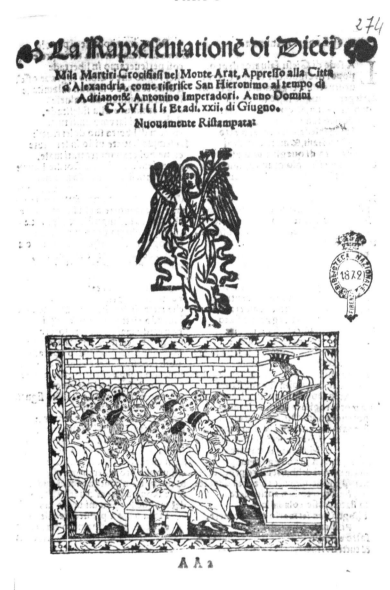

Figure 12. Representation of the practice of solo singing to the viol

wrote to Niccolò Michelozzi in Florence and instructed him to "go and
find Maestro Antonio della Viuola, and if he wants to come—as we in-
form him by means of a sonnet—borrow Sassetto's mule on my behalf,
and if it's not to be had, see to it that Antonio is provided with a good

mount, either from the house or elsewhere";[49] among Michelozzi's other letters that document Lorenzo's interest in having Antonio present is an especially illuminating one that records Clarice de' Medici's wistful recognition that Antonio's presence in Lorenzo's entourage would have the effect of delaying her husband's return to Florence: "M.° Antonio's arrival this morning causes her to lose some hope of an early return."[50] Antonio was a friend of Poliziano's, who wrote an *epigramma* in his honor (*epigr. lat.* 23), and of Pulci's, whose explicit reference to him in the *Morgante* (28.144) contains a slightly veiled allusion to Vallombrosa, which, on occasion, served as a retreat for Lorenzo and members of his retinue:

> Ed oltre a questo, e' ne verrà il mio Antonio,
> per cui la nostra cetra è gloriosa,
> del dolce verso materno ausonio
> (bench'è si stia là in quella valle ombrosa,
> che fia del vero lume testimonio).[51]

Among the members of Piero's entourage on the occasion of his visit to Rome in 1492 were "il chonpare della viola" and "il chardiere della viola";[52] "il chardiere" is presumably to be identified with Johannes Cordier, whose musical activity as an intimate of Piero's is also attested by Ascanio Condivi in his life of Michelangelo: "Frequenting Piero's house was a certain Cardiere who delighted 'il Magnifico' with his marvelous improvisatory singing to the lyre, of which 'il Magnifico' was also a practitioner, so that he played almost every evening after dinner."[53]

Giuliano di Lorenzo's sonnet *Perchè hai Serafin, Morte, offeso tanto?*, written "Pro morte Seraphini. Agosto 1500," suggests that the most famous of the lutenist-singers, Serafino Aquilano, may also have been an intimate of the Medici.[54]

And that the tradition of improvisatory singing in Medici circles continued into the sixteenth century is suggested not only by the stanzas in Nardi's play: "We have elected you lutenist in perpetuity," the members of the Sacred Academy of the Medici wrote in 1515 to "Atalanti de Miglioroctis," who had been in Medici service in 1490. The Academy, one of the quintessentially Florentine societies that were to have such a marked influence on Florentine cultural and political life in the early sixteenth century, at one time included among its members Lodovico Alamanni, Michelangelo Buonarotti, Jacopo Nardi, Palla Rucellai, Lorenzo Strozzi, and Bartolomeo Cerretani, whose history of Florence has already proved to be an important source of information about the musical life of the time and will prove to be more important still. That a personal relationship between the lutenist-singer Migliorotti and Jacopo Nardi is demonstrated by the reference is suggestive and documents Nardi's conversance with the musical tradition Migliorotti represented (although the reference postdates the performance of *I due felici rivali* by two years).[55]

Finally, a *pasquinata*—one of the scurrilous verses posted annually on the statue of Pasquino in Rome—suggests how widely known was Leo X's preference for extemporaneous singing and demonstrates that "literary" reflections of the practice are not limited to Poliziano's and Pulci's sophisticated allusions to Antonio di Guido: "Deliras, Pasquille, lyrae si carmina jungas; / Dives eris solum si cytharedus eris."[56]

The stanzas in Nardi's *I due felici rivali* served the same function as those in honor of Cardinal Francesco Gonzaga in Poliziano's *Orfeo* of 1480, and they may well have been clothed in similar musical dress, which, as Pirrotta suggested, may have resembled the music of Pesenti's setting of Horace's *Integer vitae* (see example 3):[57] the setting is entirely syllabic, and the melodic writing is marked by an almost exclusive reliance on conjunct motion; the rhythmic design derives directly from the accentuation of the text, so that accented syllables are set uniformly to a longer value (a breve) and unaccented syllables to a shorter one (a semibreve). The dedicatory function of the text, in short, would presumably have dictated the characteristics of its musical setting, and the all-important objective of rendering the text intelligible would have resulted in a musical design in which the text's "phonological" properties were simply musically heightened.

Example 3. Michele Pesenti, setting of Horace's ode *Integer vitae*, *Frottole libro primo* (Venice: O. Petrucci, 1504), fol. 44[r]

Canti carnascialeschi and improvisatory singing to the lute or viol were characteristically Florentine modes of musical expression; that they were featured prominently among the artistic elements of the festivities in 1513 suggests that in its musical as in its political practices the restored regime was content with the forms and methods it had inherited from Lorenzo "il Magnifico" and saw no reason to refuse his legacy; culturally and politically, "restoration" Florence, to no small extent, was in the grasp of the past.

CHAPTER 3

THE ELECTION OF LEO X

GIOVANNI CAMBI'S response to the extravagance of the Carnival festivities could hardly have been atypical; but if he and others who reacted similarly hoped for a restoration of the Republic, they were to be frustrated. Within a month, Cardinal Giovanni was elected pope, and one could argue in retrospect that his election, more than any other single event in the history of Florence, ensured the continuity of the Medici regime and would thus serve to transform Florentine political and cultural life in ways that no contemporary could then have imagined.

Nonetheless, whatever concerns Florentine republicans may have had, many of their fellow citizens responded enthusiastically at first to the news of Leo's election; he was, after all, the first Florentine pope, and although jealousies and resentments were at play in Florentine political life, to be very sure, most Florentines would have acknowledged readily that they regarded Leo's election as a compliment to their city—of which, justifiably, they were fiercely proud. At least one contemporary historian suggested, however, that in some instances their response may be explained by less disinterested considerations: Francesco Vettori observed, cynically, that "because the Florentines are devoted to trading and the pursuit of gain, all were thinking of being obliged to profit from this pontificate."[1] Indeed, within days of Leo's election, a representative of the Mantuan court in Rome reported to Isabella d'Este Gonzaga that "Rome is *piena piena* of Florentines," and on April 20, some five weeks after the election, he repeated his observation: "The entire Apostolic Palace is full of Florentines."[2] The initial reaction in Florence, therefore, can hardly be said to have been selflessly motivated in all cases. Cerretani and Masi both furnished detailed accounts:

> The Ten issued the edict that there would be three successive days of *feste*. Each night, a *trionfo* was drawn by oxen from the Medici garden in Piazza San Marco down the Via Larga, and they stopped when they reached the Palazzo Medici. And a beautiful song glorifying the pope and his family was ordered—that is, a *canto* "delle Palle." And when the song was finished, the aforementioned *trionfo* was set afire by means of fireworks.

The specificity of Masi's account permits us to determine the location of the festivities more precisely than in the case of the February Carnival

42

feste, although one has to be aware that the Medici owned several houses in the Via Larga and one cannot be certain, therefore, that the festivities took place directly in front of what is today Palazzo Medici-Riccardi.[3]

Cerretani's account offers more detailed information as to the themes of the *trionfi* and the music's explanatory function:

> The first night there were two *carri*, one representing Discord and the other Peace, with appropriate explanatory songs, and trumpet fanfares and torches. Finally the *trionfo* representing Discord was burned. The next night there was a *trionfo* representing Peace and another representing War, with songs, trumpet fanfares, torches, and fireworks; finally they burned the *trionfo* representing War. The third night there was a *trionfo* representing Suspicion and Fear, and trumpet fanfares, torches, and artillery, and in another was Tranquility, and having sung, they burned the *trionfo* representing Suspicion and Fear with such a popular clamor that Florence was turned upside down, and it seemed that the entire city was ablaze because there was a bonfire at each *campanile*, tower, and house. And thus the city was engaged in the greatest of celebrations for several days.[4]

Like one of Leo's election capitulations, the themes of the Florentine *trionfi* reflected the expectation that Leo would assume his father's role as diplomat and the hope that he would enjoy similar success. The texts of two of Heinrich Isaac's motets invoke similar themes: the opening of one of his elegies for Lorenzo "il Magnifico," *Quis dabit pacem populo timenti*, alludes obliquely to Lorenzo's diplomatic activity, and *Optime pastor*, written to celebrate Leo's election, sets several related texts, one of which is "Da pacem Domine in diebus nostris." And although Cerretani's account itself permits no such inference, there must also have been the expectation, or at minimum the hope, that Leo would also assume his father's role as patron of the arts and letters, and that with his election artists and literati in Medici employ would again enjoy a cultural and intellectual *ambiente* that prompted comparison with that of fifth-century Athens.[5]

As for the texts and music of the "canti a proposito" to which Cerretani alluded, I can only say that despite the existence of several *canti* whose texts are appropriate to the occasion, none of them, in my view, can be unequivocally associated with the celebrations for Leo's election. Federico Ghisi associated a *canto* "delle Palle" specifically with the festivities, but his thesis, I believe, is not fully substantiated by the available evidence.[6] A likelier candidate for performance on the occasion of the celebrations, in view of the title of its printed source, is a piece whose text was published by Alessandro d'Ancona from a print entitled *Castellanus de Castellanij j. v. doctor, In laudibus sanctiss. p. Leonis de Medicis noviter creati*:

Palle, Palle, viva viva,
Grida il mar, la terra, il cielo,
Venga ognun con pronto zelo
A dir Palle, e viva, viva[7]

Roberto Ridolfi suggested, I believe more plausibly still, that the *canto* "degli spiriti beati" of Machiavelli, newly pardoned in March of 1513, may have been composed for the occasion; its references to war and peace (lines 6 and 9) and the flock's "new shepherd" (lines 26–27) are appropriate to the historical circumstances of the moment and correspond closely to the chroniclers' descriptions of the festivities, as Ridolfi himself remarked:

Spiriti beati siano,   [1]
che da' celesti scanni
sian qui venuti a dimostrarci in terra,
poscia che noi veggiano
il mondo in tanti affanni
e per lieve cagion sí crudel guerra;
e mostra a chi erra,
sí come al Signor nostro al tutto piace
che si ponghin giú l'arme e stieno in pace.

L'empio e crudel martoro   [10]
de' miseri mortali,
il lungo strazio e 'nrimediabil danno,
il pianto di costoro
per li infiniti mali
che giorno e notte lamentar gli fanno,
con singulti e affanno,
con alte voci e dolorose strida,
ciascun per sé merzè domanda e grida.

Questo a Dio non è grato,   [19]
né puote essere ancora
a chiunche tien d'umanitate un segno;
per questo ci ha mandato,
che vi dimostriam ora
quanto sie l'ira sua giusta e lo sdegno:
poiché vede il suo regno
mancar a poco a poco, e la sua gregge,
se pe 'l nuovo pastor non si corregge.

If Ridolfi's inferences are correct, Machiavelli's *canto* may be among the first artistic expressions of Leo's papacy of themes that were to be of central importance in his iconography; in its allusions to peace and to Leo as pastor, it conflates references that were invoked repeatedly throughout his papacy and utilized in some of the most important works his artists were to execute for him.[8] As for the music's characteristics, that the *canti* performed on the occasion of the celebrations for Leo's election served an explanatory function similar to that of Alamanni's and Nardi's *canti* of several weeks before and were performed under similar conditions suggests, at minimum, that they were stylistically related, poetically and musically, to the earlier examples.

Meanwhile, in Rome, the elaborate ceremonies occasioned by the election of the new pope also included musical elements:

> And the following morning, March 11, 1513, at two hours after sunrise, the window of the conclave, which had been walled up, having been broken open, a statement was issued in a loud and intelligible voice by the R. Alessandro Farnese, cardinal-deacon of S. Eustachio: "Gaudium magnum nuntio vobis, papam habemus, reverendissimum dominum Joannem de Medicis, diaconum cardinalem Sanctae Mariae in Domenica, qui vocatur Leo decimus." The statement having been issued, for two hours there was heard, in the Castel Sant'Angelo and the Apostolic Palace, much shouting, and sounds of mortars, and other artillery, and the playing of various instruments, and the ringing of bells, and the voices of people crying "Viva Leo" and "Palle, palle"; it truly seemed that the heavens were resounding and thundering.
>
> Not long thereafter, the pope, seated in a *Cathedra Pontificale*, was led from the said conclave, with great magnificence and a group of all the clergy and religious singing "Te Deum Laudamus," into the Church of St. Peter to the main altar, and there he was enthroned by the cardinals of the Holy Church. Come the evening of the said day, and for eight continuous days throughout our beloved city of Rome, there were bonfires, and torches, and flares as a sign of rejoicing. And in various places, principally among the noble Florentine merchants, money was distributed, and bread, and many full barrels of wine set out in the middle of the *piazze* and streets, and every kind of instrument was played in front of their houses and palaces, and there were the greatest celebrations, such that Rome was never more joyous.
>
> The solemn coronation was scheduled for the nineteenth of the aforementioned month. A large and spacious wooden platform was constructed above the marble steps of the Church of St. Peter, and eight most beautiful columns erected there, above which one saw a well-constructed cornice, with reliefs, which truly seemed of marble. On the morning of the said day, the pope was led by his relatives and the entire College of Cardinals, archbishops, bishops, and prelates from the Apostolic Palace to the Church of St. Peter and seated in

the Chapel of the Apostle Andrew; the morning psalms and orations were solemnly sung. The praises having been completed, he was adorned in priestly dress in order to celebrate mass, at the conclusion of which he was led to the platform described above; and a triple-crowned tiara, adorned with many other pearls and jewels, was placed on his head by two cardinals, namely the cardinals Farnese and d'Aragona; and he was crowned, to the great tumult of *tubicine* and other instruments, and the rejoicing of the people.[9]

On April 11, there followed the Lateran *possesso*, the ceremony in which the pope, as bishop of Rome, took possession of his cathedral, the Church of S. Giovanni in Laterano (see figure 13).[10] The event was scheduled so as to occur on the first anniversary of the battle of Ravenna, which had resulted in Cardinal Giovanni's capture by the French and his subsequent escape; Leo, characteristically, chose to ride the same horse he had ridden at the battle.[11]

Among the hundreds of participants in the elaborate procession, which was reported to have lasted some five hours, were "about twenty-five of the pope's singers," "clothed in surplices and on horseback"[12] and "various instrumentalists dressed in the uniform or livery of the pope, some in velvet, others in the finest cloth, that is, white, red, and green; and on their chest most excellent gold embroidery: there was a diamond with three feathers, one white, one green, and one red, bound at the quill by a *brevicello* on which was written the word *Semper*, and behind, on their back, was a yoke, with this or similar lettering, as above."[13]

The *possesso* is important for our purposes not only because it served to introduce new topoi into the corpus of Medicean conceits but also because of the distinctive character of its principal artistic element: characteristically Roman triumphal arches (see, for example, figure 14),[14] which, unlike the Florentine carnival *carri*, were "static" elements, later to be utilized by Florentine artists on the occasion of one of the most celebrated festive events of the entire century, Leo's 1515 Florentine *entrata*.[15] In the order of the procession, the principal such elements of the *possesso*, which were the products of individual initiative, were the following:[16] an elaborate *apparato* constructed in front of the house of Ceccotto Genovese in the Borgo, which may have spanned the width of the Via Alessandrina (or Borgo Nuovo);[17] the gate in the wall that connected the Castel Sant'Angelo with the Tiber, whose ephemeral decoration served to convert it temporarily into a kind of triumphal arch;[18] an arch at the Ponte Sant'Angelo constructed under the auspices of the *castellano*, Raffaello Petrucci, the bishop of Grosseto;[19] an arch constructed at the behest of the Sienese banker Agostino Chigi in front of his *palazzo* in the Via de' Banchi;[20] at the *Zecca* (the mint) an extraordinary double arch whose

Figure 13. Representation of Leo's
Lateran *possesso*

components had been constructed at the behest of the Florentine mercan-
tile community and "Messer Johanni Zincha Teutonico, master of the
Mint of the *Romana Camera* and *Sede Apostolica*";[21] an arch in Piazza di
Parione (now Piazza di Pasquino) in front of the house of Ferdinando
Ponzetti, *Chierico di Camera*;[22] an arch in front of the house of Bishop
(later Cardinal) Andrea della Valle, opposite the site of the Church of S.
Andrea della Valle;[23] a floral arch in Via Pellicciaria, which corresponded
to Via Cesarini, subsequently absorbed into the Corso Vittorio Emanuele
II;[24] and, on the return route from the Lateran, an arch erected under the
auspices of the Genovese merchants the Sauli, at their house near the
Cancelleria.[25] Other individuals—among them the goldsmith Antonio di
San Marino and the Roman aristocrat Evangelista de' Rossi—resorted to
the less costly expedient of decorating their homes with sculpture.[26]

When Leo was elected, he inherited an extraordinarily rich store of
papal conceits, adapted in some instances to make more uniquely specific
reference to him. Several of the inscriptions that the arches bore invoked
familiar themes that cannot, therefore, be considered specifically Leonine;
others utilized elements of a rapidly developing Leonine iconography

Figure 14. Design for a triumphal arch, attributed to
Baldassare Peruzzi. Possibly the one constructed at
the behest of Agostino Chigi for Leo's *possesso*

that were subsequently to find more mature artistic expression in other
works of art executed for Leo. Available to the various individuals for
whom the *ephemerae* were created, therefore, was an exceptionally large
complex of images—sacred and secular, Christian and classical—which
afforded them almost limitless possibilities. Perhaps inevitably, the content of the corpus of themes embodied in the ephemeral elements of the
possesso accordingly had nothing like the kind of organic integrity and coherence that characterized the "programs" for the 1513 Carnival or the 1514
Triumph of Camillus, for reasons that one scholar has described as attrib-
utable to the effects of "private enterprise . . . that . . . confused the
themes."[27] One should say, however, that it is not the simultaneous appearance of Christian and classical elements on a single arch that leads one
to describe the *possesso*'s themes as "confused," since in an era that would
have been much less likely than ours to see such a combination as
anomalous, there were indeed a great many instances of the use of sacred
and secular references in combination. It is rather that the iconographic

material embodied on the succession of arches seems not to have been organized according to a kind of program.

The arch constructed at the Ponte Sant'Angelo, for example, included among its various elements not only a representation of Christ's donation of the keys to St. Peter and the inscription "LEONI. X. PONT. MAX. UNIONEM ECCLESIASTICAM INSTAURANDI CHRISTIANOQUE TUMULTUS SEDANDI STUDIOSO," but also Apollo with his lyre.[28] Agostino Chigi's arch, similarly, bore the inscription "LEONI. X. PONT. MAX. PACIS RESTITUTORI FELICISSIMO," and thus reflected the same expectation regarding Leo's diplomatic activity that inspired the Florentine *canti* of the preceding month; it was also decorated with representations of mythological figures: Apollo, Mercury, Pallas, centaurs, and nymphs. Bernice Davidson has observed that Apollo was depicted at least six times in the works of art executed for the *possesso*, and, further, that in Vergil's *Eclogue* 4 (line 10), he is proclaimed king of the Golden Age. His representation on the arches may therefore have been intended as a reference to the same topos that was invoked during the festivities for the February carnival.[29]

At the *Zecca*, the arch "bordered the house on two sides, one in the Via *Pontificum*, by which the pope proceeded to the Lateran, the other in the Via Florida, by which he returned."[30] At this point, the permanent facade of the *Zecca* was subsequently to be constructed according to Antonio da San Gallo the Younger's design, which called for a three-dimensional arch raised on a rusticated base, in apparent reference to the ephemeral structure of April 1513. The location of the *Zecca* at the junction of the Vie *Pontificum* and *Peregrinorum* (or Florida) gave it considerable importance, positioned as it was at the point where the processional and recessional routes converged. Accordingly, the statue atop the arch of the Florentine merchants, which spanned the Via *Pontificum*, faced the papal entourage as it proceeded along Via de' Banchi; the statue atop the arch that spanned Via Florida faced the entourage as it returned from the Lateran ("alli dui summitate delli archi si riposava sopra ciascuna una figura . . . , le quale quella che era sopra l'arco de via Pontificum havea volto verso banchi, et l'altra dalla via Florida havea volte le spalle"); between the two were the papal arms.[31] Among the inscriptions contained in the *tondi* and octagons that the arch of the Florentine merchants featured were "Tamquam Moyses" and "Tamquam Aron," which invoked the traditional themes of the *principatus* of Moses and the *pontificatus* of Aaron, a distinction in spheres of authority suggested by texts in Exodus; that the arch employed the traditional references in combination, however, signified that in the New Covenant, *principatus* and *pontificatus* coexist in the heirs to Moses and Aaron, St. Peter and his successors.[32] The arch also featured "a nude Christ, and St. John, protector of our city, who was baptizing him."[33]

That it was precisely at this point in the procession—where "[the two streets] were empty"—that "verses were sung"[34] was appropriate, given the importance of its location in the processional route and the fact that that importance was signaled by the elaborate character of the ephemeral architectural element; there was, in short, a kind of concentration of artistic elements of various kinds—architectural, literary, and musical—which served to underscore the importance of its position. Although the account in Sanuto's diaries fails to specify the verses' content, they could easily have explicated any of the inscriptions contained in the *tondi* or octagons that the structure featured; its thematic content, in short, furnished adequate material for musical elaboration (it is also possible, though in my view unlikely, that the verses' text bore no relationship to any of the various inscriptions on the arch). It is not clear from the reference whether the verses were sung during the course of the procession to the Lateran or upon the return (indeed, the account in Sanuto confuses the various components of the arch and fails to distinguish between its two parts). If they were sung upon the return, they would most likely have explicated material inscribed on the part of the arch constructed at Zincha's behest rather than the part erected for the Florentine merchants. Sanuto's account also does not reveal who performed the verses, and is so brief that we can only speculate as to the stylistic properties of the music. The papal singers could have dismounted and sung the verses; alternatively, other singers—either members of the papal chapel who did not participate in the procession or of another of the city's musical establishments—might have been stationed at the arch. As for the characteristics of the verses' musical setting, I would say that a less spare and simple musical design than that of the February *canti carnascialeschi* would not have been inappropriate, especially if the singers were indeed not participants in the *possesso*'s principal "dynamic" or "kinetic" element, the procession itself, but were instead positioned at the arch. Moreover, as in the case of Leo's 1515 *entrata*, as I suggest below, the verses presumably explicated material inscribed on the arch, so that witnesses' understanding of the content of the verses did not depend exclusively on their being aurally intelligible in performance.

Next in the order of the procession was the arch constructed at the behest of Bishop della Valle, which was decorated with antique statues that formed part of his collection and were later depicted in the border of one of the Cappella Sistina tapestries executed according to Raphael's design.[35]

If the representation of the donation of the keys and the references to Moses and Aaron on the arch of the Florentine merchants invoked traditional themes, other *apparati* employed a more distinctively Medicean and Leonine iconography. On the arch in the Piazza di Parione, for example, Leo as cardinal was depicted as engaged in disputation ("era picto in

habito cardineo el Papa in sedia, et parea che con certi vecchi disputassi"),
an apparent reference to the *disputa* Cardinal Giovanni conducted in
Rome around 1511 on the one theological problem on which he is known
to have expressed his views—the immortality of the soul.[36] During the
course of its return to the Vatican upon the conclusion of the ceremonies
at the Lateran, the papal entourage passed the arch at the Casa de' Sauli
(see figure 15), which similarly employed a Leonine conceit of fundamental importance, as the principal narrative account of the *possesso* reveals:

> And the procession having passed the Cancelleria, at the house of the
> Sauli, Genovese merchants, *depositarii* of *Sua Santità*, was erected an
> unusually ingenious arch. Beneath the arch, in its underside, which
> was divided into eight sections, one saw the arms of the pope in an
> octagon in the middle. The octagon, as Leo passed by it, was raised
> up, and from there emerged a *palla*, which opened, and inside was a
> young boy who, with bold spirit and cheerful expression, recited
> these verses: "Si fuerat dubium superis an regna daretur, / Am-
> biguum princeps optimus omne levat, / Nam rebus nemo fessis
> adhibere salutem, / Nec melius medicus sciret habere manus." The
> said verses having been recited, the *palla* withdrew inside, and the
> arms returned to their place.[37]

The Sauli's arch employed the image of Leo as a "medicus" who would
cure the ills of the Church, an image whose success depended in good
part, of course, on the coincidence that Leo was a Medici. It was invoked
repeatedly in literary works composed during Leo's pontificate and finds
expression, for example, in the text of Isaac's motet *Optime pastor ovili
tandem qui laceri medicus gregis ulcera sanes*, among a great many other
texts.[38]

Zincha's *apparato* also utilized specifically Leonine material. In each of
the eight octagons was depicted one of the principal events of Leo's life;
an explanatory Latin verse inscribed on the arch indicated that each occurred on the eleventh day of the month, although, in fact, only four of
them did. Their importance to Leonine imagery is suggested by the fact
that six of the events depicted were later to be represented as well in the
borders of the tapestries for the Cappella Sistina: Cardinal Giovanni's
entry into Florence on March 10, 1492, after his Investiture with the cardinalate on the previous day; the entry into Rome for the conclave, which
resulted in his election on March 11, 1513; his flight from Florence on November 9, 1494, following the exile of his brothers Piero and Giuliano; his
capture at the battle of Ravenna on April 11, 1512; his subsequent escape;
and events in the restoration of 1512—that is, his return to Florence on
September 14 and the *parlamento* in Piazza della Signoria on the sixteenth
(the arch constructed in Piazza di Parione—which was also decorated
with representations of Apollo, Bacchus, Hercules, Mercury, and

Figure 15. Baldassare Peruzzi, design for a
triumphal arch, possibly the one constructed
at the behest of the Sauli for Leo's *possesso*

Venus—similarly depicted the cardinal's escape from captivity; the presence of an angel in the scene served to suggest the miraculous nature of
the escape). Zincha's *apparato* further depicted Leo's birth, which occurred on December 11, 1475, and the Lateran *possesso* itself, which occurred on April 11.[39]

Subsequently,

> the pope passed the arch of Agostino Chigi and of the *castellano*,
> with the sounds of instruments and artillery discharges, and thus
> having joyously returned to the Borgo and passed the *adornamento*
> of Cecchotto, he reentered the Apostolic Palace; the cardinals of the
> Holy Church having thus been dismissed, and all the other prelates,
> each returned to his residence, and with bonfires and other signs of
> rejoicing one demonstrated one's happiness all night in *feste*, the
> playing of instruments, and song.[40]

Celebratory *canti* and the "suoni di varj instrumenti" were suitable
responses to Leo's election; he ought to have been gratified.

GIULIANO DE' MEDICI'S
CAPITOLINE
INVESTITURE

AFTER LEO's election, a new set of themes was featured prominently in works of art and literature executed for Medici patrons: in addition to the themes of return and regeneration that one finds expressed in works composed during the first months of the restoration, there were allusions to the Roman citizenship of the Medici and to the unity of Florence and Rome. It scarcely needs to be said that throughout the entire period of the Renaissance, classical references were of absolutely central importance to artistic programs of the type under consideration here; as we have seen, they were important to the program for the 1513 Carnival. Clearly, one cannot say, therefore, that such elements as were utilized by the artists responsible for the ceremonies for Giuliano's 1513 Investiture with Roman citizenship[1] were in any way novel. Nonetheless, Leo's election served to encourage—and legitimize—the use of conceits that made reference, for example, to the Florentines' Roman ancestry. Among the works that utilized such topoi were quasi-dramatic scenes staged during the ceremonies for the 1513 Capitoline Investiture, scenes in which Leo's and Giuliano's Roman mother, Clarice Orsini, was represented, and the unity of Florence and Rome was symbolized by allegorical figures that personified the Arno and Tiber rivers; in addition, Leo's personal device, the yoke, was seen to unite Romulus and Remus, the legendary founders of Rome, with the constellation Ursa (i.e., "Orsini") Major.[2]

The ceremonies on the Capitoline also involved important musical elements, some of which are of unusual interest not only for what they tell us about the specific contexts in which music figured in such festivities but also for the insights they afford into the variety of musical practices in Medici circles and perhaps even for the relationship of these practices to those of other patrons.

Two individuals of exceptional importance to Roman cultural and intellectual life, among others, were charged with responsibility for the festivities: Tommaso Inghirami *detto* "Fedra," professor of rhetoric at the University of Rome, Vatican librarian, secretary of both the conclave of

1513 and the Lateran council, assumed responsibility for the program for the decoration of the temporary theater constructed for the event, and perhaps for its architectural program, as well as for the direction of Plautus's *Poenulus*, performed on the fourteenth of September;[3] Camillo Porzio, *oratore*, poet, jurist, and Latinist, assumed responsibility for the succession of floats that served to convey the event's political meaning.[4]

Each of the principal chroniclers—Marcantonio Altieri, who himself was one of those responsible for planning the festivities, Paolo Palliolo, and Francesco Chierigati—provided unusually detailed information about the ceremonies. And the general agreement of the three accounts as to the various elements of the festivities serves once again to increase one's confidence in their accuracy, although I should point out that even though the accounts agree reasonably closely as to the content of each of the dramatic scenes, they differ as to the order in which they were presented; moreover, Chierigati's letter states that the final scene before the performance of Plautus's *Poenulus* was presented at the end of the first day, whereas Palliolo's account—which is the fullest and the one I generally follow—suggests that it took place on the second day, immediately before the performance of the comedy. How might one explain such disparities among the accounts? In some instances, "retrospective" narratives were based upon "prospective" programs drafted prior to the events in question; changes that came about subsequent to the drafting of the programs may therefore not be reflected in accounts based closely on them. Indeed, as we shall see, the program for Leo's 1515 Florentine *entrata* prescribed seven triumphal arches. Jacopo Nardi's description of the *entrata* corresponds closely to the prescriptions in the program and differs accordingly from other accounts that record a greater number of ephemeral architectural elements than the program provided for. John Shearman has suggested, plausibly, that Nardi himself may have been the author of the program; alternatively, the program may have been one of his sources.[5]

Altieri reported:

> On the thirteenth of September, the magnificent Signor Giovangiorgio Cesarini, *gonfaloniere* of the *Popolo romano* and the *capo della festa*, proceeded with an infinite number of wind players and trumpeters to the papal palace where Giuliano was staying. And thus received, Giuliano was accompanied throughout the entire city with the endless and varied playing of the aforementioned instruments.[6]

The piazza was already crowded with observers when the procession reached the Capitoline Hill, where the temporary theater had been constructed in the corner formed by the Palazzi Senatorio and de' Conservatori.[7] In 1513, of course, the Capitoline had yet to be transformed according to Michelangelo's design into the remarkable assemblage of ar-

Figure 16. Anonymous representation of the Capitoline prior to reconstruction
according to Michelangelo's design

chitectural and sculptural monuments one sees today. On the contrary,
the site was marked, in the words of James Ackerman, by "muddy foot-
paths" and a "disorderly complex" of "dilapidated palaces" (see figure 16).
"Perhaps [Michelangelo's] project," Professor Ackerman continued, "was
visualized as a translation into permanent materials of those arches, gates,
and facades of wood and canvas erected in the sixteenth century for the
triumphal entries and processions of great princes."[8]

In 1513, in the absence of any such permanent structures appropriate to
the importance of the occasion, the city officials resorted to the expedient
of an ephemeral structure, and an elaborate one (see figures 19–22). The
theater measured some thirty-seven by thirty-one meters and was approx-
imately eighteen meters high.[9] It was covered by an awning striped in
white, blue, and green.[10] Constructed of wood, its building materials had
been decorated so as to resemble marble.[11] The theater's facade and interior walls bore paintings *all'antica* in chiaroscuro, imitating reliefs, and
framed by fluted and gilded columns (see figures 19, 20, and 22). The facade paintings represented the foundation of Rome, of the Capitoline
(*The Surrender of the Tarpeian Rock to the Sabines*) and of the Temple of
Jupiter (see figure 19).[12] Vasari reported that different artists were responsible for the scenes and that Baldassare Peruzzi's painting was judged the

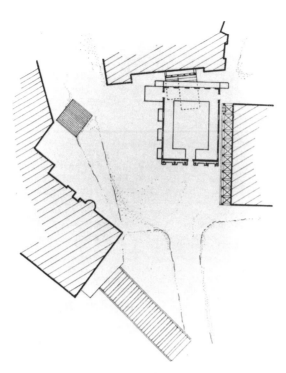

Figure 17. Plan of the Capitoline in 1513 showing the location of the temporary theater constructed for the Investiture ceremonies: the Church of the Aracoeli is to the left, the Palazzo de' Conservatori to the right, and the Palazzo Senatorio at to

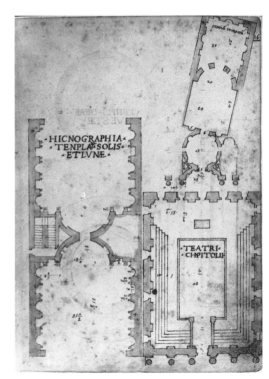

Figure 18. Preliminary design for the plan of the theater

Figure 19. Hypothetical reconstruction of the design of the theater's facade

Figure 20. Hypothetical reconstruction of the design of the wall opposite the
theater's entrance

most successful of them: "that by the hand of Baldassare, twenty-eight
braccia high and fourteen broad, showing the betrayal of the Romans by
Julia Tarpeia, was judged to be without a doubt better than any of the
others."[13] Above the paintings were various allegorical figures: on one

Figure 21. Hypothetical reconstruction of a longitudinal section of the theater

side the she-wolf with Romulus and Remus and a figure representing the Tiber, on the other the Florentine lion with a *palla* under one of its paws and a figure representing the Arno.[14] The far wall of the theater's interior—whose architectural features included five doors, closed by gold curtains, which opened onto the steps of the Palazzo Senatorio and thus afforded the actors access to the theater[15]—had been similarly decorated (see figure 20), and, like some elements of the facade decoration and the narrative content of several of the dramatic scenes, reflected the theme of Florentine-Roman unity: depicted were relations between the Etruscans—the putative precursors of the Florentines—and the ancient Romans. Above were friezes that displayed traditional Medicean devices: *palle*, yokes, diamonds, and lions.[16] Covered benches lined the walls on three sides of the theater's interior. On the fourth side, against the wall opposite the entrance, was constructed a platform that served, successively, as the site of the celebration of the mass, the orations delivered in Giuliano's honor, the banquet, the presentation of the scenes, and the performance of *Poenulus* (see figure 22).[17]

The benches provided space for perhaps fifteen hundred to two thousand observers; many others stood. Others still—Roman nobles—had had benches constructed in the space between the theater and the Church of the Aracoeli, from which they viewed the proceedings through the theater's windows; on the other side, similarly, there were observers positioned at the windows of the Palazzo de' Conservatori. There were even those who had opened holes in the walls of the theater so that they could witness the festivities. In all, there were probably around three thousand observers.[18]

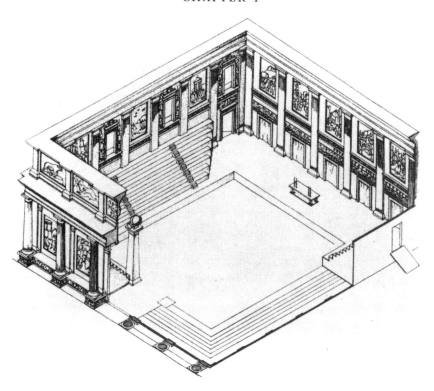

Figure 22. Hypothetical reconstruction of the theater's interior

Various introductory ceremonies were concluded; Giuliano and the members of his retinue and numerous Roman officials, ambassadors and other attendees were arranged on either side of the altar. Then, "the most remarkable music having quieted everyone," "in a manner suited to such solemnity, the priests and singers began the polyphonic mass,"[19] "which was sung by Joannes Dominici, the bishop of L'Aquila"[20] and "which all attended devoutly."[21]

Absent more specific information, one can only speculate as to the identity of the "infinito numero de bifari e trombette" who furnished the music for the procession and of the singers who performed the "solenne messa in canto figurato." That various institutions in the city maintained establishments whose members were capable of assuming responsibility for the performances, however, is clear. For many years, perhaps for centuries, the municipal government had maintained bands of instrumentalists—identified variously as musicians of the Capitoline or the Senate—

the participation in 1513 of whose early cinquecento incarnation would have been entirely appropriate, given that the city itself was formally responsible for the decision to confer Roman citizenship on the honoree. That the instrumentalists' responsibilities specifically included performance at dinners—indeed, two musicians were dismissed in 1530 for having failed to fulfill such obligations satisfactorily—further suggests that the city musicians may have been those who performed for Giuliano's Investiture, since the elaborate banquet formed an important part of the ceremonies.[22] As for the singers, one might be inclined to speculate that they were members of the Cappella Sistina, especially since the honoree's brother was the pope. Here again, however, it is important to recognize that there were protocols that Leo was anxious to honor. The participation of the Cappella Sistina might well have served to obscure a distinction between the prerogatives of the civic government and those of the papacy—a delicate distinction that both parties would certainly have wished to maintain (indeed, the very fact that the Capitoline itself had been selected as the location for the ceremonies suggests that such political considerations were at issue).[23] One of the earliest documents that records the existence of a corps of instrumentalists in the employ of the *Popolo Romano* specifies that there were "two choruses of musicians, one of voices and the other of instrumentalists." And although the earliest sixteenth-century archival reference fails to mention vocalists, it is nonetheless perfectly conceivable that the city also had singers in its employ who were responsible for performing the polyphonic mass. As for the music the instrumental and vocal ensembles performed, I can do no more than point to the existence of documents demonstrating that on occasion the Capitoline instrumentalists did indeed purchase books of music, although the references are from considerably later.[24] It is not difficult to imagine how the singers might have come into possession of the polyphonic mass they performed, whatever their identity.

After the mass, there followed the conferring of Roman citizenship on Giuliano. A lectern covered in gold cloth was placed on the platform from which Lorenzo Valli, *scriba perpetua* of the Roman Senate, and Mario Scapuccio, prior of the *Conservatori*, delivered celebratory orations; Giuliano expressed his thanks.[25] Then, "the *Conservatori* and *Magistrati* had the privilege of citizenship, which had been granted to Giuliano by the Roman Senate and people, loudly proclaimed. It having been read, so great was the noise of trumpets, *pifari*, and artillery discharges that not only the Capitoline and Rome but also the surrounding region reverberated."[26]

There followed a short interval, during which the altar and lectern were removed from the platform in order to prepare for the magnificent banquet, which consisted of more than eighty courses, announced by instrumental fanfares; one of the chroniclers was careful to note that "the old custom of playing and singing after the banquet was not omitted."[27]

Then the Roman authorities and their Florentine guests retired briefly to the Palazzo de' Conservatori while the platform was readied for the playing of the scenes. Giuliano and the Florentines who formed his entourage were seated to the right of the platform; the *carri* entered from the theater's leftmost door—the large door in the wall closest to the Church of the Aracoeli—and exited to the right after the enactment of the scenes at the center of the platform.[28] The actors who played the various roles in the scenes and in the performance of *Poenulus*—including the roles for women—were boys, young Roman aristocrats; all of the texts were recited or sung in Latin:[29] "Various kinds of instrumental music were heard, after which there appeared a lady representing Rome, who recited an oration."[30] "And then, the nymphs who were with her having sung other beautiful verses in honor of his Holiness and the aforementioned magnificent Giuliano,"[31]

> Rome and the nymphs with her exited, accompanied by the sounds of trumpets, *piffari*, and other harmonies. The playing having ceased, an eclogue was recited, in which two peasants took part. They sang many verses in rustic style to a lute, one in honor of his Holiness, the other in praise of the magnificent Giuliano. This was the conclusion of the eclogue, after which followed the music of *piffari*.[32]

As one sees, instrumental interludes served to introduce and conclude the recitations and the staging of each of the "dramatic" presentations. In addition to the music that set off the various scenes, instrumental and vocal performances were incorporated into the presentations themselves. The recitation of the eclogue, for example, involved the singing of verses to the lute (the practice of solo singing to string accompaniment is thus documented in Medici circles once more). Nor, by any means, were the presentation of the first of the dramatic scenes and of the eclogue the only such to involve music:

> A large mountain followed, from which, in the presence of Giuliano, exited Monte Tarpeio, who was dressed in Carthaginian style and had a large beard, and he was clothed in garments of paper, which had been made in such a way as to resemble the mountain and which looked like a small hill, and he had Rome on his shoulders. He sang several verses in honor of his Holiness. Then, Rome and the Romans having been commended to Giuliano, Monte Tarpeio withdrew inside the mountain and moved on.[33]
>
> A *carro* entered accompanied and conducted by eight soldiers, armed in ancient Roman style, and a good many nymphs. In the

middle of the *carro* sat Rome; to the right sat Justice; to the left sat Fortitude. The nymphs and soldiers made the sweetest music, after which they exited together with the *carro*, Rome, Justice, and Fortitude.[34]

Evening was approaching, and before the playing of the following scene, torches were carried into the theater and placed about the proscenium. Then:

> After a short interval, many Corybants entered, priests of Cybele, who came distributing gold and playing various instruments. These were the musicians of Cardinal Ippolito d'Este of Ferrara, and they, too, sang a good many verses to the sweetest of music. After them there followed a *carretta*, made in the antique way; two lions were drawing it. In it was seated Cybele, in front of whom was a great ball, made so as to resemble the earth [see figure 23]. The ball divided in two and from it emerged Rome in the form of a most beautiful young woman, dressed in gold and crowned. Having exited, she sang several verses.[35]
>
> Another gilded *carro* followed on which was a lady representing Florence, who recited several verses, complaining that Rome had deprived her of his Holiness and the magnificent Giuliano. She stepped down and approached Giuliano, feigning tears because he had abandoned Florence, which had sustained and educated him until that time. She fell to her knees before Cybele, who wanted Rome and Florence to become one. And the union was realized. As a sign of rejoicing, several newly composed hymns were sung and played by the musicians of the cardinal d'Este.

Although the scene's dramatic situation, to be sure, would not have warranted gestures as emphatic as those depicted in Raphael's *Death of Ananias*, we might nonetheless concur with the suggestion that Raphael's cartoon employs the "visual language" of contemporary Roman theater, in whose practices Inghirami was a figure of central importance. If the suggestion is indeed applicable in this instance, it assists in our attempts to visualize the performance of the quasi-dramatic scenes.[36]

We have already seen one text that documents the presence of Cardinal Ippolito d'Este of Ferrara on the occasion of a musical performance in Medici Rome,[37] and we shall see yet another;[38] the three references suggest not only that Ippolito enjoyed a personal relationship with Leo, but that one of the bases for that relationship may have been a common interest in music. Ippolito is one of the few cardinals of the period whose activities as music patron are documented in any detail;[39] Michele Pesenti, one of the musicians known to have been in his employ in 1513 who

Figure 23. Baldassare Peruzzi, design for a triumphal
carro, possibly the one for the dramatic scene that
depicted the goddess Cybele

may therefore have been among the members of the "musica del Cardinale di Ferrara" who performed for the Capitoline festivities, subsequently entered Leo's service, and the decision to do so may have resulted
from a professional acquaintance first made in 1513.[40] More important,
such a personal relationship between Ippolito and Leo would surely help
to explain some Ferrarese-papal musical connections reflected in roughly
contemporary musical sources.[41] As for Chierigati's use of the term
"hymni," I believe his precision was specious and that one can conclude
little about the genre of the pieces performed from his use of the term,
other than that they were presumably in relatively simple homophony,
perhaps with instrumental accompaniment played "colla parte."

On the afternoon of the fourteenth of September, the last of the scenes
involving musical elements was staged, as was Plautus's *Poenulus*: "The
following day, instrumental music of various kinds was heard throughout
the theater. When at last there was silence, a very ornate *carro* entered,"[42]
"led by four of the pope's white horses with four nymphs mounted on
them."[43]

On it, toward the front, was a pelican. Around its neck it was wearing a yoke. On the right side was a she-wolf with Romulus and Remus nursing, on the left the celestial Orsa. In the middle of the *carro* was planted a beautiful laurel. Resting against the base of this laurel was an elegant chair, in which was seated the goddess Clarice of the Orsini, mother of the magnificent Giuliano, descended from heaven and dressed in gold. Father Tiber was lying nearby, to the right, Arno to the left, both with white beards and hair.[44] Standing on the *carro*, all three sang several verses.[45]

Two nymphs in Clarice's service came on foot behind the *carro*. And when the *carro* came before the magnifcent Giuliano, Clarice, singing, addressed many verses to him. One of the said nymphs who followed the *carro*, seeing everything to be festive and joyful, invited her companions to sing verses of this sentiment together: "O, nymphs, inhabitants of the Tiber and inhabitants of the Arno, let us sing together. O, Tiber and Arno nymphs, let us sing together." Finally the nymphs began the sweetest of music.[46]

That the Tiber and Arno nymphs joined in song captured the essential political message of the Investiture ceremony perhaps more effectively than any other of its artistic elements, their "sweetest of music" a metaphor for the similarly harmonious political relationship between Rome and Florence.

Chierigati added: "The *festa* was concluded and before leaving, the four nymphs on horseback sang a *frottola* in honor of the magnificent Giuliano."[47] In this instance, too, I do not believe that we can infer from Chierigati's account that the piece concluding the scene was necessarily a *frottola* and that it therefore displayed some of the musical characteristics typical of the genre. Chierigati was a Mantuan agent, and his letter was directed to the marchesa Isabella d'Este Gonzaga. He used a term that would have been familiar to him, and his conversance with the musical traditions of the Mantuan court would likely have led him to describe many secular pieces indiscriminately as *frottole*, unless he was considerably better informed about music than many others who held similar positions at the time. His use of the term is especially interesting in that he specified further that all four of the "nimphe" participated in the performance ("le quatro nimphe . . . cantorno una frotola"); accordingly, the work evidently did *not* display one of the most characteristic features of the genre—the opposition of a solo vocal line to string accompaniment. At minimum, one can conclude from his reference that the piece was a setting of a secular text whose stylistic properties were similar enough to those of works in the *frottola* repertory that Chierigati did not hesitate to use the term.

The principal account continues: "After much playing of trumpets and *pifari*, *Penulo*, a comedy by Plautus, was performed, not translated into Italian, but in Latin."[48] Notwithstanding the unmagnanimous judgment of a Mantuan observer, who reported to the marchese that "the theater *apparato* and costumes were not to be compared in any way to your Excellency's,"[49] Baldassare Peruzzi's stage scenery was said by Vasari to have elicited an extraordinary response: "what amazed everyone most was the perspective-view or scenery for a play, which was so beautiful that it would be impossible to imagine anything finer, seeing that the variety and beautiful manner of the buildings, the various *logge*, the extravagance of the doors and windows, and the other architectural details that were seen in it, were so well conceived and so extraordinary in invention, that one is not able to describe the thousandth part."[50]

> The actor who was to recite the prologue appeared on stage. And having finished the recitation of the prologue, he exited as he had entered. There then began the sweet harmony of *pifari*, which lasted for a good while; thereafter neither other choruses nor music nor instrumental playing was heard during the performance of the comedy, except for the trumpet of the crier when he addressed the people. And in this they approximated the method of performing comedies maintained in Plautus's times and also Terence's, according to which the chorus had no place, but only *pifari*—otherwise called *tibie*—were employed.[51]

Scrupulous fidelity to what was presumed in this instance to be classical tradition precluded a practice that was subsequently to become standard: the performance of instrumental or vocal music—*intermedii*—between the acts of dramatic works. That theatrical performances in Medici circles were soon to include such elements is attested by evidence that documents performances of Lorenzo Strozzi's "Commedia in versi" in the Palazzo Medici in September of 1518 on the occasion of Lorenzo II's wedding, of Ariosto's *I suppositi* in the Vatican Palace in 1519, of Machiavelli's *La Clizia* at the home of Jacopo di Filippo Falconetti *detto* "il Fornaciaio" outside the walls at San Frediano in January of 1525, a performance whose witnesses may have included Alessandro and Ippolito de' Medici, and of Lorenzino de' Medici's *Aridosia* in the Loggia de' Tessitori in June of 1536 on the occasion of Alessandro's wedding. The comedies of Terence and Plautus, of course, are of particular importance in the history of Italian Renaissance theater; and in Medici Rome, as in other centers, there was a flourishing tradition of performances of works by both classical authors: in April of 1514, for example, there was a performance of Plautus's *Asinaia* following a dinner whose attendees, once again, included Giuliano de' Medici.[52]

The theatrical performance concluded at sunset on the fourteenth; the actors assembled on the platform anew, and thus the many satisfied members of the audience were afforded the opportunity to see them one last time. So successful was the entire *festa* that the pope wished to have it repeated, and on the eighteenth of September, the "prose, versi, musiche et comedia" were performed once again at the Apostolic Palace.

One cannot argue on the basis of evidence that documents a single such event that the Capitoline Investiture was in any way typical in its use of music; nevertheless, a single reference alludes specifically to polyphonic music, amid references to the instrumental accompaniment to the procession, instrumental fanfares that followed the conferring of Roman citizenship on Giuliano, instrumental interludes that served to articulate the sequence of recitations and the staging of the scenes, solo singing to the lute, and vocal and instrumental performances whose specific musical characteristics are, for the most part, not otherwise detailed, apart from the presumably specious references to "hymni" and "una frotola." Of course, one should bear in mind that the music formed part of an elaborate political and social event that dictated its "language," its stylistic features. Despite the methodological hazards of arguing from the absence of evidence to the contrary, I would argue, nonetheless, that many of the references presented thus far—those pertaining to the 1513 Carnival as well as to the Capitoline Investiture—testify to musical practices that in one sense may be construed as relatively circumscribed in character, in the relative absence of performances of polyphonic music, but in another sense document a musical culture of considerably greater variety than the surviving practical sources suggest.

LEO X'S 1515 FLORENTINE
ENTRATA

THE ARTISTIC and musical elements of the Capitoline Investiture expressed the topos of Florentine-Roman unity. That Florence and Rome were ever more closely connected after 1513, culturally and politically, is reflected as well in the artistic elements of the festivities organized for Leo's 1515 Florentine *entrata*, though in a very different way. In 1513, in part perhaps because of its newness, the political relationship between the two cities was invoked explicitly, in precise textual references in the *canti* and the didactic symbolism of the allegorical figures in the quasi-dramatic presentations. The explicitness and "self-consciousness" of the references also resulted from the occasional nature of the event as well as from the relative newness of the political circumstances that formed its background. In 1515, conversely, Florentine-Roman political associations were reflected less overtly in the program for the ephemeral works of art created for the occasion, though they were nonetheless evident. Indeed, the significance of the character of the artistic program was not lost on contemporaries, even if the political relationship between Florence and Rome was not expressly detailed as in the case of the Capitoline Investiture, though some contemporaries may have been too willing to attribute a significance to the works of art that they may not have had: an ephemeral structure at the corner of Via Tornabuoni and Via Porta Rossa—which bore an inscription to the effect that Florence was under the protection of two lions (the *marzocco*, one of the city's traditional symbols, and Pope Leo) and two Johns (John the Baptist, the city's patron saint, and Giovanni de' Medici)—was thought by Masi to have resembled the Castel Sant'Angelo;[1] another chronicler remarked repeatedly that Florence resembled Rome.[2] To some extent, the relationship is suggested even by the very type of *ephemerae* created: in February of 1513, the works of art ornamented Carnival *carri*, quintessentially Florentine in character; in November of 1515, there were instead triumphal arches of the type used during Leo's Lateran *possesso*, inscribed with texts explicated by verses of *canti*.[3] To be sure, the works were created for the visit of the pope, who, in addition to being a Medici, now possessed clear Roman associations. Upon his election he inherited an elaborate ceremonial protocol, which served in good part to determine the character of such events as the 1515 *entrata*. As we shall see, subsequent festivals organized in Florence made use of traditionally Florentine elements, and one should certainly attribute the distinctive character of the 1515 *ephemerae* in part to the fact that the pope was the dedicatee.[4]

The *entrata* was occasioned by the French victory at Marignano over the Swiss and their allies, who included the Florentines and the pope, and the consequent need for a conciliatory meeting between Leo and King Francis I.[5] There was some discussion as to where the meeting ought to take place. One possibility entertained was Florence itself, but the Medici would not have forgotten the political circumstances that occasioned Charles VIII's elaborate Florentine *entrata* of 1494, shortly after their exile, and they opted for Bologna. Ever cognizant of the potential benefits of a successful *festa*, Leo and his relatives decided that he instead would enter Florence by means of a formal *entrata*.[6]

It promised to be an unusually memorable such event. The considerable financial resources of the papacy afforded the Medici the means to indulge whatever taste they may have had for extravagant public ceremony, certainly, but Leo's election had had another, more symbolic (and less material) consequence: however reluctant the family may have been for political reasons to indulge such tastes during the fifteenth century, Leo's election liberated and emboldened them. As pope, he could afford to behave in ways that some of his ancestors, prudently, had avoided. And the city of Florence, similarly, was more willing to countenance such behavior in a Medici who was vicar of Christ, and thus to respond in kind:

> There were orders given for *trionfi* and *apparati* designed to honor him as much as possible. His Holiness departed from Rome, and Lorenzo, having returned from Francis's camp, set out toward the pope in turn, and in the city woodworkers and painters and other artisans were all engaged in work, and the entire city readied itself for the celebrations. On the thirtieth of November, the feast of St. Andrew, his Holiness entered Florence.[7]

One of the most informative of the sources is written "prospectively": it specifies that the triumphal arches to be constructed along the route of the procession were, according to a Renaissance convention,[8] to represent the cardinal and theologic virtues, which in this instance were interpreted as attributes of Leo's person; that an eighth arch at the Canto de' Carnesecchi would symbolize the summation of the virtues in Leo; and that explanatory verses would be sung that explicated the inscriptions each arch was to bear; at the first, "an appropriate explanatory song will be sung," at the second and third "musica," and at the Canto de' Carnesecchi

> will be a structure in the form of a triumphal arch, above which—his Holiness having acquired all of the aforementioned virtues—will be the four cardinal virtues supporting the papal throne, that is, "Prudentia" in front ("ut caveat a futuris"), "Justizia" in back ("ut satisfaciat de preteritis"), "Temperentia" to the right ("non ellevetur in Prosperis"), "Fortezza" to the left ("ne succumbat in adversis"). The throne being empty, above it will be "Fede," "Speranza," and "Carità," who will hold the tiara, and there will be beautiful music signifying that, his Holiness having taken possession of the virtues, those ladies prepared a *trionfo* for him.

Leo's residence during his stay was to be the Sala del Papa in the Church of Santa Maria Novella, and the account prescribes that "at the entry to the Sala del Papa, a most beautiful structure symbolizing human and divine happiness is prepared, and there, with music, he rests."[9] The close agreement between Jacopo Nardi's account in his *Istorie* and the prescriptions suggests that he, once again, may have been the author of the "program":[10]

> Beginning at the Porta Romana and as far as the Cathedral, seven magnificent and beautiful triumphal arches were constructed in various places; they represented the four cardinal and the three theologic virtues; at each several verses were sung in the pope's honor, which were appropriate to the particular virtue that the arch represented.[11]

That events did not unfold exactly as prescribed and as recounted by Nardi, however, is suggested by a number of the other retrospective narratives. The structure that Masi likened to the Castel Sant'Angelo was only one of several *ephemerae* that were apparently not originally envisioned: at the north end of Ponte Santa Trìnita was an obelisk that Masi and Paris de Grassis described as a copy of one at the Vatican; a column designed by Bandinelli that replicated Trajan's, according to Vasari and Ammirato, was erected in the Mercato Nuovo (these last two elements, similarly, may have prompted the observation that Florence had been decorated in such a way as to resemble Rome); Bandinelli was also responsible for a statue of Hercules in the Piazza della Signoria; and in Piazza Santa Maria Novella was an equestrian statue executed by Sarto and Jacopo Sansovino.[12]

Among detailed records of payments to the artists responsible for executing the ephemeral artistic elements is one recording payment of "fifty-six *fiorini larghi in oro* given to the singers who sang on the afore-mentioned arches," one of the instances where an "archival" reference substantiates the testimony of "narrative" accounts. Because the payment to the "cantori" was recorded in the *Libro di condotta . . . dagli Otto di Pratica* (1514ff., fol. 89ᵛ), it is reasonable to assume that they were members of the chapel of one of the city's public ecclesiastical institutions. The Florentine instrumentalists who participated are likely to have been the employees of the Signoria.[13]

As in the case of the 1513 Carnival, the documentation for Leo's *entrata* is thus exceptionally rich, and it is possible to form a remarkably vivid image of that extraordinary event and reconstruct its prominent musical element.

An account that concentrates on the *entrata*'s principal "dynamic" or "kinetic" element,[14] the procession itself, specifies that among the hundreds of richly attired participants were instrumentalists: after various members of the curia, "there followed forty-five of the pope's relatives, all magnificently dressed and very skilled riders. Thereafter, on foot, came all the artisans of Florence, in order, with four trumpeters with newly designed flags. Thereafter, the *Gonfalonieri* of the quarters of the city and the eight members of the *Signoria* on foot. Then sixteen trumpeters with flags with the arms of the city of Florence."[15]

As we have seen, the papal entourage entered the city by the Porta Romana, and at each of the arches—in order, at the Porta Romana, the Church of San Felice, the Ponte Santa Trìnita, the Piazza della Signoria, the Badia, the Canto de' Bischeri (at the corner of Via dell'Oriuolo and Piazza del Duomo), the Cathedral, where the *trionfo* took the form of a temporary facade, and the Canto de' Carnesecchi (at the corner of Vie de' Bianchi and Rondinelli) (see the accompanying plan, figure 24)—it paused as prescribed so that Leo could listen to the singing of the verses, as we learn not only from Nardi but from Paris de Grassis, the papal master of ceremonies, as well: "on these were sung various *cantilenae*, which the pope appeared to enjoy listening to."[16] (Both Cambi and Paris de Grassis also recorded that as in the case of the Lateran *possesso*, altars had been constructed at various points along the route of the procession and that clerics and members of monastic orders stationed there sang during the course of the procession.)[17] And from the descriptions of the arches in the various narrative accounts, one can draw some conclusions about the iconographic material that the explanatory *canti* elucidated.

Vasari described the arch at Porta Romana, which symbolized the virtue of "Prudentia," as "entirely historiated" and Landucci recorded four silvered columns sixteen *braccia* high, and additional pilasters. Other chroniclers variously described the decoration: one specified that the frieze contained mirrors encircled by serpents, another that the decora-

Figure 24. Plan of the route of the papal procession and location of the principal elements of the ephemeral decoration for Leo's 1515 *entrata*: A. the Cathedral of Florence; B. Palazzo Medici; C. Palazzo Vecchio; D. the Church of Santa Croce; E. Palazzo Pitti; F. the Church of Santo Spirito; G. the Church of Santa Maria Novella; H. the Church of San Lorenzo; 1. the arch at Porta Romana; 2. the arch in Piazza San Felice; 3. the arch at the south end of Ponte Santa Trinita; 4. the obelisk at the north end of Ponte Santa Trinita; 5. the *teatro* in Piazza Santa Trinita; 6. the column in the *Mercato Nuovo*; 7. Bandinelli's *Hercules*; 8. the arch in Piazza della Signoria; 9. the arch at the Badia; 10. the arch at the Canto de' Bischeri; 11. the temporary facade of the Cathedral; 12. the arch at the Canto de' Carnesechi; 13. the equestrian statue in Piazza Santa Maria Novella; 14. Bandinelli's "bellissimo edificio" at the entrance to the Sala del Papa in the Church of Santa Maria Novella

tion included representations of the fates, the baptism and temptation of Christ, and Tobias and the angel.[18]

The second arch—in Piazza San Felice—featured a figure of "Temperentia" that poured water first into one vase and then into another, and illustrative Old Testament stories, and was constructed of several pilasters and eight columns ten to twelve *braccia* in height, which were decorated so as to resemble marble and supported a "palco doro"; Cerretani and other chroniclers further recorded a portrait of Lorenzo "il Magnifico" and the inscription "Hic est filius meus dilectus" (Matthew 3.17), which was said to have brought the pope to tears.[19] The inscription thus made explicit what was surely implicit: that Leo was to be seen as Christ, and his *entrata* as Christ's triumphal entry into Jerusalem.

The third arch, at the north end of Via Maggio, symbolized the virtue of "Fortezza" and was reported to have been as wide as Ponte Santa Trìnita and constructed of six large columns that resembled serpentine and porphyry; its inscription, "LEONI .X. LABORVM VICTORI [Leo X, Victor over the Labors]", employed a Herculean metaphor that, as we shall see, was to be invoked still more explicitly later in the course of the *entrata*. Among the elements of the decoration were representations of Judith and Holofernes and Samson destroying the temple (on the side facing Via Maggio) and Joshua at Jericho, and David and Goliath (on the side facing Ponte Santa Trìnita).[20]

The ephemeral elements at the north end of Ponte Santa Trìnita, in Piazza Santa Trìnita and in the Mercato Nuovo—the obelisk, *teatro*, and column, all additions to the original program—apparently did not serve as loci for musical performances. The arch constructed in the Piazza della Signoria, on the other hand, presumably did. The structure was reportedly located where Ammanati's *Neptune* now stands and symbolized the virtue of "Justizia." The narratives variously describe either a structure that consisted of four arches arranged in the form of an *arcus quadrifrons*—each arch surmounted by a representation of "Justizia"—or, alternatively, an octagon; Landucci recorded paired columns at each corner, which were said to have been white, their lower portions fluted, their upper portions decorated with gilded foliage in relief, and surmounted by Corinthian capitals. Other features included a frieze, an inscription in gilded lettering at the summit that read "LEONI .X. PONT. MAX. PROPTER MERITA," and illustrative iconographical material appropriate to the theme of "Justizia": among other elements were representations of Daniel, Brutus, and Solomon.[21] Vasari's commentary on his fresco in the Palazzo Vecchio, which depicts the *entrata* (see figure 25), further suggests that instrumental music may have accompanied the procession of the entourage through the Piazza della Signoria: "at the windows of the Palazzo you see the *pifferi* who played and the trumpeters, each participating in the festivities, and the windows adorned with hangings."[22] The fresco also furnishes an important visual record of another of the *ephemerae* created for the occasion—Baccio Bandinelli's *Hercules*, which was fashioned of wood covered in clay and stood under the eastern arch of the Loggia de' Lanzi. In one important respect, Vasari's representation of the *ephemera* conforms to a reference in one of the retrospective narratives that specified that Hercules carried "a club on his shoulders."[23] As John Shearman suggested in his exemplary study of the *entrata*, the *Hercules*, an "addition to the original programme," "is most unlikely to have been casually chosen. There was probably a double reference—like the two Lions and the two Johns—to Florence and to the pope. Leo himself was compared with Hercules as the Tuscan hero who first bore the *signum leonis* (the lion skin, itself a symbol of *virtus*), and it is probably on this basis that Hercules appears among the hieroglyphic attributes of the Leonine pontificate on the additions Raphael made to the ceiling of the Stanza d'Eliodoro in 1514, and again in the borders of the tapestries for the Sistine Chapel, 1515–16."[24]

The arch erected at the Badia, which symbolized the virtue of "Fede," was attributed by Vasari to Baccio da Montelupo, Granacci, Aristotile da San Gallo, and Pontormo—the actual payment was made to "Francesco Granacci et altri"—and was constructed of pilasters and twenty-four gilded columns and bore the inscription "L.X.P.M. FIDEI CVLTORI." Other elements reportedly included a painting by Pontormo and representations of various biblical figures appropriate to the theme of the arch: Jacob, David, Joseph, and Joachim expelled from the temple.[25] Cambi remarked that "because a beautiful *apparato* had been constructed at the foot of the steps of the Badia, the pope paused, and his singers sang a hymn."[26] If there were indeed singers atop the ephemeral structure at the Badia who sang verses in accordance with the prescriptions of the anonymous "program," the singing of the papal choir may be seen as a kind of response, and the musical "exchange" of the two choirs anticipated a similar exchange between the papal and French Royal chapels in Bologna on December 13.

The arch at the Canto de' Bischeri, which symbolized the virtue of "Speranza" and was designed by Rosso Fiorentino, had a Doric order of twenty-seven pilasters, decorated so as to resemble porphyry and arranged in the form of an *arcus quadrifrons*; the illustrative iconographic material included representations of Shadrach and his companions in the furnace, the crossing of the Red Sea, Elisha curing Naaman's leprosy, Jacob and the angel, and Noah awaiting the return of the dove; at the summit was a sculpted group comprising Abraham and Isaac. The inscription read "SPES EIVS IN DOMINO .L.X.P.M."[27]

The decoration of the facade of the Cathedral—which served to convert it temporarily into an *ephemera* that symbolized the virtue of "Carità"—was the work of Sarto and Jacopo Sansovino and, if Vasari's account is correct, of Andrea di Cosimo Feltrini and Giovanni Rustici as well; the structure reached as high as canvas coverings that were stretched

Figure 25. Instrumentalists play from the windows of the Palazzo Vecchio in Vasari's representation of the procession of the papal entourage through Piazza della Signoria

between the Cathedral and the Baptistery and consisted of twelve wooden Corinthian columns on a high base, painted so as to resemble marble and surmounted by cornices and friezes; at the doors were triumphal arches. Various sculptural elements included Old Testament subjects by Sansovino decorated in such a way as to resemble bronze, and Apostles located in the niches between the columns, perhaps also executed by Sansovino; also featured were paintings in chiaroscuro and "grotesque" decoration executed by Sarto and Feltrini.[28] One chronicler recorded that the illustrative narratives exemplifying the virtue of "Carità" included Elijah fed by the angel and Jonah shaded by the gourd.[29] As the procession entered the Cathedral, "one heard nothing other than the sound of artillery, and bells, and *chiarini*, and trumpets, and drums of soldiers who were with the pope."[30] While there, "the pope prayed longer than was customary and at last gave the blessing, while the cardinal deacon de' Medici, the Florentine archbishop, was singing the versicles and prayer, dressed in his red cope."[31] How well Cardinal Giulio discharged his musical responsibilities that day we do not know. That he was gifted enough to have acquitted himself admirably, however, is suggested by the testimony of two observers who on other occasions commented approvingly on his musicianship: in 1530, on the occasion of the coronation of Charles V as holy Roman emperor, Giulio, then Pope Clement VII, "said the Preface, and very well, having a good voice and being a perfect musician"; and Antonio Soriano, a Venetian envoy in Rome, reported that Clement was regarded as one of the "good musicians who are now in Italy."[32]

Cardinal Giulio having sung, the entourage exited the Cathedral and proceeded to Leo's temporary residence in Santa Maria Novella, accompanied, in Landucci's words, by "a great many trumpeters and *pifferi*."[33] At the Canto de' Carnesecchi, Bandinelli's "charming and most beautiful arch had been constructed, with ten nymphs who were singing," just as the anonymous chronicler had prescribed, and at Santa Maria Novella, where Bandinelli's "bellissimo edificio" and Sansovino's and Sarto's equestrian statue had been erected,[34] the *entrata* was concluded; it had been one of the most remarkable such events in the history of Italy, if not of Europe.

The only substantial artistic element created for the occasion to have survived is Feltrini's, Ridolfo Ghirlandaio's, and Pontormo's decoration of the vault of the Cappella de' Papi in the Church of Santa Maria Novella, which is replete with Medici devices (see figure 26);[35] can one argue that some of the *ephemerae* may have been similarly decorated and that the evidence of the Cappella de' Papi may serve us, therefore, in our attempts to visualize their "grotesque" decoration?

As for the musical component, one can draw some tentative inferences from the descriptions contained in the narrative accounts. We need not

Figure 26. Leonine and Medicean devices among the elements of Feltrini's,
Ghirlandaio's, and Pontormo's decoration of the vault of the Cappella de' Papi,
Church of Santa Maria Novella, Florence

assume, first of all, that the music for the explanatory verses was necessarily as simple as for the 1513 *canti carnascialeschi*. As in the case of the
Lateran *possesso* of April 1513,[36] the verses explicated themes that were also
attested by inscriptions on the arches, and observers were not dependent
solely upon the singers' verses, therefore, for an understanding of those
themes. Moreover, performance conditions were different from those for
the *canti carnascialeschi*, precisely because the arches were "static" elements. Stationed as they were atop the arches, the singers could easily
have executed a considerably more elaborate kind of piece. Indeed, in
1539, on the occasion of yet another festive event associated with the
Medici, Eleanor of Toledo's *entrata*, twenty-four singers atop the arch of
the Porta al Prato performed Corteccia's elaborate eight-voice motet
Ingredere (see the opening measures of the work in example 4), accompanied by four trombones and four *cornetti*, and perhaps one can argue
by analogy that the settings of the explanatory verses for Leo's *en-*

Example 4. Opening of Francesco Corteccia's setting of the motet text *Ingredere* for Eleanora of Toledo's 1539 Florentine *entrata, Musiche fatte nelle nozze dello illustrissimo Duca di Firenze il signor Cosimo de Medici et della illustrissima consorte sua mad. Leonora da Tolleto* (Venice: A. Gardane, 1539), and *Thesaurus musicus continens selectissimas octo, septem, sex, quinque et quatuor vocum Harmonias, tam a veteribus quam recentioribus symphonistis compositas, & ad omnis generis instrumenta musica accomodatas. Tomi primi continentis cantiones octo vocum.* (Nürnberg: J. Montanus and U. Neuber, 1564)

trata, though presumably not as elaborate as Corteccia's densely contrapuntal *Ingredere*, may nonetheless have shared some of its stylistic characteristics.[37]

I do not believe we can conclude from Cambi's specificity that the "inno" performed by the papal singers at the Badia was necessarily a setting of a hymn text. On the other hand, because the piece was performed by participants in the "dynamic" element, it is likely that its music would

Example 4, continued

indeed have been simpler stylistically than that for the explanatory verses, and one of the spare, homophonic hymn settings in the repertory of the Cappella Sistina would have been appropriate. It is even possible that the piece was chanted, as the liturgical texts in the Cathedral certainly were. As for the singers' identities, I would say that, given the *entrata*'s duration—it was said to have lasted some seven hours—the same small group of ten singers who sang at Bandinelli's arch at the Canto de' Carnesecchi might well have been responsible for performing at all of the arches (or, more likely, several such small groups, given that the singers' compensation was substantial), and one can imagine them moving from arch to arch as the papal entourage processed slowly through the city. I can point to no actual pieces of instrumental music that may have resembled the "suoni" of the "chiarini," "tamburi," and "tronbe," but based on what may be a roughly contemporary depiction of the *entrata*, one can at least

Example 4, continued

imagine the papal instrumentalists' participation in the procession and perhaps even what they contributed to the varied sounds observers heard that day (see figure 27).[38]

Leo's stay in Florence was marked by elaborate liturgical ceremonies, several of which included important and interesting musical components. Masi reported that on December 1, the day following the *entrata*,

the pope left his aforementioned residence, and came to visit the Annunziata de' Servi of Florence. And as he entered the said chapel, he knelt and said his prayer, and as soon as he had prayed, the aforementioned figure of the aforementioned Annunziata was uncovered, and after the figure—which was uncovered three times, one after the other—was re-covered, the pope said, "aiutorium nostrum in nomine domini," and his singers, who had gone to stand opposite in the

Figure 27. Papal instrumentalists accompany the procession of the papal entourage in what is possibly a representation of Leo's 1515 Florentine *entrata*. Majolica plate

chapel of San Niccolò, responded to what he said. And after he had said certain verses that are customarily said in such places, and the singers had responded, the aforementioned pope said the Benediction.[39]

Leo's preferences with respect to his accommodations during his stay in Florence and the adaptation of Florentine ecclesiastical institutions to satisfy papal ceremonial protocol had been specified in a letter of October 22 from Baldassare Turini, Lorenzo's *oratore* in Rome, to Lorenzo.[40] The chapel in Santa Maria Novella had been decorated by Feltrini, Ghirlandaio, and Pontormo so as to serve temporarily as Leo's *cappella quoti-*

diana; it was to fulfill the same function as the chapel of Nicholas V in the Vatican apartments. The Church of San Lorenzo, on the other hand, had been adapted for the public ceremonies of the papal chapel,[41] and there, in San Lorenzo, "the singers of the pope sang a most beautiful polyphonic mass every morning, and the church was much frequented by the people, out of respect for the pope and because of the unusual magnificence."[42] Bartolomeo Masi was present on December 2 when the pope's singers performed "la bellissima messa di figurato," and his account furnishes an interesting detail that may provide an insight into contemporary Florentine performance practice: "a papal mass was begun, which Archbishop Giovanni Tedeschini-Piccolomini of Siena said, and the singers of the pope's musical chapel responded to the mass, who were other singers, not ours, and at the mass the organs were not played, and it was one of the most beautiful masses that I have ever heard or seen."[43] Masi's careful note concerning the organs suggests that the papal singers' a cappella performance on that occasion was contrary to Florentine custom.

Leo left Florence on December 3 and proceeded to Bologna for his meeting with Francis, who entered the city on December 11:[44] "At length, there came in order: first the pope's guard on horseback and the Swiss guards on foot with trumpets and drums; then followed the king's trumpeters, clothed in blue garments with gold fleurs-de-lis."[45] A number among those who witnessed Francis's impressive entry were also present on the thirteenth when Leo celebrated mass in the Church of San Petronio, and a dispatch of the twelfth conveys a note of genuine anticipation: "Tomorrow the pope sings a solemn mass in San Petronio, and his Majesty the king will wash the pope's hands, and there will be beautiful ceremonies."[46] From a French chronicle one has a sense of just how "beautiful" the ceremonies were:

And the next morning the pope sang mass as magnificently as any pope has ever sung, because *monsieur* the duke of Lorraine and all the princes of the realm served him, and there were the singers of the king and the pope, who made beautiful music, because there were two good chapels together and they sang in competition with each other.[47]

Another French source adds the detail that "the aforementioned mass began around noon and ended at four in the afternoon."[48]

Leo, too, must have been impressed by the singing of the members of the king's chapel: he subsequently granted benefices to Guillaume Cousin, Noel Galoys, Jean Richafort, and Claudin de Sermisy, and Antoine de Longueval and Jean Mouton were named apostolic protonotaries. Indeed, the presence of Francis's chapel must explain in part the enormous influx of Franco-Netherlandish music into Italian, and specifically Florentine and Roman, sources at just this time. That Mouton's representation in these sources is so substantial itself suggests the possibility of a direct relationship between their copying and the meeting of the two chapels. It is entirely plausible that Leo should have capitalized on the presence of the French chapel to obtain music. There is explicit documentation that other patrons were actively involved in procuring music from Mouton—for example, in a letter of October 29, the Ferrarese music scribe Jean Michel wrote that Mouton had given him a "motet for the victory"; by this Michel surely meant *Exalta regina galliae*, composed by Mouton for the French victory at Marignano and copied into the manuscript Florence, Biblioteca Medicea-Laurenziana, Acq. e doni 666. The presence of the motet in this Medici manuscript is surely suggestive, and it seems a promising hypothesis that the work entered Medici musical circles at the time of the meetings in Bologna in December.[49]

On December 22, Leo and his entourage returned to Florence, where he remained until February 19.[50] Though there were further musical performances, there was none that matched in splendor or historical importance the musical elements of the November 30 *entrata* or of the Bologna meetings; Paris de Grassis recorded that mass was sung on the fourth Sunday of Advent and the Feast of St. Stephen in the Church of San Lorenzo and in the Cathedral on Christmas Day when, further, the Gospel and Epistle were sung (chanted?) in both Greek and Latin.[51]

As we have seen, one of the references to musical performances during Leo's visit specifies polyphony (masses "di figurato") and the polyphonic masses in the repertory of the Cappella Sistina during Leo's time would have served; among such works were Brumel's Missa *de nostra domina*, Fevin's Misse *de Feria, Mente tota supplicamus*, and *parva*, Hylaire's Missa *sine nomine*, Josquin's Missa *Pange lingua*, Mouton's Missa *Tu es petrus*, Pipelare's Missa *Fors seulement*, and Willaert's Missa *Mente tota tibi supplicamus* (in Vatican City, Biblioteca Apostolica Vaticana, manuscript Cappella Sistina 16); Josquin's Missa *Mente tota tibi supplicamus* (in manuscript Cappella Sistina 26); and La Rue's Misse *Ave maria, Cum Jocunditate*, and *Pourquoy non* (in manuscript Cappella Sistina 45).[52] One of these (or another similar work) might have been sung when mass was celebrated in San Petronio on December 13; if so, and if the mass performed were Fevin's or Hylaire's or Josquin's or Mouton's, the irony that it was the work of a composer associated with the French royal court would surely have escaped neither Leo nor Francis. Leo favored the court's musical traditions, and a performance by the *cappella papale* of a mass by a French composer would have been an appropriate inclusion among the compliments exchanged on the occasion of the Bologna meetings.

TOWARD THE *PRINCIPATO*: LORENZO DE' MEDICI, 1513–1519

CHAPTER 6

ARCHBISHOP GIULIO'S
POSSESSO

PAPAL DIPLOMATIC initiatives inevitably intersected with developments in Florence where since 1513 Lorenzo II had been his family's principal representative. The political implications of Giuliano's ready acquiescence to the arguments of the moderates in 1512 were not lost on Leo; the pope found a more willing agent for his Florentine political agenda in his nephew Lorenzo, who was accordingly entrusted with responsibility for the restored regime. Giuliano himself needed little persuading: the prospect of residing more-or-less permanently in the Eternal City proved attractive enough, and shortly after Leo's election he followed his older brother to Rome, where he took up residence in the Vatican Palace[1] and was free to pursue his literary and musical interests.[2]

Leo evidently concluded, however, that Lorenzo had to be closely managed, and in an attempt to ensure that Lorenzo comported himself acceptably, Leo had Giuliano draft a set of instructions that was sent to Lorenzo when he assumed responsibility for the regime. Moreover, in part presumably so that he had an independent source of information about developments in Florence, Leo named his cousin Giulio archbishop of Florence in April of 1513.[3]

Giulio decided on a formal *entrata*. Masi noted in his diary that "on the fifteenth of August, our Most Reverend Monsignor Archbishop of Florence came and took possession of his archbishopric, with all the customary *ordini* and ceremonies, which was the grandest triumph and one of the most beautiful things ever done for any archbishop."[4]

Among the "ordini e cerimonie" there were indeed musical elements, as another chronicle reveals:

> They led the archbishop as far as the Piazza della Signoria where the Signoria and the gonfaloniere of justice of the Republic and of the Florentine people were sitting upon the *ringhiera*, and there, to the greatest ringing of bells and the sound of trumpets and other instruments, he was honorably received by them and honored and greeted from the aforementioned platform by the present gonfaloniere, the magnificent Giovanni de' Bernardi, and when he had arrived at the

85

marble stone placed as a marker where the blessed Zenobius, Floren-
tine bishop, wonderfully roused and revived a dead boy, after the
Versicle *Ora pro nobis Beate Zenobi* had been sung by the priest and
after the Response *Ut digni efficiamur promissionibus Christi*, the Most
Reverend Archbishop similarly sang and, singing, said the prayer of
Saint Zenobius, and afterward proceeded as far as the *angolo* de'
Pazzi, and there, turning toward the Cathedral, he arrived at the
aforementioned Florentine Cathedral Church.[5]

Masi's account concludes: "he entered by the Cathedral's central door.
While the archbishop was there, he celebrated a solemn mass, singing."[6]

An elaborate procession, the ringing of bells, instrumental fanfares, the
chanting of liturgical texts invoking the aid of a saint who figured prominently in Florentine religious practice,[7] the singing (chanting?) of mass in
the Cathedral: some of the ceremonial elements for the archbishop's
possesso witnessed by the people of Florence in 1513 were prescribed by tradition; that they and other similar elements were, as we have seen, to be
featured during Leo's 1515 *entrata* suggests that Giulio's *entrata* may have
served as one of the models for the pope's.[8]

CHAPTER 7

THE 1514 FEAST OF
SAN GIOVANNI

LORENZO, intensely ambitious, moved in the meantime to consolidate his position in Florence. He had learned some lessons well: if one needed specific examples to illustrate Savonarola's claim that "many times the tyrant occupies the people in spectacles and festivals,"[1] Lorenzo's would serve. Although he was no tyrant, it was clear to him, as to his relatives before and after him, that a successful *festa* promised potentially enormous returns, and he was determined to achieve such success with the festivities for the 1514 Feast of San Giovanni, the first since he had assumed responsibility for the government. Lorenzo's artistic sensibilities are not attested by an abundance of evidence, but whatever such qualities he may have had, one may be certain that his cultural and political objectives with respect to the *festa* were not modest and that they demanded that he adopt extravagant means: accordingly, he requested the pope's elephant, Hanno, which had been given to Leo by the king of Portugal— a request that Leo declined to honor on the grounds that Hanno's feet were too tender for the journey from Rome to Florence, which would, in any event, have taken more time than was available.[2]

The pope, nonetheless, was acutely interested in the progress of the planning for the festivities. On June 8, Baldassare Turini da Pescia, Lorenzo's agent in Rome, wrote to Lorenzo to report that "today after lunch, while walking and standing to listen to the singing, his Holiness and the Most Reverend *Monsignori* of Ferrara and Aragon and Messer Luigi Rossi drew closely together, and speaking of events in Florence, that is, the joust, *trionfi*, *cacce*, and other festivities that would take place there, his Holiness had Messer Luigi summon me, and they wanted to see the program for the *trionfo* and the provisions for the joust that I had from there and as a result they resolved that because the Most Reverend Cardinals of Ferrara and Aragon were going to Loreto, as they were within three days, they would come to see the *festa*, and be there in disguise, the vigil of San Giovanni. With the greatest of longing, one spoke of the *festa*, and in these discussions it was said that the magnificent Giuliano will also go, but in disguise";[3] and Turini's letter to Lorenzo of June 19, quoted in Chapter 1, continues as follows: "His Holiness is spending the better part of the day in his room, awaiting the festivities that will take place there, day by day."[4]

They included both religious and secular components, several of which involved music: "beginning Wednesday, the twenty-first of June, there was, according to ancient custom, a most beautiful *mostra* [or exhibition by the city's artisans and merchants], and the following morning the usual procession."[5] One may assume that such religious processions ordinarily involved the singing of the participants, which was perhaps accompanied by the playing of a portative organ, and on other similar occasions contemporary accounts reveal that there was indeed such a musical element.[6]

But the most spectacular event of the festivities was the presentation of the Triumph of Camillus, which took place—tellingly—in Piazza della Signoria; the account in Sanuto, which is the fullest, demonstrates that the discussion in Rome of June 8 had indeed succeeded in convincing Cardinals d'Aragona and d'Este to go to Florence in order to witness the festivities personally:

> All the people were assembling and all the foreigners who were there, a good many of them from Rome, among them seven cardinals, that is, Marco Cornelius, Bandinello Sauli, Bernardo Dovizi da Bibbiena, Ippolito d'Este da Ferrara, Innocenzo Cibo, Alfonso Petrucci da Siena, and Luigi d'Aragona, and our magnificent *gonfaloniere* of the Holy Church Giuliano de' Medici.[7]

"The following morning, which was Friday the twenty-third," the account continues, "the *nuvole* or *edifici* were performed, according to ancient custom, representing first when God banished Lucifer and his followers from heaven."[8] As has been observed, the use of the term "nuvole" or "clouds" in this context suggests the extent to which they were considered "the miraculous instruments of *sacre rappresentazioni*," their role "in the transformation scenes of the secular theater" a kind of "literal realization" of the imagery of the Old Testament, where "clouds are the conceptual instruments of miraculous revelation, disappearance, or transit."[9]

> And the last represented Life and Death. I don't want to neglect to tell you that before this presentation we had a *moresca*, lasting not less than an hour; it was as beautiful as has been seen. Now I don't know where to begin to bring myself to recount what we had that evening, truly something never again to be seen, representing the Triumph of Camillus, which comprised seventeen *carri* or *trionfi*. First there was a *carro* of ladders, lanterns, and other similar instruments for besieging a city, and thereafter another *carro* of shields, banners and many arms seized from the enemy; then a battering ram

used of old to breach walls, which was a beautiful and ornate *edificio*. Again there followed a *carro*, above which was a goose, which was the reason why the Romans heard the Gauls' attempt to scale the Capitoline. After these followed eleven *carri* that portrayed different acts of the triumphant Camillus: a load of clothing, a load of silver, some of goods seized, some of arms, and all were spoils of war, but very well decorated and adorned. After these followed a grander and more prominent *carro*, more highly ornate than all the others, of armed prisoners and most beautiful spoils, drawn by four pairs of oxen. Behind these came two hundred men on horseback who were well ordered into three groups by eighty armed men comprising three companies that afterward participated in the joust, and, maintaining excellent order, they formed a considerable part of the procession. (And I forgot that surrounding the first *carro*, of ladders, were one hundred *maragioli*, sappers, or miners; thereafter men at arms with their standards and all the requisite implements). There followed fifty on foot, all attired in blue cloth, with some wooden arms, with some fasces of gold rods, poles bound to these at the top with garlands of laurel in front. Finally, there came the victorious Camillus, upon a *trionfo* that was grander than any other, on which were singers who were singing.[10]

One of the contemporary narratives specifies that the "festaiuoli" were "Filippo di Benedetto de' Nerli, Francesco di Giuliano Salviati, Filippo di Filippo Strozzi, Prinzivalle di messer Luigi della Stufa e Girolamo del maestro Luca," and according to Vasari, Francesco Granacci was responsible for the artistic elements of the *trionfo* (although Vasari erroneously associated the performance with Leo's 1515 *entrata*): "Granacci was employed in the sumptuous and magnificent preparations that were made . . . by Jacopo Nardi, a man of great learning and most beautiful intellect, who, having been commanded by the . . . Eight to prepare a splendid masquerade, executed a representation of the Triumph of Camillus. This masquerade, insofar as it lay in the province of the painter, was so beautifully arranged and adorned by Granacci that no man could imagine anything better."[11] As Vasari noted, the author of the Camillus masque was again Jacopo Nardi, who was becoming increasingly expert in his role as Medici propagandist.

How may we interpret Nardi's elaborate allegory? In the *Decades*, which Nardi translated,[12] Livy wrote of Camillus as "a man of singular excellence," "foremost in peace and in war . . . , whether one thinks of the yearning of his countrymen who called on him in his absence . . . or of the success with which on being restored to his country he restored the country itself at the same time; . . . he maintained his glorious reputation, and was deemed worthy of being named next after Romulus, as Rome's second founder."[13] If Nardi's program was intended to suggest a parallel between Lorenzo II and Camillus, it was an extravagant comparison. Nonetheless, within two years, Ludovico Alamanni, who was Cerretani's and Nardi's colleague in the Sacred Academy of the Medici, was to make the comparison more explicit still: in his "Discorso . . . sopra il fermare lo stato di Firenze nella devozione de' Medici" of 1516, he suggested that Lorenzo, "being able to make himself the equal of whichever of the ancients or moderns, will want to compete more readily with Caesar and Camillus than with the impious Agathocle, the most cruel Sylla and the villainous Liverocto da Fermo."[14] If the themes of the 1513 Carnival, therefore, were more-or-less those of return and regeneration, in June of 1514 the metaphor was extended and made more oblique: implicitly, the Medici—and perhaps Lorenzo II specifically—were compared to Camillus, his city's second founder and restorer. As for Lorenzo himself, the meaning of the *trionfo* was apparently clear enough: he wrote to his envoy in France, Francesco Pandolfini, that the masquerade "in fact refers to nothing if not to the expulsion of the House of Medici and to the subsequent revocation." Lorenzo's implicit suggestion that the Medici, like Camillus, were recalled from exile is, of course, an idealized presentation of the historical reality; nonetheless, it was subsequently to find expression in the borders of the tapestries executed for the Sistine Chapel in the years immediately following. Lorenzo's objective, admittedly, was in part to ensure that the *trionfo*, which celebrated the victory of Camillus over the Gauls, not be misinterpreted by the French, and he was presumably moved to state his interpretation of the *trionfo*'s meaning explicitly in response to a letter of Turini's of June 8, which conveyed Cardinal d'Este's concern as to how the French might construe its thematic content. But in taking such care to advance his interpretation, Lorenzo, knowingly or not, revealed that there was indeed another meaning, one that many observers, certainly, would have appreciated. Nardi's program expressed a theme central to contemporary Florentine political experience, one expressed as well in Machiavelli's writings: that Italy ought to free herself from domination by barbarians from north of the Alps. Indeed, Machiavelli entitled chapter 26 of *The Prince* "Exhortatio ad capessendam Italiam in libertamque a barbaris vendicandam [Exhortation to Take Italy and Free Her from the Hands of the Barbarians]" and his "Exhortatio," like the program of Nardi's *trionfo*, evoked a theme that must have produced powerful resonances among contemporaries.[15]

The text of Nardi's *canto*, which was sung by the "cantori . . . sopra . . . [il] più che ogni altro grande triumpho," is preserved. In its references to Camillus as a "second father" (line 24) and to the "barbarian spoils" (line 18), "sacred leaves" (line 19), and evergreen laurel (lines 39–40), among others one could cite, one sees immediately its relationship to contemporary Florentine political topoi, to Nardi's probable source, that is, Livy's *Decades*, to the artistic elements of the Camillus *trionfo* as related in Sanuto's diary and even to Nardi's own earlier poetic efforts on the occasion of the 1513 Carnival:

Contempla in quanta altezza se' salita, [1]
felice, alma Fiorenza,
poiché dal ciel discesa è in tuo presenza
la Gloria e cogli esempi a sé t'invita;
la quale ha tal potenza
ch'a' morti rende vita,
onde'ella il morto già Cammillo mostra
viver ancor per fama all'età nostra.

Quell'è Furio Cammillo, il gran romano [9]
per cui Roma esaltata
fu tanto, che l'invidia scellerata
usò 'nver lui la rabbia, benché invano;
perché la patria ingrata
il consiglio non sano
conobbe poi che gli levò la soma,
e fu costretta a dir: per te son Roma.

Le pompe trionfal nel tuo cospetto, [17]
le barbariche spoglie,
le tempie ornate delle sacre foglie
mostron le laude sue; ma tal concetto
una parola accoglie,
poiché lui solo e' detto
della patria, per l'opre alte e leggiadre,
primo liberator, secondo padre.

Manca la vita in un tanto superba, [25]
mancon le sue sante ale:
la nostra dea contr' a l'ordin fatale
trae'l buon fuor del sepolcro e 'n vita il serba;
la virtú sola vale
contr'alla morte acerba,
e senza lei cercar Gloria non giova;
ma seguendo virtú, costei si trova.

Come vedete, seco insieme vanno [33]
la dea Minerva e Marte,
che colla spada, con scienza e arte

all'uom mortale immortal vita danno;
e le vergate carte
lo ristoron del danno,
perché come l'allor foglia non perde,
la storia e poesia sempre sta verde.

Dunque colui che 'n questo mondo brama   [41]
col generoso cuore
vincer l' invidia e acquistare onore,
né seco seppellir la propria fama,
porti alla patria amore;
perché colui che l'ama,
e con giustizia difende e governa,
in cielo ha vita e gloria al mondo eterna.[16]

The music for Nardi's *canto* is not preserved, though in its absence we may posit that it was stylistically reminiscent of the *canti* performed on the occasion of the 1513 Carnival, given that the *canti*'s function and their performance conditions were effectively identical on the two occasions.[17]

The festivities concluded with events of a different kind: "And the Signoria had arranged for *feste* and jousts in which one saw Giuliano with a brocade garment and thus also Lorenzo, as joyful as possible, and there was a *caccia* where there was every variety of animal and two lions and everything was done with respect to the gentlemen who came from Rome and the six cardinals in disguise."[18]

LORENZO DE' MEDICI, CAPTAIN GENERAL OF THE FLORENTINE MILITIA AND DUKE OF URBINO

INSOFAR AS the San Giovanni festivities were judged an artistic success, they may well have contributed to Lorenzo's standing among some Florentines; but such ephemeral success, inevitably, was no substitute for more tangible and enduring accomplishments. In May of 1515 Lorenzo succeeded in having himself elected captain general of a corps of some five hundred Florentine militiamen who had been recruited the previous month at the pope's behest by Lorenzo's agent, his cousin Galeotto, during one of Lorenzo's increasingly frequent absences from Florence.[1] His election violated custom: understandably fearful of the possible consequences of entrusting the position to a fellow citizen, the Florentines had never appointed anyone other than a presumably disinterested hired mercenary. No one who interpreted Lorenzo's interest in the position as evidence of aristocratic pretensions would have been accused of having reacted cynically; the trumpet fanfares that announced the "presa di bastone," the occasion on which Lorenzo received the symbols of office, must have appealed powerfully to his sense of the ceremonial:

"Copia litterarum datae Florentiae die XIII Augusti 1515." Yesterday was the muster of the company and men at arms of the magnificent Lord Lorenzo, in which this order was in great part observed, *videlicet*; it was ordered that three times at various hours on the preceding day the trumpeters were to go throughout the city, playing, which signaled that the following day all the men were to assemble in order, that they were to be mounted and that all the people were to gather together in a designated place, which was the Church of San Marco, not far from the magnificent Lorenzo's house. In order, everyone went to the Piazza della Signoria where one heard the sounds of artillery, trumpets, and bells, and everyone saying "Palle, palle!" On the *ringhiera* at the foot of the stairs outside the Palazzo Vecchio were the members of the Signoria then in residence and the magnificent Lorenzo, having dismounted, between the gonfaloniere and another of the members of the Signoria; there they heard an oration by messer Marcello, the *segretario primo* of the Signoria. *Qua expedita*, the gonfaloniere gave the standard, helmet, a horse, and *bastone* to the magnificent lord.[2]

The responses to Lorenzo's election were predictably sharp: Marino Giorgi, the Venetian envoy, reported that "this Lorenzo has been made captain of the Florentines against their laws, which do not permit any Florentine to be captain. He has become the ruler of Florence; he orders and is obeyed. They used to cast lots; now no longer; what Lorenzo commands is done. Accordingly, the power of this House of Medici is displeasing to the majority of the Florentines." On August 13, the day following Lorenzo's Investiture, Archbishop Giulio de' Medici entered Florence by means of a formal *entrata* (see figure 28),[3] and on the fourteenth, Filiberta of Savoy, Francis I's aunt, whom Giuliano de' Medici had married in Torino in February, was similarly received (see figure 29). That three such magnificent ceremonial events occurred in immediate succession surely evoked a response from the Florentines who witnessed them; it must have seemed, even to the most casual observer, that the "aristocratization"[4] of this mercantile family was rapidly nearing completion.

Lorenzo's election to the position of captain general of Florence nonetheless failed to satisfy his appetite. Even he must have recognized, reluctantly, that the Florentines were not prepared for the Medici to rule explicitly, in name as well as in fact. He accordingly began to consider other outlets for his aristocratic ambitions.

In March of 1516, the duke of Urbino was deprived of his possessions in the papal state, ostensibly for having refused to ally himself with the pope against Francis I in 1515. Lorenzo and his mother Alfonsina Orsini-Medici—who was vilified in her lifetime and thereafter for her seemingly limitless ambition—persuaded Leo to permit Lorenzo to succeed the duke, and by early June he had completed a military operation against Urbino; the Florentine Signoria responded dutifully by ordering the appropriate celebrations, but, according to Parenti, many Florentines chose not to witness the festivities for the Feast of San Giovanni,[5] whose artistic element seems to have been little more than an overt glorification of Lorenzo, and, to judge from the abruptness of Masi's account, perhaps a clumsily executed one at that:

> On Thursday, the fifth of June, one heard in Florence of the taking of Urbino with all of its castles, except for the holdings and the people; the duke fled. Monday morning the Signoria of Florence went to Santa Maria del Fiore with the Colleges and the Otto di Pratica to make an offering, and they sang a beautiful mass of the Holy Spirit.[6]

Figure 28. Francesco Granacci, design for ephemeral decoration,
possibly for Archbishop Giulio de' Medici's Florentine
entrata of August 1515

On the twenty-fifth of June, ten *trionfi* went throughout the city
of Florence and on the last was performed a *canto* that explained the
allegory: that is, that the said *trionfi* were made in honor of his Lordship Lorenzo de' Medici.[7]

Once again, Jacopo Nardi's involvement may have been solicited:
among the *canzone* preserved in the manuscript Florence, Biblioteca
nazionale centrale, Magliabechi VII, 1041, is a "Canzona di iacopo nardy"
(fol. 86ᵛ), whose topical allusions may refer to Lorenzo's military ex-
ploits—though, if so, the portrait is idealized, to be very sure:

> Pose natura ogni cosa mortale   [1]
> sotto il ciel della luna
> in ma[n] della fortuna
> onde ella è la cagio[n] del be[n] & male.
> Ma il suo poter no[n] vale
> nel'huomo in cui si aduna
> Vera virtù con son[n]o [*sic*: senno] & co[n] prude[n]za
> come oggi in te si vede, alma fiorenza.

Figure 29. Anonymous sketch of Filiberta of Savoy, the wife of
Giuliano di Lorenzo de' Medici

CHAPTER 8

Fortuna incertta piu no[n] dona o toglie   [9]
sempre come li piace
al mondo guerra o pace,
anzi è constructa a seguir l'altrui voglie
Et priva di sue spoglie
alla virtù subiace,
La qual tie[n] ferma la volubil rota
né teme più fortuna la p[er] quota.

Notate quel ch[e] mostra il laur degno   [17]
già di fronde spogliato,
hora dal destro lato
lieto racorre ogn'huo[m] sotto il suo segno,
così quel secco legno
che dal ciel fulminato
Stilla benigno a quegli il dolce mele
che pascevan già altrui d'aceto & fele.

Colui ch[e] è vero & giusto vincitore   [25]
a' sup[er]bi minaccia
et quegli abbatte & scaccia
come co[n]viensi a gieneroso core,
ma chi lassa l'errore
pietosame[n]te abbraccia
Imitando l'amor del som[m]o bene
come in q[uesta] figura si contiene.

Chi segue la virtù, come si vede,   [33]
alfin ne acquista gloria
Et di nuova victoria
dove[n]ta triompha[n]do spesso herede
Et poi morto possede
Sempre degna memoria
pur ch[e] insieme virtù co[n]iuncta sia
Con opre liberali & cortesia.

Godi hor fiorenza all'ombra del tuo lauro   [41]
ch[e] ti cuopre & defende
con lo scudo ch[e] splende
digem[m]e oriental legate in auro,
dal'indo insino al mauro
La tua fama si exstende
poi ch[e] uno tuo figlio, anzi padre, p[er] zelo
regnando in terra ha forza ancor in cielo.

Had there been no rubric in the manuscript indicating Nardi's authorship, one would have been able to make an argument for it nonetheless on the basis of the imagery: Nardi had earlier employed the same reference that appears in line 45 of the *canto* in the prologue to *I due felici rivali* (the version of the text preserved in manuscript Florence, Biblioteca nazionale centrale, Magl. VII. 1131).[8] The appropriateness of the allusions in the *canto* to the historical circumstances of the moment suggests that it might well have been the one performed in June of 1516, although the rubric that accompanies another *canzona* preserved in the same manuscript— "Canzona del frate de servi facta p[er] la medesime [*sic*] materia della rinco[n]tro"—may imply that the occasion was instead the reconquest of Urbino in 1517;[9] to my knowledge, however, we have no accounts documenting festivities at that time that included a musical element.

CHAPTER 9

THE WEDDING OF LORENZO
AND MADELEINE

THERE REMAINED only the matter of an appropriate spouse. Leo's meeting with Francis in 1515 was one manifestation of the importance to him of maintaining amicable relations with the French; Giuliano's marriage to Filiberta was another. As Francesco Vettori reported, "The pope sought to establish a good, solid friendship with King Francis. He had it arranged that Lorenzo would take a French wife."[1]

No event of Lorenzo's career resulted in more elaborate festivities than his 1518 wedding to Madeleine de la Tour d'Auvergne, an event that prompted the pope to honor his nephew with the gift of an important musical document of the "written tradition," the famous "Medici Codex."[2]

Lorenzo and Madeleine were engaged on January 25, 1518; Lorenzo departed for France on March 22, and on May 2 he and Madeleine were married.[3] They returned to Florence in August. Cerretani reported:

And we had news [August 18, 1518], Lorenzo de' Medici, duke of Urbino and our captain, having arrived in Lombardy with the duchess, the result of which was that Madonna Alfonsina, with eight heads of the government, thought to honor them, and grandly, and gave this responsibility to the Otto di Pratica, who, through their ministers, ordered *armeggierie* and *feste* and all those things that were ordinarily done for the Feast of San Giovanni. They constructed a platform in front of the door to Palazzo Medici, as wide as the street, as long as the *palazzo* and three *braccia* high, with awnings above, an *apparato* with tapestries and seats, splendidly done, and thus, sumptuously, the entrance and the *loggia*, and for the banquets they appropriated the courtyard and the *loggia de' melaranci*, which they decorated marvelously with friezes and arms and tapestries and awnings above, particularly the *loggia verde*, where the comedies were to be performed. One hundred thirty maidens between the ages of fifteen and twenty-six were invited to the banquets, fifty of whom were to be with Madonna Alfonsina at the door in order to receive the duchess on the platform.[4]

99

Figure 30. Portrait of Alfonsina Orsini-Medici, the widow of
Piero di Lorenzo de' Medici and mother of
Lorenzo di Piero di Lorenzo,
attributed to Botticelli

Figure 31. Anonymous portrait, possibly of Madeleine de la Tour d'Auvergne,
wife of Lorenzo di Piero di Lorenzo de' Medici

As in 1514, at the time of the festivities for the Feast of San Giovanni,
the preparations for the celebrations in Florence aroused considerable interest in Rome, and as on the earlier occasion, several members of Leo's
court went to Florence to witness the proceedings: "The Most Reverend

Cardinals Luigi de' Rossi and Innocenzo Cibo left here for Florence with many other members of the court—who were Lorenzo's closest relatives—in order to be present on that solemn occasion."[5] Cerretani reported that "on the twenty-fifth of August 1518 the duke arrived in Florence and left his wife at Cafaggiolo, where all the close relatives went to visit her. And on the fourth of September all of them went to Poggio a Caiano, which was decorated like a paradise."[6]

On the seventh, Madeleine entered the city:

> The wife of the duke made her *entrata* into Florence at two hours before sunset by the Porta al Prato, having paused at a monastery two miles outside the city. Her entourage entered in this order, that is: first, a few of her carriages; then, three hundred on horseback who were archbishops, bishops, protonotaries, canons, the rector of the *Studio, cavalieri*, doctors, and other gentlemen, old and young; then all the soldiers, among them Signor Giampaolo Baglioni, Vitello Vitelli, Signor Renzo da Ceri, a good many Orsini and other gentlemen; then relatives of the House of Medici.[7]

The duchess's immediate entourage was formed of "six of her maids of honor and a very few gentlemen who had come with Madeleine, who followed these between the two cardinals Cibo and Rossi, with forty young people from noble houses at her stirrup, with garments *alla tedesca* of purple satin, jackets of crimson, rose-colored braid with emblems of gold, and splendidly ordered, after which was an incalculable number of horsemen. Inside the gate, on a *carro*, was an olive tree and quantities of instrumental music [era un Ulivo con quantità di suoni]."[8]

Other festivities organized in Lorenzo's and Madeleine's honor, several involving musical elements, occurred on the eighth, ninth, tenth, and twelfth of September; Cerretani recorded that "on the eighth was the banquet with seventy young women served by the said young people and after eating they exited onto the platform that had been constructed in front of the *palazzo* where they danced under the awning all day in the presence of the people."[9] Alfonsina herself reported on the day's events to Giovanni da Poppi, Lorenzo's chancellor, in a letter that furnishes a number of richly evocative details, among them the report that Lorenzo and Madeleine, significantly, were often made visible to the Florentine *popolo*:

> Ser Joanni:

> All the young women invited who had accepted came this morning, and all very well attired, and at about one half-hour past midday they went to dinner in the garden, and with them the duchess, who was at the north end of the garden, facing the *loggia*, between the two Most Reverend Cardinals, and the duke facing her. And all four sides

of the garden were filled up. They left the table at two hours past midday and, having withdrawn inside, some in the *camera della saletta*, some in the room opposite, and others still in my room, almost all changed their attire, all most beautifully. They exited onto the platform at three hours past midday, where they danced until an hour before sunset, and even the duchess herself danced two dances, one with the duke, one with the *Maiordomo*, Francesco Vettori. And truly this day passed very happily. And God granted us beautiful weather, and to such universal satisfaction that I could not tell you. And there were truly many people, at the windows, on the rooftops, in the streets, on the platforms that had been constructed everywhere and from which one could see, such that you could not imagine the half of it. And at sunset, they went inside to rest a bit and at one half-hour past sunset began the performance of the comedy, called *Falargo* [*sic*: properly *Philargio* of Giovanni Manenti?], which was very well performed and had a very beautiful *apparato*. The comedy having been finished and they having rested a bit inside, all the young women from this morning to dinner went to dinner and the duchess with them and after dinner we didn't wish to dance. I have to tell you that the duke had [Raphael's] portrait of his Holiness and the Most Reverend *Monsignori* de' Medici and Rossi [see figure 1] placed above the middle of the table where the duchess and the other gentlemen and ladies were eating, and it truly brightened everything up.
Bene valete.
Florentiae, die VIII septembris 1518.
Alfonsina de' Medici Ursina[10]

Cerretani's account continues: "On the ninth was a banquet for the entire city and aristocratic friends who were 130 of the principal citizens, who, having eaten and a most beautiful comedy having been performed, were permitted to leave. On the tenth the members of the family banqueted and a most beautiful comedy was performed, and dancing, instrumental music, and other delights."[11]

An entry in Sanuto's diary furnishes information as to the identity of some of the actors who participated in the performances of the comedies: "All the comedians who were to be found in Rome were sent in order to perform the comedies and enrich the *festa* considerably, and among the others Cherea." The Cherea mentioned in the reference is surely Francesco de' Nobili da Lucca, *detto* Cherea, a famous comedian and the chancellor of Fracasso Sanseverino, the son of Roberto Sanseverino and brother of Giovanni Francesco Sanseverino, the count of Cajazzo (Fracasso's and Giovanni Francesco's nephew Ferrante was prince of Salerno and an important figure in the development of a tradition of theatrical performances in Naples).[12] And Vasari, in three of the *Vite*, recorded that Aristotile da San Gallo, Franciabigio, and Ridolfo Ghirlandaio were all involved in the execution of the decorations and stage scenery. Indeed, in Aristotile's *Vita* he specified that "Franciabigio and Ridolfo Ghirlandajo . . . had charge of everything" and in Franciabigio's *Vita* claimed further that the artist "acquired credit and favor" with Lorenzo "on account of . . . the method, masterly judgment and grace" with which he executed "two sets of scenery for the dramas that were performed. . . . This service was the reason that he received the commission for gilding the ceiling of the hall at Poggio a Caiano, in company with Andrea di Cosimo [Feltrini]."[13]

Francesco d'Antonio Zeffi da Empoli, priest and canon of the Church of San Lorenzo, subsequently a member of the Accademia Fiorentina, and the tutor of the sons of Filippo Strozzi the Elder, recorded a performance of a comedy in Palazzo Medici that may well be identical with one of the performances of September 1518. Zeffi was one of the authors who contributed to the poetic anthology *Lauretum*, probably issued at the time of Lorenzo's and Madeleine's wedding; others included Donato Giannotti, Alessio Lapaccini, who was perhaps present at the performance of *I due felici rivali* in 1513, Andrea Dazzi, who had authored the program for the 1513 Carnival performance of the *Diamante* company, and Ludovico Alamanni, Bartolomeo Cerretani's and Jacopo Nardi's colleague in the Sacred Academy of the Medici. That Zeffi is represented in the anthology serves, in my view, to increase one's confidence in the accuracy of his report on the performance he described, since it demonstrates that he was a member of the circle of artists and literary figures around Lorenzo II de' Medici.[14] Although I feel compelled to point out that Zeffi's account does not permit us to conclude that the performance *necessarily* took place on the occasion of Lorenzo's and Madeleine's wedding—he stated only that it took place at the behest of "Lorenzo duca di Urbino," and therefore between 1516, when Lorenzo was invested with that title, and 1519, when he died—the inference traditionally drawn about the date of the performance nonetheless seems to me to be the most logical one, especially given Zeffi's reference to Ghirlandaio's role in the design of the stage set, which seems to corroborate Vasari's remarks. If one accepts the traditional interpretation, Zeffi's account serves to identify another of the comedies performed on the occasion of the wedding festivities and its author, although it does not permit us to determine on which of the two evenings in question—the ninth or the tenth—it was staged; further, in identifying the *sala grande* of the Palazzo Medici as the location of the performance, his testimony is inconsistent with that of Cerretani, who, as we have seen, identified the site as the "loggia de' melaranci" or "verde":

Lorenzo Strozzi's first comedy was performed in the Palazzo Medici at the behest of the magnificent Lorenzo, duke of Urbino; you [i.e., Palla Strozzi] and your older brother Giovan Battista acted your parts in such a way that among the actors whose services had been solicited throughout the whole dominion, one perceived how well prepared you were in your delivery. It may be that on later occasions similar works were performed and directed more splendidly, but until that time our citizens had not yet seen a comedy directed so well. Lorenzo [Strozzi], wishing to please not so much the duke, simply, as all the people, undertook responsibility for everything that was required in order to have the comedy successfully performed, and first, in the above *sala grande* in the aforementioned palace he had a stage set designed by Ridolfo Ghirlandaio, which to all turned out to be new and marvelous.[15]

How might we resolve the inconsistency between the accounts as to the location of the theatrical performances? Cerretani and Zeffi are both authoritative witnesses, and one need not conclude in this instance that either of the reports is necessarily in error. It may simply be, instead, that one of the performances—the one Zeffi recounted—did indeed take place in the *sala grande* on the *piano nobile* of Palazzo Medici, the room that overlooked what is now Via Cavour. A surviving representation of the garden in its original state permits us to visualize the setting for the other performances.[16]

Manuscript Ashburnham 579 of the Biblioteca Medicea-Laurenziana contains the text of a comedy known to scholars as the "Commedia in versi"; the fact that the copy is accompanied by a rubric in Lorenzo Strozzi's hand—"The first comedy that I ever wrote, performed in Palazzo Medici [Laprima Comedia chio facesi mai recitata incasa e medici]" (fol. 3^r)[17]—suggests that the previous attribution of the work to Machiavelli was erroneous and that the piece is instead to be identified with the one performed on the occasion Zeffi described.[18] His report continues with a detailed account of unusual interest of the music for the *intermedii*:

After having placed a variety of instruments in different locations, he divided them in this way: before the comedy there were the *suoni grossi* of trumpets, bagpipes, and *pifferi*, so that the souls of the audience were aroused; he had the second act introduced by three richly dressed Moors with three lutes, who, in the silence, sweetly delighted all; in the third, soprano voices sang to four *violoni*, rising according to the comedy; to the tumult of the fourth, he accommodated the most acute plucked instruments; the final music was of four trombones, artfully and sweetly modulating their voices. The music was subsequently imitated; but until that time it had never come into use or consideration, because it rarely happens that the person in charge of an enterprise is equal to all of the difficulties that one encounters in it. And in the singing Lorenzo played his role with great grace, so much so that several times he appeared lascivious, especially when conferring his love to the sound of his lute.[19]

Pirrotta suggested that one might explain Zeffi's claims as to the novelty of the *intermedii* in two different ways: not only were they "visible"—the reference to the three richly dressed Moors who introduced the second act, one of whom was apparently Lorenzo Strozzi himself, demonstrates that they were indeed so—but also bore some relationship to the plot, as is suggested by the allusions to the soprano voices "rising according to the comedy" and the "tumult of the fourth" act, which elicited appropriate instrumentation.[20]

Cerretani's account of the festivities concludes: "On the evening of the twelfth there were three *trionfi*, Venus, Mars, and Minerva, with sublime songs, after which came Imeneo, god of weddings, with an appropriate explanatory song, and other most ornate songs, and thus the wedding festivities ended, to the people's small satisfaction and all caused by two things: the one, Madonna Alfonsina's great avarice, and the other, the heads and the directors of the *festa* of the dancing."[21]

Among Jacopo Nardi's *canti* is a "Canzona sopra il Carro delle tre Dee"[22] that must have been one of those performed on the evening of the twelfth, despite the fact that its text, in two respects, does not correspond precisely to Cerretani's account: Nardi's *canto* makes reference to Juno, Minerva, and Venus, while Cerretani's report specifies that there were three *trionfi* that represented Mars, Minerva, and Venus. In other respects, however, the textual allusions are so appropriate to the historical circumstances of the occasion that one can reasonably posit that Cerretani's account is in this instance erroneous. As Francesco Bausi observed in his analysis of the text,[23] its references to a dedicatee who is a non-Florentine woman (lines 36–37), a spouse (lines 13 and 30) who, by virtue of her marriage, is invested with a "corona ducale" (line 20), suggest that the event that occasioned the composition and performance of the work was Lorenzo's and Madeleine's wedding:

> Non vide 'l mondo mai sotto la luna   [1]
> donna tanto felice o tanto degna,
> perché somma fortuna
> col tuo sommo valor congiunta regna,
> ond'il ciel non ti sdegna;
> anzi, per farti di sue grazie dono,
> queste tre dee dal ciel discese sono.

Questa, che lieta innanzi all'altre viene, [8]
Vener si chiama, madre dell'amore,
qual con dolce catene
serra duo cuor gentili in un sol core;
questa col suo favore
con tal nodo t'unisce al tuo consorte
che scior nol può fortuna, tempo o morte.

Segue Giunon, regina delli dei, [15]
la qual dispensa onor, stato e richezza;
e promette costei
donarti regno, tesoro e altezza;
e perché assai t'apprezza,
di corona ducale oggi t'onora,
forse per farti piú felice ancora.

La terza dea è chiamata Minerva, [22]
per cui saggio operar, come si vede,
sol s'accosta e conserva
quel che natura e fortuna concede;
perché prudenza eccede
con sua virtú la forza delle stelle,
il savio sol non è subietto a quelle.

Dunque seguendo sempre questa dea [29]
con tutto il cor, felici e degni sposi,
Giunone e Citarea
al mondo vi faranno alti e famosi;
e di sí gloriosi
parenti, poi, la generosa prole
spargerà il nome quanto scalda il sole.

E tu ricevi, alma Fiorenza, [36]
questa preclara donna, alla qual porge
il ciel tanta eccellenza
che simil fra' mortali oggi non sorge;
perché, se 'l ver si scorge,
quel celeste favor che 'n questa abbonda,
ognor ti farà piú lieta e gioconda.[24]

Who were the instrumentalists who furnished the "quantità di suoni" during Madeleine's *entrata* and the music for the dancing on the evenings of the eighth and tenth of September and participated in the theatrical performance described by Zeffi? And who were the singers who performed the "canti divini" and "ornatissimi" that concluded the wedding festivities? That a number of instrumentalists and singers were in Lorenzo's service or otherwise associated with him in some way is demonstrable. The names of the instrumentalists Giamandrea da Brescya sonatore,[25] Gian Maria Giudeo,[26] Girolamo da Melia sonatore,[27] Tadeo musicho,[28] and Urbano sonatore[29] appear in his account books at one time or another, as do the names of several musicians who were also in the service of the public institutions: Bartolomeo degli Organi,[30] Giovannibattista d'Arezzo,[31] and Ser Vergilio cappellano.[32] Other musicians' names occur in Lorenzo's correspondence: Giangiacomo pifaro (a famous instrumentalist who passed from Lorenzo's service to Leo X's and then to Clement VII's and who, with Benvenuto Cellini, performed instrumental arrangements of motets at Clement's table, according to Cellini's own account),[33] Giovanni Como pifaro,[34] and Pierino pifaro (who may be identical with the Pierino mentioned by Vasari),[35] and, again, Bartolomeo degli Organi[36] and Vergilio.[37] Though the evidence concerning these musicians dates from various times during the second decade of the sixteenth century, at minimum it suggests that despite an earlier thesis to the contrary, Lorenzo was indeed interested in music and that his musical "establishment," though never very large by contemporary standards, may well have been large enough in 1518 to have assumed reponsibility for the musical component of his wedding festivities. We are aided in our attempts to visualize the instrumentalists' participation in the *feste da ballo* by the famous depiction of a wedding scene that decorates the front panel of a *cassone* now in the Galleria dell'Accademia in Florence (see figures 32 and 33); although the panel is not contemporary with the events in question—it dates from the fifteenth century—it nonetheless furnishes evocative pictorial evidence, especially given that some of the same decorative elements were evidently employed on the two occasions in question, as a comparison of the *cassone* panel with Cerretani's description of the events of 1518 suggests. As for the musical characteristics of the pieces performed at the *feste da ballo* and on the evening of September 10, we might speculate, first, that the ensemble for the *feste* was composed of shawm, bombard, and sackbut, the *alta capella* featured on many such occasions. The *capella* presumably made use of standard tenor patterns, above which were improvised "exuberant" counterpoints "in rhapsodic and rhythmically exciting fashion," to quote the words Daniel Heartz used in describing what is perhaps the most celebrated example of polyphonic instrumental music for the dance from Renaissance Italy (example 5); although its style would no longer have been current in 1518, it nonetheless gives some sense of the character of such music. The instrumental pieces performed on the evening of the tenth may have exemplified a similar "compositional" technique (the instrumentalists might well have made use, alternatively, of arrangements of works in the contemporary secular vocal repertory, or perhaps of such pieces as Isaac's *Palle, palle*). The *feste da*

Figure 32. Anonymous representation of a wedding scene

Figure 33. Instrumentalists accompany the *festa da ballo* in a detail from Figure 32

ballo also presumably featured the traditional pairing of stately *bassa-danza* and animated *saltarello* ("after the one the other is always performed [detro ad ella se fa sempre lui]," Antonio Cornazano claimed), and although one cannot know what specific dances Lorenzo's and Madeleine's guests performed, among them may have been two choreographed by the bridegroom's own grandfather, Lorenzo "il Magnifico"; at minimum, that the Medici delighted in dancing there can be little doubt.[38]

There is much other evidence that testifies to Lorenzo's musical patronage. There is, for example, an interesting exchange of letters between Lorenzo and Cardinal Giulio de' Medici in February and March of 1513 that documents Lorenzo's efforts on behalf of the Signoria of Florence to secure the services of a corps of instrumentalists from Cesena[39] and further evidence of his interest in instrumental music in another exchange concerning the musicians of Cardinal Luigi d'Aragona, whose services both Lorenzo and Leo were trying to obtain after d'Aragona's death.[40] Lorenzo seems particularly to have enjoyed dancing, as the accounts of the wedding festivities suggest, and for that reason he may have been especially interested in maintaining a corps of instrumentalists.[41] That he indeed derived pleasure from music is suggested not only by the evidence that documents the existence of his small "establishment" but also by other references that reveal that he was present on various occasions when music was performed.[42]

He also continued his family's long-standing tradition of involvement in the patronage practices of the Florentine public institutions: in 1518, he arranged for provisions of various kinds on behalf of Baccio Moschini and Baccio degli Organi at the Cathedral, baptistery, and Church of the Annunziata.[43] He may, moreover, have been involved in securing the services of French musicians for the papal musical establishment: Bernardo Dovizi da Bibbiena, Leo's legate in France, wrote to Lorenzo in 1518 concerning "tre putti musici" who were being sought in France so that they could be sent to Leo.[44]

As his family's principal representative in Florence after 1513, Lorenzo received a great many letters of recommendation from his relatives in Rome on behalf of various supplicants, musicians among them, and he was expected to respond in some way to any that were intended to be taken seriously and were not written simply in order to discharge a responsibility. In May of 1514, for example, Giuliano de' Medici, Baldassare Turini da Pescia, then Lorenzo's agent in Rome, and Niccolò de' Pitti, the prior of the papal chapel, all wrote to Lorenzo on behalf of Heinrich Isaac,[45] and in May of 1516 Giuliano de' Medici and Cardinals Giulio de' Medici and Antonio del Monte wrote to Lorenzo concerning Alessandro Coppini.[46]

Example 5. M. Gulielmus (?), polyphonic arrangement of the
basse dance tenor *La spagna*, Perugia, Biblioteca comunale,
MS 431, fols. 95ᵛ–96ʳ

Example 5, continued

Lorenzo also seems to have played something of a role in the transmission of music between Florence and Rome and in two instances the works transmitted were evidently composed at Lorenzo's behest; indeed, the two letters that permit this particular conclusion may be of unusual importance, since they suggest that Lorenzo was interested in polyphonic settings of Italian texts and that he requested such pieces from composers associated with Leo's musical establishment—in one instance Elzear Genet, in another perhaps Bernardo Pisano. Lorenzo, therefore, may have played a role in encouraging the experimentation with settings of Italian texts that forms the background for the emergence of the madrigal. In neither instance can we be certain of the identity of the work in question, since in one case the reference is to a setting of the text "Sono io donna" by an otherwise unidentified composer named "Zoppino," who may have been Pisano; and in the other the reference is simply to a work by the master of the papal chapel, at that time Genet. There are four extant settings of Italian texts by Genet, one of which may have been the one sent to Lorenzo, and although all may be described as "frottolesque" rather than "madrigalian" in their musical style, they do, in their use of Petrarchan texts, reflect the tendency toward more sophisticated literary expression characteristic of the early madrigal.[47]

Lorenzo, finally, seems to have had books of music copied for him: an undated letter from Baccio degli Organi to Giovanni da Poppi testifies to such activity.[48]

Even if Alfonsina's evident satisfaction with the events of the first weeks of September 1518 was not universally shared, as Cerretani's report suggests, they nonetheless contributed some enduring images to the history of Florentine public life: the *entrata* itself, accompanied by instrumental playing, in which scores of Florentine city officials participated, mounted on horseback; among the others whose involvement Cerretani recorded—the members of the Florentine militia, Lorenzo's relatives, the cardinals Innocenzo Cibo and Luigi de' Rossi—those who accompanied Madeleine on foot, attired as they were in garments of unusual elegance, seem especially to have contributed to the extraordinary visual impact the event must have had; the succession of banquets in the garden of the Medici palace on the eighth, ninth, and tenth, at one of which, at least, the pope and Cardinal Giulio were symbolically present in the form of Raphael's remarkable portrait, now in the Galleria degli Uffizi; on the eighth and tenth the *feste da ballo* on the platform designed by Aristotile, Franciabigio, and Ridolfo Ghirlandaio and constructed in front of Palazzo Medici, its various decorative elements visually impressive enough to have prompted Cerretani's detailed report; on the eighth, ninth, and tenth the performances of Giovanni Manenti's *Philargio*, Lorenzo Strozzi's "Commedia in versi," and a third, unidentified comedy, played by Cherea and his colleagues against the *loggia* that formed the south wall of the garden in the palace or in the *sala grande* on the *piano nobile*, and embellished, in the case of Strozzi's work, with elaborate musical *intermedii*; and finally, on the twelfth, the traditional procession of *carri*, the meaning they were intended to convey in part explicated by *canti*; and all of the events witnessed by hundreds of Florentines who were either in attendance or among those who observed from the streets, platforms, and rooftops.

For his part, Leo, too, must have derived some real satisfaction from the events of 1515–18, notwithstanding the premature death in March of 1516 of his beloved younger brother Giuliano. His family's relationship to the French royal family had been considerably strengthened as a result of Lorenzo's marriage to Madeleine. By 1518, Lorenzo was captain general of the Florentine Militia and duke of Urbino, and Giulio was archbishop of Florence, cardinal, legate to Bologna, and papal vice-chancellor. Within months of Lorenzo's wedding, however, the continuity of the regime was seriously threatened: Lorenzo was the last legitimate direct male descendant of Cosimo "il Vecchio" other than the pope, and on May 4, 1519, he died. Cardinal Giulio temporarily assumed responsibility for the regime.[49]

ALESSANDRO DE' MEDICI AND THE ESTABLISHMENT OF THE *PRINCIPATO*

CHAPTER 10

THE FIRST YEARS OF
CLEMENT'S
PONTIFICATE

CARDINAL GIULIO set about to reverse the effects of Lorenzo's auto-cratic behavior and ineffectual stewardship of the Medici regime, and ac-cording to most accounts achieved considerable success.[1] His political ac-complishments were matched by cultural ones: he is to be credited with a significant role in the execution of some of the most important artistic projects of the entire period, including the New Sacristy at the Church of San Lorenzo in Florence and the decoration of the *salone* at the Medici villa at Poggio a Caiano.[2] He may, in addition, have maintained a small musical "establishment" whose members possibly included Philippe Ver-delot,[3] the most important of the early madrigalists, and the famous lutenist Gian Maria Giudeo, who, as we have seen, had long been an inti-mate of various members of the Medici family.[4] Giulio demonstrably con-tinued his family's habit of involving itself in the patronage practices of the Florentine public institutions.[5] The music manuscript Cortona, Bib-lioteca comunale 95, 96/Paris, Bibliothèque nationale, Nouvelles acquisi-tions françaises 1817, was almost certainly copied for Cardinal Giulio, probably during the years he was his family's principal representative in Florence, and it may be considered one of the most important documents we possess for the evolution of the Italian madrigal, since its repertory is a kind of conspectus of premadrigalian types and would presumably have been available to Verdelot during the years that witnessed the emergence of the new genre. If these inferences are correct, Pirrotta's thesis as to Cardinal Giulio's important role in that evolution is substantiated.[6]

However, as papal vice-chancellor and incumbent, therefore, of the most important position in the Vatican hierarchy, Cardinal Giulio could not expect to reside indefinitely in Florence, and in his attempts to iden-tify a representative who could attend effectively to his family's interests in the city, he never satisfactorily realized his objective. Neither Goro Gheri, who had been Lorenzo II's chancellor, nor Cardinal Silvio Pas-serini, who succeeded him as the Medici family's principal agent, pos-sessed Giulio's manifest political abilities, and neither was destined to enjoy success comparable to Cardinal Giulio's, in part for reasons that Gheri and Passerini were unable to control: both men were non-Florentines and therefore encountered resentment among the citizens of Florence.[7]

Nor were there any members of the Medici family who might have served the family's interests more ably than Gheri or Passerini. The eldest male descendants of Cosimo "il Vecchio" were Ippolito, the illegitimate son of Giuliano di Lorenzo, and Alessandro, said to be Lorenzo II's son but who, it was whispered, was instead Cardinal Giulio's bastard. Both boys were about nine years old in 1520 and therefore not appropriate candidates to succeed Cardinal Giulio, even if they had been politically capable and responsible, which they most decidedly were not. Giulio was compelled to divide his time between Florence and Rome throughout the period between Lorenzo II's death in May of 1519 and Leo's in December of 1521, and beyond.[8]

Giulio was a candidate for the papacy upon Leo's death, but Adrian VI instead emerged victorious from the conclave. When in 1523 Adrian himself died, Giulio was elected and took the name Clement VII. His election precipitated yet another crisis in Florence, since he was clearly unable to minister personally to his family's concerns. In 1524, whatever remaining objections to Alessandro and Ippolito on grounds of youth and inadequacy having been overcome, Ippolito was sent to Florence, where he was responsible to Cardinal Passerini, and Alessandro took up residence in the villa at Poggio.[9] Pope Clement, temporarily at least, could turn his attention to other matters.

He was fated to experience what J. R. Hale has described as "almost uninterrupted humiliation. Merely to list the problems that confronted Clement in the eleven years of his pontificate . . . is to suggest that the enormity of his task precluded success. . . . Apart from Habsburgs and Valois fighting for predominance in Italy . . . they included Henry VIII bullying for his divorce; Suleiman leading his Turks into Hungary, defeating its king and threatening Vienna; Lutheranism spreading throughout the Empire and into Scandinavia; Zwingli lighting revolt against Rome in Switzerland. On those eleven years pressed the full weight of what were becoming the most pervasive spiritual and political crises Europe had experienced."[10] It was the first of these problems, ultimately, that was to have the most decisive consequences for Florence.

Clement sought to maintain the traditional alliance with France, even after the defeat of the French army at the battle of Pavia in February of 1525 and the king's capture.[11] The Treaty of Cognac, which was signed in 1526 after Francis's return from captivity, resulted in the formation of an anti-imperial league whose members included Genoa, Milan, Venice, and the papacy and, inevitably, the pope's native city, despite the fact that

Figure 34. Sebastiano del Piombo, portrait of Pope Clement VII
(Giulio di Giuliano de' Medici)

Figure 35. Titian, portrait of Ippolito di Giuliano di
Lorenzo de' Medici

Figure 36. Vasari, portrait of Alessandro di Lorenzo di Piero di
Lorenzo de' Medici

Florence was not among the treaty's formal signatories.[12] Whatever prospects for military success the League of Cognac may have enjoyed evaporated with the death of the pope's cousin, the famous *condottiere* Giovanni *delle Bande Nere*, as a number of the most important contemporary witnesses suggested, Filippo de' Nerli and Benedetto Varchi among them.[13] Clement, moreover, was openly equivocal—by diplomatic means he sought to prepare for the growing eventuality of an imperial victory—and his equivocation served to weaken the League's resolve.[14]

On May 6, 1527, the imperial army, operating essentially independently, sacked Rome. It would be almost impossible to exaggerate the effect of the sack and the dislocations it precipitated on the collective consciousness of Europe, difficult though it may be to recapture the sentiments of Europeans who lived more than four and a half centuries ago.[15] The reaction in Florence was immediate: on May 17, Ippolito and Alessandro were exiled and the republic subsequently renewed.[16] When the Medici family was restored in 1531, it was to remain until the eighteenth century.

As Professor Felix Gilbert suggested to me, given the character of Florentine political life in the years between Lorenzo II's death and the restoration of 1531, one would not expect that there were institutional innovations. In the period immediately after Lorenzo's death, Cardinal Giulio, whose objective was the papacy, was not inclined to attempt to establish himself. The years between 1523 and 1527, similarly, may be considered a period of transition, a period that witnessed an aligning of parties.[17] Nor, for the same reasons, would one expect a succession of public festivals similar to those organized in the years between the restoration of 1512 and Lorenzo's death, and, indeed, there is only one such event amply attested by contemporary evidence that matches in music-historical importance the events of the first decade of the restoration.

Donato Giannotti, Filippo de' Nerli, and Giorgio Vasari attest a performance of Niccolò Machiavelli's famous comedy *La Clizia* at the home of Jacopo di Filippo Falconetti *detto* "il Fornaciaio" in Santa Maria in Versaia, outside the gate in the Florentine city walls at San Frediano.[18] Falconetti was a member of one of the Florentine magistracies—the "dodici Buonuomini"—when he was dismissed from office by the Signoria in January of 1520 and exiled for five years "extra civitatem Florentiae et portam Sancti Frediani de Florentia." The performance of *La Clizia* formed part of the elaborate festivities occasioned by his recall on January 13, 1525, and followed a magnificent banquet "to which all of the principal citizens came and the most esteemed members of the *stato* who were then governing."[19] Vasari's account seems to suggest that Alessandro and Ippolito were among the members of the audience:

When the *Mandragola*, a most amusing comedy, was to be performed by the company of the Cazzuola in the house of Bernardino di Giordano, on the Canto a Monteloro, Andrea del Sarto and Aristotile executed the scenery, which was very beautiful; and not long afterward Aristotile executed the scenery for another comedy by the same author, in the house of . . . Jacopo at the Porta S. Fr[ed]iano. From that kind of scenery and perspective views, which much pleased the citizens in general and in particular Signor Alessandro and Signor Ippolito (who were in Florence at that time, under the care of Silvio Passerini, cardinal of Cortona), Aristotile acquired so great a name that it was afterward his principal profession.[20]

The performance was met with an exceptional response, to judge from a letter of February 22 from Nerli to Machiavelli, in which Nerli, then governor of Modena, flattered Machiavelli with an extravagant compliment that described the performance in language borrowed directly from Poliziano's *Stanze*:

> Fornaciaio and you, and you and Fornaciaio, have succeeded in such a way that the fame of your glorious accomplishments has been racing not only throughout all of Tuscany but also throughout Lombardy. I know of the garden having been leveled in order to prepare the stage set for your comedy; I know of the *conviti* not only for the leading and noblest patricians of the city but also for the middle and lower classes, things customarily done only for princes. The fame of your comedy has flown everywhere; and don't you believe that I've had these things from friends' letters; rather I've had it from travelers who go through all the streets expounding upon "the glorious displays and magnificent festivals [Le gloriose pompe e i fieri ludi]" of the *porta a San Fr[ed]iano*. I would like you to send me this comedy, which you recently had performed, as soon as you can.[21]

Among the features of the performance that must have contributed to its extraordinary reception were novel musical elements that proved to be of enduring significance: Machiavelli's texts for the *intermedii* and the *canzone* before the prologue were set to music by Philippe Verdelot in the new madrigal style. Indeed, some sense of Machiavelli's own understanding of the importance of the musical elements is conveyed by the text of the second strophe of the *canzone* before the prologue, sung by a small vocal ensemble that comprised a nymph and three shepherds: "Happy and cheerful, therefore, we shall unite our singing to your present endeavor, with a harmony so sweet you have never heard the like of it before (Pertanto, allegri e lieti, / a queste vostre imprese / farem col cantar nostro compagnia / con sì dolce armonia / qual mai sentita più non fu da voi)."[22] It was, in Pirrotta's words, "no empty boast," for the musical elements of the performance "represent the starting point of a new concept of *intermedi*": "the 'sweet harmony' of madrigalian polyphony [see example 6] replaced the introduction by a single player accompanying himself on the lyre," a tradition typified, for example, by Nardi's *I due felici rivali* of 1513.

"A further novel aspect was also at least partly musical. This was the unification of the musical pieces between the acts, achieved by having them all performed by the same group,"[23] in contradistinction to the heterogeneity of the *intermedii* for the performances of Lorenzo Strozzi's "Commedia in versi" in Florence in 1518 and Ariosto's *I suppositi* in Rome in 1519. Musical *intermedii*, of course, were fixtures of theatrical performances elsewhere; but in Renaissance Florence, where classical precepts and practices acquired virtually sacrosanct status, the *intermedii* were "real choruses, engaged in the task, once performed by the classical choruses, of commenting on the events within the play and adding an almost hieratic sense of celebration to the performance."[24]

Example 6. Philippe Verdelot, setting of Machiavelli's text for the *canzone* before the prologue of *La Clizia*, *Quanto sia lieto il giorno*, *Il primo libro de madrigali di Verdelotto* (Venice: O. Scotto, 1537), no. 1

Example 6, continued

125

Example 6, continued

Example 6, continued

THE CORONATION OF
CHARLES V

THE OUTCOME of the battle of Pavia and the sack of Rome served to demonstrate that the empire had at long last achieved undisputed hegemony in Europe. Clement could no longer afford to indulge a notorious tendency to equivocate; the events of the mid-1520s had forced his hand. That he was compelled to come to terms with Charles is vividly demonstrated by his decision to invest the emperor with the imperial crown, and the ceremonies in Bologna in late 1529 and early 1530 were, by any measure, among the most extraordinary of the entire sixteenth century.

The principal musical elements of the ceremonies were musical embellishments of specific liturgical provisions; in this instance, therefore, more so than in any other detailed thus far, they elaborated centuries-old ritual traditions that governed their stylistic characteristics. That this should have been the case is hardly surprising, given the nature of the ceremonies and the identity of the principal participants. The events, inevitably, generated an unprecedented degree of interest throughout Europe, and the extensive and elaborate descriptions they inspired thus afford their close reconstruction.

Clement arrived in Bologna on October 24, 1529, and Charles on November 5.[1] Among other, familiar ceremonial elements of Charles's elaborate *entrata*, the chroniclers recorded the participation in the procession of the instrumentalists—*pifferi*, trumpeters, and drummers—of various of Charles's lieutenants,[2] and of the emperor himself, "the emperor's *trombe* with his *pifferi* numbering eight in all, his *trombette* numbering twelve, all on horseback."[3] One chronicler reported that upon the procession's arrival in Piazza Maggiore, "so great were the sounds of voices, trumpets, drums, and artillery, that it seemed that Bologna was turned upside down."[4] Clement greeted the emperor in front of the Church of San Petronio and after various ceremonies withdrew to his temporary residence in the Palazzo Comunale; Charles, "accompanied by the cardinals, entered the Church of San Petronio to pray, where the papal chapel was singing the *Te Deum laudamus*, and upon the altar were placed all of the principal relics in Bologna."[5] The emperor in turn then retired to his apartments, which adjoined the pope's.[6]

Figure 37. Anonymous woodcut, representation of Charles V's Bolognese
entrata of 1529

    Throughout their stay in Bologna, Charles and Clement were engaged
in discussions intended to resolve various outstanding political issues,
among them, importantly, the constitutional status of the city of Florence.[7] One of the narratives records that "it was decided at Bologna to
make Alessandro de' Medici duke of Florence."[8] Throughout this period,
too, there were numerous occasions for musical performances: on November 25 and 28, mass was sung in the chapel of the Palazzo Comunale
and on December 5, the imperial musicians sang mass in the Church of
San Domenico at the behest of the emperor, who was present.[9] In the
absence of Clementine music manuscripts dating from after the sack of
Rome,[10] it is difficult to gauge the importance of the imperial chapel's
presence for the dissemination of the imperial repertory in Italy, in the
way one can trace the effects of the presence of the French chapel in 1515
in contemporary Florentine and Leonine sources.[11] Nonetheless, it is
hardly an extravagant hypothesis that some kind of exchange must have
taken place. Indeed, on February 14, 1530, some newly composed works
by the master of the imperial chapel, Adrian Thiebault *dit* Pickart, were

Figures 38 and 39. Instrumentalists accompany the procession of the imperial
entourage in a representation of Charles's *entrata*

performed by the chapel's members in the Church of S. Salvatore, and such works in particular are likely to have been among those solicited by the papal musicians. As for the identity of works sung by the papal chapel on various occasions during the meetings, one can draw some inferences from the contents of the manuscript Vatican City, Biblioteca Apostolica Vaticana, Cappella Sistina 55, copied during the previous decade, which contains such pieces as Jean Beausseron's Missa *de Feria*, Andreas Michot's Misse *de domina nostra* and *feria*, and Pierre Moulu's Misse *Missus est Gabriel* and *Stephane gloriose*.[12]

On December 23, a general peace was concluded; the treaty's signatories included the emperor and the pope, Venice, Francesco Sforza (the pretender to the duchy of Milan), Mantua, Savoy, Monferrato, Urbino, Siena, and Lucca.[13] The treaty was proclaimed in the Cathedral of Bologna on January 1,[14] and "a solemn mass was sung in the presence of the pope and the emperor and all the ambassadors who were in the city."[15] The way was cleared for the imperial coronation ceremonies.

There were actually to be two such ceremonies, one on the twenty-second of February, when Charles was to receive the Iron Crown of Lombardy, and a second on the twenty-fourth, his birthday,[16] when he was to receive the imperial crown, five years to the day after the event—the victory of his forces at the battle of Pavia[17]—which precipitated the remarkable succession of developments that culminated in the imperial coronation itself. The first of the ceremonies occurred in the chapel of the Palazzo Comunale, and from the several narrative accounts one can partially reconstruct its complex liturgico-musical element: the singing of litanies, perhaps in *falsobordone*, the solo chanting of mass Proper texts, the singing of the *Te Deum*, the choral performance of "una bela musica"—almost certainly in polyphony—after the chanting of the Gospel.

> Early on the morning of the twenty-second of February, his Majesty prepared to receive the crown of Lombardy. Accompanied by Duke Alessandro de' Medici, he went to the chapel in the Palazzo Comunale.[18]
>
> And several orations having been said, the papal singers then sang the Litanies.[19]
>
> The Introit of the mass was begun, in chant.[20]
>
> The mass proceeded as far as the Epistle, which was sung by a member of the papal chapel; meanwhile, the Most Reverend Archbishop of Zara in Dalmatia, Francesco of the House of Pesaro, took the book, and the sacristan took the lighted candle in hand, and they went before the pope as his assistants, and the pope said the Epistle, according to custom.[21]

(The passage thus substantiates the assumption that the celebrant ordinarily recited liturgical texts while they were being sung, either in chant—by a soloist or the choir—or in polyphony.)

Then, a gold pillow having been placed at the pope's feet, while the Gradual was being sung, the emperor, led by the two Most Reverend Cardinals assisting him, Girolamo Doria and Ippolito de' Medici, went to kneel upon it.[22]

The pope invested the emperor with the symbols of office: the crown, the orb, the scepter, and the sword; instrumental fanfares and the ringing of bells marked the moment of formal investiture.[23]

After the coronation, the pope began to pray, saying "Sta et retine locum," and he intoned the *Te deum laudamus*, which the singers completed,[24] the pope and the emperor standing throughout. When the singers reached the verse "Te ergo quaesumus famulis tuis subveni," the pope, the emperor, the Most Reverend Cardinals and everyone in the chapel knelt. And the Most Reverend Cardinal Hincvorth [i.e., Wilhelm Enckenvoirt], who was singing the mass, purified the altar with incense.[25]
And at the conclusion of certain orations, which were sung by the chapel,[26] the deacon took the missal and stood a short distance from the altar and sang the Gospel,[27] "Quem dicunt homines esse filium hominis,"[28] at the conclusion of which the reverend master of ceremonies, Biagio da Cesena, gave the book to his Holiness to kiss, and the Most Reverend Bishop of Orense, in Spain, Ferdinando de Valdés, gave it to the emperor to kiss.[29] And then the singers began to sing and to make beautiful music. While the singers were singing their music, the Most Reverend Cardinal Hincvorth turned with his back to the altar and took the paten in his hand. Then Caesar went to the altar. Having arrived before the Most Reverend Cardinal Hincvorth he knelt. Then his Most Reverend Eminence gave the paten to Caesar to kiss. His Majesty went to his place. At the conclusion of the mass, the pope stood and said, "Adiutorium nostrum in nomine Domini," and gave the Benediction. And the Most Reverend Cardinals began to exit from the chapel, and thus also the pope and the emperor. And the pope retired to his rooms and the emperor to his.[30]

To judge from the detailed reports one finds in contemporary accounts, the imperial coronation ceremony two days later involved considerably more elaborate liturgico-musical provisions, the featured texts and rituals redolent of ancient ecclesiastical protocol and fraught with meaning; the participants included the highest-ranking individuals in the Vatican hier-

archy. In an ingenious and poignant attempt to create physical surround-
ings that approximated those the emperor would have found had the coronation taken place, properly, at St. Peter's in Rome, the pope's artists
had decorated the interior of San Petronio;[31] space for the papal and imperial musicians had been prepared.[32] An elaborate, elevated passageway,
adorned with tapestries and garlands, had been constructed from the
Palazzo Comunale to San Petronio, by way of which the principal participants processed to the ceremony.[33] On either side of the main door of
the church a temporary wooden chapel had been erected.[34]

The papal entourage arrived first, at midmorning;[35] Clement was accompanied by eighteen cardinals and numerous bishops and members of
his court. One of the accounts records that the choir of the Church of San
Petronio "was so crowded that the pope reached his place with diffi-
culty":[36] "There followed the pope's hired mercenaries, and the pope carried in a 'sedia pontificale' and wearing his crown. And having entered the
chapel, they immediately began to sing Nones, according to custom."[37]

One imagines the papal procession moving slowly, deliberately
through the crowded church, the cardinals' brilliant dress contrasting vividly with the somber, dark-brown building materials of San Petronio, one
of the great monuments of medieval Italian ecclesiastical architecture; the
pope borne aloft, resplendent in full papal regalia, no longer the youthful,
more confident Clement of Sebastiano del Piombo's remarkable portrait
but an older, bearded Clement, his face clearly showing the chastening
effects of the events of 1527. Emotions must have run exceedingly high
that day among observers, the sense of anticipation almost palpable. It
was indeed a moment of high drama.

The imperial entourage arrived a half-hour later.[38] The marchese of
Monferrato carried the scepter; the duke of Urbino, the sword; the count
Palatine Philip, the nephew of the elector, the imperial orb; and the duke
of Savoy, the crown.[39] Charles was clothed in royal vestments and wore
the Crown of Lombardy; he was accompanied by Cardinal Deacons
Niccolò Ridolfi and Giovanni Salviati.[40] With melodramatic timing, the
elevated passageway collapsed almost immediately upon the arrival of
Charles's entourage at the church.

Various introductory ceremonies were to be completed in the temporary chapels constructed at the entrance to San Petronio. As the imperial
procession approached the main door of the church, a priest sang Christ's
words to St. Peter from the Gospel of St. John (21.17):

> Then, preceding the priest singing a certain Response that says
> "Petre, amas me?—Domine tu scis quia amo te.—Pasce oves meas
> [Peter, do you love me?—Lord, you know that I love you.—Feed my
> sheep]," he came to the great door, where the two cardinal bishops

Alessandro Farnese and Lorenzo Campeggio came, wearing their miters and copes.[41]

The Gospel text chanted two days earlier, "Quem dicunt homines esse filium hominis? (Who do men say that the Son of Man is?)," recounts the famous episode when Christ questioned his apostles as to his identity, and in response to Peter's reply, "You are the Christ, the Son of the Living God (Tu es Christus filius Dei vivi)," proclaimed, "You are Peter, and upon this rock I will build my church (Tu es Petrus et super hanc petram aedificabo ecclesiam meam)" (Matthew 16.13, 16–18). The text chanted during the procession of the imperial entourage on the twenty-fourth, like the earlier one, therefore, evoked powerful images central to Christian theology and singularly appropriate for the imperial coronation ceremony, images peculiarly suggestive of the significance of the event and of the relationship between the complementary spiritual and temporal prerogatives of the ceremony's principal participants.

Then

Cardinals Farnese and Campeggio and the emperor came to the main altar, at the foot of which a certain structure was built, so that it would resemble the lower part of the "confessio" of St. Peter's in Rome; his Majesty knelt and the two cardinal bishops came down to him; they having knelt, they sang the Litany, saying "Ora pro eo."[42]

Vasari described the ceremonies that subsequently occurred:

Then the emperor was accompanied by Cardinal Farnese, he being the eldest and deacon of the College of Cardinals, into the chapel of San Maurizio, where, the emperor's vestment having been unbuckled, his shoulder and right arm were anointed with holy oil. These things done, the solemn mass was immediately begun, with wonderful music sung *a coro doppio*, the mass celebrated by the pope; and the emperor, clothed in clerical vestments, was assisting him at the altar.[43]

The accounts in Sanuto's diaries enlarge upon Vasari's considerably and furnish a number of revealing details:

And then, all of the imperial insignia having been placed upon the altar by the papal master of ceremonies, their Lordships returned to their designated places, while the Kyrie and Gloria were being sung; and the day's Oration and another for the emperor were sung by the pope from his seat.[44]

The Epistle was sung by the Subdeacon Giovanni Alberino and another Epistle in Greek by Messer Braccio Martelli, the papal *cameriere*.[45]

The pope then invested the emperor with the symbols of his high office, the transcendent moment recorded by Vasari in his evocative fresco in the Sala di Clemente VII in the Palazzo Vecchio (see figure 40). In his commentary on the fresco in the *Ragionamento quarto*, Vasari identified the most important of the individuals portrayed in his depiction of the event:[46] Cardinals Girolamo Doria and Ippolito de' Medici,[47] who had assisted the emperor on the earlier occasion, shown kneeling on the steps immediately to the pope's left, Cardinal Campeggio,[48] shown seated directly beneath Cardinal Doria, absorbed in prayer, and, immediately to Campeggio's left, Cardinal Alessandro Cesarini,[49] who, as we shall see, was to chant the Gospel, and Cardinal Deacon Farnese,[50] shown seated at lower left, his face turned toward the viewer, gesturing with his left hand to the scene's central action (he may therefore be considered a kind of "festaiuolo," a choric figure who served, in Michael Baxandall's words, "as a mediator between the beholder and the events portrayed"[51]); the marchese of Monferrato,[52] who had participated in the procession of the imperial entourage, shown standing beneath and to the right of the choir loft, his arms fully extended toward the papal throne; in the loft, the papal and imperial musicians,[53] boys and adult males, the singer at the front right corner shown marking the *tactus* (was he intended to represent Adrian Thiebault,[54] the imperial chapel master?); at the bottom, the mounted trumpeters, whose fanfares signaled the moment of Investiture. Vasari also described some of the principal elements of the ephemeral decoration: the silk and gold cloth hangings, the several representations of Clement's coat of arms, the elaborate ephemeral *apparato*, an Ionic order of columns and cornices, fashioned of wood and decorated so as to resemble stone.[55]

Then,

The first of the apostolic subdeacons and other subdeacons and his chaplains came to the place where the Litanies are sung, where they sang praises to the emperor, saying, "Exaudi Christe," several others who were above the choir with the singers responding to them, "Domino Carolo invictissimo imperatori et semper augusto salus et victoria." The praises having been repeated three times, the first of the subdeacons said, "Salvator mundi"; and they responded, "Tu illum adiuva"; and then they said, "Sancta Maria . . . tu illum adiuva." And they sang the Litany in this form, responding always, "Tu illum adiuva."[56] And then, the master of ceremonies having appeared in the center of the chapel with the Most Reverend Alessandro Cesarino, and the requisite devotions having been completed, his Most Reverend Eminence sang the Gospel as it was ordinarily sung. At its conclusion, the master of ceremonies having appeared a

Figure 40. The imperial and papal singers and the imperial trumpeters are depicted in
Vasari's representation of the coronation of Charles V

second time with the archbishop of Rhodes, Marcus, *Ordinis Praedicatorum*, the archbishop sang the Gospel in Greek, having also performed the obligatory devotions. At the conclusion of the Gospel, the emperor sat until the Credo was sung in *canto figurato*. The Secret having been concluded, the pope said the Preface, and very well, having a good voice and being a perfect musician.

At the *Pax tecum*, the emperor left the altar, and he kissed the pope and returned to his place to kneel. And the pope left the altar and returned to his seat, as is customary, and the emperor to his as well. And meanwhile the *Agnus Dei* was sung.[57]

At the conclusion of the mass, the principals and the members of their retinues and other attendees—envoys of virtually all of the important European states[58]—exited from the church. The pope and the emperor mounted on horseback for the *cavalcata* to the Church of San Domenico, which on the occasion of the imperial coronation ceremonies served as proxy for the Church of San Giovanni in Laterano, the Cathedral of Rome; there, Charles was to preside at further ceremonies still. Vasari remarked that during the procession "one heard great shouting and the sound of the trumpets and the beating of drums."[59] The magnificent *cavalcata* is depicted in period engravings (figures 41 and 42), which assist us in our attempts to visualize what must have been regarded by contemporaries as one of the most extraordinary occurrences in recent human history.

The pope accompanied the emperor to the entrance of the church and then returned to his temporary residence.[60] At the conclusion of the ceremonies at San Domenico, during which Charles "created many knights, among them many Germans and a great many of every kind,"

the Lateran canons came to his Majesty at the main door of the Church, where the emperor was honorably received by them, and he having kissed the cross and the relics, they went before him singing *Te Deum laudamus*. And at the main altar, his Majesty gave an oration, and having arisen he kissed the altar and the crown was set down and he was received as a canon and brother of the Church of the Lateran. And then the emperor came to the Palazzo Comunale with his company by the shortest route. The route was covered with cloth hangings, all the houses furnished with arms and greenery.[61]

It was late afternoon by the time Charles had returned to his apartments.[62] That evening there was a banquet in the Palazzo Comunale:

A very large room where one was to eat adjoined the apartment of the cardinal Ippolito de' Medici and was completely adorned with tapestries. The emperor retired there casually, having sent away al-

Figure 41. Representation of the *cavalcata* to the Church of San Domenico
in Bologna following the imperial coronation

Figure 42. Representation of the *cavalcata*

most all the servants, and there he removed his cloak and dressed in a full-length garment of gold brocade. To the sound of *pifferi* and trumpets, they began to bring the dishes to the table, in marvelous order.[63]

The meal, which was most sumptuous, concluded with instrumental playing and music of various kinds.[64]

Yet other festivities followed; the "comedy of Agostino Ricchi da Lucca entitled *I tre tiranni*"—published in Venice in 1533 "with Apostolic and Venetian Privilege" and dedicated "to the Most Illustrious and Most Reverend Signor Ippolito, Cardinal de' Medici"—"was written to be performed in Bologna before his Holiness Clement VII and Charles V [in a hall in the Palazzo Comunale] on the day of commemoration of his Majesty's coronation" on March 4.[65] Ricchi's comedy furnishes an example of what Pirrotta has called the "realistic use of music in comedy," a practice in which "the inclusion of music in the main action . . . took on a realistic function: the characters could be made to sing, play, or dance on stage in those ways and in those circumstances in which singing, playing, and dancing would be plausible and acceptable in ordinary life."[66] One of the earliest and most famous instances occurs in act 4, scene 9 of Machiavelli's *Mandragola*. There, the protagonist, a disguised Callimaco, having devised an elaborate scheme in order to seduce Madonna Lucrezia, with whom he is infatuated, approaches singing the popular song "Venir ti possa el diavolo allo letto, / dapoi che io non ci posso venir io [Would that the devil could come to your bed, / Since I cannot come there myself]" to lute accompaniment; he is thereupon carried into Lucrezia's bedroom by his accomplices and Lucrezia's fatuous, unsuspecting husband Nicia, who had easily been duped into participating in the deception.[67] In Ricchi's *I tre tiranni*, the heartsick Chrisáuolo is urged by his servant Phileno in act 2, scene 5 to "take this lute, and play and sing some happy song, in order to rid yourself of such great pain." Chrisáuolo responds, "I can sing nothing other than what I feel in my heart," and he proceeds to sing the madrigal text "Non vedrà mai queste mie luci asciutte / In alcun tempo il Cielo [Never shall the heavens see my eyes henceforward dry]."[68] As Pirrotta suggested,[69] the *lauda* text "Apparecchiate la strada al Signore, / Diceva il gran Battista nel diserto" in act 4, scene 4 may also have been sung, in this instance by the repentant Philócrate, "dressed in sackcloth" and contemplating "going to San Iacopo di Galitia" in Spain "in penance for his error."[70]

Their political objectives for the moment thus realized, Charles left Bologna on March 22, and Clement nine days later; they were to meet again in 1532, but never before or since the winter of 1529–30 did the supreme pontiff and the holy Roman emperor meet under circumstances that appealed more powerfully to the European imagination.

ALESSANDRO, DUKE OF THE
FLORENTINE REPUBLIC

CHARLES'S CORONATION was only one of several consequences of
the newly established relationship between him and Clement. The political effects of Clement's reconciliation with the emperor soon manifested
themselves: the pope was afforded a means to restore his family to
Florence and to attempt a permanent resolution of its status.

When Florence was besieged by imperial troops, the outcome was all
but inevitable. The formal acts of capitulation were signed on August 12,
1530, by Ferrante Gonzaga and Bartolomeo Valori, the imperial and papal
agents, and representatives of the city. As in 1512, a *parlamento* was called
and a *balìa* of twelve members appointed, headed by Valori, who remained as the principal representative of the Medici family until the end
of the year, when he was replaced by Nicola Schomberg, the archbishop
of Capua. On February 17, 1531, the *balìa* declared Alessandro de' Medici
eligible for membership in all of the magistracies. On July 5, Alessandro
and his entourage entered the city, and on the following day an imperial
edict was issued that declared him *capo* of the city and of the government.[1]

During the winter of 1531–32, Clement was engaged in discussions with
a number of the city's principal citizens concerning the possibility of substantial constitutional reform, and at long last, on April 27, 1532, after almost a century of de facto Medici rule behind appearances of republicanism, there came the constitutional changes that served as "the charter of
the Medici principate," in Randolph Starn's words:[2] the Signoria and the
position of *gonfaloniere* were abolished; genuine authority was vested in
a newly established magistracy known as the Council of the Forty-Eight;
Alessandro was formally accorded the ambiguous title of "duke of the
Florentine Republic," which may be read as a last pathetic attempt to
preserve the fiction of republicanism; and the Medici were granted the
right of hereditary succession.[3]

The regime's security depended, of course, upon the state of its relationship to the emperor. It had been agreed that in order to reinforce that
relationship, Charles's bastard daughter, Margaret of Austria, would
marry Alessandro, who was presented to the Florentines as the illegitimate son of Lorenzo II but who, as we have seen, was rumored to have

been Clement's bastard instead. Margaret's visit to Florence in April of 1533, which may have occasioned the composition of Jacques Arcadelt's madrigal *Giovanetta regal pur innocente*,[4] also occasioned festivities whose musical elements for the most part have *not* survived. In reporting abruptly on her visit, Cambi, who was scandalized by the expense of the 1513 Carnival festivities, made little effort to conceal his sentiments concerning Alessandro's and Margaret's questionable pedigree: "On the sixteenth of April, 1533, the illegitimate daughter of the emperor Charles, nine years of age, and the fiancée of his Lordship Alessandro, the illegitimate son of Duke Lorenzo de' Medici, entered Florence."[5]

On the twentieth of April, Margaret attended a performance by the Compagnia dell'Orciuolo of the famous fifteenth-century Florentine *sacra rappresentazione* of Feo Belcari known as the *Festa di San Felice*, which was performed for the first time in some years on the occasion of her visit and had been revived specifically in her honor.[6] A manuscript in the Biblioteca nazionale centrale preserves a description of the *festa* in the form of a dialogue between Niccolò di Stefano Fabrini, a Florentine intellectual who was subsequently to be a member of the Accademia Fiorentina, and his friend Giovanni. The account specifies that the "festaiuoli" charged with responsibility for the festivities in Margaret's honor included "Filippo Strozzi et Girolamo Gu[i]cciardini." Niccolò explained that the "'festa di San Felice' signifies the *festa* of the Annunciation of the Virgin, but it is called 'of San Felice' because it is performed in that church," and in response to a question of Giovanni's, he elaborated in considerable detail on his remark to the effect that it included "melodies, instrumental playing, music, and other delights":

An angel comes and announces the *festa*, urging everyone to be attentive. Then he calls many prophets and sybils one by one, commanding each to say what he or she knows of the incarnation of the son of God, and, having come into the angel's presence, each, singing, says one verse concerning what he or she has prophesied about the birth of the Messiah. At the conclusion, the heavens open with dances, instrumental music, and *feste*, and the angel Gabriel is there, among six angels, rejoicing and dancing, and God the Father instructs the delegation that it is to address the Virgin Mary, and, descending from the cloud, it greets the Virgin and says the words of the Gospel of St. Luke, which begins, "Missus est," and here, the Virgin Mary and the angel Gabriel alternating, the Virgin at last says, "Ecce ancilla Domine," and the angel returns to heaven; the Virgin gives the Canticle *Magnificat*, the angels following it, and, they having returned to heaven with other instrumental music and songs, the heavens close, and it is finished.[7]

Figure 43. Margaret of Austria, wife of Alessandro di Lorenzo di Piero di Lorenzo
de' Medici, attributed to Gio. Gaetano Gabbiani

In arranging for the performance of a *sacra rappresentazione*, the "festaiuoli" introduced the duke's young fiancée to a genre of absolutely central importance to Florentine popular religious experience, a genre whose
effect was achieved, in the words of one scholar, "with elaborate mechan-
ical means, actors suspended on strings, great revolving disks, massed

sources of artificial light, people going up and down in wooden clouds."[8] The *Festa di San Felice* in particular had a distinguished history. The performance that Margaret witnessed was preceded by many others and she had illustrious predecessors as honorees: in March of 1471, Galeazzo Maria Sforza, the duke of Milan, attended performances of "the Annunciation of the Virgin in San Felice, Christ's Ascension into heaven in the Carmine; and in Santo Spirito when he sends the Holy Spirit to the apostles";[9] and in November of 1494, shortly after the expulsion of the Medici, King Charles VIII, similarly, was entertained by "several solemn and beautiful *feste*," among them that of the *"Vergine Annunziata*, which was performed with ingenious and marvelous artifice in the Church of San Felice in Piazza."[10] For one of the earlier fifteenth-century performances, no less a figure than Filippo Brunelleschi designed the stage machinery, which was used throughout the fifteenth century and perhaps as late as 1565.[11]

As for the music, one can distinguish between "the intoned recitation of dialogue," in Pirrotta's words (the prophets' and sybils' verses "concerning what [each] has prophesied about the birth of the Messiah" were surely performed in this manner), and "singing and playing for realistic purposes (that is, as part of the plot)," "those few instances in which the characters are represented in the act of singing, a hymn, a song, or a prayer."[12] In this particular case, alas, the references in Niccolò's and Giovanni's dialogue are imprecise, and they permit us to do little more than speculate as to the specific musical characteristics of the "suoni e canti." One can draw some more substantial inferences from Belcari's text, as Bianca Becherini suggested; the rubrics indicate that the *lauda Laudate el sommo Dio* is to be sung by the "delegation" of angels "who come in Gabriel's company" and at the conclusion of the *rappresentazione* they sing the *terza rima* text "Vergine santa immacolata e pia" to the Virgin.[13]

The *lauda* text *Laudate el sommo Dio* circulated independently and is found, for example, in the print LAUDE *fatte e composte da più persone spirituali. Et tucte le infrascripte laude ha raccolto et insieme ridocto Iacopo di maestro Luigi de' Morsi cittadino fiorentino a di primo di Marzo* MCCCCLXXXV [1486], where there is neither an attribution to Belcari nor one of the familiar "cantasi come" ("sung like") rubrics that accompany *lauda* texts in many other instances and thus serve to identify musical settings for the texts in question.[14] However, another *lauda* print, *Le Laudi* of Feo Belcari, printed in Florence around 1480, contains the text "Cristo, ver uomo e Dio," accompanied by the rubric "Cantasi come—Laudate el sommo Dio,"[15] and in Serafino Razzi's famous *lauda* collection of 1563, *Libro primo* DELLE LAVDI SPIRITVALI,[16] there is a musical setting for "Cristo, ver uomo e Dio," at the conclusion of which is the indication "All the same *canzoni* are sung to the same tune [Tutte le medesime

¶ Comincia la Rappresentatione della Annuntiatione di nostra Donna. Et prima langelo annuntia la festa.

V Oi excellenti & nobili auditori che siate alla presentia ragunati p gratia ui preghiamo / euostri cori attenti stieno honesti & costumati . a udire & uedete con grandi amori emestier sancti qui annuntiati dello incarnar di dio: & chi lha decto fermando a questo tucto lintellecto Io priegho la diuina prouidenza che doni gratia allointellecto mio

chi possa annuntiar di ásta essenza uerbo incarnato uero figluol di Dio ilqual fu pieno di somma sapienza & annuntiocci la uia del disio chi ha risponder parli con douere epropheti diranno ellor parere
Seguitano poi epropheti chiamati dallangelo: et in prima Noe. Noe il padre eterno creatore comanda che tu dica a tucta gente del nascer di Iesu nostro signore Noe dice.
El uerbo eterno e/certo stabilito dal uoler di suo padre / che uenite

Figure 44. Frontispiece, *La Festa della Annuntiatione di nostra Donna*

Canzoni si cantano in sulla medesima Aria]." A comparison of the two texts suggests that there are indeed formal and structural affinities between them, and the music for "Cristo, ver uomo e Dio" can easily have served for "Laudate el sommo Dio." As one sees below, both texts metrically are *ballate* and therefore employ the same rhyme scheme (*aABCBCcA*) and formal plan. In each instance, an opening couplet of seven- and eleven-syllable lines, which serves as the *ripresa*, is followed by a four-line *stanza* consisting of two *piedi* of two lines each and a *volta* that is related to the *ripresa* by means of the metrical and rhyme schemes: the lines are of seven and eleven syllables and the last line rhymes with those of the opening couplet (the first line of the *volta*, conversely, relates the *volta* to the second and fourth lines of the *stanza* by means of the rhyme). *Laudate el sommo Dio* thus joins the small group of extant musical works that were demonstrably performed on one of the occasions described here.

Christo ver huo[m], e Dio,	Laudate el sommo Dio,
sotto spetie di pan te ador'io,	Laudatel con fervente e buon desio.
Adoro te nell'hostia consacrata,	Laudate Dio cantando con buon zelo,
con la virtù della fede sincera,	Laudate le virtù celeste e sante,
Per le parole è transostantiata,	Laudate tutti quanti il re del cielo,
la sostanza del pane in carne vera,	Laudate le potenzie tutte quante,
l'humanitade in terra,	Dategli laude tante
e nel suo corpo Giesù Christo pio.	Quante potete ad un Signor sì pio.[17]

Musically, the *lauda* manifests some of the stylistic characteristics generally typical of the genre: syllabic text setting, homorhythms, an almost complete absence of contrapuntal devices, and a musical phrase design modeled closely on the text phrase design (see example 7). In this particular instance, one finds extreme economy in the melodic writing, the same music serving for lines 3 and 5, which are otherwise linked through rhyme, and for lines 4, 6, and 8. The musical "treatment" of the text, therefore, is no longer consistent with the fourteenth-century practice of repeating the music of the *ripresa* in the *volta*.

Although the musical element of Belcari's *sacra rappresentazione* is thus for the most part irretrievable, one can readily visualize the setting for the performance of 1533: the interior of the Church of San Felice has remained essentially unchanged since the fifteenth century.[18]

Cambi also reported that "on the twenty-third of April, 1533, the day of St. George, Duke Alessandro had a great and grand *convito*, and comedies and *moresche* were performed,"[19] and the dialogue between Niccolò and Giovanni adds further details (although its testimony is inconsistent with Cambi's as to the date of the *convito*):

Example 7. Setting of the *lauda* text *Laudate el sommo Dio* from Feo Belcari's
Festa di San Felice, Libro primo DELLE LAVDI SPIRITVALI DA DIVERSI ECCEL.
E DIVOTI AVTORI, ANTICHI E MODERNI COMPOSTE.
Raccolte dal R. P. Fra Serafino Razzi Fiorentino, . . .
(Venice, 1563), fols. 47ᵛ–48ᵛ

Example 7, continued

At the head of the said *cortile*, under the *loggia* toward Borgo San Lorenzo, was the *apparato* for a comedy with a beautiful perspective. On Thursday, the twenth-fourth of April, was a *convito* under the *logge* of the *cortile*. And after dinner there came masqueraders of various kinds, and there was dancing; that evening there was a comedy that was finished at four hours after sunset.[20]

In the fifteenth century, Alessandro's illustrious ancestor Cosimo "il Vecchio" had been careful to avoid the appearance of aristocratic behavior; but whatever diffidence may have characterized Cosimo's activity as a political figure or patron of the arts, Alessandro ruled Florence in name as well as in fact and comported himself accordingly. Such festivities as those organized in Margaret's honor could be important elements of cultural policy, evidence of the gradual transformation of Florentine political life. There was soon to be other, more material evidence of that transformation.

When the Medici were restored to Florence in 1512, Paolo Vettori advised Cardinal Giovanni that although his ancestors had ruled more with skill than with force, he would be compelled to rule more with force than with skill.[21] In the mid-1530s, Vettori's counsel was to find expression in the Fortezza da Basso, which for many Florentines became the very symbol of the end of Florentine liberty.[22] "There was nothing in the popular or aristocratic tradition of the city that prepared the way for controlling it by force," J. R. Hale has written; "so radical a break with Florentine convention"[23] therefore calls for explanation. Threatened from without by a group of *fuorusciti*, the regime was more than ever receptive to the advice of those—Luigi Guicciardini, Filippo Strozzi, and Francesco Vettori among them—who argued as Paolo Vettori had some two decades before.[24] Moreover, there is evidence that the emperor was concerned for his young daughter's safety: when, after Clement's death in September of 1534, Alessandro pressed him concerning the marriage, Charles responded that the date, to some extent, would depend upon the state of completion of the Fortezza, which by then was already under construction.[25]

After a series of surveys it had been decided that the fortress would be located at Porta a Faenza, perhaps because it was nearest of the city gates to Palazzo Medici.[26] The foundation stone was laid on July 15, 1534. Giovanfrancesco Camaiani wrote to Luigi Guicciardini that "this morning at one hour and twenty-five minutes after sunrise the foundation of the Fortezza was begun,"[27] and an anonymous chronicler described the ceremony in considerable detail:

> A platform was constructed alongside the excavation with an altar at the head of the platform, where Duke Alessandro and Signor Alessandro Vitelli, the commander of the duke's guard, and other gentlemen went with the entire court and guard and the Most Reverend Monsignor Agniolo Marzi, bishop of Assisi, who said the mass at the said altar [Camaiani adds the detail that "his Excellency having arrived, they began to sing the solemn mass"], and the mass having been said, the bishop was attired in vestments in the excavation where the laying of the foundation of the *cittadella* was ordered, the bishop singing hymns and other texts; and finally he blessed it.[28]

In less than a year and a half, the project was brought essentially to completion. The ceremony for the installation of the garrison on December 5, 1535 may have included a more substantial musical element still, if one can trust Vasari's account, its elaborate prose florid and playful by turns:

Most Divine Messer Pietro Aretino,

The Most Reverend Agniolo Marzi having arrived, he waited to sit; he was removed of his ordinary garments, singing psalms with antiphons and responsories and other psalms throughout, whereupon they began to clothe him in priestly garments with the greatest of ceremony; and then a group of voices began *Spiritus Domini super orbem terrarum* [*sic*: properly *Spiritus Domini replevit orbem terrarum*] in polyphony, purifying the altar in particular with incense fragrant with perfumes and thereafter the flags that were to be flown at the Fortezza. I heard a Kyrie, which seemed to be sung by heavenly voices, and the very earth seemed pleased with the Gloria that I heard intoned by the Most Reverend Bishop, who was answered by a multitude of trombones, *cornetti*, and voices, so that one inclined one's head owing to the sweetness as when one grows sleepy around the fire. At the conclusion of the oration, the *Veni, Sancte Spiritus* was begun by harmonies of trombones; and then the Gospel was concluded, after which, intoning the Credo, it was answered with a good deal more noise of the sort that is only heard during Lent at the Ponte Vecchio around a basket of fish. The singers finished and, re-freshed, began anew with the Verse, which follows, so that we ar-rived at the Preface with many ceremonies.[29]

As one sees, the performance of the polyphonic settings of the liturgical texts included the (presumably) *colla parte* accompaniment of brass instru-ments, appropriate to an outdoor performance.

At the Elevation, the members of the garrison began to appear, "equipped with the most divine armor, which resembled the triumph of Scipio in the second Punic war. The mass was finished with a Benediction that seemed to come from heaven." Finally, at "one hour and three min-utes after midday," the captain of the guard was formally invested with the symbols of office, the standard and *bastone*: "one heard the sound of artillery and of trumpets and arquebusses and shouts, such that it ap-peared that the heavens and earth and the whole world were collapsing, and many horses that were frantically neighing out of fear and owing to the noise, such that one waited an hour before their faces were clearly visible, because of the amount of smoke," and the garrison moved inside the Fortezza for the first time.[30]

The impulse that had earlier led the anxious young duke to consult the astrologers in order to determine the most auspicious moment for the installation ceremony and, indeed, to undertake the construction of the Fortezza in the first instance may also explain the ceremony's liturgical elements: Vasari's specificity concerning the texts that were sung serves to identify the mass as an invocation to the Holy Spirit. "Spiritus Domini replevit orbem terrarum" is a scriptural text from the *Liber Sapientiae* (1.7), used in various liturgical contexts on Pentecost Sunday and suc-ceeding feast days and in the Votive Mass of the Holy Spirit; *Veni, Sancte Spiritus*, similarly, is the famous Sequence for Pentecost. Like the "solemn polyphonic mass" sung during the Capitoline ceremonies of 1513, therefore, and the "beautiful mass" sung in the Cathedral of Florence at the time of the conquest of Urbino[31]—also a mass of the Holy Spirit, notably—the musical elements of the ceremonies for the laying of the foundation stone of the Fortezza and the installation of the guard exemplify the ways in which liturgico-musical elements were employed on occasions of principally political significance, the ways in which ritual means served manifestly political ends.

THE WEDDING OF
ALESSANDRO AND
MARGARET

HOWEVER MUCH the regime's stability may have been enhanced by virtue of Alessandro's betrothal to the emperor's daughter and the construction of the Fortezza da Basso, it continued to be threatened. There remained a large group of dangerously disaffected citizens; among them had been the duke's own cousin, Cardinal Ippolito, whose sudden death in August of 1535 prompted the speculation, inevitably, that he had been assassinated at Alessandro's behest.[1]

The festivities in Naples for Alessandro's and Margaret's wedding did not, therefore, occur under the most auspicious of circumstances; the regime's opponents took advantage of the emperor's presence in order to press their concerns, and the recently completed Fortezza figured prominently in the debate.[2]

The emperor had acceded to the requests of Ferrante and Pietro Antonio Sanseverino, the princes of Salerno and Bisignano, and of Alfonso d'Avalos, the marchese of Vasto, to visit the kingdom and its capital upon his return from the North African campaign. He disembarked at Reggio di Calabria and was first the guest of Pietro Antonio and then of Ferrante. On November 25, 1535, he arrived in Naples, and the city received him in a manner appropriate to his status as the most powerful monarch in Europe.[3] Among the elements of the ephemeral decoration were triumphal arches; one of the accounts specifies that "at the sixth was a representation of Joy, crowned with flowers, with several nymphs who were singing."[4] Gregorio Rosso, the author of one of the most important Neapolitan narratives of the entire period and an eyewitness to the events described here, recorded that

> the emperor went from the Porta Capuana to the archbishopric, where, he having arrived, the vicar who came with him gave him the holy water, and, the emperor wanting to kneel, it was my responsibility to give him the pillow; and he having prayed while the *Te Deum laudamus* was being sung with most solemn music, Antonio

Mormile, *Electus* of Portanova, presented the open missal—I holding the *capitoli* of the city—and Ettore Minutolo, *Electus* of Capuana, administered the oath, saying that it was customary for all the kings and emperors to affirm on similar joyous occasions that they would observe the privileges and favors granted by their predecessors to their vassals; hearing that, the emperor arose and, having placed his hand on the missal, swore to observe—and to have observed—everything, inviolably; as a sign of rejoicing, the trumpets sounded and artillery pieces were discharged.[5]

Later during the course of the *entrata*, Charles, mounted "on his large and beautiful horse," paused "in the middle of the street amidst many shouts of 'Imperio, Imperio' and the trumpets, *cornetti*, pifferi, and *cantanti a ballo*. A great, sweet melody was above the royal Porta Capuana; there were many other trumpeters positioned on the towers and the walls were full of women and men."[6]

Rosso's account continues:

Throughout the entire time the emperor was there, the city looked beautiful and was full of many personages: in addition to the Spanish, there came the duke of Ferrara, the duke of Urbino, the duke of Florence, and Don Ferrante Gonzaga, prince of Molfetti, and Don Francesco d'Este, marchese of Padula, was still in Naples at that time.[7]

Among the members of the large retinue that accompanied Alessandro were the archbishop of Pisa and the bishops of Pistoia and Saluzzo, Francesco Guicciardini (it was Guicciardini who was to counter the exiles' demands so very effectively), Francesco Vettori, the duke's two young cousins Lorenzo di Pierfrancesco, who was to be his assassin, and Cosimo di Giovanni *delle Bande Nere*, who was to be his successor,[8] and "five hundred select arquebusiers on horseback and fifty helmeted lancers with their lances at their thighs; beyond this he had five hundred other cavalry."[9] Under the circumstances, Alessandro's overt show of ecclesiastical, military, and political force was understandable: Rosso left no doubt as to the nature of the pending agenda.

The duke of Florence had come for the promised marriage, which several Florentines were seeking to prevent, and also the cardinals Giovanni Salviati and Niccolò Ridolfi, imploring the emperor with words of supplication to deign to restore liberty to Florence, accompanying their requests with expansive promises; but they accomplished nothing, because the emperor truly bore ill will toward the Florentines, as a people wholly disposed toward the French.[10]

There were happier moments, however. Indeed, Rosso remarked that that entire winter didn't seem winter at all, but one continuous spring, without cold, without rain, without wind, the sky always serene, such that it seemed to rejoice with the spirit of the Neapolitans. On December 19, the viceroy, Don Pietro da Toledo, hosted a most solemn banquet for the emperor in the garden of the villa at Poggioreale, from which the emperor derived the greatest of pleasure and particularly from an eclogue or pastoral farce that, to us, was very humorous. On January 6 was a most beautiful joust in the Piazza Carbonara. That evening, there were balls in the Castel Capuano, and they continued similarly for quite a few days, occasioned by the wedding of Madama Margherita of Austria, the emperor's daughter, to the duke of Florence, although she was very young. While the *Sindaco* and the *Deputati* assembled at S. Lorenzo every day in order to attend to public matters, the emperor was engaged in *conviti* and *feste* throughout that entire carnival season, hosted by the prince of Salerno, the prince of Bisignano, and the viceroy, who prepared a beautiful masquerade and *festa* one day at the home of the treasurer Alonso Sances, his confidant, to which he invited all the beautiful women and ladies of Naples.[11]

Another of the contemporary accounts suggests that there may indeed have been some substance to Benedetto di Falco's seemingly extravagant claim that "with regard to music, beyond that natural instinct with which it seems that heaven has endowed every Neapolitan spirit, almost everyone supplements nature with art, so that various harmonies of an exquisite sweetness are heard both day and night in different places, sometimes with voices, sometimes with instruments."[12] In a dispatch of January 23 to the duke of Mantua, Count Nicola Maffei, a Mantuan envoy, described the musical events that occurred one day during Carnival and furnished a number of evocative details. Maffei, whose own enthusiastic response to the music he heard is conveyed in his remark that "it seemed that paradise had revealed each of its beauties and harmonies," recorded that the emperor rode through the streets in disguise, and that groups of musicians competed with one another in singing "rustic pieces as they sing them here" or "madrigal pieces very well concerted," that they wandered throughout the city improvising verses and songs in honor of the women whom they saw at the windows and "rendered sweet harmony to the delight of those who could hear it."[13]

Events crowded in on one another: "On the second of February, the emperor went to Monte Oliveto, where the entire nobility and Neapolitan and foreign *signoria* then in Naples assembled. That morning, the emperor ate at the home of Ferrante Sanseverino, prince of Salerno, where that evening there came all the ladies and gentlewomen of Naples, and a most beautiful comedy was performed."[14] Ferrante, the nephew of Fracasso Sanseverino and Giovanni Francesco Sanseverino, the count of Cajazzo, seems to have inherited his uncles' cultural and intellectual interests, for he, like them, was responsible for promoting a tradition of theatrical performances.[15]

The wedding ceremony itself and the magnificent *convito* that followed occurred on the evening of February 29, at the Castel Capuano. The roster of attendees alone conveys some sense of the extravagance of the event: Ercole II d'Este, duke of Ferrara; Guidobaldo della Rovere, duke of Urbino; Andrea Doria, prince of Melfi; Pierluigi Farnese, duke of Benevento; the cardinal legates Santacroce and Cesarini; Ferrante and Pietro Antonio Sanseverino, princes of Salerno and Bisignano; the marchese and marchesa of Vasto; Donna Isabella Villamarina and Donna Giulia Orsini, princesses of Salerno and Bisignano; and Donna Maria di Cardona, marchesa of Padula.[16] The wedding occasioned a succession of balls, masked receptions, and other such festivities;[17] an anonymous Florentine chronicler recorded that "the emperor ordered a joust for the wedding festivities in which he also participated, armed *alla moresca*, and, masked, he danced."[18] Rosso's remark that "the carnival season concluded in continuous masquerades, entertainments, banquets, music, comedies, farces, and other recreations, his Majesty often disguising himself, sometimes in the company of the viceroy, sometimes with the marchese del Vasto"[19] was not hyperbole, to be very sure.

At long last the dizzying succession of ceremonies and celebrations in Naples came to an end. On March 11, Alessandro returned to Florence.[20] Charles himself left Naples on March 22 in the company of some six thousand Spanish infantrymen and one thousand cavalry and followed Alessandro to Florence, where he was received by means of a magnificent ceremonial *entrata* on April 28.[21] His visit to Florence, however, was to be brief relative to his Neapolitan sojourn, and on May 4, at midafternoon, he departed.[22]

Margaret, too, was to have a Florentine *entrata*, like Madeleine de la Tour d'Auvergne before her, and like Madeleine she went first to the Medici villa at Poggio a Caiano; Vasari reported to Aretino on June 3 that "on the twenty-eighth of May she arrived at Poggio, which astounded her, seeing such a building. A great many rooms were adorned with gold silk cloth and other cloths and stamped leather." On May 31, Margaret entered the city by the Porta al Prato, like Madeleine de la Tour again. Her entourage proceeded to the Cathedral by way of the Borgo Ognissanti, the Canto degli Strozzi, Via Tornabuoni, and the Canto de' Carnesecchi. During the course of the *entrata*, the aid of the Holy Spirit was

invoked once more: the procession paused in the Cathedral, "and an oration having been said, the Benediction given, and the *Veni Sancte Spiritus*
sung, it exited" and continued to Margaret's temporary residence at the
home of Alessandro's cousin Ottaviano, which had been richly decorated
with works of art from the Medici collection.[23]

On June 13 were the nuptial mass and other concluding festivities of
the wedding celebrations, as Benedetto Varchi reported; the festivities
thus conformed to contemporary practice as described by Klapisch-
Zuber: "in order to be *perfetto* (completed), public signs of the celebration" that had taken place in Naples "still had to be given to the entire
community." There followed, therefore, the "highly-ritualized festive
phase" in Florence, the "'publicizing' ceremony, during which the bride
was transported to the house of her husband, whose kin and friends wel-
comed her with feasting and festivities that sometimes spread over several
days":

> And on the thirteenth, Margaret, together with her husband the
> duke, heard the nuptial mass in San Lorenzo, which was sung by
> Messer Antonio Pucci, the cardinal of Santi Quattro; and then they
> went to Palazzo Medici, where a most beautiful *convito* was prepared,
> and after eating they danced a bit; thereafter a comedy was per-
> formed.[24]

Varchi's account suggests that the comedy was performed in Palazzo
Medici and in that respect is erroneous: Lorenzo di Pierfrancesco de'
Medici's *Aridosia* was in fact performed in Via San Gallo, in the *loggia* of
the Compagnia de' Tessitori (see figure 45), and Vasari's illuminating account reveals that there were musical elements:

> The duke ordered that a comedy be performed for his wedding with
> Madama Margherita of Austria, with scenery by Aristotile, in the
> company of the Tessitori, which is joined to the houses of the mag-
> nificent Ottaviano de' Medici . . . in the Via di S. Gallo. Now
> Lorenzo di Pierfrancesco de' Medici, having himself written the
> piece that was to be performed, had responsibility for the whole per-
> formance and the music. . . . Where the steps of the scenery and the
> stage floor ended, he had the wall . . . reduced to a height of eighteen
> *braccia*, intending to build a room like a pocket in that space, which
> was of considerable size, and a platform as high as the stage proper,
> which would serve for the vocalists. Above this first stage he wished
> to make another for harpsichords, organs, and other such instru-
> ments that cannot be moved or changed with ease, . . . all of which
> pleased Aristotile, because it . . . left the stage free of musicians, but
> he was by no means pleased that the rafters supporting the roof . . .

Figure 45. Loggia dei Tessitori, Via San Gallo, Florence

should be arranged other than with a large double arch, . . . whereas Lorenzo wished that it should be supported by some props and by nothing else that could in any way interfere with the music.[25]

As we have seen, Aristotile had earlier designed the set for the performance of Machiavelli's *La Clizia* staged in January 1525, at the home of Jacopo di Filippo Falconetti *detto* "il Fornaciaio."[26] According to Vasari, Lorenzo di Pier Francesco's differences of opinion with Aristotile concerning the designs for *Aridosia* were not motivated by aesthetic considerations; Lorenzo, "self-woundingly ambitious," in J. R. Hale's words,[27] intended to murder his cousin Alessandro and he hoped that the structural inadequacies of the stage set would result in its collapse.[28] But if he was frustrated on the occasion of the performance of *Aridosia*, he was soon to succeed: in January of the following year, Lorenzo stabbed his unsuspecting cousin to death.[29]

John Walter Hill has proposed, not implausibly, that several of Arcadelt's madrigals whose texts form a cycle and are appropriate for a theatrical performance, as Pirrotta suggested, may have served as the *intermedii* for *Aridosia*: *Dai dolci campi Elisi ove tra' fiori, Foll'è chi crede la
prudenz'e gli anni, Ecco che pur doppo sí lungh'affanni*, and *Quanto fra voi
mortali*, to cite them in the order in which, in Pirrotta's view, they are
most likely to have been performed (see example 8).[30] If Hill's inferences
are correct, they demonstrate that within a decade of Verdelot's first ex-
periments with *intermedii* of the type utilized in the 1525 performance of
La Clizia, the practice he apparently inaugurated had evolved into a tradition of considerable vitality, a tradition whose principal feature was the
use of identical performing resources for each of the *intermedii*, which
served to alter the character of the frame by means of the imposition of a
symmetry absent from earlier examples.

"Alchadelte franzese" is known to have been in Alessandro's employ in
1535, and the document that records his presence in the Medici household
also records the presence of "Dua putti cantori," the instrumentalists Giovanni *tronbetto*, Mattio di Giovanni, *tronbetto*, Orlando *tronbetto*, Pietro
grecho, *tronbetto*, and Santi *tronbetto*, and several musicians whose functions are otherwise unspecified: Messer Antonio da Lucha, Giovanni da
Lucha, Lodovico musico, and Richardo franzese.[31] Messer Antonio da
Lucha is surely to be identified with the Antonio da Lucca mentioned
in Girolamo Parabosco's *La notte* (Venice, 1546), Carlo Lenzoni's *In
difesa della lingua fiorentina, et di Dante* (Florence, 1556), Cosimo
Bartoli's *Ragionamenti accademici* (Venice, 1567), and Vasari's life of Giovann'Antonio Lappoli.[32] Whether these musicians participated in the
festivities for Alessandro's wedding one does not know; that he at one
time had a musical "establishment" capable of assuming responsibility for
the musical element of the festivities, however, the document of 1535 es-
tablishes beyond a doubt.

With Cosimo I's succession in January of 1537, we conclude our long
"narrative account" of the principal Medicean festivals that occurred in
Florence and elsewhere during the transition from republic to duchy. Cosimo's election inaugurated a new era in Florentine political and cultural
history, one marked by fundamentally different circumstances that serve
to give it a coherence and identity of its own and thus to distinguish it
from the period of transition; it is characterized, above all, by the decisive
establishment of the Medici *principato*. To some extent, of course, it is
only in retrospect that one can so describe the period of Cosimo's rule,
and the kind of "foreshortening" in which historical perspective inevitably results can impoverish one's understanding of a historical reality that
was considerably more complex. At the beginning of Cosimo's rule, cer-

Example 8. Jacques Arcadelt, setting of the madrigal text *Dai dolci campi Elisi, ove tra'*
fiori, perhaps employed as one of the *intermedii* for the 1536 performance of
Lorenzino de' Medici's *Aridosia, Il terzo libro de i madrigali novissimi*
d'Archadelt a quattro voci (Venice: G. Scotto, 1539)

CHAPTER 13

Example 8, continued

Example 8, continued

160

Example 8, continued

tainly, his contemporaries can have had no idea that his election was simply one event in a process that would ultimately result in "the drowsy
acceptance of near-absolutist rule" in Hale's words,[33] however much one
might in retrospect so perceive that event. The various phases in Cosimo's gradual assumption of power—"election," "survival," "affirma-
tion," "consolidation," "elaboration," and "triumph," to borrow the
terms of Eric Cochrane's stimulating account of Cosimo's career[34]—suggest that that result was at first anything but predictable. Yet in another
sense, of course, one is impressed that Alessandro's distant relative was
elected at all. So compelling had the tradition of Medici rule become that
Alessandro's succession by another member of his family *was* all but inev-

itable, whatever prospects for survival he might initially have enjoyed. With the conclusive achievement of the *principato*, Florentine cultural life was to undergo a more substantive transformation still, one distinguished by an idealization of the previous century of de facto Medici rule and a glorification of Cosimo's most illustrious ancestors, an apotheosis of the House of Medici.

TOWARD A TYPOLOGY OF
FLORENTINE FESTIVAL
MUSIC OF THE EARLY
CINQUECENTO

WHAT CONCLUSIONS can one draw from the foregoing chapters? My objective was a reconstruction of the principal festivals in early cinquecento Florence for which there was a prominent musical component—not a complete reconstruction, certainly, since such would have been beyond the scope of this study, but complete enough to permit one to define precisely the contexts in which musical performances figured on such occasions, the relationship of the musical elements to others, artistic and literary, the interplay of those various elements, and the distinctive roles each played in the artistic program as a whole. With the evidence thus before us, we can attempt a summary of those contexts and of the specific ways in which music was employed on such occasions in Medici circles, a typology of the music making that occurred.

Concerning the political circumstances that occasioned the festivities in the first instance, I need add little to what has already been said, other than to observe once again that the festivities are a kind of artistic reflection of the most important political developments of the entire period. They reflect those developments not only in the specific sense that many of the artistic elements of the festivals—the celebratory and dedicatory *canti* among them—invoke contemporary political conceits and topoi, but also in the more general sense that the fact that the festivals were organized at all is a result of and an expression of those developments, a celebration of them. The restoration of the Medici to Florence in 1512 was celebrated, obliquely and overtly, in the Carnival festivities of 1513. Leo's election a month later, which as J. R. Hale has suggested must be considered one of the most important events in the history of Medicean Florence,[1] was similarly celebrated within weeks of the Carnival festivities. Leo's election, as Hale argued, afforded the Medici a means of achieving a "rapid . . . aristocratization" of the family,[2] all of the various phases of which are documented by public festivals. Shifting Florentine-papal diplomatic alliances resulted in Leo's meeting with Francis I in 1515, and in his extraordinary ceremonial *entrata* that occurred in November of that year, in Clement's decision to invest Charles V with the imperial crown, and in a series of marriages arranged for political purposes—marriages that in turn occasioned public celebrations: Filiberta of Savoy's ceremonial *entrata* of August 1515, and the festivities of September 1518, and of January through June 1536, organized in order to celebrate the weddings of Lorenzo and Alessandro to members of the French royal and imperial families. To be sure, there were important public festivals that occurred during the quarter-century between the restoration and the decisive establishment of the *principato* that did *not* originate in the principal political developments of the time; but it is the festivals that resulted from those developments that seem especially to have appealed to the imaginations of contemporary chroniclers and to have engaged their literary talents.

As for the precise ways in which music was employed on those occasions—and the specific contexts in which musical performances figured—I offer the classification scheme proposed below. It is offered tentatively, however. No scheme of this sort can claim to be flawless; all such schemes risk oversimplification. Nonetheless, it may serve provisionally as a means of ordering the various modes of musical expression available to Florentines of the early sixteenth century, of reducing them to a relatively few types and classifying them in categories that have a kind of coherence and cogency.

At the "low" end of the spectrum of stylistic practices that constituted the "acoustical landscape" was the kind of *spontaneous instrumental playing or singing*, the "free, ecstatic deliveries"[3] that were the expression of one's personal, public response to an important political development, the kind of music making, if one can call it that, that occurred on the evening of Leo's election, for example, when the ready availability of "many full barrels of wine" is a matter of record. For an American of the late twentieth century, perhaps the closest, most revealing analogy would be to the kinds of sounds one would expect to hear on New Year's Eve in Times Square or perhaps on the Fourth of July. Leo's election seems to have prompted many such responses, to judge from the contemporary accounts, and in attempting to imagine such events as the Lateran *possesso*, for example, one must bear in mind that among the other acoustical elements of such events, including those that are justifiably of far greater interest to musicologists, were the "free, ecstatic deliveries" of amateur instrumentalists—not to mention the ringing of bells, the neighing of horses, and the shouting of observers. Examples of other, similar instances include the playing of instruments in response to the announcement of Leo's election, the presumably spontaneous playing that accompanied the procession of the papal entourage as it passed Agostino Chigi's triumphal arch upon its return from the Lateran and the "suoni et canti" one heard throughout that evening. But such modest "works" indeed need not detain us long. Only the "rustic pieces" sung by the strolling Neapolitan singers during the 1536 Carnival are of exceptional interest, since they in part form the background for the tradition of artful reworkings of such pieces at the hands of Adrian Willaert and his contemporaries.[4]

Of considerably greater importance ceremonially, if not musically, were the *instrumental fanfares* that served as a means of communication, which announced a ceremony or articulated its sequence of events and underscored and enhanced the ceremonial significance of particular moments during that sequence: the trumpet fanfares that articulated the succession of *carri* on the occasion of the celebrations in Florence for Leo's election, the instrumental playing that signaled the moment of his coronation, the trumpet fanfares that greeted Archbishop Giulio de' Medici in the Piazza della Signoria during his *possesso* of his archbishopric in August of 1513, the "most remarkable music" that "quieted everyone" so that the singers could begin the polyphonic mass on the occasion of Giuliano's Capitoline Investiture, the instrumental fanfares that signaled that Roman citizenship had been formally conferred upon him and announced the arrival of the courses at the banquet, the instrumental music that preceded and concluded the playing of several of the quasi-dramatic scenes (the scenes may therefore be considered a series of episodes, panels in a frieze "framed" by instrumental playing), the trumpet fanfares that announced Lorenzo's *presa di bastone* in 1515, the instrumental playing that marked the moments when Charles V was formally invested with the Iron Crown of Lombardy and the imperial crown, the trumpet fanfares on the occasion of the installation of the garrison at the Fortezza da Basso that signaled the garrison commander's Investiture with the symbols of his office, and the trumpet fanfares that concluded the ceremonies at the Cathedral of Naples in 1535 during Charles's *entrata*. Such sounds, too, must have formed an important part of the "acoustical landscape," although they, too, do not often engage our attention.

A related category is formed by *pieces that served for triumphal processions and entries*; within this category, however, one can imagine a considerable stylistic range. On the one hand, there was the instrumental playing that accompanied the "dynamic element," the processions themselves: the playing that accompanied the procession of Giuliano's entourage on the occasion of his Investiture, the playing of the instrumentalists of the Florentine Signoria that accompanied the procession of the papal entourage through the Piazza della Signoria in November of 1515, the playing of the papal instrumentalists on that same occasion and of the instrumentalists that accompanied the procession of Madeleine de la Tour d'Auvergne's retinue in September of 1518, the instrumental accompaniment to Charles V's Bolognese *entrata* of 1529, depicted in contemporary engravings, and to the *cavalcata* to the Church of S. Domenico following the imperial coronation. On the other hand, there was the music associated with the "static element," the triumphal arches, which served to explicate verses inscribed on the arches—music of presumably far greater complexity and technical sophistication to judge from the example of Corteccia's *Ingredere*; none of the music of this type apparently survives from our period, but the narratives attest at least three such instances: the singing of verses at the elaborate double arch constructed for Leo's Lateran *possesso* under the auspices of the Florentine mercantile community and the master of the papal mint, the singing of verses by singers stationed atop the eight arches constructed for Leo's Florentine *entrata*, and the singing of the "several nymphs" at one of the arches constructed along the route of Charles's Neapolitan *entrata* of 1535. A special category is formed by the music sung by the clerics stationed at altars along the route of the papal procession during the Lateran *possesso* and Leo's 1515 Florentine *entrata*.

At a demonstrably higher cultural level than the music that served to accompany the dynamic element of triumphal processions were *the musical elements of processions of carri*, quintessentially Florentine in character. The narrative sources document at least five instances of such occasions when music was performed, and we are in possession not only of the actual texts that were sung on several of the occasions in question but in one instance pieces of music as well: the 1513 Carnival, the festivities in Florence for Leo's election, the 1514 Feast of San Giovanni, the celebrations for the 1516 conquest of Urbino, and the procession of *carri* for the festivities for the wedding of Lorenzo and Madeleine. These pieces are at a "demonstrably higher cultural level" not so much by virtue of their musical style, which, as we have seen, was relatively simple; it is rather that they contributed importantly, by means of the sophisticated allusions and topoi they invoked, to fulfilling the political and artistic objectives of the *feste*—indeed, they were principally responsible for conveying the political "meanings" that the festivals' organizers intended to convey. In some instances they sustain a multiplicity of readings that serve to demonstrate how ramified their content could be on occasion: just as the Medici appropriated images of return and renewal central to the Florentine literary tradition in order to suggest implicitly an identity between the family and the city of Florence—images that were invoked in Nardi's 1513 *canto carnascialesco* and introductory stanzas to *I due felici rivali*—so, after 1513, were images employed that can be read as embodying both Florentine and Roman meanings, so as to suggest an identity between the two cities.

The surviving texts also afford another observation: the political developments that occasioned these festivals determined the iconographic content of the artistic "material," certainly, but it was often "clothed in antique dress," transformed and expressed in terms that evoked the classical tradition, which continued to be of fundamental importance to Florentine cultural experience. The processions of *carri* also employed musical elements of other kinds: Cerretani's account records that trumpet fanfares articulated the succession of floats constructed for the festivities in Florence for Leo's election, as we have seen, and the payments to the Signoria's trumpeters and *piffari* in 1516 suggest that the celebrations for the conquest of Urbino made use of similar elements.

A category of exceptional importance is formed by *the pieces that had theatrical uses*. In this instance, we are aided in our attempts to classify them by Pirrotta's remarkable study of music in the Italian Renaissance theater,[5] and, indeed, many of the instances described here were cited by Pirrotta as examples of the various uses he detailed. There is, first of all, the example furnished by the introductory stanzas to Nardi's *I due felici rivali*; such stanzas ordinarily served dedicatory, hortatory, or didactic purposes, and as instances of the practice of extemporaneous solo singing, moreover, they exemplify a tradition of exceptional importance not only to the history of Italian Renaissance theater but to the history of Italian Renaissance music as well. Further, in the *intermedii* for Ariosto's *I suppositi* and Lorenzo Strozzi's "Commedia in versi" on the one hand and those for Machiavelli's *La Clizia* and, perhaps, Lorenzino de' Medici's *Aridosia* on the other, one sees the transition from the kind of heterogeneity of style characteristic of earlier cycles of *intermedii* to the kind of homogeneity characteristic of the tradition as it evolved in Florence in the 1520s and 1530s. Agostino Ricchi's *I tre tiranni* furnishes instances of what Pirrotta has called the "realistic use of music in comedy"[6] and perhaps one should include the "trumpet of the crier when he addressed the people" in Plautus's *Poenulus* in the same category. The tradition of the *sacra rappresentazione* and the music for the quasi-dramatic presentations during the Capitoline ceremonies of 1513 form special categories. In the first instance, one can distinguish between the "recitative" style presumably employed for the "narrative" elements and the "realistic uses of music" for the more elaborate "set pieces": dances, the instrumental playing that accompanied the opening of the heavens and concluded the *festa*, and the singing of the *lauda Laudate el sommo Dio*. Perhaps one can similarly distinguish among the various kinds of musical elements of the Capitoline festivities: on the one hand, one imagines that the verses sung by Monte Tarpeio, for example, or those addressed to Giuliano by the player impersonating his mother Clarice were in a kind of improvisatory style; on the other hand, the more formal set pieces certainly invoked different treatment: the singing and playing of the musicians of Cardinal Ippolito d'Este who represented the priests of Cybele, for example, or the singing of the Arno and Tiber nymphs. The terms Chieregati used with rare precision—"frotola" and "hymni"—terms that, as I suggested earlier, one might mistakenly invest with specious authority, should perhaps be interpreted simply as an attempt to identify such set pieces and distinguish them from the more recitativelike delivery of the verses.

There are, further, the many instances of what one might call *convivial uses*: the playing of the instrumentalists of the Florentine Signoria in honor of Cardinal Giovanni de' Medici in September of 1512, the music for the *feste da ballo* on the eighth and tenth of September 1518, during the festivities for Lorenzo's and Madeleine's wedding, the instrumental playing that took place after the banquet on the evening of Charles V's coronation, the *moresche* and instrumental music that accompanied the dancing on the occasion of Margaret's visit to Florence in April of 1533, the extemporaneous singing to the viol of the Catalan woman at the home of the princess of Salerno in January of 1536, and the singing of Antonia, the daughter of the count and countess of Culisano—these last two occasions recounted by Nicola Maffei—and the music for the *feste da ballo* on February 29 and June 13, 1536, on the occasion of Alessandro's and Margaret's wedding celebrations. Of the precise musical characteristics of the pieces that served such convivial uses, whose setting was often the intimacy of one's home, we know relatively less (although hypotheses about the use of instrumental arrangements of contemporary secular vocal works and improvised counterpoints to standard tenor patterns are certainly plausible); but such pieces must have been of absolutely central importance to the musical experiences of the various members of the Medici family profiled here.

Finally, there are the many, many *liturgical and other sacred, but nonliturgical, uses*—uses of such antiquity, variety, and richness that only the briefest of summaries may be attempted. It will be obvious, first of all, that in an age of virtually universal belief, it was inevitable that many of the occasions under consideration here would have been solemnized by religious observances; and events in which the principals were ecclesiastical figures were likelier still to include liturgico-musical provisions of especial complexity and fullness. One may assume, too, that the works exemplified a wide range of compositional practices, from various chant styles, to *falsobordone*, to polyphony of varying degrees of complexity. There are, first, the many instances of the singing of the mass, whether in chant or in polyphony, and, indeed, in the absence of specific references one cannot be certain about the frequency of polyphonic performances; what is certain is that among the components of a great many of the festivals described here was the singing of the mass: it was sung during Archbishop Giulio's *possesso* of his archbishopric in August of 1513 and on the occasion of the Capitoline Investiture; it was sung several times during Leo's stay in Florence following his ceremonial *entrata* of 1515—on at least one occasion, demonstrably, in polyphony—and on the occasion of the conquest of Urbino in 1516; there are also performances documented during the meetings between Clement and Charles in Bologna in 1529–30 and in 1534 and 1535 on the occasions of the laying of the foundation for the Fortezza da Basso and the installation of its garrison; and, finally, mass was sung in the Church of San Lorenzo on the occasion of the ceremonies for the wedding of Alessandro and Margaret. Of the other texts sung on various occasions, the *Te Deum* seems to have occupied an especially prominent place. In other instances, the liturgical texts were uniquely specific to the provisions of the day, as we have seen: the texts sung during Archbishop Giulio's *possesso* reflected the importance to Florentine religious experience of St. Zenobius; on other occasions, the aid of the Holy Spirit was invoked with texts appropriate to that purpose. None of the festivals featured liturgico-musical elements that were richer in meaning or more powerfully suggestive of the symbolic significance of the event than the imperial coronation ceremonies; for that reason, perhaps, those elements were described with unusual care and rare specificity, the description extending to details of performance practice. But as in the case of the convivial uses described above, most of the liturgical uses are similarly inaccessible, in the absence of precise references and sufficiently full accounts (to be sure, however, they exemplify the tradition with which musicologists are most conversant); and as in the case of the convivial uses, we may assume that liturgical uses of music were among the most important of those familiar to the historical figures whose musical experiences are detailed here.

So very few actual pieces of music remain, therefore, that one simply cannot offer many very well substantiated conclusions about the precise stylistic characteristics of the actual pieces performed on most of these occasions (although the inferences one can draw by means of analogy with extant contemporary repertories are surely plausible). Indeed, though a great many of the pieces would have been improvised, and exemplified practices that would not have required notation, one is nonetheless struck by the sheer extent of the losses; various elements of an exceptionally rich musical culture remain relatively unattested by actual musical documents (it may be, of course, that more of the works performed on these occasions survive and that we are simply unable to identify among surviving works those that were intended for the contexts defined here, the topical references in their texts having been eliminated or altered in order to appropriate them for other uses). How does one explain such losses? How does one explain the relative "fullness" of the "documentation" for the 1513 Carnival—the *canti* and several of the decorative panels executed for the *carri* are extant—and the relative absence of artistic, literary, and musical documents for subsequent festivals? Perhaps it is that the richer documentation for the 1513 Carnival is a consequence of the recent restoration of the Medici or of the greater magnificence of the festivities, and the sparer documentation for subsequent festivals is a consequence of the increasing frequency of such events, which may have led to an impoverishment of the artistic element. The abruptness of Bartolomeo Masi's report on the 1516 Feast of San Giovanni suggests that this may indeed have been the case. With the decisive establishment of the *principato*, moreover, there was among Florentines "a tendency to close in on themselves with a self-sufficiency and aloofness that was the exact contrary of the mental openness of the great Florentine artists and intellectuals of the past," as Giuliano Procacci suggested in another connection.[7] "If one considers late sixteenth-century Florentine intellectual life as a whole, paying more attention to the norm than to the exceptional summits, it is bound to seem less energetic than it had been; it shows a marked tendency to withdraw into contemplation of its own past."[8] It may be, therefore, that with the increasingly frequent calls for artistic, literary, and musical contributions to events of ever more overtly political significance, the talents of Florentine artists were increasingly less fully engaged, and the ephemeral products of their creativity, therefore, were deemed less worthy of being preserved. (On the other hand, one should moderate Procacci's remarks with Eric Cochrane's, which may serve as useful correctives. In the preface to *Florence in the Forgotten Centuries*, Cochrane wrote that he had been led "to question the validity of several generally accepted historical concepts. The first is one that would seem as strange to a citizen of Chicago in 1971 as it has seemed obvious to Tacitus, to Leonardo Bruni, and to many modern historians of Florence: that monarchical regimes are incompatible with intellectual or cultural creativity."[9] And in the prologue to *Historians and Historiography in the Italian Renaissance*, he thus characterizes the historiographic assumptions underlying a recent study of sixteenth-century Florentine political and historical thought: "The fall of the Florentine Republic in 1530, the author affirms, represents 'the last flicker of the attempt of Italians to save themselves from the excessive power of the Hapsburg emperor.' All efforts at creative thought thereafter, he continues, were hopelessly compromised by the all-embracing 'decadence' of Italian culture and by the inability of even the best historians to discern higher purpose for their works than that of 'praising the power and the political sagacity' of foreign and domestic despots."[10])

To return to the few extant pieces of music demonstrably performed on one of these occasions: what one *can* infer from them, and from the narrative descriptions that permit us to draw some conclusions about lost works, is that the contexts indeed served in part to determine musical style, that the didactic functions of many of these works indeed influenced musical language. The *canti* for the 1513 Carnival, the *lauda Laudate el sommo Dio*, even Verdelot's madrigals for the 1525 performance of *La Clizia* manifest stylistic properties that suggest that their function of providing commentary in part dictated the result.[11] One can imagine exceptions, of course: in the case of well-known liturgical texts, for example, which in many instances must have elicited sophisticated contrapuntal treatment in accordance with time-honored compositional tradition, or when the topos being invoked or the themes being explicated were also attested by texts inscribed on arches that could simultaneously be read. Moreover, it is perhaps that the relative absence of polyphony is in part to be explained in other ways as well: Pirrotta has brilliantly described humanistic antipathy for polyphony—an antipathy that resulted not only from a concern about the intelligibility of the texts of polyphonic works but also from a conviction that the "simultaneous sounding of many melodic lines had the result of neutralizing the expressive message, the ethos that each one of them taken singularly might have conveyed."[12]

As for the contribution of the musical element generally, one can say that although many of these festivals would have been successful even in its absence, it was clearly thought to be critically important to their success; its use in combination with the other artistic elements led to an enhancement or intensification of observers' experience of the festivals. Its distinctive contribution was in part a function of its essential character as a "dynamic" phenomenon. For all that one can speak of a viewer's gradual "apprehension" of a painting or sculpture, the moment-to-moment substance of such a work of art remains the same; it is a "static" entity. The moment-to-moment substance of a work of music, on the other hand, changes as the work unfolds in performance; it is quintessentially "kinetic," which made it ideally suited to such occasions, featuring movement prominently as many of them did. Some of the festivals conflated dynamic musical elements and static artistic elements—obscured the distinction between them—as in November of 1515, for example, when the singers positioned atop the triumphal arches sang verses explicating the inscriptions. A procession of carnival *carri*, on the other hand, is essentially a kinetic phenomenon, and the strophic musical treament of *canto carnascialesco* verse might be seen as an effort to create the illusion of stasis among artistic elements that were otherwise predominantly dynamic in nature. The singing of the Arno and Tiber nymphs during the Capitoline festivities of 1513, finally, is a particularly suggestive illustration of the distinctive character of music's efficacy as an art form, of its ability to convey messages that other media perhaps communicate less effectively. That the Arno and Tiber nymphs joined in song to produce the "sweetest of music"—that they exploited music's distinctive ability to present disparate materials simultaneously yet harmoniously—served as the musical representation of the metaphorical fusion of Florence and Rome of which the frescoes at Poggio a Caiano are the visual representation. The metaphor in both instances is all the more effective precisely because it is expressed efficiently, and implicitly rather than explicitly.

The many references collected and analyzed here considerably advance our understanding of the contexts in which musical performances figured in early modern Europe and, to some extent, of the relationship between context and musical language. "We know remarkably little about the occasions when music was performed during the Renaissance," Howard Mayer Brown has written.[13] The testimony of the Florentine narratives of the sixteenth century goes a very long way toward providing some answers to the question Brown's remark implicitly raises, at the very least with respect to the experiences of what J. R. Hale has called "the most provocative of Italian cities and the most famous of Italian families." Since most of the music is no longer extant—or no longer identifiable—it is only by means of an act of historical imagination, an act based on the contemporary accounts, that one can reconstruct the various acoustical elements of the occasions recounted above. As I suggested at the beginning of this study, to fail to attempt such a reconstruction would be to risk an incomplete understanding of the musical culture of early modern Florence. Even if only by means of such an act of the imagination, the acoustical elements of the early cinquecento Florentine festivals can indeed be restored to their rightful place alongside the corresponding visual elements, the surviving examples of which still exercise powerfully evocative effects—even four and a half centuries after the events that inspired their creation.

INTRODUCTION

1. Gilbert, *Machiavelli and Guicciardini: Politics and History in Sixteenth-Century Florence* (Princeton, 1965), pp. 305–15.

2. See Klapisch-Zuber, *Women, Family, and Ritual in Renaissance Italy*, trans. Lydia Cochrane (Chicago, 1985), pp. 94–116, 310–29, 68–93, and 178–212.

3. Anthony Newcomb, *The Madrigal at Ferrara, 1579–1597*, 2 vols. (Princeton, 1980).

4. The relevant texts are to be found in Cummings, "Medici Musical Patronage in the Early Sixteenth Century: New Perspectives," in *Studi musicali* 10 (1981): 197–216, especially pp. 205 and 207; "Gian Maria Giudeo, Sonatore del Liuto, and the Medici," in *Fontes Artis Musicae* 38 (1991); Richard Sherr, "Lorenzo de' Medici, Duke of Urbino, as a Patron of Music," in *Renaissance Studies in Honor of Craig Hugh Smyth*, 2 vols. (Florence, 1985), vol. 1, pp. 627–38, especially p. 634 nn. 8 and 11, p. 635 nn. 12, 14, 17, and 19, p. 636 nn. 21–23, 25–28, and 30, and p. 637 nn. 33–34 and 36; Sherr, "Verdelot in Florence, Coppini in Rome, and the Singer 'La Fiore,'" in *Journal of the American Musicological Society* 37 (1984): 402–11, especially p. 406 n. 13 and pp. 409–11; Howard M. Brown, "Chansons for the Pleasure of a Florentine Patrician," in *Aspects of Medieval and Renaissance Music: A Birthday Offering to Gustave Reese*, ed. Jan LaRue (New York, 1966), pp. 56–66, especially p. 64 n. 22; Frank D'Accone, "Heinrich Isaac in Florence," in *Musical Quarterly* 49 (1963): 464–83, especially p. 481; F. Ghisi, *I canti carnascialeschi nelle fonti musicali del XV e XVI secoli* (Florence, 1937), p. 43 n. 4, and p. 44; D'Accone, "A Documentary History of Music at the Florentine Cathedral and Baptistery during the 15th Century," 2 vols. (Ph.D. dissertation, Harvard University, 1960), vol. 2, p. 141; H. Colin Slim, "Gian and Gian Maria, Some Fifteenth- and Sixteenth-Century Namesakes," in *Musical Quarterly* 57 (1971): 562–74, especially p. 565; D'Accone, "Some Neglected Composers in the Florentine Chapels, ca. 1475–1525," in *Viator, Medieval and Renaissance Studies* 1 (1970): 263–88, especially p. 282 n. 85; Cesare Guasti, "Le carte strozziane del R. Archivio di Stato in Firenze, Inventario," in *Archivio storico italiano*, 4th ser., 7 (1881): 51 (appendix); D'Accone, "Alessandro Coppini and Bartolomeo degli Organi—Two Florentine Composers of the Renaissance," in *Studien zur italienisch-deutschen Musikgeschichte* 4, Analecta musicologica, vol. 4 (1967): 38–76, especially p. 51 nn. 69–71, and p. 75; Pietro Canal, "Della musica in Mantova," in *Memorie del R. Istituto Veneto di Scienze, Lettere ed Arti* 21 (1879): 665–774, especially p. 677; and H. Colin Slim, "Arcadelt's 'Amor, tu sai' in an Anonymous Allegory," in *I Tatti Studies* 2 (1987): 91–106, especially p. 99.

5. J. R. Hale, "The End of Florentine Liberty: The Fortezza da Basso," in *Florentine Studies*, ed. Nicolai Rubinstein (London, 1968), pp. 501–32, especially p. 504.

6. Monroe C. Beardsley and William K. Wimsatt, Jr., "The Intentional Fallacy," in *Sewanee Review* 54 (1946): 468–88, especially p. 472.

7. Nino Pirrotta, *Music and Theater from Poliziano to Monteverdi* (Cambridge, 1982), p. 53.

8. The paradigmatic article on the "unwritten tradition" is Pirrotta's "Music and Cultural Tendencies in 15th-Century Italy"; others include "New Glimpses of an Unwritten Tradition," "The Oral and Written Traditions of Music," and "Novelty and Renewal in Italy: 1300–1600"; all of these are now conveniently available in *Music and Culture in Italy from the Middle Ages to the Baroque* (Cambridge, Mass., 1984), pp. 51–71, 72–79, 80–112, and 159–74. See also *Music and Theater from Poliziano to Monteverdi* (full citation given in n. 7), pp. 21–24.

9. The phrase is Schoenberg's; he, however, used it in a very different way and in a very different context; see Carl Dahlhaus, "Harmony," in *The New Grove Dictionary of Music and Musicians*, ed. Stanley Sadie, 20 vols. (London, 1980), vol. 8, pp. 175–88, especially p. 179.

10. The phrase is Paula Higgins's; see her review of Reinhard Strohm's *Music in Late Medieval Bruges* (Oxford, 1985), in *Journal of the American Musicological Society* 42 (1989): 150–61, especially p. 152.

11. See Klapisch-Zuber, "The 'Mattinata' in Medieval Italy," in *Women, Family, and Ritual* (full citation given in n. 2), pp. 261–82.

CHAPTER I

1. On the family's exile and restoration, see, most recently, J. N. Stephens, *The Fall of the Florentine Republic, 1512–1530* (Oxford, 1983), pp. 24–73.

2. Ibid.

3. Ibid.

4. "Addì 14. di Sett. 1512. il dì di S. Croce, entrò . . . in Firenze, per la porta affaenza il Chardinale de' Medici, e benchè fussi Leghato del Papa di tutta Toschana, non volle entrare colle procissioni, chomè di chostume, e di Chonpagnia di ciptadini, ma in ischanbio di quelle, huomini darme, e fanteria assai di Romagnia, et Bolognia, et andò a schavalchare a chasa sua. Dipoi laltro giorno avea detto dandare a visitare la Signoria doppo mangiare; e la Signoria richiese molti ciptadini andassino per lui; di che mutò proposito, et disse, vandre' di notte, per mancho cirimonie, et chosì fecie; et la Signoria gli mandò el prexente ordinario dun Leghato del Papa, ellui donò loro fior. 50. larghi; et dipoi vandorono e' trombetti, e pifferi a visitarlo, con magnie sonate, e alsì alloro diè buona mancia." Giovanni Cambi, "Istorie," ed. Fr. Ildefonso di San Luigi, 4 vols., in *Delizie degli eruditi toscani*, vols. 20–23 (Florence, 1786), vol. 2, pp. 323–24. Cardinal Giovanni's return to Florence in 1512 is depicted in a fresco of Vasari's in Palazzo Vecchio and in the border of one of Raphael's tapestries for the Sistine Chapel; on the importance of the event to Florentine political experience and its "interpretation" in Vasari's and Raphael's works, see (on the fresco) Charles Davis, "Frescos by Vasari for Sforza Almeni, 'Coppiere' to Duke Cosimo I," in *Mitteilungen des Kunsthistorischen Institutes in Florenz* 24 (1980): 127–202, especially p. 153, and (on the tapestry) John Shearman, *Raphael's Cartoons in the Collection of Her Majesty the Queen and the Tapestries for the Sistine Chapel* (London, 1972), p. 85 and fig. 17.

5. Stephens, *The Fall of the Florentine Republic* (full citation given in n. 1), pp. 24–73. On the methods employed by the Medici to "rule" Florence during the

fifteenth century, see Nicolai Rubinstein's *The Government of Florence under the Medici (1434–1494)* (Oxford, 1966), which has achieved the status of a classic.

6. That the two instrumentalists were in Leo's employ before 1513 is suggested by the texts of documents of May 1513: "etiam dum cardinalatus honore fungebamur." See Herman-Walther Frey, "Regesten zur päpstlichen Kapelle unter Leo X. und zu seiner Privatkapelle," in *Die Musikforschung* 9 (1956): 46–57, 139–56, and 411–19, and 8 (1955): 58–73, 178–99, and 412–37, especially pp. 417–18 and 427, on the documents pertaining to Gian Maria and Baldo, and, on the instrumentalists in the establishment, 8 (1955): 412–37, and 9 (1956): 46–52; ad hoc payments to instrumentalists are published in 9 (1956): 54–57 and 139–46. Gian Maria Giudeo's presence in Florence is documented in 1492, when he was wanted for murder (see H. Colin Slim, "Gian and Gian Maria, Some Fifteenth- and Sixteenth-Century Namesakes," in *Musical Quarterly* 57 [1971]: 562–74, especially pp. 572 and 574); that he was in Cardinal Giovanni's employ in the period before Giovanni's election to the papacy might well have been known to members of the Florentine Signoria. On Gian Maria, see now my "Gian Maria Giudeo, Sonatore del Liuto, and the Medici," in *Fontes Artis Musicae* 38 (1991).

7. See "LEONIS X. PONT. MAX. VITA, AUCTORE ANONYMO CONSCRIPTA." in William Roscoe, *The Life and Pontificate of Leo the Tenth*, 6 vols. (London, 1806), vol. 6, pp. 314–33, especially p. 329: "Leo vero ex conviviis ingentem capiebat voluptatem, eaque delicatissimis epulis, ac variis vinorum generibus referta consulto protrahebat, inter cachinnos et scurrarum jocos quo pleniori voluptate perfunderetur, quibus tandem expletis, cantu vocum atque nervorum omnia compleri, nocturnisque praesertim conviviis, musicis instrumentis totum fere palatium personare, pontifexque eis omnes sensus totamque animam concedere; tantaque interdum dulcedine capi, ut plerumque animo deficere, peneque se ipsum linquere videretur, ac summisso quodam murmure eadem que audiebat interdum ipse decantabat; erat enim musicae artis peritissimus, ac propterea ejus professoribus, qui ad eum undecumque eruditissimi confluxerant, magna salaria praestitit, ac Johannem Mariam quendam Hebraeum, tangendis fidibus clarum, Verrutio oppido condonatum, comitatus dignitate exornavit."

8. "Heri andai dal Nostra Santità, qual ritrovai a Belvedere . . . cum . . . l'Arcevescovo di Fiorenza [Giulio de' Medici]. In l'anticamera era el Reverandissimo Cardinale de Ferrara [Ippolito d'Este] et Monsignore Cardinale de Ancona v[i]site el Nostro Santità et poi la musica di violini che fece Zoanne Maria Zudeo." See William Prizer, "Lutenists at the Court of Mantua in the Late Fifteenth and Early Sixteenth Centuries," in *Journal of the Lute Society of America, Inc.* 13 (1980): 5–34, especially pp. 22 and 33; the translation is Prizer's. Alessandro Gabbioneta was archdeacon of Mantua and the marchese's emissary to the papal court; see Prizer, *Courtly Pastimes: The Frottole of Marchetto Cara* (Ann Arbor, 1980), p. 17.

9. "Nostro Signore si sta la maggior parte del dì in la stantia sua ad giocare ad scacchi et udire sonare." William Roscoe, *Vita e Pontificato di Leone X, con annotazioni e documenti inediti di L. Bossi*, 12 vols. (Milan, 1816–1817), vol. 6, p. 221. Turini was Lorenzo II's agent in Rome.

10. "Mangioli cum Sua San.^ta Adriano [Castellesi de Corneto, cardinal of San Crisogono], Auns [i.e., Francois Guillaume de Clermont, bishop of Aux, cardinal

of Santo Stefano in Celimontana], [Bandinello] Sauli [Cardinal of Santa Sabina], [Marco] Cornaro [i.e., Cornelius, cardinal of Santa Maria in Via Lata], et [Giulio de'] Medici, et el S. Ant.° M.ª et Frate Mariano [Fetti, buffoon at Leo's court], et il Protho ge intraveneno cum la sua musica." See John Shearman, "A Note on the Chronology of Villa Madama,"in *Burlington Magazine* 129 (1987): 179–81, especially p. 180; the identifications of the individuals mentioned in Costabili's letter are Shearman's. The "Protho" mentioned may be the "Proto da Lucca," a jester at Leo's court, mentioned in a *pasquinata*; see *Pasquinate romane del Cinquecento*, ed. Valerio Marucci, Antonio Marzo and Angelo Romana, 2 vols. (Rome, 1983), vol. 1, p. 87 n. 15, and vol. 2, p. 1052. The quotation of de Beatis's letter is taken from Alessandro Luzio, "Isabella d'Este nei primordi del papato di Leone X e il suo viaggio a Roma nel 1514–1515," in *Archivio storico lombardo*, 4th ser., 6 (1906): 99–180, 454–89, especially p. 160: "Concludo ad V. S. Ill.ᵐᵃ che il Papa et de caccia et de musica de flauti piferi etc. ha piacer grandissimo del spesso [*sic*] a le spese de Aragona, et casa nostra triumpha ogni giorno de suono de piferi flauti storti [crumhorns] cornetti et omni genere musicorum." On de Beatis, see *The Travel Journal of Antonio de Beatis*, ed. J. R. Hale, trans. J. R. Hale and J.M.A. Lindon (London, 1979), p. ix.

11. Frey, "Regesten" (vol. 9) (full citation given in n. 6), pp. 143–44: "E più a quello sono la lira in la Rocha di Viterbo duc. dui Duc.——2." "E più a uno sonava la citara duc. uno nel Isola, disse messer Iulio di M.° Arcangiolo——Duc. 1" "A tre sonatori de arpa, tamborino et violetta, che sonorono el dì de S. Ioanni innanti a N. S. ducati cinque——D. 5."

12. "Non val niente, si no di sonar liuto." Marino Sanuto, *I diarii*, vol. 17 (Venice, 1886), col. 164. The translation is Gustave Reese's; see his translation of André Pirro, "Leo X and Music," in *Musical Quarterly* 21 (1935): 1–16.

13. "Hodie mihi papa pro mantia donavit pulcherimum clavicembalum sive monochordum optimum quod ipsemet in sua camera tenere solatus [*sic*] est valoribus centum ducati[;] hoc autem ideo dixit se libenter servisse quia intellexit me multum in tali sono delectari prout in veritate delector." The reference (MS Vat. Lat. 5636, fol. 249ʳ, December 26, 1518) is published in John Shearman's excellent piece *The Vatican Stanze: Functions and Decoration*, Italian Lecture, British Academy, 1971 (London, 1972), p. 21. I assume the instrument Paris's reference documents is identical to that referred to in Angelo Fabroni's life of Leo cited in Pirro, "Leo X and Music" (full citation given in n. 12), especially p. 15 n. 79. I do not know whether it is identical to the instrument documented by a letter of March 7, 1514 from Lorenzo da Pavia to Isabella d'Este, in which Lorenzo described an instrument he had recently completed for the pope, which he intended to transport to Rome after Easter: "Confeso a quela como io al presente ò finito uno belisimo clavincinbalo grande co' doi registri che gà comencai. E così, solicitado da Papa Lion, l'ò finito e spera, fato Pasqua, andare a Roma con dito instromento. E veramente l'è reusito la pù mirabile cosa che maie pù abia fato: l'è ben la vera armonia. Quanto contento averei e che quela lo podesa sentire." See Clifford M. Brown and Anna Maria Lorenzoni, *Isabella d'Este and Lorenzo da Pavia: Documents for the History of Art and Culture in Renaissance Mantua* (Geneva, 1982), pp. 130–31, and the conveniently accessible English translation of the letter in Julia Cartwright, *Isabella d'Este*, 2 vols. (New York, 1903), p. 29. See also William

Prizer, "Isabella d'Este and Lorenzo da Pavia, 'Master Instrument Maker'," in *Early Music History* 2 (1982): 87–127.

14. Castiglione's letter is in Ludwig Pastor, *Geschichte der Päpste seit dem Ausgang des Mittelalters* (Freiburg im Breisgau, 1906), vol. 4, part 1, p. 401 n. 4: "Non tacerò ancor questa nova che da Napoli è stato portato al papa un organo di alabastro, el più bello et il migliore che mai sia stato visto ne udito."

15. The gift of d'Aragona's organ is documented by a letter by the Ferrarese ambassador Alfonso Paolucci published in Alessandro d'Ancona, *Origini del teatro italiano*, 2 vols. (Torino, 1891), vol. 2, pp. 88–91: "et seduto il popolo, che potea essere in numero di due mila uomini, sonandosi li pifari si lasciò cascare la tela; dove era pinto Fra Mariano con alcuni Diavoli che giocavano con esso da ogni lato della tela; et poi a mezzo della tela vi era un breve che dicea: *Questi sono li capricci di Fra Mariano*; et sonandosi tuttavia. . . . Si recitò la Comedia, . . . et per ogni acto se li intermediò una musica di pifari, di cornamusi, di due cornetti, di viole et leuti, dell'organetto che è tanto variato di voce, che donò al Papa Monsignore Illustrissimo di bona memoria [d'Aragona], et insieme vi era un flauto, et una voca che molto bene si commendò: vi fu anche un concerto di voci in musica, che non comparse per mio juditio così bene come le altre musiche. L'ultimo intermedio fu la moresca, che si rappresentò la favola di Gorgon, et fu assai bella." In *Raffaello nei documenti* (Vatican City, 1936), pp. 93–94, V. Golzio published several texts documenting Raphael's involvement in the production; on p. 93, for example, there is a reference that in February and March of 1519 Raphael was "occupato in certo aparato di Comedia di messer Lodovico Ariosto." That some of the *pifari* who participated in the performance had been in d'Aragona's service we might infer from interesting and important texts located in the Archivio di Stato in Florence by Richard Sherr (see "Lorenzo de' Medici, Duke of Urbino, as a Patron of Music," in *Renaissance Studies in Honor of Craig Hugh Smyth*, 2 vols. [Florence, 1985], vol. 1, pp. 627–38, especially pp. 629 and 635–36); the pope's nephew was interested in procuring the services of the late cardinal's instrumentalists in 1519 for his own musical establishment, and the *pifari* are thus the subject of a correspondence between Leo's and Lorenzo's agents.

16. The payments for the organ stored in the Guardaroba ("per manifacture sue de uno organo" and "per resto di pictura del organo di guardaroba") are recorded in Archivio di Stato Romano, Camerale I, 1489, fols. 28ʳ and 52ʳ, and are published in Frey, "Regesten" (vol. 9) (full citation given in n. 6), p. 142, and Shearman, *The Vatican Stanze* (full citation given in n. 13), p. 55 n. 140.

17. On the Antico print, see Pirro, "Leo X and Music" (full citation given in n. 12), pp. 11–12 n. 59; Pirrotta, "Rom," in *Die Musik in Geschichte und Gegenwart*, vol. 11 (1963), cols. 702–6, especially col. 706; Knud Jeppesen, *Die italienische Orgelmusik am Anfang des Cinquecento* (Copenhagen, 1943), pp. 56–87 and (for an edition of part of the contents) pp. 3*–25*, and plates 1–3; *Frottole intabulate per sonare organi*, ed. Giuseppe Radole (Bologna, 1970); Radole, "Le frottole intabulate da sonar organo (1517) di Andrea Antico," in *Quadrivium* 9 (1968): 103–10; and Dragan Plamenac, "The Recently Discovered Complete Copy of A. Antico's *Frottole intabulate* (1517)," in Jan La Rue, ed., *Aspects of Medieval and Renaissance Music: A Birthday Offering to Gustave Reese* (New York, 1966), pp. 683–92.

18. On the purchase of the instruments from Nuremberg see the document of

September 30, 1517, Archivio Segreto Vaticano, Introitus et Exitus, 557, fol. 157ᵛ ("pro uno horologio et certis instrumentis musicis per eum datis S. D. N. et auro, et argento laboratis," as edited in Shearman, *The Vatican Stanze* [full citation given in n. 13], p. 21), and Pirro, "Leo X and Music" (full citation given in n. 12), p. 15 n. 79.

19. Shearman's thesis as to the function of the Stanza della Segnatura is stated on p. 21 of *The Vatican Stanze* (full citation given in n. 13).

20. Shearman, *Raphael's Cartoons* (full citation given in n. 4), p. 12 n. 73.

21. See Florence, Archivio di Stato, Libro delle provvisioni della repubblica dall'anno 1509 al 1510, c. 57, as published in Paolo Minucci del Rosso, "Di alcuni personaggi ricordati dal Vasari della Vita di Gio. Francesco Rusticci," in *Archivio storico italiano*, 4th ser., 3 (1879): 475–82, especially p. 482: "che a dì cinque Dicembre 1509 furono deputati al servizio della signoria Giovanni di Benedetto Fei, detto Feo e Michele di Bastiano detto Talina sonatori di zuffolo e di tamburino." It is Minucci del Rosso's claim that Michele di Bastiano was turned out of office by the Medici in 1512; he gave no source for his assertion, and in the interest of objectivity I am compelled to point out that a Bastiani (that is, the son of a Bastiano) is listed in 1513 as an instrumentalist of the Signoria in Monte Comune, Camerlingo del Monte, Entrata e Uscita, no. 1877, fol. 410 (see Keith Polk, "Civic Patronage and Instrumental Ensembles in Renaissance Florence," in *Augsburger Jahrbuch für Musikwissenschaft* 3 [1986]: 51–68, especially p. 68). The reference could be to Michele di Bastiano.

22. Vasari's life of Rustici contains an account of the activities of the Compagnia della Cazzuola; see *Le opere*, ed. Gaetano Milanesi, 9 vols. (Florence, 1878–85), vol. 6, pp. 611–19. At various times other members of the Compagnia, which was to play an important role in Florentine cultural life, included the following: (1) Bartolomeo *trombone*, who possibly is to be identified with the trombonist Bartolomeo mentioned in *Dialogo della musica di Antonfrancesco Doni*, ed. G. F. Malipiero (Vienna, 1965), p. 265; Cosimo Bartoli's *Ragionamenti accademici* (Venice, 1567); and Carlo Lenzoni's *In difesa della lingua fiorentina, et di Dante* (Florence, 1556); on the references from Bartoli and Lenzoni, see Andrew C. Minor and Bonner Mitchell, *A Renaissance Entertainment* (Columbia, Mo., 1968), pp. 52–53; and, on Bartoli, James Haar, "Cosimo Bartoli on Music," in *Early Music History* 8 (1988): 37–79. I say "possibly" rather than "probably" because the reference in Vasari is to a company formed in 1512, whereas the other references are from later in the century; Bartoli's, Doni's, and Lenzoni's Bartolomeo is likelier to have been the messer Bartolomeo di Luigi trombone listed among the musicians in the employ of Duke Cosimo de' Medici in 1543, 1559, and 1564, his name spelled various ways; see Frank D'Accone, "The Florentine Fra Mauros. A Dynasty of Musical Friars," in *Musica disciplina* 33 (1979): 77–137, especially pp. 134 doc. 83, and pp. 136–37 docs. 87 and 88. Keith Polk, "Civic Patronage and Instrumental Ensembles" (full citation given in n. 21), cites a Bartolomeo *trombone* of Venice in the service of the Signoria of Florence in 1520; Vasari's Bartolomeo may have been identical to the one documented by Polk; (2) Feo d'Agnolo *pifaro*, who is perhaps to be identified with the Giovanni di Benedetto Fei, detto Feo, who entered the Signoria's service in 1509; see the preceding note; (3) Giovanni *trombone*; see Polk, "Civic Patronage and Instrumental Ensembles," for references to

a Giovanni *trombone*, an instrumentalist in the service of the Florentine Signoria in 1513 and 1520, who may be identical to Vasari's Giovanni; (4) Pierino *pifaro*, who may later have been in Lorenzo de' Medici's service; see my chapter 9; (5) the famous composer and singer Bernardo Pisan[ell]o; (6 and 7) the painters Andrea del Sarto and Francesco Granacci, who made many contributions to the artistic elements executed for Medici festivals in the early cinquecento; (8) Ser Raffaello del Beccaio, Heinrich Isaac's brother-in-law; (9) Giovanni Gaddi, a member of a famous Florentine family, several of whose other members maintained close relations to the Medici (three important Florentine music manuscripts—Biblioteca nazionale centrale [hereafter cited as BNC], MS II. I. 232 and II. I. 285, and Banco rari 229—were all in the possession of the Gaddi at one time; see my study "A Florentine Sacred Repertory from the Medici Restoration," in *Acta musicologica* 55 (1983): 267–332, specifically pp. 270–72), and three heralds of the Signoria: (10) Domenico Barlacchi; (11) M. Giovan Battista di Cristofano Ottonaio, who was granted his request to be permitted to publish music in 1515 (see Martin Picker, "A Florentine Document of 1515 Concerning Music Printing," in *Memorie e contributi alla musica dal medioevo all'età moderna offerti a F. Ghisi*, 2 vols., *Quadrivium* 12 [1971]: 283–90; and (12) Maestro Jacopo del Bientina. Interestingly, the documents published by D'Accone (pp. 134 and 136–37) list a Bastiano di Michele *sonatore d'arpa* whose name is similar, though *not* identical, to the Michele di Bastiano detto Talina *sonatore di tamburino* hired by the Signoria in 1509; could one of the documents have reversed his names and misidentified his instrument?

CHAPTER 2

1. Shearman, *Andrea del Sarto*, 2 vols. (Oxford, 1965), vol. 1, p. 18.

2. Guicciardini's letter is in Francesco Guicciardini, *Le lettere*, ed. Pierre Jodogne, 2 vols. (Rome, 1986–), vol. 1, p. 325: "Giuliano, circa un mese et mezo fa, fondò una compagnia di stendardo, dove sono molti huomini da bene. Chiamonla el Diamante. Et il simile fecie Lorenzo, figliuolo di Piero, dove sono molti giovani suoi choetanei. Chiamono questa il Bronchone. Doverranno questo charnesciale fare feste e buon tempo." For additional testimony to the Medici's role in organizing the festivities, see a letter of January 29, 1513 from Fra Mariano Fetti to the marchese of Mantua in Alessandro Luzio, "Federico Gonzaga, ostaggio alla corte di Giulio II," in *Archivio della R. Società Romana di Storia Patria* 9 (1886): 509–82, in particular pp. 551–52: "Ex S. Marcho de Florentia, die 29 januarij 1513. Giunsi adì 20 del presente in Firenze citato da nostro Sr R^{mo} Legato rallegrandomi della sua entrata, dove continuamente siamo in ricordare le cronache passate, ricordando tutti li capricci facti in questa palazo et in questa magna città, ordinando in questo carnovale triomphi comoedie et moresche di mano dello Abbate di Gaieta principe et inventore d'una nuova pazia, et così andiamo ritrovando li incapriccati ingegni." On the "comoedia" performed during Carnival, see below. Cerretani's text reads as follows (Bartolomeo Cerretani, "Sommario e ristretto cavato dalla historia di Bartolomeo Cerretani, scritta da lui, in dialogo delle cose di Firenze, dal'anno 1494 al 1519," Florence, BNC, MS II. IV. 19, fol. 17^v, collated with the corresponding passages of Cerretani, "Storia in dialogo della mutazione di Firenze," Florence, BNC, MS II. I. 106): "Papa Giulio . . . commesse alLegato

[Cardinal Giovanni] che s'inviasse all'imp[re]sa di Ferrara, . . . et così fe', raccomandando a tutti gl'amici e pare[n]ti Giuliano suo fratello, il quale creò p[er] nostro ordine una Compagnia come haveva Lorenzo Vecchio, et chiamossi il Diamante p[er]chè tra loro era impresa vecchia. Hebbe p[ri]ncipio in questo modo: che facemo una list[a] de' trenta sei, quasi tutti figli de' quei padri che, con Lorenzo Vecchio, furono nel Zampillo, o, [se] volete, ne' Magi, e fatti li richiedere p[er] una sera in casa e Medici dove si cenò, parlò Giuliano, ramentando come la casa loro, con quelle di chi vi si trovò presente, havevono felicemente goduta la città, e p[oi]ch[e] quel medesimo haveva a essere, confortò et offerì et ordissi feste p[er] il futuro carnovale, pensando di dare ordine che questa compagnia governassi la città, et di già no[n] si faceva magistrato dove no[n] fussi alcuno di noi. Cominciò la benignità di Giuliano, non vi vincendo alcuno con la presuntione dalquanti, a chiedere di gratia ch[e] il tale vincessi di sorte ch[e] si mescolò quel seme stretto di giovani, ch[e] erano del'età sua, come si era fatto de vecchi. Accadde che in questa lor[o] tornata venne Lorenzo, figlio di Piero et di Madonna Alfonsina Orsini, di età d'anni diciotto in circa, allevato in Roma, non riccamente ma liberale. Non mancò chi lo p[er]suadesse che egli era figlio di Piero, . . . et che a lui s'apparteneva lo stato della città, 'sendo stato di suo padre, il che lo spinse a volere fare una Compagnia, et feciela, e chiamolla il Broncone, tutti suoi pari di età e delle p[ri]me case, et ordinorono fare anche una mummiera che havevamo fatto noi già." Several matters call for comment. The verb "godere" (past participle "goduta") can mean both "to enjoy" and "to possess," as the contrasting translations of Humfrey Butters and John Shearman suggest (Butters, *Governors and Government in Early Sixteenth-Century Florence* [Oxford, 1985], p. 208 and corresponding n. 112; and Shearman, "Pontormo and Andrea del Sarto, 1513," in *Burlington Magazine* 104 [1962]: 478–83, especially p. 478). I have chosen to adopt Butters's translation because of the sense of the political ambitions of the Compagnia members that the remainder of the passage conveys. On the company of the Magi in the fifteenth century, see Rab Hatfield's excellent article "The Compagnia de' Magi," in *Journal of the Warburg and Courtauld Institutes* 33 (1970): 107–61, especially p. 140 n. 161.

3. Giovanni Cambi, "Istorie," ed. Fr. Ildefonso di San Luigi, 4 vols., in *Delizie degli eruditi toscani*, vols. 20–23 (Florence, 1786), vol. 3, p. 2.

4. The principal sixteenth-century source for the Carnival is Vasari's life of Pontormo, *Le Opere*, ed. Gaetano Milanesi, 9 vols. (Florence, 1878–1885), vol. 6, pp. 245–89, especially pp. 250–55. I have borrowed extensively from Gaston Du C. de Vere's translation of *Lives of the Most Eminent Painters, Sculptors, and Architects*, 3 vols. (New York, 1979), vol. 2, pp. 1511–42, especially pp. 1515–18. The music is published in the text and in Joseph Gallucci, ed., *Florentine Festival Music 1480–1520*, Recent Researches in the Music of the Renaissance, vol. 40 (Madison, 1981), pp. 20–22 and 23–25; on p. xv, Gallucci furnishes information about the sources. However, Gallucci, following Vasari, incorrectly associated Alamanni's and Nardi's *canti* with the festivities for Leo's election; Shearman, in "Pontormo" (full citation given in n. 2), p. 478, offers a persuasive explanation for Vasari's statement.

5. The reference to the torchbearers is in Cerretani, MS II. IV. 19 (full citation

given in n. 2), fol. 19ᵛ; the floats are described in Vasari's account of the life of Pontormo, *Lives* (de Vere translation) (full citation given in n. 4), pp. 1515–18. See figure 4 for a representation of the *Carro della Zecca*, which the Carnival *carri* of 1513 may have resembled; to my knowledge there are no surviving representations of the 1513 Carnival *carri* themselves and we are therefore dependent upon representations of floats used for other, similar occasions, "which may help in the visualization of those of 1513," as John Shearman suggested in his exemplary study of the Carnival ("Pontormo and Andrea del Sarto" [full citation given in n. 2], p. 479 n. 20).

6. Vasari, *Lives* (de Vere translation) (full citation given in n. 4), p. 1516.

7. See Cox-Rearick, *Dynasty and Destiny in Medici Art* (Princeton, 1984), pp. 26–27 and 97–98, for an analysis of the iconography of the *trionfi*, especially of the first and last floats of the Broncone *trionfo*. See also Felix Gilbert's analysis of their meaning in *Machiavelli and Guicciardini: Politics and History in Sixteenth-Century Florence* (Princeton, 1965), pp. 142–44.

8. Vasari, *Lives* (de Vere translation) (full citation given in n. 4), p. 1518.

9. See Cox-Rearick, *Dynasty and Destiny* (full citation given in n. 7), pp. 26–27 and 97–98.

10. Butters, *Governors and Government* (full citation given in n. 2), p. 208 and corresponding n. 110. The source for Butters's assertion is a document in the BNC, Florence, MS Nuovi acquisti 985, Priorista Fiorentino dal 1282 al 1562, which contains the following marginal note on fol. 274ʳ: "Giuliano de medici p[er] corroborare lo Stato suo ordinò una compagnia in casa sua di 13 Giovani. . . . io ho visto l'ordinale sottoscritto da loro et Gli nomi sono Gli infrascriti M[esser] Giulio di G:[iulia]no di p:[ie]ro di Cosimo de Medici Giuliano di lorenzo di p:[ie]ro di cosimo de Medici. . . . Chiamossi la Compagnia del diamante."

11. Cambi, "Istorie" (full citation given in n. 3), vol. 3, pp. 2–3: "trionfo di Giuliano, e sua compagnia, andò il dì di Charnovale a' dì 8. di Febraio 1512. [1513] da hore dua di notte per insino a hore 8. di notte."

12. On Dazzi, see Francesco Bausi, "Politica e poesia: il 'Lauretum,'" in *Interpres* 6 (1985–86): 214–82, especially pp. 270–71.

13. Ibid., pp. 269–70. The poem may be found in Niccolò Machiavelli, *Opere letterarie*, ed. Luigi Blasucci (Milan, 1964), p. 361. In it, Machiavelli is visited by one of the muses, who, in response to his answer to her question about his identity, remarks: "Niccolò non se', ma il Dazzo, / poiché ha' legato le gambe e i talloni, / e sta' ci incatenato come un pazzo," and, further, "Va al barlazzo, / con quella tua commedia in guazzeroni." Bausi argued (pp. 269–70) that the reference to a "commedia" suggests that one of Dazzi's comedies may have been performed during the Carnival season; although we have explicit documentation only for the performance of the evening of February 17, presumably of Nardi's *I due felici rivali* (see n. 30), Mariano Fetti's letter, quoted in n. 2, refers to "comoedie."

14. Vasari, *Lives* (de Vere translation) (full citation given in n. 4), p. 1516.

15. Julian Kliemann, "Vertumnus und Pomona," in *Mitteilungen des Kunsthistorischen Institutes in Florenz* 16 (1972): 293–328, especially p. 318 and corresponding n. 97.

16. Cerretani, MS II. IV. 19 (full citation given in n. 2), fol. 19ᵛ: "erasi p[er] la Compagnia del Diamante . . . fatto una compagnia di maschere dove furono più di cinquecento torchi."

17. Vasari, *Lives* (de Vere translation) (full citation given in n. 4), pp. 1516–18, and Shearman, "Pontormo" (full citation given in n. 2), p. 479.

18. Shearman, "Pontormo," p. 479 n. 15, and n. 22 of my chapter 1.

19. Shearman, "Rosso, Pontormo, Bandinelli, and Others at SS. Annunziata," in *Burlington Magazine* 102 (1960): 152–56, passim.

20. Shearman, *Andrea del Sarto* (full citation given in n. 1), vol. 1, p. 79.

21. Idem, "Pontormo" (full citation given in n. 2); and Luciano Berti, "Addenda al Pontormo del Carnevale 1513," in *Scritti di storia dell'arte in onore di Ugo Procacci* (Milan, 1977), vol. 1, pp. 340–46, passim. See also Shearman's *Andrea del Sarto* (full citation given in n. 1), vol. 1, catalog entries for plates 31 and 33; Sydney Freedberg, *Andrea del Sarto*, 2 vols. (Cambridge, Mass., 1963), vol. 1, pp. 22–23, and vol. 2, pp. 40–42; and Freedberg, *Painting of the High Renaissance in Rome and Florence*, 2 vols. (Cambridge, Mass., 1961), vol. 1, pp. 446–47. All of the surviving decorative panels associated with the 1513 Carnival have been reproduced here as figures 5–11.

22. Shearman, "Pontormo" (full citation given in n. 2), pp. 479–80.

23. Cambi, "Istorie" (full citation given in n. 3), vol. 3, pp. 2–3: "ciaschuno de' detti dua trionfi avevano un chanto della finzione de' trionfi, alle chase di chi gli aveva fatti fare, ho loro amici, andavano cantando."

24. The source is a print in the BNC, Florence; it is entitled *Canzona della Morte. Canzona del bronchone. Canzona del Diamante & della Chazuola.* (n.p., n.d.). Nardi's *canto* for the Carnival is found on fols. 4ʳ–5ʳ. The description of the floats reads as follows: "Triompho primo Saturno Iano con .xii. Pastori Numa Pompilio con .xii. Sacerdoti Tito Mallio Torquato & Gaio Attilio Vulgo con xii. Senatori. Agusto con .xii. Poeti Tito & Vespasiano con .xii. Militi. Traiano con .xii. huomini iusti. Elsecol doro co[n]la Pace. Iustitia & verita. & Pieta. & Divinita. & Verecu[n]dia. & Innoca[n]tia."

25. On *canto carnascialesco* poetry, see the introduction to Gallucci's edition, *Florentine Festival Music 1480–1520* (full citation given in n. 4). I am grateful to Professor Pirrotta for observations concerning the text of Nardi's *canto*.

26. Cerretani, MS II. IV. 19 (full citation given in n. 2), fol. 19ᵛ: "al popolo pareva che fussino tornati i tempi di Lorenzo Vecchio c[irc]a alle feste."

27. Cambi, "Istorie" (full citation given in n. 3), vol. 3, pp. 2–3: "spesono fior. 1700. Et chosì el popolo si pascieva di frasche, et pazzie, et di fare penitenzia non si ragionava. . . . Spese questa seconda quanto e' prima, e tutto feciono, perchè detto Giuliano, e Lorenzo de' Medici erano ritornati alla loro patria, chapi della Ciptà, chome furono e' padri loro, dov'erano stati sbanditi anni 18."

28. Vasari, *Lives* (de Vere translation) (full citation given in n. 4), p. 1518.

29. Marino Sanuto, *I diarii*, 59 vols. (Venice, 1879–1903), vol. 15, col. 572: "a dì 17 [Vittorio Lippomano, a Venetian *oratore*] arivò in Fiorenza. . . . E subito andò dal magnifico Juliano, el qual se levava in quello, e li feze bona ziera, e fe' chiamar Lorenzino suo nepote, fiol che fo di Pietro. . . . Poi lo menò dal reverendissimo cardinal, el qual li feze molte careze venendoli contra fino a la porta di la sua camera, e lassò tutti che era con lui, e stete zercha tra quarti di hora a rasonar: e

nel partir suo, si voltò a quelli erano in camera, che erano più di 25 de li primi citadini di Fiorenza. . . . La sera fu facto una comedia per Lorenzino in una sala di sopra. El cardinal lo mandò a chiamar e volse li sentasse apresso; et ne era assa' citadini, i quali tutti lo ringraziava di quello havea facto a caxa di Medici. E compita la comedia, il cardinal lo tenia per la mano e lo menò a zena con lui."

30. See Jacopo Nardi, *I due felici rivali*, ed. Alessandro Ferrajoli (Rome, 1901), pp. ix (on the identification of the *comedia* mentioned in the account with Nardi's play) and vii–viii (on the possible members of the audience). Nardi's comedy has now been republished in an edition by Luigina Stefani, *Tre commedie fiorentine del primo 500* (Ferrara and Rome, 1986). Fortunato Pintor, in his review of Ferrajoli's edition of *I due felici rivali* in *Giornale storico della letteratura italiana* 41 (1903): 113–25, especially p. 123, correctly observed that Fetti's letter of January 29, 1513 refers to comedies and that one cannot be certain that the reference in Sanuto necessarily pertains to the performance of *I due felici rivali*; it could refer to the performance of one of the other comedies. In my view, however, the references in the dedication and stanzas correspond so closely to the details related in the account of Lippomano's visit to Florence as to suggest that Ferrajoli's identification is probably correct.

31. MS Vatican Barberini Lat. 3911 (*olim* XLV. 5). On fol. 1^r the piece is described as having been "Laurentii Medicis auspiciis acta." The illuminations constitute a border in the left margin of fol. 2^r. Another of the comedy's manuscript sources extends the references to the Medici; see Luigina Stefani's edition of the comedy, pp. 5–6 and pp. 64–65 nn. to lines 25–32: "perche io piu dun cognosco /Nel bel paese tosco / Che ha grande obbligo meco / Qual se io nonfussi seco /Divirtute e si netto / cheinon sarebbe accepto / A questo cor gentile / che renuova e lostile / e ilnome di quel dellauro / che gia dallo Indo alMauro / Lodor sparse e lafama / siche ilmodo ancora lama." Nardi later made use of the same references: see n. 8 to my chapter 8.

32. MS Vatican Barb. Lat. 3911, fol. 24^r: "Le infrascripte stanze si cantorono sula lyra in p[er]sona di Orpheo poeta, venuto da campi elisii, Quando la predetta comedia fu recitata nel co[n]specto del R[everendissi]mo Mons[igno]re Car[dina]le et il Mag[nifi]co Giuliano & Lorenzo de Medici." Although Ferrajoli, in his edition cited in n. 30 of this chapter, printed the stanzas at the end of the text of the comedy, Pirrotta has argued, certainly correctly, that they must have preceded the performance of the comedy; see *Music and Theatre from Poliziano to Monteverdi* (Cambridge, 1982), p. 121.

33. Ibid.

34. Because neither Ferrajoli's nor Stefani's edition of Nardi's play is easily accessible (see n. 30 of this chapter), I have taken the liberty of reproducing the complete text of the opening stanzas here as they appear in MS Vatican Barb. Lat. 3911, fol. 24^r. Ferrajoli, p. xxxix, observed that the line "Dapoi che il mondo & i secul sirennuova" is reminiscent of the lines in Nardi's Carnival *canto*. On images of renewal and regeneration in Medici art, see also Cox-Rearick, *Dynasty and Destiny* (full citation given in n. 7); and my article "Giulio de' Medici's Music Books," in *Early Music History* 10 (1991): 65–122. On Nardi's references to Augusto and Mecenate in *L'amicitia*, see Pirrotta, *Music and Theater* (full citation given in n. 32), pp. 120–21 and corresponding n. 5. On the comparisons drawn between the

three members of the Medici family and the classical figures, see also Bausi, "Politica e poesia" (full citation given in n. 12), p. 262. Bausi sees a reflection of the metaphor in lines 3–4 ("Foecundis alii scripserunt carmina fibris, / et Mecoenati te posuere parem") of Basilius Lancellotus's *epigramma* in the collection *Lauretum* (n.p., n.d.), printed around the time of Lorenzo II's wedding in 1518. For observations about the "iconographic" content of Nardi's stanzas, I am grateful to Professor Pirrotta.

35. On Lorenzo's use of the conceit, see E. H. Gombrich, "Renaissance and Golden Age," in *Norm and Form* (London, 1966), pp. 29–34, especially p. 32. On its various literary manifestations, see *The "Stanze" of Angelo Poliziano*, trans. David Quint (Amherst, 1979), pp. x and xxii–xxiii n. 4; Kliemann, "Vertumnus und Pomona" (full citation given in n. 15), p. 307 n. 55; Cox-Rearick, *Dynasty and Destiny* (full citation given in n. 7), pp. 20–21; and, most important, the classic article by G. Ladner, "Vegetation Symbolism and the Concept of the Renaissance," in *De artibus opuscula XL: Essays in Honor of Erwin Panofsky*, ed. M. Meiss, 2 vols. (New York, 1961), vol. 1, pp. 303–22, where many of the texts that employ the conceit are assembled.

36. Ibid.

37. Ibid.

38. On the passage from Vergil, see the references cited in n. 35 of this chapter. I have quoted the passage from *Eclogue* 4 from Karl Kappes, *Vergils Bucolica und Georgica* (Leipzig, 1876), p. 17. On Poliziano's *Stanze*, see Cox-Rearick, *Dynasty and Destiny* (full citation given in n. 7), p. 222; and David Quint's edition of the *Stanze* (full citation given in n. 35), p. 36.

39. On Giuliano as poet, see the edition of his *Poesie*, ed. Giuseppe Fatini (Florence, 1939).

40. On extemporaneous singing, see, above all, Pirrotta's brilliant piece "Music and Cultural Tendencies in 15th-Century Italy," in *Music and Culture in Italy from the Middle Ages to the Baroque* (Cambridge, Mass., 1984), pp. 80–112. Figure 12 reproduces a typical representation of the practice that aids us in our attempts to visualize the performance of the stanzas that introduced Nardi's comedy.

41. Pulci's letter of August 8, 1468 ("Habbiamoti mandata la vihuola") is in Franca Brambilla Ageno, "Una nuova lettera di Luigi Pulci a Lorenzo de' Medici," in *Giornale storico della letteratura italiana* 141 (1964): 107.

42. Other references documenting that Lorenzo sang to the viol are published in Mario Martelli, *Studi laurenziani* (Florence, 1965), p. 181 and corresponding n. 8, and pp. 188–89 and corresponding n. 40, among which is the letter of August 28, 1472 to Niccolò Michelozzi in Florence, in which Lorenzo wrote: "la viuola e l'altre cose aspetto, e a ogni modo fate di portarnele con voi." For still other references to Lorenzo's extemporaneous singing, see the letters of Ficino to Paolo Antonio Soderini and Bernardo Rucellai (in Arnaldo della Torre, *Storia dell'Accademia platonica* [Florence, 1902], p. 792; and Luigi Parigi, *Laurentiana* [Florence, 1954], p. 12): "Cum nocte superiore Laurentium Medicem audivissemus Apollinis instar in tranquillo Mammolae quasi musarum choro divina mysteria de amore canentem, ego et alter" and "Audivi quandoque Laurentium Medicem nostrum nonnulla horum similia ad lyram canentem, furore quondam

divino, ut abitro, concitum." There is also Braccio Martelli's interesting letter of April 27, 1465 (Archivio di Stato, Florence, *fondo* Mediceo avanti il principato [hereafter cited as MAP], XXII, 29), written in code to the young Lorenzo, who was then still a boy, which describes a festive evening and records the participation of many of Lorenzo's friends and "lo Spagnuolo col liuto"; singing, dancing, and instrumental music seem to have been featured prominently among the evening's events, as Martelli described them to the absent Lorenzo (see Isidoro del Lungo, *Gli amori del Magnifico Lorenzo* [Bologna, 1923], pp. 29–42).

43. The reference to the circumstances of Poliziano's death is in Pietro Bembo's poem *Politiani tumulus, Carmina libellus* (Venice, 1552), p. 45; the reference to Piero's improvisatory singing is in *Epistole inedite di Angelo Poliziano*, ed. Lorenzo d'Amore (Naples, 1909), pp. 38–40: "Canit etiam, vel notas musicas, vel ad cytharam carmen."

44. Poliziano, *Prose volgari inedite e poesie latine e greche*, ed. Isidoro del Lungo (Florence, 1867), p. 78; and Mario Martelli, *Studi laurenziani* (full citation given in n. 42), p. 146: "Udii cantar improviso, non ierser l'altro, Piero nostro, che mi venne assaltare a casa con tutti questi provisanti." For another reference to Piero's (and Lorenzo's) improvisatory singing, see the letter of May 12, 1490 from Lorenzo's chancellor Alessandro Alessandri to Piero in MAP XVIII, 22 (as published in Isidoro de Lungo, *Florentia, Uomini e cose del Quattrocento* [Florence, 1897], p. 307 n. 4): "E voi, come per la vostro vego, non avete dimenticato lo stare a cantare la nocte improviso; che da chi viene da costà, benchè a me non sia nuovo, v'è dato la corona de' dicitori. Noi, ogni dì vostro padre ci dà anche egli un poco di consolazione a udirlo cantare; e tanto più canterà ora, quanto che iarsera venne Baccio Ugolini, che gli terrà compagnia. . . . Al Bagno a Vignone, a dì xij di maggio 1490. Vostro servidore Alexandro Alexandri" (on Baccio, see the text and documentation in n. 46). Pirrotta, *Music and Theater* (full citation given in n. 32), pp. 35–36 and corresponding nn. 82–84, printed an English translation of another letter of Poliziano's, which may have been written in Rome in 1488 on the occasion of Piero de' Medici's marriage to Alfonsina Orsini; it offers further witness still to Piero's conversance with the practice and unusually illuminating insights into humanist musical tastes and the humanistic preference for the musical tradition discussed here.

45. On Baccio, see Pirrotta, *Music and Theater*, p. 24.

46. The reference to Baccio's extemporaneous singing is in "Raphaelis BRANDOLINI LIPPI junioris de musica et poetica opusculum in quo Conradolum Stangam prothonotarium apostolicum perpetua oratione alloquitur," quoted in Adrien de la Fage, *Essais de Diphtherographie Musicale* (Paris, 1864), p. 64: "Cum mirifica publicarum privatarumque rerum peritia, tum salibus atque facetiis, tum maxime vernaculis ac perjucundis canendis ex tempore ad lyram versibus et Laurentii Medicis elegantissimi ingeniorum spectatoris animum sibi devinxit, et Alphonsi secundi, Neapolitanorum regis, benevolentiam et gratiam usque adeo inivit ut Cajetani ad eo promeruerit praesulatum."

The documentation for Baccio's musical activity is especially rich and illuminating; see, for example, Baccio's letter of December 5, 1459 to the Marquis of Mantua in della Torre, *Storia dell'Accademia platonica* (full citation given in n. 42), p. 798; and in Isidoro del Lungo, *Florentia* (full citation given in n. 44), pp. 308–

9 n. 2. A 1489 letter of Poliziano's to Francesco Pucci in Naples contains the following reference, which attests to Baccio's musical talents: "Quid postremo carminibus illis sive quae ad citharam canit ex tempore, sive quae per otium componit, dulcius, mundius, limitius, venustius?" (see della Torre, *Storia dell'Accademia platonica* [full citation given in n. 42], p. 798). Several letters in the *fondo* MAP contain references that attest to Baccio's relationship to Lorenzo. In 1476, for example, Baccio wrote to Lorenzo from Cultibono as follows (MAP XXXIII, 545, as published in della Torre, *Storia dell'Accademia platonica*, p. 799): "El vermiglio è qui migliore assai che ad Vallombrosa, el bianco, se non superiore, almeno equale. Il manchamento de freschi si raguaglia col crescere della sete. Sonci l'ombre de abeti et mormorii dell'acque. La viola mi mancha per ripescare hyla summerso dalle invidiose ninphe. Però prego la M^tia vostra, me ne mandi una per lo aportatore, acciocchè passi con meno durezza il tempo che ho a stare senza voi." As Brandolini's remarks quoted here suggest, Baccio's musical talents earned him a favorable response at the Neapolitan court, where he was Florentine envoy in the 1490s. On April 22, 1491, for example, Baccio reported that "Cavalcai un poco seco [the duke of Calabria] verso Bagnolo et ragionamo insieme assai, più però cose jocose che serie.... Domandomi sio volea andare seco a Lanciano con la lyra. Risposi che lyra non havea . . . ; ma che era parato ad andare stare et fare quanto me accennasse." See MAP XLIX, 280, 281, 345, 379, as cited in della Torre, *Storia dell'Accademia platonica*, p. 800, the last of which records King Alphonso's satisfaction with Baccio's service at the Neapolitan court. While in Naples, Baccio also arranged to have a lyre made for Lorenzo, as we learn from one of his letters addressed to Lorenzo himself (MAP XLIX, 269, as published in della Torre, *Storia dell'Accademia platonica*, p. 800; April 7, 1491): "Sio credessi che li poemi del Galeoto non vi fossero più molesti che le sue medaglie grate, vi farei confortatore che lo intratenessi de una piccola letteruzza in risposta et aviso della receptione della cose mandatevi; perchè li Spasima di questo desiderio, et certo con questo mezo crederei cavarne talora qualche altra antiquità per la M. V. Et sono ancho seco in una praticha di fare fare una lyra ad vostro nome, che se riuscisse, come una ne ha facta fare per sè, certo saria degna di stare fralle cose vostre et per belleza et per dolceza. Ma quandio penso quanto e delicati orechi aborriscono lo udire limare una sega, resto ancipite in questo mio consiglio quale sia più o la pena o il diletto. Pure si porriano partire le cose di costui in questo modo, che la viola et li intagli fossero vostri e i versi di Mariotto." Della Torre, *Storia dell'Accademia platonica*, p. 799, also cited some literary references to Baccio's musicianship, as did del Lungo, *Florentia* (full citation given in n. 44), p. 308 n. 1; the reference del Lungo cited (Antonio Cammelli *detto* il Pistoia, *Rime* [Livorno, 1884], p. 54) also attests to Lorenzo's, Piero's, and Poliziano's literary activity: "Chi dice in versi ben, che sia toscano?— / Di'tu in vulgare?—In vulgare e in latino.— / Lorenzo bene, e'l suo figliuol Pierino; / Ma in tutti e dui val più il Poliziano.— / Poi?—Il Beneveni con la penna in mano, / E con la lira il mio Baccio Ugolino."

47. On the tradition of the *cantimpanche* of San Martino, which must have been of absolutely central importance to the popular musical culture of *quattrocento* Florence, see Francesco Flamini, *La lirica toscana del rinascimento anteriore ai tempi del Magnifico* (reprint, Bologna, 1977), pp. 152ff. Flamini's classic study

also contains much information pertaining specifically to the career of Antonio di Guido; see especially pp. 158–73.

48. Sforza's letter to his father is in Bianca Becherini, "Un canta in panca fiorentina, Antonio di Guido," in *Rivista musicale italiana* 50 (1948): 243–44.

49. Lorenzo's letter to Michelozzi is in his *Lettere*, ed. Riccardo Fubini, 4 vols. (Florence, 1977–), vol. 1, pp. 467–68; and in Martelli, *Studi laurenziani* (full citation given in n. 42), p. 122: "Andrete a trovare maestro Antonio della Viuola, e se vuole venire, come lo avisiamo per uno sonetto, accattate per mia parte la mula del Sassetto; e, quando non si potessi havere, fate che, o di casa o d'altrove, lo proveggiate di buona cavalcatura." See also Fubini's nn. 3 and 4 and the sources he cites. Michelozzi's interesting response, which refers to the sonnet enclosed in Lorenzo's letter, was excerpted by Fubini (nn. 3 and 4) and printed in full in Martelli, *Studi laurenziani*, p. 122, and Guglielmo Volpi, "Lorenzo il Magnifico e Vallombrosa," in *Archivio storico italiano*, 7th ser. 22 (1935): 121–32, especially pp. 122–23; Martelli (p. 123) also offered a brief commentary on the correspondence.

50. Excerpts from other letters documenting Lorenzo's interest in having Antonio present on various occasions are in Fubini, *Lettere*, nn. 3 and 4, and in Martelli, *Studi laurenziani* (full citation given in n. 42), p. 123 n. 136; among them is Michelozzi's letter concerning Clarice: "Madonna Clarice s'è rallegrata molto di quello ha inteso, ci avete ad essere domandassera e confortavene quanto sa, benché la venuta di stamani di M° Antonio gliene fa perdere un poco la speranza di sì pronta tornata."

51. On the literary references to Antonio di Guido, see Volpi, "Lorenzo il Magnifico" (full citation given in n. 49), especially p. 125 n. 2. I have quoted the passage from the *Morgante* from the edition of Franca Ageno (Milan and Naples, 1955), p. 1110. Finally, I would observe that the diarist Luca Landucci chose Antonio di Guido as his representative of the practice of improvisatory singing: "E in questi tenpi vivevano questi nobili e valenti uomini: . . . maestro Antonio di Guido, cantatore inproviso, che ha passato ognuno in quell'arte." See Landucci, *Diario fiorentino*, ed. Iodoco del Badia (Florence, 1883), pp. 2–3.

52. The document recording the presence of the two "violists" in Piero's entourage is Archivio di Stato, Florence, *fondo* Mediceo avanti il Principato, CIV, fol. 85f, as quoted in Aby Warburg, "Bildniskunst und florentinisches Burgertum," in *Ausgewählte Schriften und Würdigungen*, ed. Dieter Wuttke (Baden-Baden, 1980), pp. 65–102, especially p. 96; for more on the tradition of improvisatory singing in Lorenzo's circle, see also Warburg's accompanying discussion. Paolo Orvieto, "Angelo Poliziano 'compare' della brigata laurenziana," in *Lettere italiane* 25 (1973): 317–18, has speculated that the unnamed "chonpare della viola" was Poliziano. Other members of Piero's entourage on the occasion of the trip to Rome included three representatives of the "polyphonic tradition"—Colinet, Isaac, and Pietrequin (see Frank D'Accone, "Some Neglected Composers in the Florentine Chapels, ca. 1475–1525," in *Viator* 1 [1970]: 273)—and Allan Atlas and I have speculated that Agricola may have been in contact with Piero in Rome at the time, since both were present in the city; see "Agricola, Ghiselin, and Alfonso II of Naples," in *Journal of Musicology* 7 (1989): 540–48.

53. The quotation from Condivi's life of Michelangelo is in Parigi, *Laurentiana* (full citation given in n. 42), p. 103 n. 6: "Praticava in casa di Piero un certo,

chiamato per soprannome Cardiere, del quale il Magnifico molto piacer si pigliava per cantare in sulla lira all'improvviso meravigliosamente, del che anch'egli profession faceva; sicchè quasi ogni sera dopo cena in ciò si esercitava." On Cordier, see also Reinhard Strohm, *Music in Late Medieval Bruges* (Oxford, 1985), pp. 37–38.

54. Giuliano's sonnet for Serafino is published in his *Poesie* (full citation given in n. 39), p. 75.

55. On Migliorotti's Medici service in 1490, see Pirrotta, *Music and Theater* (full citation given in n. 32), pp. 289–90 n. 15, and Prizer, *Courtly Pastimes: The Frottole of Marchetto Cara* (Ann Arbor, 1980), p. 6 (on a letter in the Archivio di Stato of Mantua, Archivio Gonzaga, busta 2438, fol. 333ʳ, dated October 29, 1490, from which one learns that Atalante was sent for from Florence, presumably to participate in a comedy to be presented) and p. 8 (on a letter in busta 2241 of the same *fondo*, dated February 3, 1492, which reveals that "G. F. Picenardi [il poeta]" and "il Fiorentino che canta in lira," whom Prizer identifies with Atalante, were sent to Francesco Gonzaga). H. Colin Slim ("The Lutenist's Hand," in *Achademia Leonardi Vinci* 1 [1988]: 32–34, especially p. 32) stated that Leonardo da Vinci taught Migliorotti to improvise on the *lira*, probably before ca. 1483. The letter from the members of the Sacred Academy of the Medici is in Paul Oskar Kristeller, "Francesco da Diacceto and Florentine Platonism in the Sixteenth Century," in *Studies in Renaissance Thought and Letters* (Rome, 1956), pp. 287–336, especially p. 335: "vi habbiamo electo perpetuo cytharedo della nostra Sacra Academia." The reference to the membership of the Academy is from pp. 302–3 n. 60. I would also make note of the fact that one of the letters Kristeller printed in the appendix is addressed to Lorenzo II as "Magnifice domine et benefactor noster."

Although the evidence is thus far limited, I think that societies like the Sacred Academy of the Medici and the Orti Oricellari must have been of absolutely first-rank importance in Florentine musical life of the early cinquecento. On the Orti Oricellari, see Delio Cantimori "Rhetoric and Politics in Italian Humanism," in *Journal of the Warburg and Courtauld Institutes* 1 (1937): 83–102; Felix Gilbert, "Bernardo Rucellai and the Orti Oricellari: A Study on the Origin of Modern Political Thought," in ibid., 12 (1949): 101–31; and H. Colin Slim, *A Gift of Madrigals and Motets*, 2 vols. (Chicago, 1972), vol. 1, pp. 50–51 and 54–55. See also n. 22 of the preceding chapter on one of the various *Compagnie* and societies; I hope to prepare a separate study on the importance to Florentine musical life of such organizations as the *Compagnie* of the Broncone, Cazzuola, and Diamante, and the Orti Oricellari and Sacred Academy of the Medici.

56. On the *pasquinata*, see Domenico Gnoli, *La Roma di Leon X* (Milan, 1938), p. 371 and corresponding n. 2; and Franca Camiz Trincheri's informative catalog entry no. 50, pp. 80–82, in *Raffaello in Vaticano* (Milan, 1984). For further references to the tradition as practiced in Medici and specifically Leonine circles, see Pirro, "Leo X and Music," in *Musical Quarterly* 21 (1935): 1–16, especially p. 2 and corresponding nn. 8 and 9, and p. 13 and corresponding nn. 67–69, and a letter of February 18, 1520 from Alfonso Paolucci, in Rome, to the duke of Ferrara, as published in Fabrizio Cruciani, *Teatro nel Rinascimento, Roma 1450–1550* (Rome, 1983), p. 484: "Zobia fui da poi pranzo in castello e trovai il Papa in mensa che audiva Strassino, con la sua citara, dicendo all'improvviso."

57. See Pirrotta, *Music and Theater* (full citation given in n. 32), pp. 29–31; choices about the text underlay and other matters pertaining to the transcription are indebted to Pirrotta's transcription. I should note that a *contrafactum* exists with an Italian text that may be the original, and that the appropriateness of the musical setting to the rhythmic characteristics of the Latin text has been questioned; see William Prizer, "Isabella d'Este and Lucrezia Borgia as Patrons of Music," in *Journal of the American Musicological Society* 38 (1985): 1–33, especially pp. 28–29 and corresponding nn. 101–4.

CHAPTER 3

1. Vettori, "Sommario della storia d'Italia dal 1511 al 1527," in *Archivio storico italiano*, 1st ser., Appendice, vol. 6 (1848): 259–387, especially p. 300: "e perchè li Fiorentini sono dediti alla mercatura ed al guadagno, tutti pensavano dovere trarre profitto di questo pontificato."

2. "Roma è piena piena di fiorentini." Although one hardly needs more evidence of Leo's musical interests, the same letter that records that "tucto palazo è pieno di fiorentini" also observes that "ode spesso musica N. S. e di quella summamente si delecta." For both letters, see Alessandro Luzio, "Isabella d'Este nei primordi del papato di Leone X e il suo viaggio a Roma nel 1514–1515," in *Archivio storico lombardo*, 4th ser., 6 (1906): 99–180 and 454–89, especially pp. 457 and 462.

3. "I Dieci mandorono bando che si facessi festa tre dì alla fila." Bartolomeo Cerretani, "Sommario e ristretto cavato dalla historia di Bartolomeo Cerretani, scritta da lui, in dialogo delle cose di Firenze, dal'anno 1494 al 1519, Florence, BNC, MS II. IV. 19, fol. 21ᵛ, collated with the corresponding passage in "Storia in dialogo della mutazione di Firenze," Florence, BNC, MS II. I. 106. "Ogni sera uscì un trionfo, tirato da' buoi, del loro [i.e., the Medici] giardino di sulla piazza di santo Marco, e venivono giù diritto per la via Larga, e quando giugnievono in sul canto de' Medici si fermava. Et . . . era ordinato un bel canto a gloria del pontefice e della casa sua, cioè della palle; e mediato ch'el canto era finito, per ordine di fuoco lavorato s'attaccava fuoco nel sopradetto trionfo." Bartolomeo Masi, *Ricordanze di Bartolomeo Masi, Calderaio fiorentino, dal 1478 al 1526*, ed. Giuseppe Odoardo Corazzini (Florence, 1906), p. 119. On the Medici "compound" in the fifteenth and sixteenth centuries, see John Shearman, "The Collections of the Younger Branch of the Medici," in *Burlington Magazine* 117 (1975): 12–27, especially p. 16 and corresponding nn. 12–14.

4. "Fecesi la p[ri]ma sera due carri, l'uno della Discordia e l'altro della Pace, con canti a proposito, con molitudine di trombetti et di torchi. Ultimamente si arse la Discordia. L'altra sera un trionfo della Pace con la Guerra in su un altro trionfo, con canti, trobbe, torchi e fuochi lavorati; arsano ultimamente la Guerra. La 3.ª sera un trionfo col Sospetto et la Paura et trombe, torchi, arteglierie et in un altro era la Quiete, et cantato che hebbero arsano il Sospetto et la Paura con grida popolari di sorte che gl'andava sossop[r]a Firenze, et pareva che tutta ardesse p[er]chè ciascuno campanile, torre e casa haveva fuochi. E così stette la città in festa grandissima q[ua]lche giorno." Cerretani, MS II. IV. 19 (full citation given in n. 3), fol. 21ᵛ, collated with the corresponding passage in MS II. I. 106.

5. On Isaac's *Quis dabit pacem*, see Albert Dunning, *Die Staatsmotette 1480–1555* (Utrecht, 1970), pp. 22–23. On the relationship of the texts of the pieces to expectations concerning Leo's potential diplomatic role, see John Shearman's remarks in *Raphael's Cartoons in the Collection of Her Majesty the Queen and the Tapestries for the Sistine Chapel* (London, 1972), pp. 14–15; on *Optime pastor*, see also Dunning, pp. 46–53, for an interpretation of the motet's text that relates it to a visit of Matthaeus Lang to Rome in 1513. On the characterization of Laurentian Florence as a New Athens, see Shearman, *Raphael's Cartoons*, p. 73 n. 164, and the literature he cites there.

6. Gallucci ("Festival Music in Florence, ca. 1480–ca. 1520: Canti carnascialeschi, Trionfi, and Related Forms," 2 vols. [Ph.D. dissertation, Harvard University, 1966], vol. 1, p. 306, and vol. 2, pp. 168–72) printed the text and music of a piece entitled *canto* "della pace," which may have been one of the "canti a proposito" to which Cerretani referred; it is preserved in the print *Canzona della Morte. Canzona del bronchone. Canzona del Diamante & della Chazuola* (n.p., n.d.), which, as we saw in chapter 2, also contains Nardi's *canto* for the February Carnival; in the print, interestingly, the *canto* "della pace" is entitled *La chanzona del diamante* and may therefore have been performed by the *Compagnia del Diamante* on a particular civic occasion, but I do not believe that there is sufficient evidence to permit us to identify which occasion it was. More interesting still, the author of its text, according to one of the sources (Florence, Biblioteca Riccardiana, MS Riccardiano 2731), was Giovanni Battista dell'Ottonaio, one of the heralds of the Florentine Signoria, who was Giuliano de' Medici's colleague in the *Compagnia della Cazzuola* (see n. 22 of chapter 1). The "Chazuola" referred to in the title of the print surely refers to the *Compagnia della Cazzuola*. (From the various sources, principally literary in nature, there thus emerges, often with remarkable clarity, a picture of a small group of Florentine artists, literati, and musicians and their patrons, most of whom were known personally to one another by virtue of their membership in the different *Compagnie* and societies, who were responsible for the artistic activity of the first months of the restoration.) Gallucci (vol. 1, p. 307, and vol. 2, pp. 178–83) printed the text and music of the *canto* "delle palle," which Ghisi (*I canti carnascialeschi* [Florence, 1937], p. 70) associated specifically with the festivities in celebration of Leo's election.

7. On the poem published by d'Ancona, see *La poesia popolare italiana* (Livorno, 1878), pp. 55–56. D'Ancona (p. 55) also printed another text, "Sempre Palle, e Lega lega / Ciascun gridi con gran festa," which surely celebrates events of the first few months of the restoration; on the text's source, the second edition of a print entitled *Sonetti capitoli in laude della inclita casa de medici*, see Roberto Ridolfi, "Stampe popolari per il ritorno de' Medici," in *La bibliofilia* 51 (1949): 28–36, especially p. 28 n. 1; Ridolfi also described other prints that contain verses celebrating the restoration and printed the texts of two of them. On the festivities in Florence in celebration of Leo's election, see also Dunning, *Die Staatsmotette 1480–1555* (full citation given in n. 5), pp. 32–35; Dunning refers to Ghisi's remark concerning the *canto* "delle palle" and its possible association with the festivities and discusses Andreas de Silva's motet *Gaude felix Florentia*, certainly composed in celebration of Leo's election.

8. Ridolfi's thesis about Machiavelli's *canto* is in *The Life of Niccolò Machiavelli*, trans. Cecil Grayson (London, 1963), p. 139 and corresponding n. 21. I have taken the text of the poem from *Trionfi e canti carnascialeschi toscani del Rinascimento*, ed. Riccardo Bruscagli, 2 vols. (Rome, 1986), vol. 1, p. 30 (Bruscagli, however, accepts the traditional interpretation that the text refers not to Leo's election, as Ridolfi suggested, but to Clement VII's). I have not reproduced the entire text of the *canto* but only that portion that serves to suggest an association with Leo's election. On the references employed in Machiavelli's *canto* and their importance in Leonine iconography, see Shearman, *Raphael's Cartoons* (full citation given in n. 5), pp. 81–82 nn. 208–9. Yet another possible candidate for performance on the occasion of Leo's election is discussed in n. 9 of chapter 5.

9. "Et la mattina seguente [March 11, 1513], ad hore XIV, rotta la finestra del conclave, quale era murata, forno per el r. Alessandro de Farnesio, diaco, cardinale de S. Eustachio, tal parole con alta et intelligibile voce publicate: 'Gaudium magnum nuntio vobis, papam habemus, reverendissimum dominum Joannem de Medicis, diaconum cardinalem Sanctae Mariae in Domenica, qui vocatur Leo decimus.' Finite de publicare le dicte parole, fu sentito per spatio de hore doi, nel castello Adriano et il palazzo apostolico, tanto strepito et romore de bombarde at altre artiglierie, et suoni di varii instrumenti, et campane, et voce di populo gridare VIVA LEONE, et PALLE, PALLE, che parea proprio il cielo tonitruasse, o fulminasse. Non molto da poi assentato in una cathedra pontificale del detto conclave, con grande triumpho et comitato di tutto il clero et religiosi, cantando *Te Deum laudamus*, in la chiesa di Pietro al magiore altare condutto fu, et quivi dalli cardinali dalla sacra chiesa fu intronizato. Pervenuta la sera del detto dì, et per octo continui giorni per tutta l'alma città di Roma furono fatti fuochi, lumi et razi in segno di allegrezza; et in diversi lochi precipue tra nobili mercanti fiorentini furno buttati denari, et dispensato pane, et molte botte piene di vino in mezzo delle piazza e strade si poneano; et di ogni sorte de instrumente da sonare davanti allor case et palazzi si sonavano, et facevansi grandissime feste, attal che Roma non mai fu più si lieta. Fu preparata di fare la solenne coronatione a dì XIX del prefato mese. Sopra delle scale marmoree del principe deli apostoli fu constructo un grande et amplo palco ligneo, et erectovi octo columne bellissime, et sopra di esse un cornicione rilevato si vedea ben fabricato che veramente marmoreo parea. Venuta la mattina del prefato giorno fu condotto dalli suoi, insieme con tutto il sacro collegio de cardinali, archiespiscopi, episcopi, et prelati, del suo apostolico palazzo in la chiesa di San Pietro, et quivi in la capella dello apostolo Andrea posato, furon cantati solennemente li mattutinali psalmi et orationi. Perfecte le decantate laude, fu adornato de habito sacerdotale per celebrare la messa . . . , la qual finita si condusse al palco sopranarrato, et . . . fu da doi cardinali, cioè il cardinale Farnesio et de Aragona, sopra del suo capo imposto un regno di tre corone circundato, et di molte altre varie perle et gioie adornato, con gran tumulto di tubicine et altri instrumenti, et allegrezza di populo, fu coronato." See Jacopo Penni, *Cronica delle magnifiche et honorate pompe fatte in Roma per la creatione et incoronatione di papa Leone X, pont. opt. max.*, now readily available in Fabrizio Cruciani's excellent and very useful volume *Teatro nel rinascimento, Roma 1450–1550* (Rome, 1983), pp. 390–405, especially p. 391.

10. The principal sources for the Lateran *possesso* are (1) Penni, *Cronica* (full citation given in the preceding note), the title page of which is reproduced here as figure 13 (John Shearman, ["The Vatican Stanze: Functions and Decoration," in *Proceedings of the British Academy* 57 (1971): 369–424, especially p. 384] has suggested that Raphael's fresco *Leo the Great and Attila* in the stanza d'Eliodoro [see Shearman, *Raphael's Cartoons* (full citation given in n. 5), fig. 12] may be a permanent record of Leo's *possesso*, as is suggested by the fresco's similarity to Penni's title page); (2) Sebastiano di Branca Tedallini, "Diario romano dal 3 maggio 1485 al 6 giugno 1524 . . . ," in Ludovico Antonio Muratori, ed., *Rerum italicarum scriptores* (Città di Castello and Bologna, 1900–42), vol. 23, part 3, pp. 230–446, especially p. 340; and (3) Marino Sanuto, *I diarii*, 59 vols. (Venice, 1879–1903), vol. 16, cols. 160–66 and 678–90. For my purposes, the most useful discussion of the ephemeral artistic elements is John Shearman's penetrating analysis of their iconography—from which I have borrowed extensively—in *Raphael's Cartoons* (full citation given in n. 5), pp. 17 and 48–49 and corresponding n. 20, pp. 72–78 and corresponding n. 187, pp. 84–86 and corresponding nn. 220–31, and pp. 88–89 and corresponding n. 246.

11. See Shearman, *Raphael's Cartoons*, p. 17.

12. "Cantori dil Papa zercha 25, con le cotte et bene a cavallo." See Sanuto, *I diarii*, vol. 16, col. 161.

13. "varii sonatori vestiti alla divisa, over livrea del Pontefice, chi de velluto, chi de finissimo panno, cioè biancho, rosso et verde, et in nel pecto un dignissimo richamo de oro facto vi era un diamante con tre penne, una biancha, l'altra verde, e l'altra pavonaza, legate al piè con un brevicello, nel qual vi era questa parola scripta, SEMPER: et derieto nelle rene un jugo, con questa over simel littera di sopra N." Penni, *Cronica* (full citation given in n. 9), p. 392.

14. Figure 14 reproduces a sketch that may depict one of the arches executed for the occasion, possibly that executed at the behest of the Sienese banker Agostino Chigi, which was erected in front of his house. See Hermann Egger, "Entwürfe Baldassare Peruzzis für den Einzüg Karls V. in Rom: Eine Studie zur Frage über die Echtheit des sienesischen Skizzenbuches," in *Jahrbuch der Kunsthistorischen Sammlungen des allerhöchsten Kaiserhauses* 23, no. 1 (1902): 1–44, especially pp. 19–20; and Christoph Luitpold Frommel, *Baldassare Peruzzi als Maler und Zeichner*, supplement to *Römisches Jahrbuch für Kunstgeschichte* 11 (1967–1968): 75–76, catalog entry no. 32. Federico Gonzaga's letter of April 11, 1513, which specifies that the procession lasted five hours (see the text accompanying n. 12) also records seven arches, although other sources suggest that the ephemeral architectural elements (arches and other similar structures) were actually greater in number than Gonzaga suggested. See Luzio, "Isabella d'Este nei primordi del papato di Leone X" (full citation given in n. 2), especially pp. 463–65.

15. On the Roman characteristics of triumphal arches as ephemeral festival elements—and their relative novelty for Florentine artists—see John Shearman, "The Florentine *Entrata* of Leo X, 1515," in *Journal of the Warburg and Courtauld Institutes* 38 (1975): 136–54, especially p. 143. Shearman suggests that some elements of Leo's 1515 *entrata* may have been derived from the 1513 *possesso*. Indeed, as Paris de Grassis, the papal master of ceremonies, recorded, altars were constructed at various points along the route of the procession in 1513 ("ordinatum fuit et

factum quod omnes ecclesiae Urbis collocare faciant altaria aequis distantiis a
Vaticano ad Lateranum, et cantent et suffumigent, et sonent, transeunte pompa";
see Cruciani, *Teatro nel rinascimento* (full citation given in n. 9), p. 388, and Penni,
Cronica (full citation given in n. 9), p. 400, for his reference to the altars), a feature of the ephemeral decoration subsequently utilized by the Florentine authorities on the occasion of the 1515 *entrata*. I have borrowed Shearman's useful terms
"static" and "dynamic" to refer to the two principal, contrasting elements of the
possesso: respectively the arches and the procession.

16. I have borrowed extensively from Allan Ceen's and Ludwig Pastor's useful
summaries and analyses of the ephemeral decoration in *The Quartiere de' Banchi*
(New York and London, 1986), pp. 143–63 and *History of the Popes from the Close
of the Middle Ages*, trans. Ralph Francis Kerr, vol. 7 (St. Louis, 1913), pp. 40–42.

17. Ceen, *The Quartiere de' Banchi*, p. 143.

18. Ibid., p. 146.

19. Ibid., and Pastor, *History of the Popes* (full citation given in n. 16), pp. 40–
41.

20. Ceen, ibid., pp. 146–47, and Pastor, ibid., p. 41.

21. Ceen, ibid., pp. 147 and 162, and Pastor, ibid., p. 41. The reference to
"messer Joanni Zincha Teutonico, patrone della zeccha, della romana camera et
sede apostolica" is from Penni, *Cronica* (full citation given in n. 9), p. 399. In
"Baldassare Turini da Pescia: Profilo di un committente di Giulio Romano
architetto e pittore," in *Quaderni di Palazzo Te* 2 (1985): 35–43, especially p. 42 n.
16, Claudia Conforti reported on a document, a register of Leo's expenses, which
records the contribution of Turini, who was to become Lorenzo II's agent in
Rome, to the expenses incurred by the Florentine community for the *possesso*. To
my knowledge, the document—which Marcello Fagiolo and Maria Luisa Madonna first reported on—has not been made available. Elsewhere (*Baldassarre Peruzzi: pittura scena e architettura nel Cinquecento* [Rome, 1987], pp. 747–51),
Fagiolo and Madonna announced a study of the *possesso* that has not, to my knowledge, appeared.

22. Ceen, *The Quartiere de' Banchi*, p. 153, and Pastor, *History of the Popes*, p. 42
(full citations for both works given in n. 16).

23. Ceen, ibid., p. 155, and Pastor, ibid.

24. Ceen, ibid., p. 156, and Pastor, ibid.

25. Ceen, ibid., p. 162, and Pastor, ibid.

26. Pastor, ibid., pp. 41 and 42.

27. Shearman, "The Florentine *Entrata*" (full citation given in n. 15), p. 140.

28. Shearman, *Raphael's Cartoons* (full citation given in n. 5), pp. 88–89 and
corresponding n. 246, and Pastor, *History of the Popes* (full citation given in n. 16),
pp. 40–41.

29. On Chigi's arch, see Shearman, ibid., pp. 88–89 and corresponding n. 246,
and Pastor, ibid., p. 41. Bernice Davidson's observation is in *Raphael's Bible* (University Park and London, 1985), pp. 20–22.

30. "Cingevano la caxa a due bande, uno per via *Pontificum*, per la quale andò
il Papa [to the Lateran], l'altra per via Florida, per la quale ritornò." Sanuto, *I
diarii* (full citation given in n. 10), col. 686.

31. On the structure at the junction of the Vie Pontificum and Peregrinorum,

see Ceen, *The Quartiere de' Banchi* (full citation given in n. 16). I have borrowed from Ceen's description of the structure and his interpretation of the importance of its location. On p. 307 is a diagram that illustrates Ceen's proposed reconstruction of the double arch. The description of the positioning of the statues is from Penni, *Cronica* (full citation given in n. 9), p. 398.

32. Shearman, *Raphael's Cartoons* (full citation given in n. 5), pp. 48–49 and corresponding n. 20.

33. "Un Christo nudo, et sancto Joanni, protector della nostra cità . . . , che lo battezava." Penni, *Cronica* (full citation given in n. 9), p. 398.

34. "Questo era un archo belissimo che piava tute doe strade, et lì erano vacui, dove furon cantati versi." Sanuto, *I diarii* (full citation given in n. 10), col. 164.

35. Pastor, *History of the Popes* (full citation given in n. 16), p. 42, and Shearman, *Raphael's Cartoons* (full citation given in n. 5), p. 89 and corresponding n. 249.

36. On the *disputa*, see Shearman, *Raphael's Cartoons*, p. 73 and corresponding n. 156. The quotation is from Penni, *Cronica* (full citation given in n. 9), p. 401.

37. "Et essendo passato la cancellaria alla casa de Sauli, merchanti genovesi, depositarii de sua santità, era uno arco da profundo ingenio erecto. . . . Sotto del arco nel suo celo ad octo amguli compartito, si vedea nel mezzo in un octangulo una arme del Papa. . . . Lo octangulo del mezzo . . . , al passare di esso si levò via, et di quello loco uscì una palla, la qual se aperse, e eravi dentro un putto, che questi infrascripti versi con audace animo et ilare fronte recitò: Si fuerat dubium superis an regna daretur, / Ambiguum princeps optimus omne levat, / Nam rebus nemo fessis adhibere salutem, / Nec melius medicus sciret habere manus. Recitato li dicti versi la palla se ritirò dentro, et l'arme al luogo suo ritornò." Penni, *Cronica* (full citation given in n. 9), p. 402. Figure 15 reproduces a sketch that may depict the arch executed for the Sauli; see Frommel, *Baldassare Peruzzi* (full citation given in n. 14), p. 76, catalog entry no. 34.

38. Shearman, *Raphael's Cartoons*, pp. 77–78 and corresponding n. 187.

39. Ibid., pp. 17 and 84–86 and corresponding nn. 220–31.

40. "Il Papa . . . ripassò l'arco de Augustino Chisi, et dal casteliano, con suoni et tonitrui de artiglieria . . . , et così allegramente nel borgo retornato, passato lo adornamento di Cecchetto, nel suo apostolico palatio reintrò; et così licentiati li cardinali della sacra chiesa, et tutti li altri prelati, ciascuno tornò alle loro habitatione, et con fuochi et altri segni di alegrezza si mostrò lieto in tutta quella notte, in festa, suoni et canti." Penni, *Cronica* (full citation given in n. 9), p. 404.

CHAPTER 4

1. Roman citizenship was also accorded to Lorenzo II, who was, however, absent. The event was also understood to be a celebration of the *Palilia*, or birthday of Rome, which properly is April 21; implicitly, therefore, the Medici papacy and the Investiture of the pope's brother with Roman citizenship were represented as signaling a rebirth of Rome.

2. I have taken this synopsis of the principal Medicean elements of the iconography from Janet Cox-Rearick, *Dynasty and Destiny in Medici Art* (Princeton,

1984), p. 184. For another instance of the evocation of the topos of the identity of Florence and Rome, see, for example, John Shearman, *Andrea del Sarto*, 2 vols. (Oxford, 1965), vol. 1, pp. 78–89; and Matthias Winner, "Cosimo il Vecchio als Cicero," in *Zeitschrift für Kunstgeschichte* 33 (1970): 261–97, on the *salone* at the Medici villa at Poggio a Caiano, several of whose frescoes can be interpreted as embodying both a Florentine and a Roman meaning; for this example, I am indebted to Sheryl Reiss. In a letter to Lorenzo II, Cardinal Giulio described the Church and Florence as "essendo . . . due membri in un solo corpo" (Archivio di Stato, Florence, MAP, CXVII, 109).

3. Arnaldo Bruschi, "Il teatro capitolino del 1513," in *Bollettino del Centro internazionale di Studi di architettura Andrea Palladio* 16 (1974): 189–218, especially p. 190. Inghirami was called Fedra because he had played that role in Seneca's *Ippolito* in Rome; see Nino Pirrotta, "*Commedia dell'arte* and Opera," in *Music and Culture in Italy from the Middle Ages to the Baroque* (Cambridge, Mass., 1984), pp. 343–60 and 465–70, especially p. 467 n. 19. On Inghirami, see Fabrizio Cruciani, "Il teatro dei ciceroniani: Tommaso 'Fedra' Inghirami," in *Forum italicum* 14 (1980): 356–77.

4. Bruschi, "Il teatro," pp. 189–218.

5. Altieri's "Avviso" and Palliolo's "Narratione" are both published in Fabrizio Cruciani's excellent volume entitled *Il teatro del Campidoglio e le feste romane del 1513* (Milan, 1968), pp. 4–20 and 21–67; Francesco Chierigati's "Descriptione de la pompa . . . fatta in Roma il dì che 'l signor . . . Juliano di Medici . . . fu fatto cittadino et barone romano" is in Cruciani, *Teatro nel Rinascimento 1450–1550* (Rome, 1983), pp. 416–19. Altieri was the author of a treatise on marriage rituals, an important source for Klapisch-Zuber's essay "Zacharias, or the Ousted Father" cited in my introduction above. My account is based entirely on excerpts from these three principal narratives, although there are several others printed in full or excerpted by Cruciani; some of these others also contain reference to the musical elements. See, for example, Marino Sanuto, *I diarii*, 59 vols. (Venice, 1879–1903), vol. 17, cols. 73–74. A synopsis based on Chierigati's account may be found in M. Creighton, *A History of the Papacy during the Period of the Reformation*, vol. 4 (London, 1887), p. 197. Also, the unpublished diary of Cornelius de Fine (Rome, Biblioteca Apostolica Vaticana, Ottob. Lat. 2137) contains references to the musical performances that formed part of the banquet on the evening of the thirteenth; for this reference I am grateful to Sheryl Reiss.

For useful discussion on the question of disparities among accounts of the same festival, I am grateful to Dr. Julian Kliemann of Villa I Tatti, the Harvard University Center for Italian Renaissance Studies in Florence. For John Shearman's thesis concerning Nardi's possible authorship of the "program" for Leo's 1515 *entrata*, see "The Florentine *Entrata* of Leo X, 1515," in *Journal of the Warburg and Courtauld Institutes* 38 (1975): 136–54, especially p. 139 and corresponding n. 9.

I think it is important to add that my account is a kind of patchwork, based as it is on references drawn from all three narratives. I have been careful to specify which account provides which references, and do not wish to convey the impression that any one of the narratives contains an account that corresponds exactly to the one provided here. The authors had different interests and objectives and would therefore have been inclined to report selectively. For useful discussion on this point I am grateful to Professors Patricia Rubin of the Courtauld Institute of Art at the University of London and Daniel Bornstein of Texas A&M University.

6. Altieri, in Cruciani, *Il teatro del Campidoglio* (full citation given in n. 5), p. 10: "alli XIII di settembre, . . . il Magnifico Signor Giovangiorgio [Cesarini, *gonfaloniere* of the *Popolo romano* and *capo della festa*] . . . , con infinito numero de bifari e trombette si conduss'al palazzo del Papa dov'il Magnifico dimorava. E quello, così ricevuto, s'accompagnò per tutta la Città con infiniti et assai diversissimi suoni de' prenominati istromenti."

7. On the theater, see, above all, Bruschi "Il teatro" (full citation given in n. 3).

8. Ackerman, *The Architecture of Michelangelo* (Baltimore, 1970), pp. 147 and 153.

9. Bruschi "Il teatro" (full citation given in n. 3), p. 191.

10. Ibid.

11. Ibid.

12. See the useful summary descriptions of the theater in Cox-Rearick, *Dynasty and Destiny* (full citation given in n. 2), pp. 98 and 100, and Nino Pirrotta and Elena Povoledo, *Music and Theater from Poliziano to Monteverdi* (Cambridge, 1982), p. 315 n. 8.

13. Vasari, *Lives of the Most Eminent Painters, Sculptors, and Architects*, 3 vols., trans. Gaston Du C. de Vere (New York, 1979), p. 998. Vasari erroneously associated the festivities with those for the occasion on which Giuliano received the symbols of office as *gonfaloniere* of the Church. On Peruzzi's contribution to the ephemeral artistic elements for the occasion, see also Christoph Luitpold Frommel, *Baldassare Peruzzi als Maler und Zeichner*, supplement to *Römisches Jahrbuch für Kunstgeschichte* 11 (1967–68): 76–78, catalog entries nos. 36–38.

14. Cox-Rearick, *Dynasty and Destiny* (full citation given in n. 2).

15. Bruschi, "Il teatro" (full citation given in n. 3), p. 197, and Cruciani, *Teatro nel Rinascimento* (full citation given in n. 5), p. 410.

16. Cox-Rearick (full citation given in n. 2).

17. Bruschi (full citation given in n. 3), pp. 193 and 195.

18. Ibid., pp. 195–96.

19. Altieri, in Cruciani, *Il teatro del Campidoglio* (full citation given in n. 5), p. 11: "racquetati tutti con una singolarissima musica." Palliolo, in ibid., p. 35: "Li sacerdoti et cantori dedero principio alla solenne messa in canto figurato con modi condecenti a tanta celebrite."

20. Chierigati, in idem, *Teatro nel Rinascimento* (full citation given in n. 5), p. 417: "quale fu cantata . . . per lo episcopo de l'Aquila [Joannes Dominici]."

21. Palliolo, in idem, *Il teatro del Campidoglio* (full citation given in n. 5), p. 35: "alla quale tutti stettero devotamente."

22. Alberto Cametti, "I musici di Campidoglio," in *Archivio della Società romana di storia patria* 48 (1925): 95–135, passim.

23. See Bruschi, "Il teatro" (full citation given in n. 3), pp. 189 and 190, and Cruciani, *Teatro nel Rinascimento* (full citation given in n. 5), p. 408.

24. Cametti, "I musici" (full citation given in n. 22), pp. 118–19; on the reference to the "two choruses of musicians" ("due cori di musici, uno di voci e l'altro di stromenti"), see especially p. 97.

25. Bruschi, "Il teatro" (full citation given in n. 3), p. 213 n. 5.

26. Palliolo, in Cruciani, *Il teatro del Campidoglio* (full citation given in n. 5), p. 37: "gli Conservatori e Magistrati . . . fecero . . . leggere ad alta voce el privilegio del patritiato concesso dal Senato e Populo Romano allui [Giuliano]. . . . El quale letto . . . , tanto grande fu il romore et strepito delle trombe, pifare et artigliarie discaricate, che non solo il Campidoglio et Roma, ma anchora le circostanti regioni ne ribombavano."

27. Ibid., p. 44: "Lo antiquo instituto de' suoni et canti dopo el convivio non è stato omesso."

28. Bruschi, "Il teatro" (full citation given in n. 3), p. 214 n. 5, and Cruciani, *Teatro nel Rinascimento* (full citation given in n. 5), p. 412.

29. Cruciani, ibid., p. 412.

30. Palliolo, in idem, *Il teatro del Campidoglio* (full citation given in n. 5), p. 45: "In tanto varii suoni se sentivano, dopo gli quali . . . apparse una . . . Madonna. . . . Questa Madonna rappresentava Roma, la quale recitò una oratione."

31. Chierigati, in idem, *Teatro nel Rinascimento* (full citation given in n. 5), p. 417: "Et puoi, havendo anche le nimphe [who were with her] cantate altri bei versi in laude del nostro signore et del prefato Magnifico."

32. Palliolo, in idem, *Il teatro del Campidoglio* (full citation given in n. 5), pp. 47–48: "De poi Roma et le nymphe con lei se partirono accompagnate da gran suoni di trombe, pifare et altre armonie. Cessati gli suoni . . . , fu recitata una egloga . . . in la quale intervengono duo villani. . . . al suono di [una] cithara cantano molti versi al modo rusticano, l'uno in laude di Nostro Signore, l'altro in commendationi del . . . Magnifico Juliano. Questa fu la conclusione del egloga, dopo la quale seguì la musica di pifare." Donna Cardamone had earlier cited the portion of Nocturno Napolitano's poetic account of the Capitoline festivities concerning the recitation of the eclogue (*Triumphi de gli mirandi Spettaculi* [Bologna, 1519]) as evidence of the interest in rustic poetry, which forms the background for the emergence of the *canzone villanesca alla napolitana: The "canzona villanesca alla napolitana" and Related Forms, 1537–1570*, 2 vols. (Ann Arbor, 1981), vol. 1, p. 35 and p. 239 n. 11. See also Cardamone's discussion of the tradition that the "rustic" *eclogue* exemplifies in ibid., p. 34.

33. Chierigati, in Cruciani, *Teatro nel Rinascimento* (full citation given in n. 5), p. 417: "Seguitò una montagna grande de la qual, alla presentia del Magnifico, uscì el Monte Tarpeio, qual era vestito da punico cum una gran barba, et havea una vesta di carta fatta come la montagna che parea un monticello, et havea Roma su le spalle. . . . et cantò alcuni versi in laude del nostro signore. Poi, raccomandato Roma et gli romani al Magnifico, ritornò ne la montagna et passò ultra." Chierigati's account differs from that of Palliolo, who described the "mountain" that first entered as the Monte Tarpeio, from which emerged the Capitoline god; see Palliolo in Cruciani, *Il teatro del Campidoglio* (full citation given in n. 5), p. 48.

34. Palliolo, in ibid., pp. 50–51: "intrò . . . un carro accompagnato et menato da VIII militi armati alla usanza antiqua de' Romani et alquante nimphe. Sopra il carro sedeva in mezzo Roma . . . ; dalla destra li sedeva la Justitia . . . , dalla sinistra la Fortezza. . . . le nimphe e militi . . . fecero una suavissima musica. Dopo la quale uscirono . . . , insieme con el carro, Roma, Justitia et Fortezza."

35. Ibid., p. 52: "Dopo breve intervallo, intraro . . . molti coribanti [priests of Cybele], quali andavano spargendo oro et sonando varii instrumenti. Questa era

la musica del Cardinale [Ippolito d'Este] di Ferrara, et similmente cantavano con soavissime modulationi alquanti versi. . . . Dietro a loro seguiva una carretta al modo antiqua formata, duo leoni la tiravano. Sedeva in essa Cybele con una gran palla inante, fatta alla similtudine del mondo. Allhora la palla in due parte fu divisa. . . . Della palla uscì Roma in forma de una bellissima giovene, de oro vestita et incoronata. . . . Uscita Roma della palla, cantò alcuni versi." At this point, the MS Bologna, Biblioteca universitaria 3816, whose readings Cruciani's edition generally follows (see the critical notes in ibid., pp. 131 and 134), gives the actual Latin verses that were sung, rather than the Italian paraphrase that Palliolo's account ordinarily provides: "Questa era la musica del Cardinale del Ferrara et similmente cantaro con soavissime modulationi gl'infrascritti versi. Florida florenti floret Florentia flore / Aeternum et Medices decus orbis clara propago; / Auspicijsque tuis iterum nunc Roma resurget, / Magne Leo, amissosque animos excelsa resumet," as published in Paolo Palliolo Fanese, *Le feste pel conferimento del patriziato romano a Giuliano e Lorenzo de' Medici*, ed. O. Guerrini (Bologna, 1885), p. 107. Many of the Latin texts that were recited and sung are contained in another of Palliolo's accounts of the *festa* (see Cruciani, *Il teatro del Campidoglio* [full citation given in n. 5], pp. 69–94); if one's objective, therefore, were a complete reconstruction of the *festa*, one could certainly integrate the Latin texts with the material contained in the narrative accounts. (I have checked the incipits of the Latin verses in the second of Palliolo's accounts against the alphabetical index of texts in Knud Jeppesen, *La frottola*, 3 vols. [Copenhagen, 1968–70], vol. 2, pp. 207–62, in an attempt to locate musical settings that may have been composed for the Capitoline ceremonies, but in no way can I claim to have conducted an exhaustive, systematic search. The festival merits a more detailed reconstruction than was possible here.) On the drawing that may be a sketch for the Cybele *carro*, reproduced here as figure 23, see Frommel, *Baldassare Peruzzi* (full citation given in n. 13), pp. 77–78, catalog entry no. 37, and Philip Pouncey and J. A. Gere, *Italian Drawings in the Department of Prints and Drawings in the British Museum*, 2 vols. (London, 1962), vol. 1, p. 141, catalog entry no. 243, and vol. 2, plate no. 217.

36. Chierigati, in Cruciani, *Teatro nel Rinascimento* (full citation given in n. 5), p. 418: "Sequia un altro carro dorato . . . , sopra el quale era una donna . . . che representava Fiorenza, qual recitò alcuni versi dolendosi et querelandosi de Roma che l'havesse privata de . . . el nostro signore et el Magnifico. Smontò poi et venne avanti el Magnifico, . . . simulando lacrime perché lui havea abbandonata epsa Fiorenza qual havealo nutrito et educato fino a questi tempi. Si butò in genochio avanti Cibelle. . . . La qual . . . voleva che Roma et Fiorenza fussero una cosa medema. . . . et fu fatto la confederatione. In segno de leticia fu cantato et sonato per la musica del cardinale [d'Este] alcuni hymni novi." For the suggestion about Raphael's cartoon as a record of contemporary dramatic practice, see John Shearman, *Raphael's Cartoons* (London, 1972), p. 131 and plate 21.

37. See my chapter 1.

38. See my chapter 7.

39. See Lewis Lockwood, "Adrian Willaert and Cardinal Ippolito I d'Este," in *Early Music History* 5 (1985): 85–112.

40. Michele Pesenti was in Ippolito's employ in 1513 and later in Leo's; see

Lockwood, ibid., especially p. 112, and Herman-Walther Frey, "Regesten zur päpstlichen Kapelle unter Leo X. und seiner Privatkapelle," in *Die Musikforschung* 8 (1955): 58–73, 178–99, and 412–37, and 9 (1956): 46–57, 139–56, and 411–19, especially pp. 140–42.

41. See Lewis Lockwood, "Jean Mouton and Jean Michel: French Music and French Musicians in Italy, 1505–1520," in *Journal of the American Musicological Society* 32 (1979): 191–246, especially pp. 243–46.

42. Palliolo, in Cruciani, *Il teatro del Campidoglio* (full citation given in n. 5), pp. 55–56: "El dì sequente.... varii suoni per il theatro se sentivano. Fatto finalmente silentio, intrò . . . un carro molto ornato."

43. Chierigati, in idem, *Teatro nel Rinascimento* (full citation given in n. 5) p. 418: "condotto da quatro chinee bianche del Papa cum quatro nimphe sopra epse."

44. Palliolo, in idem, *Il teatro del Campidoglio* (full citation given in n. 5), p. 55: "sopra esso, in la parte anteriore, stava el pelicano . . . ; sopra il collo portava un giogo, dal lato destro haveva una lupa con Romulo et Remulo alle mamme, dalla sinistra la celeste Orsa. In mezzo . . . era piantato un bello lauro. . . . Al pedale di questo lauro appoggiava un polito seggio, nel quale era la diva Clarice, madre del Magnifico Juliano, del sangue Orsino, da cielo discesa, vestita de oro. . . . Da man dritta li giaceva apresso il patre Tiberino, da man manca Arno, ambo con barba bianca et capelli canuti."

45. Chierigati, in idem, *Teatro nel Rinascimento* (full citation given in n. 5), p. 418: "Stando sul carro cantorno tutti tre alcuni versi."

46. Palliolo, in idem, *Il teatro del Campidoglio* (full citation given in n. 5), pp. 56 and 58–59: "apresso el quale [the *carro*] andavano a piedi . . . due nimphe per il servitio di Clarice. Et quando [the *carro*] fu pervenuto nel conspetto del Magnifico Juliano, lei [Clarice], cantando, gli disse molti versi. . . . Una della dette nimphe [who followed the *carro*], vedendo ogni cosa essere piena de allegrezza et festa, invitò le compagne a cantare inseme con versi di questa continentia: 'O nimphe habitatrici de Tibre et habitatrici di Arno, cantiamo inseme. O nimphe Tibricole et Arnicole, cantiamo inseme.' Finalmente le nimphe . . . diedero principio ad una soavissima musica."

47. Chierigati, in idem, *Teatro nel Rinascimento* (full citation given in n. 5), pp. 418–19: "Poi fu finita la festa . . . et avanti partissero le quatro nimphe [on horseback] . . . cantorno una frotola in laude del Magnifico." Altieri (in idem, *Il teatro del Campidoglio* [full citation given in n. 5], p. 18) described the conclusion of the last scene (which he identified as that representing "un fanciullo in forma di Roma," rather than, as in Palliolo's account, that representing Clarice de' Medici) as follows: "Finisse poi in quell'atto la ripresentatione con haver ogni homo sommamente dilettato, et interpostasi molto eccellente musica, come nella maggior parte de gli altri atti s'era fatto della rappresentatione, si terminò al fine con impeto di trombe, biffari, tambori et infinito altro numero d'instrumenti alla fama di questa solennità quasi per tutta Italia concorsi, che per la copia e diversità de' tuoni pareva che'l mondo subissasse."

48. Palliolo, in idem, *Il teatro del Campidoglio* (full citation given in n. 5), p. 59: "Dopo molti suoni di trombe et pifare, fu recitato il *Penulo*, comedia di Plauto, non tradotta vulgare ma latina."

49. On the report of the Mantuan observer concerning the theater, see Alessandro Luzio, "Isabella d'Este nei primordi del papato di Leone X e il suo viaggio a Roma nel 1514–1515," in *Archivio storico lombardo*, 4th ser., 6 (1906): 99–180 and 454–89, especially p. 127: "il teatro apparato et habiti non furono da comparare a quelli de V. Ex. in conto alcuno."

50. Vasari, *Lives* (full citation given in n. 13), p. 998. On Peruzzi's design of the stage scenery, see also Frommel, *Baldassare Peruzzi* (full citation given in n. 13), pp. 76–77, catalog entry no. 36. However, see also Bruschi, "Il teatro" (full citation given in n. 3), pp. 196–97, and Cruciani, *Teatro nel Rinascimento* (full citation given in n. 5), p. 414; both argue that Vasari's account is erroneous in this instance.

51. Palliolo, in Cruciani, *Il teatro del Campidoglio* (full citation given in n. 5), p. 62: "Uscì . . . lo recitore del prologo. . . . Et fatto fine al recitar del prologo, reintrò onde era uscito. Allhora fu dato principio ad una soave concento di pifare, el quale durò per buon spatio; né altro choro, musica né suono in tutta questa comedia fu udito, excetto la tromba del precone quando al popolo fece audientia. Et in questo si sonno accostati al modo servato in fare le comedie a' tempi de Plauto et anchor di Terentio, apresso li quali non ha luogo nessuno il choro, ma solo se li adoperavano le pifare, altramente nominate tibie."

52. On the use of *intermedii* in the subsequent performances, see my chapters 1, 9, 10, and 13. Interestingly, by the middle of the sixteenth century, opinion as to the appropriate use of music in performances of classical comedies, particularly of Terence, had apparently changed: as Colin Slim noted (*A Gift of Madrigals and Motets*, 2 vols. [Chicago, 1972], vol. 1, p. 102 and corresponding n. 172), an illustration from an Italian edition of 1561 of Terence's *Heautontimorumenos* shows three musicians—two singers and a player of the viola da gamba. The illustration is reproduced as plate 24 in Pirrotta, *Music and Theater* (full citation given in n. 12). On the performance of *Asinaia* in 1514, see Claudia Conforti, "Baldassarre Turini da Pescia: Profilo di un committente di Giulio Romano, architetto e pittore," in *Quaderni di Palazzo Te* 2 (1985): 35–43, especially p. 43 n. 24. Finally, on the importance of the comedies of Terence and Plautus to the development of Italian Renaissance theater, see Pirrotta, *Music and Theater*, chapter 2, passim.

CHAPTER 5

1. On the *entrata*, see, above all, John Shearman's masterful study "The Florentine *Entrata* of Leo X, 1515," in *Journal of the Warburg and Courtauld Institutes* 38 (1975): 136–54. Professor Shearman's command of the primary material is so thorough—and his analysis of it so incisive—that one could hardly improve on it materially, and I will have occasion to refer to it repeatedly in the course of this chapter; indeed, I have borrowed liberally from it, as will be clear from the following notes. On the ephemeral structure at the juncture of Vie Tornabuoni and Porta Rossa, see especially p. 140 and p. 149 n. 41. I should say that Ilaria Ciseri's *L'ingresso trionfale di Leone X in Firenze nel 1515*, Biblioteca Storica Toscana, a cura della Deputazione di Storia patria per la Toscana, XXVI (Florence, 1990), appeared too recently for me to take account of its contents.

2. Shearman, "The Florentine *Entrata*," p. 140.

3. Ibid., p. 143.

4. Ibid.

5. Ibid., p. 148 n. 37.

6. Adriano Prosperi, "Clemente VII," in *Dizionario biografico degli italiani*, vol. 26 (Rome, 1982), pp. 237–59, especially p. 241.

7. "Sommario et ristretto cavato dalla historia di Bartolomeo Cerretani . . . in dialogo delle cose di Firenze, dal'anno 1494 al 1519," Florence, BNC, MS II. IV. 19, fol. 37^r, collated with the corresponding passage in MS II. I. 106: "E fessi ordini p[er] i trionfi et apparati p[er] honorarlo quanto fusse possibile. Partissi Sua Santità [from Rome] . . . e Lorenzo de' Medici, tornato dal Re [Francis], s'inviò alla volta del Papa, e nella città leg[niaiuo]li e dipintori et altri artigiani erono tutti in op[er]a, e tutta la città faceva festa. . . . Addì 30 di novembre 1515, il dì di S[an]to Andrea . . . entrò in Firenze Sua Santità."

8. Shearman, "The Florentine *Entrata*" (full citation given in n. 1), p. 145 n. 27.

9. "Sette Archi Triomphali, che se ne fa uno al entrar de la porta de S^{to} Pietro Gattolino . . . et li se cantara una Canzone al Proposito. . . . A .s. Felice in Piazza serà el secondo . . . cum musica. . . . Alla parte [*sic*] de la trinita el tercio . . . cum Moti et musica. . . . Al Canto de Carneschi sara uno edificio ad uso de Triompho, che havendo N. S. acquistato tutte le soraditte virtu, sopra del quale seranno poste quattro [i.e., the cardinal virtues] che tenghino la sedia [i.e., the papal throne], cio è la parte de nanti, la Prudentia: ut caveat a futuris: la parte de drieto: la Justicia, ut satisfaciat de preteritis: la Temperancia a dextris, non ellevetur in Prosperis: La Fortezza a sinistris, ne succumbat in adversis: La sedia essendo vota sopra de quella saranno eminenti, la Fede, speranza et charita che tenerano in mane, un regno [i.e., the tiara], et vi sera una musica bella, significante, che [the pope] havendo posseduto [the virtues]: quelle donne li hano preparato un Triompho. . . . Uno apparato bellissimo dal principio de la via de la scala sino alla porta de la sala del Papa: ove se prepara un bellissimo edificio figurante, la felicità humana, et divina, et in quello cum musiche se repossi." "Archi, et spectaculi Preparati a Fiorenza per la entrata de Papa Leone X^{mo} . . . ," British Library, MS Harley 3462, fols. 194^{r-v}, as edited in Shearman, "The Florentine *Entrata*" (full citation given in n. 1), pp. 145 and 147–48.

In "Un'occasione in cui la storia detta il canto alla festa," in *Il teatro dei Medici, Quaderni di teatro, Rivista trimestrale del Teatro Regionale Toscano* 2, no. 7 (1980): 114–34, Maria Luisa Minio-Paluello (and following her *Trionfi e canti carnascialeschi del Rinascimento*, ed. Riccardo Bruscagli, 2 vols. [Rome, 1986], vol. 1, pp. 286–88) relates a *canto carnascialesco* entitled the *Canzona di Firenzuola* to the festivities for Leo's visit to Florence. I feel compelled to say that I am not convinced by her argument, in part because I can find no appropriate place for the *canto* among the musical elements of the *entrata* as described in the narrative accounts (it would not have been appropriate for performance at one of the triumphal arches, for example, because its text seems to me not to correspond to the content of any of the iconographic material reportedly inscribed on the arches). Moreover, it makes oblique reference to the *Compagnia* of the *Broncone*, which, by November of 1515, had already been in existence for some three years, and which apparently played no part in the festivities for Leo's visit to Florence. The reference to the *Broncone* suggests to me that the *canto*—which also refers to "il signor nostro" (line 11), the "figlio di Clarice [Orsini-Medici]" (line 53); i.e., Pope Leo X—was likelier among those performed in March of 1513 to celebrate Leo's election (on which see my chapter 3), an event in which the Broncone company might well have participated, given that it had recently been formed and had performed only a few weeks earlier, at the time of the February Carnival.

10. Shearman, "The Florentine *Entrata*" (full citation given in n. 1), p. 139 n. 9.

11. "Cominciando alla porta (di San Pietro Gattolini [the present Porta Romana]) insino alla chiesa cattedrale erano edificati in diversi luoghi per tutta la strada sette magnifichi e begli archi trionfali, che rappresentavano le quattro virtù cardinali e le tre virtù teologiche. A ciascuno de' quali erano cantati in sue lodi e esaltazione alcuni versi accomodati e convenienti alla virtù che in quello arco si rappresentava." Nardi, in Shearman, "The Florentine *Entrata*," p. 139 n. 9.

12. On these elements, see Shearman, "The Florentine *Entrata*" (full citation given in n. 1), pp. 140 and 149–50 and corresponding nn. 40–42.

13. "Et fiorini cinquantasei larghi in oro dati a cantori che cantorno in su decti archi." Ibid., pp. 136–37 n. 2 and p. 147 n. 34. On the membership of the Cathedral's and baptistery's chapels in the early sixteenth century, see Frank D'Accone, "The Musical Chapels at the Florentine Cathedral and Baptistery during the First Half of the Sixteenth Century," in *Journal of the American Musicological Society* 24 (1971): 1–50. On the Signoria's instrumentalists, see Keith Polk, "Civic Patronage and Instrumental Ensembles in Renaissance Florence," in *Augsburger Jahrbuch für Musikwissenschaft* 3 (1986): 51–68, especially p. 68.

14. I have borrowed the useful terms "dynamic" and "static" from Shearman, "The Florentine *Entrata*" (full citation given in n. 1).

15. "Succedeano .xlv. parenti del papa vestiti tutti molto richamente: Et molto ben à cavallo. . . . successive veniano à piedi tutti gli artifici de Fiorenza per ordine. con .iiij Trombetti . . . con gli penoni di nova foggia. . . . doppoi li Confaloni de li quarteri. Et li .Signori otto di Firenza à piedi. Item .xvi. Trombetti con li penoni viz: con le arme de la communita di Fiorenza." Francesco Chiericati, "Descriptione de la Entrata de la s.ta di N. S. papa Leone X.mo . . . ," British Library, MS Harley 3462, as edited in Shearman, "The Florentine *Entrata*," pp. 150–51.

16. "Super istis erant [sung] cantilenae diversae, quas Papa libenter audire videbatur." Paridis de Grassis, *De ingressu Summi Pont. Leonis X. Florentiam*, ed. Dominico Moreni (Florence, 1793), p. 9. Elsewhere (pp. 16–18) Paris adds "& iste fuit ordo procedendi a Porta ad Ecclesiam S. Reparatae, in qua via fuerunt per me ordinati cives, qui per spatia, ut dixi, custodirent, ne qua fieret pressura, aut scandalum, aut mora, ut solet quando que a Iuvenibus Mulierum inspectoribus. Pontifex primo accepit Regnum in capite, quod cum gravaretur in media via illo deposito, accepit leve Regnum, & delectabatur, cum in quolibet arcu triumphali cantaretur aliquid in suam laudem, & firmabat gressum, ut omnia audiret, & intelligeret."

17. Giovanni Cambi, "Istorie," ed. Fr. Ildefonso di San Luigi, 4 vols., in *Delizie degli eruditi toscani*, vols. 20–23 (Florence, 1786), vol. 3, pp. 86–87: "dipoi [in the processional order] ne venono Preti soli di S. Maria del Fiore, e S. Lorenzo, e frati e Monaci di tutte le reghole; si feciono altari, e stettono insu'

canti in luoghi dove parve loro a vederlo passare, e chantavano dove passava dalloro." Paris, *De ingressu* (full citation given in the preceding note), pp. 7–8: "Quo autem ad sacram Processionem ordinavi, quod omnes de Clero Civitatis, quantumcumque exempti venirent sub poenis pecuniariis per me impositis exceptis Monialibus, licet etiam Papa dedit Monialibus volentibus venire, & videre licentiam veniendi, ad loca honesta, ita ut viderent, sed non viderentur, prout multa Collegia Monialium Claustralium venerunt, & aliquae omnino abstinuerunt, multi etiam Religiosorum Conventus se excusare voluerunt, ne venire cogerentur, sed omnino venerunt, & comparuerunt, non tamen per vias ambulaverunt in processionibus illis, sed feci quod Vicarius Archiepiscopi assignavit singulis Regulis locum suum, in quo unaquaeque Regula suum Altare quam festivissime erigeret, & ibidem stantes cantarent, dum aequitatus Papalis transiret a principio usque ad finem, quod placuit Papae, & Cardinalibus, ac etiam Civibus universis, & si qua contentio erat inter aliquos, ut saepe solet, Vicarius eas concordaret, & factum est de facili."

18. Shearman, "The Florentine *Entrata*" (full citation given in n. 1), p. 145 n. 27.

19. Ibid., n. 28.

20. Ibid., n. 29.

21. Ibid., p. 146 n. 30.

22. "Vedete alle finestre del palazzo [della Signoria] i pifferi che suonano, ed i trombetti, che ognuno fa festa, ed è adorno le finestre di tappeti." Vasari, *Le opere*, ed. Gaetano Milanesi, 9 vols. (Florence, 1878–1906), vol. 8, p. 145.

23. Shearman, "The Florentine *Entrata*," (full citation given in n. 1), pp. 149–150 n. 41.

24. Ibid. On the significance of images of Hercules, see also Shearman, *Raphael's Cartoons in the Collection of Her Majesty the Queen and the Tapestries for the Sistine Chapel* (London, 1972), pp. 89–90; Shearman, "The Vatican Stanze: Functions and Decoration," in *Proceedings of the British Academy* 57 (1971): 369–424, especially p. 385 and corresponding n. 123; Janet Cox-Rearick, *Dynasty and Destiny in Medici Art* (Princeton, 1984), pp. 146–47; and Virginia Bush, "Bandinelli's *Hercules and Cacus* and Florentine Traditions," in *Studies in Italian Art and Architecture, 15th through 18th Centuries*, ed. Henry A. Millon, Studies in Italian Art History, vol. 1, Memoirs of the American Academy in Rome 35 (1980): 163–207, especially pp. 170–72.

25. Shearman, "The Florentine *Entrata*" (full citation given in n. 1), p. 146 n. 31. Vasari, in the lives of Baccio da Montelupo and Andrea del Sarto, wrote, in one instance, that Baccio was responsible for an arch constructed between the Palazzo del Podestà (what is today known as the Bargello) and the Badia, and, in the other, that Aristotile cooperated with Granacci on an arch opposite the door of the Badia (see Vasari, *Le opere* [full citation given in n. 22], vol. 4, p. 541, and vol. 5, p. 24); elsewhere (vol. 6, pp. 255 and 436), he records Pontormo's involvement. However one interprets Vasari's statements, Cambi's reference (see n. 26) is to this structure.

26. "Perchè era fatto un bello aparato appie le schalee di Badia si fermò il Papa, e chantossi un inno da sua chantori." Cambi, "Istorie" (full citation given in n. 17), pp. 86–87.

27. Shearman, "The Florentine *Entrata*" (full citation given in n. 1), pp. 146–47 n. 32.

28. Ibid., p. 147 n. 33, and idem, *Andrea del Sarto*, 2 vols. (Oxford, 1965), vol. 2, pp. 317–18.

29. Shearman, "The Florentine *Entrata*" (full citation given in n. 1), p. 147 n. 33.

30. "Non si sentiva altro che colpi d'artiglierie, e suoni di canpane e chiarini e tronbe e tamburi di soldati che erono col sopradetto Ponteficie." *Ricordanze di Bartolomeo Masi, Calderaio fiorentino, dal 1478 al 1526*, ed. Giuseppe Odoardo Corazzini (Florence, 1906), pp. 172–73.

31. "Papa diutius solito oravit, & tandem Cardinalis de Medicis Diaconus, qui erat Archiepiscopus Florentinus in Cappa sua rubea cantante versiculos, & orationem, Papa benedixit." Paris, *De ingressu* (full citation given in n. 16), p. 18.

32. Marino Sanuto, *I diarii*, 59 volumes (Venice, 1879–1903), vol. 52, col. 648 ("disse el prefatio et molto bene, per haver bona voce, et esser perfeto musico"); and Eugenio Alberi, ed., *Relazioni degli ambasciatori veneti al Senato*, 2d ser., vol. 3 (Florence, 1846), p. 278 ("delli buoni musici che ora siano in Italia").

33. "Tronbe e pifferi assai." Luca Landucci, *Diario fiorentino dal 1450 al 1516 continuato da un anonimo fino al 1542*, ed. Iodoco del Badia (Florence, 1883), p. 353.

34. "Era fatto un vago e belliss[im]o arco, con dieci nimphe che cantavano." Cerretani, BNC, MS II. IV. 19 (full citation given in n. 7), fol. 39ᵛ. For Landucci's decription of Bandinelli's arch, see Shearman, "The Florentine *Entrata*" (full citation given in n. 1), p. 147 n. 34. The equestrian group in Piazza Santa Maria Novella stood on an ornate brick base four *braccia* high. The horse was made of gilded clay and reared over an armed and gilded figure beneath its hooves; the fallen figure was reported to have been nine *braccia* long. See Shearman, *Andrea del Sarto* (full citation given in n. 28), vol. 2, pp. 318–19, and Shearman, "The Florentine *Entrata*" (full citation given in n. 1), p. 150 n. 42.

35. See idem, "The Florentine *Entrata*," p. 148 n. 36.

36. See my chapter 3.

37. For a discussion of Corteccia's motet, see Andrew Minor and Bonner Mitchell, *A Renaissance Entertainment: Festivities for the Marriage of Cosimo I, Duke of Florence, in 1539* (Columbia, Mo., 1968), pp. 58 and 103.

38. The singers were paid fifty-six large gold florins. If there were only ten of them, each would have been paid just under six florins each. In 1521, two new appointees to the musical chapel at the Annunziata earned annual salaries of eighteen florins (see D'Accone, "The Musical Chapels" [full citation given in n. 13], p. 41, doc. 9). Payments of around six florins for singing during Leo's *entrata*, therefore, would have been the equivalent of a third of one's annual salary, and it seems unlikely that the total would have been disbursed among so small a number of singers. On the majolica plate, which Shearman dates prior to the event, see Shearman, "The Florentine *Entrata*" (full citation given in n. 1), pp. 153–54 and corresponding nn. 62–67.

39. "El . . . Ponteficie uscì della sopradetta abitazione sua . . . , e venne a vicitare la Nunziata de' Servi di Firenze. . . . E come egli entrò in detta cappella, si pose ginocchioni e fecie sua orazione, e mediato ch'egli ebbe orato, si scoperse la sopradetta figura della sopradetta Nunziata. . . . e dipoi che la sopradetta figura fu

ricoperta, che si scoperse tre volte l'una dopo l'altra, el . . . ponteficie disse *aiutorium nostrum in nomine domini,* e' cantori sua, e quali s'erono arrecati ritti al dirinpetto, nella cappella di santo Nicolò, rispondevano a ciò ch'e' disse. E dipoi ch'egli ebbe ditto cierti versetti ch'egli usono dire in simili luoghi, e ch'e' cantori ebbono risposto, el sopradetto Ponteficie detta la benedizione." *Ricordanze di Bartolomeo Masi* (full citation given in n. 30), p. 173. Masi's reference is to the famous "annunciate Virgin," one of the most revered of Florentine religious images, on which see Richard Trexler, "Florentine Religious Experience: The Sacred Image," in *Church and Community, 1200-1600* (Rome, 1987), pp. 37–74, especially p. 41, and John Shearman, *Pontormo's Altarpiece in S. Felicita* (Newcastle upon Tyne, 1971), p. 10.

40. The relevant portion of Turini's letter (Archivio di Stato, Florence, *fondo* MAP, CV, 15) reads as follows; he specified that Leo wanted to reside at "S. M. Novella e quivi stare due giorni, ma poi venire a starsi così in casa sua e continuare abitarsi lì, e dice che si servirebbe della Chiesa di San Lorenzo per farvi la Cappella e che voleva tutta la casa libera e che tutti voi altri potervi andare a stare in casa di Giovanfrancesco." See Claudia Conforti, "Baldassarre Turini da Pescia: Profilo di un committente di Giulio Romano architetto e pittore," in *Quaderni di Palazzo Te* 2 (1985): 35–43, especially p. 43 n. 24.

41. Shearman, "The Florentine *Entrata*" (full citation given in n. 1), p. 153 n. 60.

42. "Et ogni mattina cantarano e cantori del Papa la bellissima messa di figurato allo altare di decto sacramento et era questa chiesa molto frequentata da populi per rispecto del Papa et di tante magnificentie." Florence, Archivio Capitolare di San Lorenzo, Giornale "A" della Sagrestia dal 1506–21, fol. 305ʳ, as edited in Frank D'Accone, "Heinrich Isaac in Florence," in *Musical Quarterly* 49 (1963): 464–83, especially p. 482. Interestingly, as Sheryl Reiss observed, the same document suggests that one of Donatello's famous bronze pulpits in San Lorenzo was converted into a *cantoria* for the use of the singers on the occasion of Leo's visit.

43. "Si cominciò . . . una Messa papale, la quale disse l'arcivescovo [Giovanni Tedeschini-Piccolomini] di Siena. E cantori della cappella della musica del papa rispondevono alla sopradetta Messa, che sono altri cantori che non sono i nostri; et a detta Messa non si sonò organi, che fu una delle più belle Messe ch'io udissi o vedessi mai." *Ricordanze di Bartolomeo Masi* (full citation given in n. 30), p. 175.

44. Shearman, "The Florentine *Entrata*" (full citation given in n. 1), p. 153 n. 61.

45. "*Tandem*, vene l'ordene: Prima la guarda del Papa a cavallo e li svizeri [Guards] a pede con trombe e tamburi; da poi seguitavano li araldi dil Re con le trombe, vestiti a gigli d'oro in campo d'azuro." Sanuto, *I diarii* (full citation given in n. 32), vol. 21, cols. 392–93. The participation of instrumentalists is also noted by Andrea Bernardi, *Cronache Forlivesi*, 2 vols., ed. Giuseppe Mazzatinti (Bologna, 1895–97), vol. 2, p. 428.

46. "Quella dia cantar una messa solenne in San Petronio, et la Majestà dil Re le darà l'acqua a le mano, e vedrasse belle cerimonie." Ibid., col. 383.

47. "Et lendemain au matin le Pape chanta la messe en la plus grande triumphe que jamais pape chanta, car mons[ieu]r le duc de Lorraine et tous les princes du royaulme de France le servoient, et y estoient les chantres du Roy et du Pape,

lesquelz faisoient bon ouyr, car c'estoient deux bonnes chapelles ensambles et chantoient à l'envye." Robert de la Marck, Seigneur de Florange, *Mémoires du Maréchal de Florange, dit le petit aventureux*, 2 vols. (Paris, 1913–24), vol. 1, p. 211. I am grateful to Marianne Waterbury for assistance with the translation of the original French.

48. "Commancea ladicte messe environ midi et fynit à quatre heures du soir." Jean Barrillon, *Journal de Jean Barrillon, secrétaire du Chancelier Duprat 1515–1521*, 2 vols. (Paris, 1897–99), vol. 1, p. 174.

49. On the benefices and graces extended to members of the royal chapel, see Richard Sherr, "The Membership of the Chapels of Louis XII and Anne de Bretagne in the Years Preceding their Deaths," in *Journal of Musicology* 6 (1988): 60–82, especially pp. 66–67, 71, 74, and 77–79.

Ludwig Finscher and I have both argued that the meeting of Francis's and Leo's chapels may account for the appearance of French music in Italian manuscripts dating from the period after the meeting; see Cummings, "Medici Musical Patronage in the Early Sixteenth Century: New Perspectives," in *Studi musicali* 10 (1981): 197–216, especially p. 214 n. 53. See also Lewis Lockwood, "Jean Mouton and Jean Michel: French Music and French Musicians in Italy, 1505–1520," in *Journal of the American Musicological Society* 32 (1979): 191–246, especially pp. 202–4 and 211–17, on the document recording that Mouton gave Michel some motets in October of 1515.

Albert Dunning, *Die Staatsmotette 1480–1555* (Utrecht, 1970), pp. 108–20, discusses the meetings in Bologna (and the political developments that precipitated them) and associates several important polyphonic works with the events: Bruhier's and Mouton's motets *Vivete foelices, Exalta Regina Galliae* and *Exultet coniubilando Dei*. Earlier (p. 47), Dunning had proposed that Isaac's *Quid retribuam tibi* was for Leo's visit to Florence.

50. Shearman, "The Florentine *Entrata*" (full citation given in n. 1), p. 153 n. 61.

51. Paris de Grassis, *De ingressu* (full citation given in n. 16), pp. 26 ("Domenica quarta de Adventu habita est Missa Papalis in Ecclesia Sancti Laurentii Florentiae, quam solitis Ceremoniis cantavit Archiepiscopus Neapolitanus novus Assistens, & non est habitus sermo"), pp. 27–29 ("Missa Major in die Nativitatis Christi Pontifice officium faciente Florentiae. Item dixi Papae, an Canonici preparare debeant Bursellam sicut Canonici Sancti Petri de Urbe, quam donant Pontifici post missam cantatam. . . . Petrutius Cardinalis cantavit Evangelium latinum, Episcopus Nucerinus Graecum, latinam Epistolam cantavit Dom. Hieronymus Senensis, Livius Cubicularius Papae cantavit Graecam, Cardinalis Sanctorum quatuor fuit assistens in sinistra, & nihil unquam principaliter fecit"), and p. 30 ("In die Sancti Stephani. Hanc Missam cantavit Reverendissimus Dominus Cardinalis de Flisco in Ecclesia Sancti Laurentii").

52. See Jeffrey Dean, "The Scribes of the Sistine Chapel, 1501–1527" (Ph.D. dissertation, University of Chicago, 1984). I have listed only those masses that, according to Dean's analysis of the physical characteristics of the Cappella Sistina manuscripts, might have been copied *before* the events of November and December 1515, so as not to beg any questions about what the repertory of the Sistine Chapel might have been at that time.

CHAPTER 6

1. For evidence that Giuliano resided in the Vatican Palace, see Karl Frey, "Zur Baugeschichte des St. Peter," in *Jahrbuch der Preussischen Kunstsammlungen* 31 (1910): supplement, 1–95; 33 (1913): supplement, 1–153; and 37 (1916): supplement, 22–135; especially 31 (1910): 21–22, for example, and elsewhere.

2. Documentary references of various kinds testify to Giuliano's musical interests. That he collected music manuscripts, for example, is clear. In October of 1513, he wrote from Rome to Lorenzo II as follows: "N[ostro] S[igno]re vorrebbe certi miei libri di musica che restorono costi et maxima uno di messe" (for Giuliano's letter and Lorenzo's response, see my study "Medici Musical Patronage in the Early Sixteenth Century: New Perspectives," in *Studi musicali* 10 [1981]: 197–216, especially p. 205). He was, moreover, in possession of two music manuscripts that are still in existence: Vatican City, Biblioteca Apostolica Vaticana, Cappella Giulia XIII. 27 (on which see Allan Atlas, *The Cappella Giulia Chansonnier* [Rome, Biblioteca Apostolica Vaticana, C. G. XIII. 27], 2 vols., Musicological Studies, no. 27 [Brooklyn, 1975]), and Florence, Biblioteca Medicea-Laurenziana, Mediceo Palatino 87, the famous "Squarcialupi Codex" (on the inscription that records Giuliano's ownership—"Si Reverendissimo Cardinali de Medicis Organa Antonii Squarcialupi avi mei grata extitere, non minoris puto fore librum hunc Juliano fratri suo optimo. Vade igitur, liber, et in eiusdem bibliothecam te confer. Meque et meos sibi et familie sue commenda"—see Johannes Wolf, ed., *Der Squarcialupi Codex* [Lippstadt, 1955], unpaginated introduction). That Giuliano may also have made a practice of honoring political figures with gifts of music manuscripts is suggested by documentary evidence that on one occasion, at least, he did so: in January of 1515, he sent a book of music to the king of Portugal (see A. Pellizzari, *Portogallo e Italia nel secolo XVI* [Naples, 1914], pp. 150–51; Pellizzari erroneously identified Giuliano with his cousin Cardinal Giulio; for this reference, I am indebted to Sheryl Reiss. The same text may be found on p. 611 of vol. 2 of the series *As gavetas da Torre do Tombo*, 12 vols. [Lisbon, 1960–77], published by the Centro de Estudos Historicos Ultramarinos; for this reference, I am indebted to Bonnie J. Blackburn and Leofranc Holford Strevens).

Giuliano also wrote letters from Rome to Lorenzo II in Florence on behalf of musicians associated with the Medici family; in May of 1514, for example, he wrote on Isaac's behalf (see Frank D'Accone, "Heinrich Isaac in Florence: New and Unpublished Documents," in *Musical Quarterly* 49 [1963]: 464–83, especially p. 481; and F. Ghisi, *I canti carnascialeschi nelle fonti musicali del XV e XVI secolo* [Florence, 1937], pp. 43–44) and in May of 1515 he wrote on behalf of Alessandro Coppini (see Richard Sherr, "Verdelot in Florence, Coppini in Rome, and the Singer 'La Fiore,'" in *Journal of the American Musicological Society* 37 [1984]: 402–11, especially p. 410).

Giuliano also seems to have maintained a small musical establishment, if a document in the Carte strozziane indeed pertains to him; see the text of the document in Edward E. Lowinsky, ed., *The Medici Codex of 1518*, 3 vols., Monuments of Renaissance Music, vols. 3–5 (Chicago, 1968), vol. 1, p. 32 n. 24, and, for the argument that the document pertains to Giuliano and not to Lorenzo II, as had been assumed, see Richard Sherr, "Lorenzo de' Medici, Duke of Urbino, as a Patron of Music," in *Renaissance Studies in Honor of Craig Hugh Smyth*, 2 vols., ed. Andrew Morrogh et al. (Florence, 1985), vol. 1, pp. 627–38, especially p. 627.

That Giuliano indeed delighted in performances of music is suggested not only by the existence of his small corps of instrumentalists but by references in contemporary correspondence as well, which provide glimpses into his musical experiences; in the Archivio di Stato, Mantua, Archivio Gonzaga, Busta 2993, L. 14, fol. 71^r, for example, is a letter of December 21, 1502 from Isabella d'Este to Francesco Gonzaga, which reads as follows: "Gionsi qui . . . uno Monsignore de Bilocho, francese et homo del nostro Christianissimo Re. . . . essendo heri convidata a cena cum Madonna Francisca Torella, lo condussi meco insieme cum il Magnifico Juliano Medici, quale passando per qui s'è firmato quatro giorni a vedere Mantua. Il spasso che gli ho dato questi dui dì è Marchetto [Cara] e la mogliere, quali meritamente gli sono ultra modo piaciuti." See William Prizer, *Courtly Pastimes: The Frottole of Marchetto Cara* [Ann Arbor, 1980], p. 42. And in November of 1514, Isabella d'Este reported once again on a convivial evening that included musical performances: "Marti el R.^{mo} Mr Cardinale nostro fratello mi fece uno bonissimo disinare a Therme, poi disinare stettimo in grandissima festa con Mons. R.^{mo} de Aragona, S. Maria di Portico, Cornaro et Cibo, li dui M.^{ci} Juliano et Laurentio [de' Medici], sig. Franceschetto [Cibo] et molti altri signori et gentilhomini in canti et suoni de varie sorte." See Alessandro Luzio, "Isabella d'Este nei primordi del papato di Leone X e il suo viaggio a Roma nel 1514–1515," in *Archivio storico lombardo*, 4th ser., 6 (1906): 99–180 and 454–89, especially p. 148.

Finally, I refer the reader to the text and notes of my chapter 2 for material concerning Giuliano's role in organizing the Carnival festivities of 1513, which, as we have seen, involved musical performances, and for evidence that he may have been associated with Serafino Aquilano, one of the premier lutenist-singers of the Quattrocento.

3. On Giuliano's instructions to Lorenzo, see "Instructione al Magnifico Lorenzo," in *Archivio storico italiano*, 1st ser., Appendice, vol. 1 (1842–44): 299–306; and Humfrey Butters, *Governors and Government in Early Sixteenth-Century Florence, 1502–1519* (Oxford, 1985), p. 203 and corresponding n. 93. Information pertaining to Giulio's biography is drawn from Adriano Prosperi, "Clemente VII," in *Dizionario biografico degli italiani*, 32 vols. (Rome, 1960–), vol. 26, pp. 237–59.

4. "A' dì xv d'agosto . . . , el nostro reverendissimi monsignore arcivescovo di Firenze . . . venne e prese la tenuta del suo arcivescovado . . . , con tutti gli ordini e cerimonie che si costuma fare, che fu un trionfo grandissimi et una delle più belle cose che mai più si faciessi a nessuno arcivescovo." See Giuseppe Odoardo Corazzini, ed., *Ricordanze di Bartolomeo Masi, Calderaio fiorentino, dal 1478 al 1526* (Florence, 1906), pp. 132–33.

5. "Ipsum [the archbishop] duxerunt . . . usque in plateam magnificorum Dominorum, ubi supra ringheria erant sedentes excelsi Domini, & Vexillifer Iustitie Reipublice, & Populi Florentini, & ibidem maximo cum sonitu campanarum, tubarum, & aliorum instrumentorum fuit ab eis honorabiliter receptus, & honoratus, & salutatus ex ringhiera predicta a magnifico Iohanne de Bernardis moderno Vexillifero Iustitie Populi Florentini . . . . & cum pervenisset ad lapidem

marmoreum, positum in signum, ubi Beatus Zenobius Episcopus Florentinus mirabiliter excitavit, & seu resuscitavit quemdam puerum mortuum . . . ; decantato a Clero versiculo: Ora pro nobis Beate Zenobi, & responso: Vt digni efficiamur promissionibus Christi: idem Reverendissimus Dominus Archiepiscopus decantavit, & decantando dixit orationem Sancti Zenobii, & postmodum . . . perressit . . . ad Angulum de Pazzis, & ibidem se volvens versus Ecclesiam Florentinam, . . . pervenit ad Ecclesiam Cathedralem Florentie predicte." See Giovanni Lami, *Sanctae Ecclesiae Florentinae Monumenta*, 3 vols. (Florence, 1758), vol. 3, p. 1760. For this reference I am grateful to Sheryl Reiss.

6. "Entrò per la porta del mezzo di santa Maria del Fiore. . . . mentre che v'era l'arcivescovo, si celebrò una solenne Messa, cantando." *Ricordanze di Bartolomeo Masi* (full citation given in n. 4), pp. 132–33.

7. Saint Zanobi also had special meaning for Archbishop Giulio: his name as entered on his baptismal record was "Giulio et Zanobi di Giuliano." Giulio was born on May 26, 1478; the Feast of Saint Zanobi is May 25. For this information I am grateful, once again, to Sheryl Reiss.

8. The manuscripts Florence, BNC, Magl. XIX. 121 (fols. 15^v–16^r) and Banco rari 230 (fols. 134^v–135^r) contain a *canto* on a text by Machiavelli, which opens "Già fumo hor non più spiriti beati." Ghisi (*I Canti carnascialeschi* [Florence, 1937], p. 72; and "Poesie musicali italiane," in *Note d'archivio per la storia musicale* 16 [1939]: 68–73, especially p. 70) argued that the *canto* celebrates Giulio's appointment to the position of archbishop of Florence. However, the print *Laude vecchie e nuove* contains a work, *Già fummo eletti, ed or siam riprovati*, which carries the indication that it is to be sung to the music of a *canto* "de' diavoli," and formal and linguistic characteristics of the text suggest that the indication refers to the music of Machiavelli's *Già fumo hor non più spiriti beati*. The *Laude vecchie e nuove* is undated but was reprinted in Venice in 1512 by Giorgio Rusconi. Since the music for Machiavelli's *canto* was therefore in circulation by that date at the latest, the *canto* cannot have been composed for the occasion that Ghisi cited, which occurred in 1513. See Bonnie J. Blackburn's excellent article "Two 'Carnival Songs' Unmasked: A Commentary on MS Florence Magl. XIX. 121," in *Musica disciplina* 35 (1981): 121–78, especially pp. 129–30 and corresponding nn. 20–22 and the references she cites there. Renato Chiesa, "Machiavelli e la musica," in *Rivista italiana di musicologia* 4 (1969): 3–31, especially p. 8, and, following him, Mario Fabbri (in *Il luogo teatrale a Firenze* [Milano, 1975], p. 75) attributed the music for Machiavelli's *canto* to Alessandro Coppini, on what basis I do not know.

CHAPTER 7

1. "Molte volte il tiranno . . . occupa il popolo in spettacoli e feste," in Massimo Bontempelli, *Il Poliziano, il Magnifico, Lirici del Quattrocento* (Florence, 1917), p. 289.

2. See W. Roscoe, *Vita e pontificato di Leone X*, ed. L. Bossi, 12 vols. (Milan, 1816–17), vol. 5, p. 43, and vol. 6, p. 217; and John Shearman's useful discussion in "The Florentine *Entrata* of Leo X, 1515," in *Journal of the Warburg and Courtauld Institutes* 38 (1975): 136–54, especially p. 154 and corresponding nn. 63–65.

3. See Roscoe, *Vita e pontificato* (full citation given in n. 2), vol. 5, p. 43, and

vol. 6, p. 217: "Hoggi dopo pranzo passegiando Sua Santità et stando a udire cantare si strinsero insieme quella et Monsignori Reverendissimi di ferrara et de Aragona et messer Luigi de rossi et parlando delle cose di Firenze cioè della giostra, triomphi, caccie, et altre feste che si faranno li, Sua Santità mi fece chiamare da M. Luigi et volseno vedere la nota del triompho, et delli capitoli della giostra, che ho avuto di là, et in conclusione si risolverno, che andando li prefati Reverendissimi Ferrara et Aragona ad Loreto, come vanno fra III. dì, di venire ad vedere la festa, et essere li stravestiti, la vigilia di S. Giovanni. . . . con grandissimo desiderio si parlò di quella festa, . . . et in questi ragionamenti si disse, che il Magnifico Juliano anchora lui verrà, ma stravestito." Although I am aware of the methodological risks of doing so, I have translated "nota" as "program," because it is clear that Turini's letter refers to a written document in his possession and that it contains a description of some kind of the forthcoming Triumph of Camillus. For useful discussion on the term "program," I am grateful to Dr. Julian Kliemann of Villa I Tatti, the Harvard University Center for Italian Renaissance Studies in Florence. On Turini, see Claudia Conforti, "Baldassarre Turini da Pescia: Profilo di un committente di Giulio Romano architetto e pittore," in *Quaderni di Palazzo Te* 2 (1985): 35–43. Turini was Lorenzo's *oratore* at the papal court; sometime between the end of February and the middle of March 1514, he received the "commissione ufficiale di oratore," as is suggested by his letter of March 20 to Lorenzo, which also makes clear that he resided in Alfonsina Orsini-Medici's household in Rome—i.e., the Palazzo Madama (Conforti, "Baldassarre Turini da Pescia," p. 39). A portion of the text of the letter (Florence, Archivio di Stato, *fondo* Mediceo avanti il principato, CVII, n. 3) was published by Conforti in "Architettura e culto della memoria: La committenza di Baldassarre Turini datario di Leone X," in *Baldassarre Peruzzi: pittura scena e architettura nel Cinquecento*, ed. Marcello Fagiolo and Maria Luisa Madonna (Rome, 1987), pp. 603–28, especially p. 605.

4. Roscoe, *Vita e pontificato*, vol. 6, p. 221: "Nostro Signore si sta la maggior parte del dì in la stantia sua . . . , aspectando ad la giornata quello si farà lì, dì per dì de quelle feste."

5. Marino Sanuto, *I diarii*, 59 volumes (Venice, 1879–1903), vol. 18, col. 313: "cominzando, Mercoredì, a di 21 Zugno, secondo l'uso anticho, si feze bellissima mostra, e la matina seguente la solita devota processione."

6. Giovanni Cambi, "Istorie," ed. Fr. Ildefonso di San Luigi, 4 vols., *Delizie degli eruditi toscani*, vols. 20–23 (Florence, 1786), vol. 3, pp. 44–45, also describes the procession. For evidence that the musical elements of processions may have included the playing of a portative organ, see Luigi Parigi, *Laurentiana: Lorenzo dei Medici cultore della musica* (Florence, 1954), p. 21 and corresponding n. 22. Bartolomeo Masi's diary contains a long passage that conveys a clearer sense of the musical component for such religious processions, in this instance one that occurred on the occasion of Leo's calling of a crusade against the Turks in 1518: "Andò el bando per tutto Firenze, da parte de' nostri magnifici signiori, . . . come in detta mattina [May 3, 1518] . . . si direbbe la sopradetta Messa [Masi had earlier written that 'si cantò, nella chiesa di santa Maria del Fiore . . . , una solenne Messa'], e che tutto el popolo andassi . . . a udirla, per comandamento . . . del nostro santissimo papa Leone, pregando Iddio che gli dia . . . vettoria contro agli

infideli. E cosi per inpetrare grazia da dio, la santità del Papa ordinò e fecie una solenne procissione nella città di Roma. . . . E cosi ancora in Firenze s'è fatto, questo dì x di maggio mdxviii, . . . una solenne pricissione quanto mai si faciessi in Firenze. . . . [E]ntrò . . . in santa Maria del Fiore, e quivi si cantò, tornato che fu detta procissione, una solenne Messa con moltissimi orazioni, più che non si suole per l'ordinarie Messe. Et a detta procissione non andò altri religiosi che preti secolari, e tutti e frati e monaci di tutti conventi che sono in Firenze e presso a Firenze a tre miglia. . . . e mentre che durò a passare detta procissione, senpre cantorno inni e salmi e cose divote i' lalde di Dio. Et ancora tutte le chiese parrocchiale . . . , a' dì vij a' dì viij del presente mese di maggio, andorno a procissione per tutti e Popoli loro, et accozzavasi insieme una chiesa di priorìa con tutte quelle chiese che gli sono sottoposte, o vo' dire più propinque, come se santo Lorenzo con tutti e sua preti, et ancora tutti e preti che fussino in chiese parrocchiale vicino a detto santo Lorenzo. E dette chiese di priorìa portavano la crocie, e non l'altre, e passavano per tutte le vie di loro Popoli, cantando inni e salmi e cose i' lalde di Dio." *Ricordanze di Bartolomeo Masi, Calderaio Fiorentino, dal 1478 al 1526*, ed. Giuseppe Odoardo Corazzini (Florence, 1906), p. 230. Cambi, in "Istorie," vol. 3, p. 138, also reported on these events and added the further detail that "addì 3 detto . . . la Signoria di Firenze fecie chantare la Messa . . . in S. Maria del Fiore, . . . e chantolla Mess. Francesco di Mess. Tomaxo Minerbetti Arcivescovo nel Reame di Napoli."

7. That the Triumph of Camillus was presented in Piazza della Signoria is suggested by the account published in Filippo di Cino Rinuccini, *Ricordi storici*, ed. Giuseppe Aiazzi (Florence, 1840), p. 180, as quoted in Cesare Guasti, *Le feste di S. Giovanni Batista in Firenze* (Florence, 1908), p. 29: "E in Piazza vi venne da venti Carri trionfali; cosa ricca e magna: e intorno a questi Carri v'era circa a mille cavagli, tutti bene a ordine come San Giorgi." Guasti, in *Le feste*, pp. 30–47, also printed a long poetic account of the festival. The reference to the cardinals' attendance is in Sanuto, *I diarii* (full citation given in n. 5): "concoreva tutto el populo e quanti forestieri vi si trovava, che da Roma ce n'è assai, fra quelli 7 cardinali, zoè [Marco] Cornaro [i.e., Cornelius], [Bandinello] Sauli, [Bernardo Dovizi da] Bibiena, [Ippolito d'Este da] Ferara, [Innocenzo] Cibo, [Alfonso Petrucci da] Siena et [Luigi d'A]Ragona e il nostro magnifico confaloniero di Santa Chiexia [Giuliano de' Medici]."

8. Sanuto, ibid.: "La matina seguente, che fu Venerdì, a dì 23, secondo l'anticho costume furon fate le nuvole overo hedificii, rappresentando prima quando Dio cazò Luzifero e soi seguazi dal cielo." The term *edifici* refers to wheeled platforms that bore individuals who represented allegorical figures and who on occasion enacted quasi-dramatic scenes; see Joseph J. Gallucci, Jr., "Festival Music in Florence, ca. 1480–ca. 1520," 2 vols. (Ph.D. dissertation, Harvard University, 1966), vol. 1, pp. 12–20.

9. John Shearman, "Correggio's Illusionism," in *La prospettiva rinascimentale: Codificazioni e trasgressioni*, vol. 1, ed. Marisa Dalai Emiliani (Florence, 1980), pp. 281–94, especially p. 292.

10. Sanuto, *I diarii* (full citation given in n. 5), cols. 313–14: "e per l'ultimo el vivo e'l morto. . . . E non vo' lassar de dirvi che, inanzi a questa rapresentatione, havemo avanti a questa una moresca durante non mancho de una hora; fu bella

quanto mai fusse veduta. Hora non so da che capo mi fare a dire quello che la sera havemo, cossa veramente giamai non più veduta, rapresentando il triumfo di Camillo, qual furono 17 cari, over triumphi. Prima ne veniva un caro di scale, lanterne e altri simili instrumenti da sforzar una città, e apresso uno altro caro di rotele, pavesi e molte arme predate da i nimici; di poi uno ariete che antichamente usavano ad abater le mure, ch'era bello e ornato hedificio. Seguiva ancora un caro dove era sopra una ocha, che fu causa che romani sentirono lo [Gauls'] scalare del Capitolio. Apresso a questi seguiva 11 cari, che significavano di diversi atti di questo triumphante Camillo: quale era caricho di veste, qual era caricho di argento, qual di presoni, qual di arme, e tutte erano spoglie de i nimici, ma tanto bene ornati e abiliati. . . . Seguiva apresso questi più eminente e magior caro più che tutti gli altri ornatissimo, di pregioni armati e belissime spoglie, tirato da 4 para di boy. . . . Venivano drieto a questi circha 200 cavali, ch'era da 80 homeni d'arme compartiti per hordine benissimo in tre parte, ch'eran tre compagnie che hanno di poi servito a la zostra, e con bellissime hordine tenivano lungo spazio. Et erami scordato che, intorno al primo caro di scale, eran 100 maragioli, over guastatori . . . ; apresso poi a la gente d'arme con loro stendardi e ogni arnese necessario. Seguiva 50 a piedi vestiti tutti di panno azuro con certe arme di legno, con certi fassi di verge d'oro a quelle aste ligate in capeglii con girlande de lauro in testa. Ultimamente ne veniva, sopra un più che ogni altro grande triumpho, el victorioso Camillo, sopra quale triumpho erano e cantori cantando."

11. The reference to the "festaiuoli" is in the account in Rinuccini, *Ricordi storici* (full citation given in n. 7); Vasari's reference to Granacci and Nardi is in *Lives of the Most Eminent Painters, Sculptors, and Architects*, trans. Gaston Du C. de Vere, 3 vols. (New York, 1979), vol. 2, p. 1211. On other evocations of the Camillus allegory in Florentine art and literature, see Janet Cox-Rearick, *Dynasty and Destiny in Medici Art* (Princeton, 1984), pp. 35–36 and corresponding n. 79, and pp. 239 and 253.

12. *LE DECHE DI T. LIVIO, PADOVANO, DELLE HISTORIE ROMANE, Tradotte nella lingua Toscana, da M. IACOPO NARDI cittadino Fiorentino,* . . . (Venice, 1562).

13. Nardi's translation (*LE DECHE*, fol. 102ᵛ) reads as follows: "fu huomo vnico . . . : il primo in pace, & in guerra, . . . o pel desiderio, che di lui hebbe la città: laqual essendo suta presa, . . . o ver per la felicità: p[er] laqual restituito alla patria, esso la medesima patria seco restitui. Fu poi pari al titolo, . . . & fu giudicato degno d'esser dopo Romolo, chiamato il secondo edificatore della città di Roma." My English translation of the original Latin is taken from *Livy*, trans. B. O. Foster, vol. 3(New York, 1924), p. 359.

14. See Alammani's "Discorso" in Rudolf von Albertini, *Firenze dalla repubblica al principato* (Turin, 1970), pp. 376–84, especially p. 380: "potendo epsa . . . rendersi pare ad qualunche delli antichi et de' moderni, vorrà piú presto giostrare con Cesare et Camillo che con lo impio Agathocle, col crudelissimi Sylla et con lo scelerato Liverocto da Fermo." For more on the Camillus allegory, see Kurt W. Forster, "Metaphors of Rule: Political Ideology and History in the Portraits of Cosimo I de' Medici," in *Mitteilungen des Kunsthistorischen Institutes in Florenz* 15 (1971): 65–104, especially p. 73.

15. For Lorenzo's letter to Pandolfini, see A. Giorgetti, "Lorenzo de' Medici, Duca d'Urbino, e Jacopo d'Appiano," in *Archivio storico italiano*, 4th ser., 8 (1881):

222–38 and 305–25, especially p. 236: "narrando et leggendo loro et interpretando ad che fine sia facto questo triompho . . . , che in facto non allude se non alla cacciata et dipoi alla revocatione della casa de' Medici." See also Julian Kliemann, "Politische und humanistische Ideen der Medici in der Villa Poggio a Caiano" (Ph.D. dissertation, Ruprecht-Karl-Universität, Heidelberg, 1976), pp. iii–12 n. 131; and Cox-Rearick, *Dynasty and Destiny*, p. 36 n. 82. For the evocation of the suggestion that the Medici were recalled from exile, see John Shearman, *Raphael's Cartoons in the Collection of Her Majesty the Queen and the Tapestries for the Sistine Chapel* (London, 1972), p. 85. Turini's letter ("El quale triumpho, per essere contra Franzesi, è stato di quà notato da alchuno homo da bene, et detto che è da advertirci per rispecto de' Franzesi, che sono molto sensitivi, et quando V. S. lo potessi mutare, o subtacere il nome, non sarebbe male; quella è prudentissima, et credo haverà ben pensato tutto; questo gli ho detto, perchè Monsignore Reverendissimo di Ferrara me ne ha advertito questa mattina, che dice cognoscere in qualche parte la natura Gallica. Io ne ho detto con Monsignore Reverendissimo nostro, et anchora lui dice, che quando si potessi mutare, non sarebbe male; tamen tutto sia rimesso ad la prudentia di V. S.") is in Roscoe *Vita e pontificato* (full citation given in n. 2), vol. 6, no. 113. On the theme expressed in the title of chapter 26 of *The Prince*, see, most recently, Sebastian de Grazia's stimulating biography of Machiavelli, *Machiavelli in Hell* (Princeton, 1989), pp. 30, 152, and 348. Professor J. R. Hale reminds me that Machiavelli's *Prince* was not published until considerably later; nonetheless, it had recently been composed and its evocation of the theme reflected in the title of chapter 26 is therefore an expression of contemporary political concerns.

16. My edition of the *canto* text is taken directly from Riccardo Bruscagli, ed., *Trionfi e canti carnascialeschi toscani del Rinascimento*, 2 vols. (Rome, 1986), vol. 1, pp. 74–75; see Bruscagli's notes for an explication of various references.

17. The MS Florence, Biblioteca Riccardiana, Ed.r.196, contains a *lauda* text (fol. 5^r [= fol. 121^r]), "Vergine gloriosa in ciel beata," accompanied by the rubric "Di messer Castellano [Castellani] sopra la Canzona del triompho di Camillo"; see Giuseppe Corsi, "Laude di Castellano Castellani," in *Giornale storico della letteratura italiana* 150 (1973): 68–76, especially p. 73 and corresponding n. 21. It is an instance, therefore, of the common practice of using the same music for secular and sacred (if nonliturgical) texts. Giulio Cattin ("Musiche per le laude di Castellano Castellani," in *Rivista italiana di musicologica* 12 [1977]: 183–230, especially pp. 202–3) remarked on the formal and structural affinities between the *lauda* text and the text of the anonymous *trionfo* "delle tre Parche," for which there is a musical setting preserved in MS Florence, BNC, Banco rari 230 (fol. 90^v). If Cattin is correct, it may be that the musical setting for the *Trionfo delle tre Parche* also served for Nardi's *canto* for the 1514 Feast of San Giovanni. Without contemporary evidence that the music for the *trionfo* "delle tre Parche" indeed served for the *lauda* text, however, I would be reluctant to advance an argument that it also served for the text of Nardi's *canto* for the Triumph of Camillus, based, as such an argument would be, on inferences about formal affinities among the texts.

18. "Et Li S[ignori] fecion fare feste et giostre in su le quali si trovò Giuliano con saione di broccato, et così Lorenzo con tanta festa quanto fu possibile, et fecesi una caccia dove fu di ogni spezie d'animali et due lioni, et tutto si fe' ris-

petto a' signori che vennero da Roma e sei cardinali travestiti." Bartolomeo Cerretani, "Sommario et ristretto cavato dalla historia . . . , in dialogo delle cose di
Firenze," BNC, Firenze, MS II. IV. 19, fol. 27ᵛ. Three of the other narrative accounts (Sanuto, *I diarii* [full citation given in n. 5], Cambi, "Istorie" [full citation
given in n. 6], and Luca Landucci, *Diario fiorentino dal 1450 al 1516*, ed. Iodoco del
Badia [Florence, 1883], pp. 345–48) provide considerably fuller information than
does Cerretani about the concluding festivities that took place on subsequent
days. Because those festivities did not include musical elements, however, they are
less important for my purposes here and I have opted, therefore, to provide Cerretani's abbreviated account.

CHAPTER 8

1. Francesco Bausi, "Politica e poesia: il 'Lauretum,'" in *Interpres* 6 (1985–86):
214–82, especially p. 224 n. 23.

2. Marino Sanuto, *I diarii*, 59 volumes (Venice, 1879–1903), vol. 20, cols. 530–
31: "'Copia litterarum datae Florentiae die XIII Augusti 1515.' Heri se fece qui la
monstra de la compagnia e gente d'arme del signor magnifico Lorentio, in la
quale fu observato questo ordine in gran parte, *videlicet*; fu ordinato che tre volte
in diverse horo li trombetti andasseno sonando per la terra, *videlicet* una avanti
giorno, che significava [that the following day] ogni homo mettersi in hordine, . . . che se montasse a cavallo, . . . [and] che tutte le gente fussero in ordinanza unite tutte in uno loco deputato. . . . che è el templo de San Marco, non
molto sopra la casa de epsi [i.e., Lorenzo II]. . . . tutti in ordinanza se transferirno
in piaza ove se sentivano gran sonari de artegliare, trombe, et campane, et voce
universale dicente: 'Palle, palle!' Erano questi . . . signori in residentia in la ren-
giera a piede de le scale fori del palazo, et smontato el signor Magnifico prefato fra
el Confaloniero et uno altro de' signori, dove audirno una oratione fatta da
missier Marcello secretario primo de loro signorie. . . . *Qua expedita*, el confaloniero dette lo stendardo, elmetto, uno cavallo et il bastone al signore Magnifico."

3. For the report of the Venetian envoy, see Eugenio Alberi, ed., *Relazioni
degli Ambasciatori veneti al Senato*, 2d ser., vol. 3 (Florence, 1846), pp. 52–53:
"questo Lorenzino è stato fatto capitano dei Fiorentini contro le loro leggi, che
non permettono che alcun Fiorentino sia capitano. . . . Egli si è fatto signor di
Fiorenza; egli ordina ed è obedito. Si imbossolava; ora non si fa più; quello che
commanda Lorenzino è fatto. . . . Sicchè alla più parte dei Fiorentini non piace la
potenza di questa casa dei Medici." My translation is based in part on J. R. Hale's;
see his *Florence and the Medici: The Pattern of Control* (London, 1978), p. 99. On
Giulio's ceremonial *entrata* on the thirteenth, see Sanuto, *I diarii* (full citation
given in the preceding note), col. 532. The entry in the *Libro ceremoniale* of the
herald of the Signoria, Angelo di Lorenzo Manfidi da Poppi, furnishes a few interesting details about music performed on the occasion of Cardinal Giulio's visit
to Florence in mid-August: "A dì XV d'agosto . . . , che fu el dì della Donna, la
reverendissima signoria del legato [i.e., Giulio] e così la excelsa Signoria andorono alla messa in Santa Reperata che fu solenne, la quale cantò el vescovo de'
Pagagniotti. L'ordine dello andare fu questo. Parechi tavolaccini innanzi. Dipoi

e tronbetti che ci erano, perchè parte ne era a Siena alla festa. Dipoi quattro donzelli, apresso e pifferi." There followed the granting of gifts to the Signoria's instrumentalists: "A 6 pifferi cioè prima e tronbetti ducati dodici" and "A 8 tronbetti ducati dodici et ½." See Richard Trexler, ed., *Francesco Filarete and Angelo Manfidi, The Libro Cerimoniale of the Florentine Republic* (Geneva, 1978), pp. 120–21. Sheryl Reiss suggested to me that the sketch reproduced here as figure 28 may have been for an element of the ephemeral decoration for Archbishop Giulio's ceremonial entry.

4. The phrase is Hale's; see *Florence and the Medici* (full citation given in the preceding note) p. 87.

5. Humfrey Butters, *Governors and Government in Early Sixteenth-Century Florence* (Oxford, 1985), pp. 276–78.

6. Giovanni Cambi, "Istorie," ed. Fr. Idelfonso di San Luigi, 4 vols., in *Delizie degli eruditi toscani*, vols. 20–23 (Florence, 1786), vol. 3, p. 99: "Giovedì a' dì di 5. di Giugnio ci fu in Firenze la presa di Urbino con tutte sua Chastella, salvo lavere, elle persone el Signore se ne fuggi. Il lunedì mattina la Signoria di Firenze andorono a hoferta cho' Chollegi, e Otto di Praticha a S. Maria del Fiore, e chantorono una bella Messa dello Spirito Santo."

7. Giuseppe Odoardo Corazzini, ed., *Ricordanze di Bartolomeo Masi, Calderaio Fiorentino, dal 1478 al 1526* (Florence, 1906), p. 205: "a dì xxv detto [i.e., of June], si andò per Firenze, . . . dieci trionfi, . . . et insu l'utimo trionfo v'era [performed] uno canto, che dichiarava la similtudine . . . : [cioè] che detti difizi erono fatti in lalde del signore Lorenzo de' Medici." Cesare Guasti, *Le feste di S. Giovanni Batista in Firenze* (Florence, 1908), pp. 50–58, printed records of payments made to various individuals for their contributions to the festivities, which serve to substantiate Masi's account; among the payments are the following, which record the participation of Baccio degli Organi, one of the foremost Florentine composers of the time, who perhaps was being paid for having composed the musical setting of the explanatory *canto*, and of the *pifferi* and trumpeters of the Signoria: "Stephano Tomasii, miniatori, pro carris XI, pro triunphis et cantoribus, libras mille quatuorcentas triginta quinque piccioli. . . . L. 1435 s.—d.—Ac etiam quod solvat Bartholomeo degli Orghani libras octuaginta quatuor. . . . 84 s.—d.—Ac etiam stantiaverunt quod solvat Pifferis Palatii libras octo et solidos octo piccioli. . . . 8 s. 8 d.—Ac etiam solvat Trombettis libras septem piccioli. . . . 7 s.—d.—"

8. I have transcribed the text from the manuscript source. My transcription differs in some respects from Bausi's (see the reference in n. 1 to this chapter); I welcome the opportunity to thank Dott. Gino Corti for checking it. As Bausi observed (p. 233 n. 48), the text is also found in the manuscript Florence, Biblioteca riccardiana, 2731, where it is attributed to Guglielmo Angiolini. Charles Singleton, who did not collate the redaction in Magliabechi VII, 1041, published the poem as Angiolini's in *Canti carnascialeschi del Rinascimento* (Bari, 1936), pp. 223–24; Riccardo Bruscagli, following Singleton, recently republished the poem as Angiolini's (*Trionfi e canti carnascialeschi del Rinascimento*, 2 vols. [Rome, 1986], vol. 1, pp. 44–46). I am inclined to agree with Bausi's thesis that it is Nardi's poem, in part for the reason he advances—that it is found in MS Magl. VII, 1041 with two other *canti* whose attributions to Nardi are not in doubt—and also for

the reason I advance in the text—that it contains a reference reminiscent of another of Nardi's literary efforts: on the earlier use of the image employed in line 45, see lines 25–32 of the prologue to *I due felici rivali* in the version of MS Florence, BNC, Magl. VII. 1131, as edited in Luigina Stefani, *Tre commedie fiorentine del primo 500* (Ferrara and Rome, 1986), pp. 5–6 and pp. 64–65 nn. to lines 25–32; see also n. 31 to my chapter 2. As Giulio Cattin observed in "I 'cantasi come' in una stampa di laude della Biblioteca riccardiana (Ed. r. 196)," in *Quadrivium* 19 (1978): 5–52, especially pp. 25–26, there are structural affinities between *Pose natura* and the *lauda Madre del sommo ben Gesù*, which suggest that the music for the one may have served for the other; unfortunately, however, there is not known to be an extant musical setting for the *lauda* text.

9. Bausi, "Politica e poesia." Moreover, the second *canzona* refers to a *duca*, and since Lorenzo was not formally invested with the title until August 18, 1516 (see Butters, *Governors and Government* [full citation given in n. 5], p. 278), Bausi's thesis that the two *canzone* date from after the reconquest may well be the correct one. I take the liberty of including the entire text of the *canzona* "del frate de' Servi," which is replete with Medicean conceits; it was clearly intended to accompany a procession of *carri*: see the reference to "L'ultimo carro" in the sixth strophe. I am very grateful to Gino Corti for the transcription: "Hoggi iubila el cielo con gran letitia / qual tu, Fiorenza, in terra / poiché per tuo [*sic*] virtù, senno e militia, / di catena si sferra / la tanto stata in servitù iustitia. / Hay gloriosa guerra / per il cui sancto e salubre restauro / iustitia in ciel triumpha e in terra el lauro. [second strophe] L'arbore offesa sì dalla saeta / per invidia e livore / d'arbore antiqua or facta arbore electa, / stilla dolce liquore. / El mel ch'l troncho del sancto arborgetta, / mostra drento e di fiore / lei ben per mal pietosamente rendere / a chi l'offese o a chi la volse offendere. [third strophe] Colei che segue al grande arbore apresso / è la virtù victrice, / la genuflexa e col volto dimesso / è fortuna infelice /ch'a llei s'arrende e dello error commesso / humil sua colpa dice / e giura di tener per sempre a ghalla / la già da lei sì rotolata palla. [fourth strophe] El lauro nel vexillo fighurato / fra nugoli e 'l sereno, / mostra che chi l'à già rotto e sfrondato / mentre bel tempo avieno, / poi ne' bisogni lor che el ciel turbato / sotto a lui ricorrieno, / lui generosamente ogniuno achoglie / alla sacra ombra delle sue sancte foglie. [fifth strophe] El degno duca che in arme si splende / tra vivi e morti armati, / mostra che morte per suplicio rende / a' superbi obstinati, / e suplici subietti in favor prende / da lui poi vezeggiati, / el che par che gran gloria al duca serbi, /clemente agli umili, rigido a' superbi. [sixth strophe] L'ultimo carro spargie ognior texoro / come fa l'acque un fiume, / che' 'l gentil sangue del sacrato alloro /sempre hebbe per costume / largho far gratie e largo spargier l'oro. / El regnante oggi nume / gli antici avanza in versar l'oro in terra, / che tutto il mondo in la sua palla serra."

1. Francesco Vettori, "Sommario della storia d'Italia dal 1511 al 1527," in *Archivio storico italiano*, 1st ser., Appendice, vol. 6 (1848): 259–387, especially p. 327: "Il Papa, . . . cercò di fare una buona e solida amicizia con Francesco re di Francia. . . . [F]ece praticare che Lorenzo togliesse moglie in Francia."

2. On the "Medici Codex," see (for the thesis that it was Francois Ier's gift to Lorenzo) Edward E. Lowinsky, "The Medici Codex, A Document of Music, Art, and Politics in the Renaissance," in *Annales musicologiques* 5 (1957): 61–178; idem, ed., *The Medici Codex of 1518: A Choirbook of Motets Dedicated to Lorenzo de' Medici, Duke of Urbino*, 3 vols., Monuments of Renaissance Music, vols. 3–5 (Chicago, 1968); and idem, "On the Presentation and Interpretation of Evidence: Another Review of Costanzo Festa's Biography," in *Journal of the American Musicological Society* 30 (1977): 106–28; and (for the much more plausible thesis that it was Leo's gift to Lorenzo) Joshua Rifkin, "Scribal Concordances for Some Renaissance Manuscripts in Florentine Libraries," in ibid., 26 (1973): 306–9, especially p. 306; David Crawford, "A Review of Costanzo Festa's Biography," in ibid., 28 (1975): 102–11; Ludwig Finscher's review of Edward E. Lowinsky, ed., *The Medici Codex*, in *Die Musikforschung* 30 (1977): 468–81; Lewis Lockwood, "Jean Mouton and Jean Michel: New Evidence on French Music and Musicians in Italy," in *Journal of the American Musicological Society* 32 (1979): 191–246, especially pp. 241–46; Leeman Perkins's review of Edward E. Lowinsky, ed., *The Medici Codex*, in *Musical Quarterly* 55 (1969): 255–69; idem, ed., Johannes Lheritier, *Opera omnia*, Corpus mensurabilis musicae, vol. 48 (n.p., 1969), pp. xli–xlii; and Martin Staehelin's review of Edward E. Lowinsky, ed., *The Medici Codex*, in *Journal of the American Musicological Society* 33 (1980): 575–87. There were other reflections of the event in the "written tradition," as Albert Seay suggested: see "Two Datable Chansons from an Attaignant Print," in ibid., 26 (1973): 326–28.

3. Francesco Bausi, "Politica e poesia: il 'Lauretum,'" in *Interpres* 6 (1985–86): 214–82, especially p. 228.

4. "Sommario et ristretto cavato dalla historia di Bartolomeo Cerretani, scritta da lui, in dialogo delle cose di Firenze, dal'anno 1494 al 1519," Florence, BNC, MS II. IV. 19, fols. 49^v–50^v: "Et havemo nouve [August 18, 1518] Lorenzo d'Urbino de' Medici, Duca et Cap[itan]o nostro, essere giunto in Lombardia con la donna, il che causò che M[adonn]a Alfonsina, con otto capi del governo, pensorono honorarli et grandeme[n]te et dettono questa cura agl'Otto di Pratica, i quali, p[er] loro ministri, ordinorono armeggierie e feste e tutte quelle cose che si solevan fare p[er] San Giovanni. Feciono un palco avanti la porta del palagio, largo quanto la via, lungo quanto la casa, alto braccia tre, con le tende di sop[r]a, apparato con arazzerie et sedie splendidamente et così l'entrata e la loggia riccamente, et p[er] fare i conviti destinorno la corte e loggia de melaranci, la quale con fregi et armi, et arazzi e tende sopra mirabilmente feciono bella, massime la loggia verde dove si destinò fare le commedie. In mentre che i conviti si facevano invitossi cento trenta fanciulle non maritate da' 15 in 26 anni, delle quali ne hebbono cinquanta con Madonna Alfonsina alla porta a riscievere la sposa in sul palchetto." Several items call for comment. Cerretani's term *armeggerie* refers to staged military maneuvers that men performed outside the houses of the women whom they were courting; see Joseph J. Gallucci, Jr., "Festival Music in Florence, ca. 1480–ca. 1520," 2 vols. (Ph.D. dissertation, Harvard University, 1966), vol. 1, pp. 12–20. I assume the "loggia de melaranci" (or "loggia verde"), which Cerretani specified as one of the sites of the *conviti*, refers to the *loggia* in the garden of the *palazzo*, as is also suggested by the text of Alfonsina Orsini Medici's letter of September 8, on which see n. 9 to this chapter and the corresponding text, in which she specified

that one of the *conviti*, at least, took place in the garden (for useful discussion on this point, I am grateful to Dr. Christine Sperling of Bloomsburg University of Pennsylvania, my fellow *borsista* during the 1989–90 academic year at Villa I Tatti, and to Dr. Wolfger Bulst of the Kunsthistorisches Institut in Florence). Cerretani's text seems to distinguish the courtyard from two *logge*: the "loggia de melaranci" (or "verde") and another, otherwise unidentified *loggia* ("et così l'entrata e la loggia"), and his pairing of the terms *entrata* and *loggia* may signify that he had in mind the *loggia* on the corner of the Vie de' Gori and Cavour, traditionally said to have been reconstructed according to Michelangelo's design the preceding year; does Cerretani's text permit us to argue that the traditional dating is in error and that in 1518 the *loggia* still existed in its original state? On the dating, see James Ackerman, *The Architecture of Michelangelo* (Baltimore, 1970), p. 307 and plate 32. Finally, on the term *braccio* (plural *braccia*) and its metric equivalent, see Wolfger Bulst, "Die Ursprüngliche Innere Aufteilung des Palazzo Medici in Florenz," in *Mitteilungen des Kunsthistorischen Institutes in Florenz* 14 (1970): 369–92, especially p. 374 n. 14.

5. Marino Sanuto, *I diarii*, 59 volumes (Venice, 1879–1903), vol. 26, col. 19: "De qui sono partiti [September 4] per Fiorenza li reverendissimi cardinali [Luigi de'] Rossi et [Innocenzo] Cibo con molti altri cortesani per ritrovarsi a questa solenità; i qual sono soi [Lorenzo's] parenti stretissimi."

6. Cerretani, MS Florence, BNC, II. IV. 19, fols. 49ᵛ–50ᵛ: "Alli 25 d'agosto 1518 giunse il Duca in Firenze et lasciò la donna in Cafaggiuolo, dove andorono tutte le parente e parenti stretti a visitarla. E addì 4 di [settem]bre n'andorono tutti al Poggio a Caiano dove era adornamente come d'un paradiso." Obviously, Lorenzo's relatives who resided in Rome and departed from there on the fourth of September (see the preceding note) were not among those who visited Madeleine on the twenty-fifth of August and the fourth of September.

7. MS Florence, BNC, II. I. 313 (Magl. XXV. 17), "La Città di Firenze," fols. 117ᵛ–118ʳ: "la moglie del Duca fece la sua entrata in firenze a hore 22 p[er] la porta al Prato, 'sendosi posata a' un' munistero discosto dalla città dua miglia. [Her entourage] Entrò con questo hordine, cioè: prima, pochi sua carriaggi, di poi 300 cavalli che erano Arcivescovi, vescovi, Protonotarii, Canonici, il Rettore dello Studio, Cavalieri, Dottori, et altri gentilhuomini vecchi e giovani, di poi tutti e soldati tra quali il sig[no]r Giampaolo Baglioni, Vitello Vitelli, il Sig[no]r Renzo da Ceri [a member of the Orsini family], Orsini assai et altri sig[no]ri in quantità, dipoi e parenti et affini di casa Medici." The virtually verbatim dependence of portions of the text of this manuscript on Cerretani's makes it clear that one of the author's sources was Cerretani's history, although I have found no acknowledgment to that effect in the manuscript itself.

8. Cerretani, MS Florence, BNC, II. IV. 19, fols. 49ᵛ–50ᵛ, collated with the corresponding passage of Cerretani's history in MSS Florence, BNC II. I. 106 and II. I. 313: "sei Donzelle sua, e pochissimi gentilhuomini venuti con lei doppo i quali ne veniva in mezo a dua Cardinali [Cibo and Rossi] con 40 giovani di case nobile alla staffa con veste alla Tedescha di raso pavonazzo, giubbone di chermisi, tocche rosate con immagine doro e riccamente a hordine, e dietro un numero innumerabile di cavalli. Drento alla porta in su un carro era un Ulivo con quantità

di suoni." I am uncertain how to interpret the reference to the "Ulivo"; presumably, it refers simply to the decoration of the *carro* that bore the instrumentalists whose music accompanied the procession, and, to interpret its imagery conventionally, it may have been intended to symbolize the state of diplomatic relations between Florence and France, of which Lorenzo's and Madeleine's marriage was a manifestation.

9. MS Florence, BNC, II. I. 313 (full citation given in n. 7): "Adi 8 di sett[emb]re 1518 si fece il convito a 70 fanciulle servite da detti giovani e doppo desinare vennono in sul Palco che era fatto nella via dinanzi al Palagio sotto le tende dove si ballò t[u]t[t]o il di presente il popolo."

10. "Ser Jo[anni]. . . . vennero questa mactina tucte le fanciulle invitate che havevano acceptato, et tucte benissimo abbigliate, et circa alle XVIII hore e mezzo andorono a tavola nel Giardino, et la Duchessa con loro, ma in quella [north] testa di sopra riscontro alla loggia in mezo delli due Reverendissimi, et el Duca di fuori, riscontro. Et si empierono tucte le quattro faccie del giardino. Levoronsi di tavola circa alle XX hore, et ritiratesi parte in camera della salecta et parte nella camera riscontro, et parte ancora qua su in camera mia; quasi tucte si mutorono di veste, tucte bellissime. . . . Andorono fuori su el palco alle XXI hore, dove danzorono fine alle XXIII hore, et la Duchessa anche lei ballò dua danze, una col Duca, l'altra col Maiordomo [Francesco Vettori]. Et veramente questo dì si è passato molto allegramente. Et Dio ci ha serviti d'una tempo bellissimo, et con tanta satisfactione dello universale che non ve lo potrò dire. Et veramente ci è stato tanto el popolo, per le finestre, per li tecti, per le strade, per li palchetti che si erano facti in ogni luogo donde si poteva vedere, che non vi imagineresti mai mai la metà. Et alle XXIIII se ne entrorono nelle camere a riposarsi un poco, et a una meza hora di nocte si cominciò la comedia, detta, falargho, quale è stata molto bene recitata, et con bellissimo apparato. . . . Finita la comedia et riposatesi alquanto in camera andorono a tavola tucte le fanciulle di questa mactina, et la Duchessa con loro et dopo cena non habbiamo voluto che si balli. . . . Hovvi a dire che la Pictura [by Raphael] di N. S. et Monsignor reverendissimo de' Medici, et Rossi, el Duca la fece mectere sopra alla tavola, dove mangiava la Duchessa et li altri signori, in mezo, che veramente rallegrava ogni cosa. Bene valete. Florentiae, die VIII septembris 1518. Alfonsina de' Medici Ursina." I have taken the text of Alfonsina's famous letter from Alessandro Parronchi, "La prima rappresentazione della Mandragola," in *La bibliofilia* 64 (1962): 37–62, especially pp. 52–53. In Sergio Bertelli and Piero Innocenti, *Bibliografia Machiavelliana* (Verona, 1979), pp. xxii and corresponding n. 2, the comedy to which Alfonsina referred is identified as Giovanni Manenti's *Philargio*, on the basis of a passage in Sanuto, *I diarii* (full citation given in n. 5), vol. 37, cols. 559–60: several "savii dil Consejo andono a veder provar una comedia . . . , di la qual è autor Zuan Manenti. . . . Et fo principiada a hore 24; duroe fino a le 6. Fo 9 intermedii, et tre comedie per una fiata in prosa per Zuan Manenti, ditta Philargio et Trebia et Fidel." The identification is made more plausible by evidence that suggests an association between the Venetian Manenti and Machiavelli (see Manenti's letter to Machiavelli of February 28, 1526, published in Niccolò Machiavelli, *Opere*, ed. Franco Gaeta, vol. 3 (Turin, 1984), pp. 575–77. In "Angelo Beolco da Ruzante a Perduoçimo," in *Lettere ita-*

liane 20 (1968): 121–200, especially p. 137 and corresponding n. 78, Giorgio Padoan offered an emended reading of the passage in Sanuto, on which basis he argued that the reference is to a single comedy, properly entitled *Philargio et Trebia et Fidel*: "Fo 9 intermedii et tre comedie, per una fata in prosa per Zuan Manenti, ditta 'Philargio et Trebia et Fidel.'" On Manenti, see Emilio Lovarini, *Studi sul Ruzzante e la letteratura pavana*, ed. Gianfranco Folena (Padua, 1965), p. 90. It would seem that Alfonsina's account lends itself to the following interpretation: Madeleine was seated facing the *loggia* that formed the south wall of the garden of Palazzo Medici, the wall that bordered on Via de' Gori and faced the Church of San Giovannino degli Scolopi. Lorenzo was seated across the table from her, with his back to the *loggia*. If other tables were indeed placed against the four walls of the garden, and if Cerretani was correct in identifying the garden *loggia* as the site for some of the theatrical performances, the tables against the *loggia* would have been removed for the performances, certainly. On the portrait of Leo, Giulio, and Luigi de' Rossi displayed on the occasion of the banquet, see, most recently, Richard Sherr, "A New Document Concerning Raphael's Portrait of Leo X," in *Burlington Magazine* 125 (1983): 31–32. Sherr observed that a letter of September 2, 1518 from Benedetto Buondelmonti in Rome to Goro Gheri in Florence suggests that the portrait was painted expressly for the purpose of being displayed at the banquet.

11. MS Florence, BNC, II. I. 313 (full citation given in n. 7): "A di 9 detto si fece il convito a tutto lo stato, et amici nobili che furno 130 cittadini de primi i quali desinato che hebbono et fatto una bellissima commedia furno licentiati. A di 10 detto si convitò e parenti, e fecessi una belliss[im]a commedia, [and] balli, suoni, et altri piaceri."

12. Sanuto, *I diarii* (full citation given in n. 5): "Sono *etiam* stà mandati tutti li buffoni che in Roma si ritrovavano, et tra li altri è andato Cherea per far comedie, per ornare tanto più la festa." Pirrotta, *Music and Theater*, p. 40 n. 9, argued that Cherea was "the man most instrumental in establishing the custom of performing comedies in Venice. In Fracasso's home, on the Giudecca, in 1513, 'was demonstrated a certain shepherds' comedy, by his chancellor Cherea [fu fato certa demonstratione di comedia di pastori per il suo Cherea],' as Marin Sanudo, *Diarii*, vol. xv (Venice 1889), p. 531, reports." For further witness to Cherea's professional activity, see, again, Sanuto, *I diarii*, vol. 32 (Venice, 1892), col. 458, a reference that attests a performance of Machiavelli's *Mandragola* on February 13, 1522 ("In questa sera, a li Crosechieri fo recitata una altra comedia in prosa, per Cherea luchese e compagni, di uno certo vechio dotor fiorentino che havea una moglie, non potea far fioli etc. Vi fu assaissima zente con intermedii di Zuan Pollo e altri bufoni, e la scena era piena di zente, che non fu fato il quinto atto, perchè non si potè farlo, tanto era il gran numero di le persone"; see also Sergio Bertelli, "When Did Machiavelli Write *Mandragola*?" in *Renaissance Quarterly* 24 [1971]: 317–26, especially p. 317 and corresponding n. 3); Pirrotta, *Music and Theater*, p. 94; and, above all, Alessandro d'Ancona, *Origini del teatro italiano*, 2 vols. (Torino, 1891), vol. 2, pp. 111–22.

13. Vasari, *Lives of the Most Eminent Painters, Sculptors, and Architects*, 3 vols., trans. Gaston Du C. de Vere (New York, 1979), vol. 2, p. 1121, and vol. 3, pp. 1610 and 1666. John Shearman, in *Andrea del Sarto*, 2 vols. (Oxford, 1965), pp. 82–83 n.

4, suggested that Vasari's claim that "one commission followed from the success of the other is at least as likely to be a plausible sequence of his own invention as a piece of concrete information."

14. On Zeffi, see Bausi, "Politica e poesia" (full citation given in n. 3), p. 250; and Lorenzo di Filippo Strozzi, *Le vite degli uomini illustri della casa Strozzi* (Florence, 1892), p. vii; and, on the poetic anthology, Bausi, "Politica e poesia." Bausi ("Jacopo Nardi, Lorenzo duca d'Urbino e Machiavelli: L'occasione' del 1518," in *Interpres* 7 [1987]: 191–204, especially pp. 196ff.) suggested that Zeffi's contributions to the publication bear some relationship to Jacopo Nardi's *canzone* for the wedding festivities, on which see nn. 22–24 to this chapter, and the corresponding text.

15. "La prima [*commedia* of Lorenzo Strozzi] fu recitata nel Palazzo de' Medici ad istanza del Magnifico Lorenzo duca di Urbino: dove voi [Palla Strozzi] ed il maggior vostro fratello [Giovan Battista] vi portaste nel recitare la parte vostra in tal maniera, che tra li istrioni che per tutto il dominio si eran procacciati, si conobbe evidente la prontezza della pronunzia vostra. Può essere, che altra volta si sieno di poi recitati e condotti simili poemati più riccamente, ma infino a quel tempo la memoria de' nostri cittadini non aveva ancora vistone una commedia si bene condotta. Imperocché volendo Lorenzo non solo al principe satisfare, quanto a tutto il popolo, prese sopra le sue spalle tutto quello che a condurre onorevolmente la Commedia si richiedeva. E prima nella sala grande di sopra in detto Palazzo fece nelle scene apparire una prospettiva per le mani di Ridolfo del Grillandaio, [che] a tutti nuova e maravigliosa." I have taken the text of Zeffi's account from Parronchi, "La prima rappresentazione" (full citation given in n. 10), especially pp. 80–81.

16. See Ernst Steinmann, ed., *Die Portraitdarstellungen des Michelangelo*, Römische Forschungen der Biblioteca Hertziana, vol. 3 (Leipzig, 1913), pp. 72–73 and table 72. I am grateful to Wolfger Bulst for having brought this representation of the garden to my attention and for very useful discussion about the Palazzo Medici generally. See his article cited in n. 4 to this chapter. Dr. Bulst informs me that the phrase "sala grande di sopra" need not necessarily refer to the room on the *piano nobile*; it was also used to refer to the room immediately above, on the second floor. In Dr. Bulst's view, however, it seems likelier in this context to refer to the *piano nobile*, and here I have assumed that Zeffi was referring to that room.

17. See Pio Ferrieri, "Lorenzo di Filippo Strozzi e un codice Ashburnhamiano," in Pio Ferrieri, ed., *Studi di storia e critica letteraria* (Milan, Naples, and Rome, 1892), pp. 221–332, especially p. 224 n. 2: the rubric is in the same hand as the corrections in MS Ashb. 606, which are autograph.

18. The comedy was published as a work of Machiavelli's in vol. 8 (Milan, 1805) of the series Classici italiani. Machiavelli copied the text into a manuscript now preserved in the BNC (Banco rari 29 [*olim* Magl. VIII.1451bis; n. 336 degli in—4° della strozziana); see Parronchi, "La prima rappresentazione" (full citation given in n. 10), p. 71 and corresponding n. 2, and Lorenzo di Filippo Strozzi, *Commedie: Commedia in versi—La Pisana—La Violante*, ed. Andrea Gareffi (Ravenna, 1980), p. 36. The text is accompanied by the rubric "ego Barlachia recensui" (see Fortunato Pintor, "Ego Barlachia recensui," in *Giornale storico della letteratura italiana*

39 [1902]: 103–9; and Parronchi, "La prima rappresentazione," p. 71 n. 2, and p. 73), a reference, certainly, to Domenico Barlacchi, the herald of the Signoria, who was a member of the Compagnia della Cazzuola; see n. 22 to my chapter 1.

Ashburnham manuscript 579 contains the rubric (fol. 2^r) "Commedia del Sr Lorenzo Strozzi recitata in Casa i Medici circa il 1506." In his edition of the "Commedia in versi," Gareffi claimed (pp. 37–38) that a comma is to be understood in the inscription on fol. 3^r of the manuscript, and that it should thus read as follows: "La prima commedia ch'io facessi, mai recitata in casa e Medici." He observed that the inscription is thus inconsistent with that which appears on the preceding folio, fol. 2^r ("recitata in Casa i Medici circa il 1506") and, further, that Zeffi's account is also inconsistent with the inscription on fol. 2^r, since Giovan Battista Strozzi, whose participation in the performance Zeffi recorded, would have been only two years old in 1506; these anomalies, he suggested, resulted from a confusion among Strozzi's contemporaries between the work that was his first and another, different work that was performed in Palazzo Medici. That the "Commedia in versi" was indeed the first is suggested not only by the inscription on fol. 3^r of MS Ashb. 579 but also by lines 43–45 of the prologue: "perché io so ch'afirmare per certo posso / ch'un tal poeta è nuovo, e l'invenzione / al tutto e' nuova." Gareffi's proposed resolution to the various inconsistencies posed by the two inscriptions is that Zeffi erroneously believed that Strozzi's first comedy was not the "Commedia in versi" but instead *La Pisana*, that it was *La Pisana* that was performed in 1518, and that the "Commedia in versi" had been performed earlier. I prefer to accept the testimony of the inscription as it appears on fol. 3^r ("Laprima Comedia chio facesi mai recitata incasa e medici") and thus to identify the "Commedia in versi" with the work Zeffi described ("la prima [of Strozzi's comedies] fu recitata nel Palazzo de' Medici ad istanza del Magnifico Lorenzo duca di Urbino").

19. Zeffi, in Parronchi, "La prima rappresentazione" (full citation given in n. 10), especially pp. 80–81: "Dipoi avendo di vari luoghi fatta la provvisione di diversi strumenti, gli divise in questo modo: che avanti la commedia incominciassero i suoni grossi, come trombe, cornamuse, pifferi, che destassero gli animi degli auditori: il secondo atto fece introdurre tre Mori riccamente abbigliati con tre liuti, che nel silenzio dilettarono soavemente ciascuno: nel terzo cantarono su quattro violoni, voci soprane, alzandosi secondo la Commedia. Al tumulto che nel quarto romoreggiava, accomodò li più acuti strumenti di penna: la ultima musica, furono quattro tromboni, modulano artificiosamente e con dolcezza le lor voci. Le quali musiche di poi sono state più volte imitate: ma per allora non erano mai venute in uso, né forse in considerazione; perché rade volte interviene che un principe, il capo di qualche impresa, sia alto a tutte le circostanze, che in quella si ricercano. E Lorenzo . . . nel cantare adempiva con molta grazia la parte sua, tanto che alcuna volta pareva lascivo, massime quando col suo leuto conferiva i suoi amori." My translation is in part adopted from Karen Eales's; see her translation of Pirrotta, *Music and Theater from Poliziano to Monteverdi* (Cambridge, 1982), pp. 122–23, n. 8. Howard M. Brown, *Sixteenth-Century Instrumentation: The Music for the Florentine Intermedi*, Musicological Studies and Documents, no. 30 (n.p., 1973), p. 87, attempted a reconstruction of the instrumentation of the

intermedii based on Zeffi's account; his translation of the references to the instruments differs in some details from that offered here.

20. Pirrotta, *Music and Theater* (full citation given in the preceding note).

21. Cerretani, MS Florence, BNC, II. IV. 19, fols. 49ᵛ–50ᵛ: "Addì 12 . . . la sera vennero tre trionfi, Venere, Marte e Minerva, con ca[n]ti divini, dopo i quali venne Imeneo, dio delle nozze, con canto a proposito, et [other] canti ornatissimi, e così furono finite le nozze con pochissima satisfatione delle genti e tutto causorono due cose, l'una avaritia grandissima di Madonna, l'altra i capi e guide della festa de' balli." At this point I would like to observe that there are substantive differences among the various redactions of Cerretani's text. The manuscript Parronchi used (see n. 10 to this chapter) contains the references to the *convito* and *festa da ballo* of the eighth of September and the *convito* and theatrical performance of the ninth; it omits the references to the events of the tenth and, further, assigns the presentation of the *trionfi* to the evening of the ninth rather than the evening of the twelfth. I have followed the chronology suggested by the text in MS II. I. 313: on the seventh, the *entrata*; on the eighth, the banquet and *festa da ballo* (and, according to Alfonsina, the performance of Manenti's *Philargio*); on the ninth, the banquet and theatrical performance (perhaps Strozzi's "Commedia in versi"); on the tenth, a banquet, theatrical performance (perhaps Strozzi's "Commedia in versi"), *festa da ballo* and performance of instrumental music; and on the twelfth, the presentation of the *trionfi* and *canti* (probably including Jacopo Nardi's "Canzona sopra il Carro delle tre Dee," on which see the following text and notes). I am not qualified to offer an opinion concerning the thesis advanced by Parronchi that Machiavelli's *Mandragola* was one of the three works performed during the wedding festivities; see Parronchi, "La prima rappresentazione" (full citation given in n. 10), and Pirrotta, *Music and Theater* (full citation given in n. 19), pp. 122–24. I can point out, however, that although Zeffi mentioned only one comedy, as Pirrotta correctly observed, which is surely to be identified with Lorenzo Strozzi's so-called "Commedia in versi," as Pirrotta also observed, Cerretani referred to "le commedie" in his account of the decorations in Palazzo Medici, and Vasari, in the *Vite* of Aristotile, Franciabigio, and Ghirlandaio, implied that there was more than one comedy performed.

22. See Bausi, "Jacopo Nardi" (full citation given in n. 14), especially pp. 191–92.

23. Ibid., especially p. 193.

24. I have taken the text of the *canzone* from Bausi, ibid., pp. 191–92.

25. Richard Sherr, "Lorenzo de' Medici, Duke of Urbino, as a Patron of Music," in *Renaissance Studies in Honor of Craig Hugh Smyth*, 2 vols. (Florence, 1985), vol. 1, pp. 627–38, especially p. 637 n. 34. Also, on the city's instrumentalists who may also have served as members of Lorenzo's "establishment," see Keith Polk, "Civic Patronage and Instrumental Ensembles in Renaissance Florence," in *Augsburger Jahrbuch für Musikwissenschaft* 3 (1986): 51–68, especially p. 68.

26. H. Colin Slim, "Gian and Gian Maria, Some Fifteenth- and Sixteenth-Century Namesakes," in *Musical Quarterly* 57 (1971): 562–74, especially p. 565.

27. Sherr, "Lorenzo de' Medici" (full citation given in n. 25).

28. Ibid.

29. Ibid. An "Urbano sonatore" is also mentioned in correspondence of the Strozzi family (see Richard Agee, "Filippo Strozzi and the Early Madrigal," in *Journal of the American Musicological Society* 38 [1985]: 227–37, especially pp. 229–30 and corresponding nn. 13–15); further, an "Urbano sonator liuti" is listed as a resident of Rome in a census taken during Clement VII's pontificate (see D. Gnoli, "Descriptio Urbis e censimento della popolazione di Roma avanti il sacco borbonico," in *Archivio della R. Società romana di storia patria* 18 [1894]: 467); might either (or both) have been the same instrumentalist who was in Lorenzo de' Medici's employ?

30. See Frank D'Accone, "Alessandro Coppini and Bartolomeo degli Organi—Two Florentine Composers of the Renaissance," in *Studien zur italienisch-deutschen Musikgeschichte* 4, Analecta musicologica, vol. 4 (1967): 38–76, especially p. 51 nn. 69–71.

31. Sherr, "Lorenzo de' Medici" (full citation given in n. 25), p. 637 n. 33.

32. D'Accone, "Some Neglected Composers in the Florentine Chapels," in *Viator* 1 (1970): 263–88, especially p. 282 n. 85.

33. On Giangiacomo, see my article "Gian Maria Giudeo, Sonatore del Liuto, and the Medici," in *Fontes Artis Musicae* 38 (1991).

34. Sherr, "Lorenzo de' Medici" (full citation given in n. 25), p. 635 n. 19.

35. Ibid., p. 635 n. 19 and p. 636 n. 30. On Vasari's reference to a Pierino pifaro who was a member of the Compagnia della Cazzuola, see n. 22 to my chapter 1. A Pierino who was an instrumentalist is also mentioned in the autobiography of Benvenuto Cellini (see *The Life of Benvenuto Cellini*, trans. J. A. Symonds [New York, 1924], pp. 12–15); it is possible that these three instrumentalists named Pierino (or any two of the three) were identical.

36. D'Accone, "A Documentary History of Music at the Florentine Cathedral and Baptistery during the 15th Century," 2 vols. (Ph.D. dissertation, Harvard University, 1960), vol. 2, p. 141; and D'Accone, "Alessandro Coppini and Bartolomeo degli Organi" (full citation given in n. 30), p. 75. On Baccio's relationship to Pope Clement VII, see my article "Gian Maria Giudeo, Sonatore del Liuto, and the Medici" (full citation given in n. 33).

37. D'Accone, "A Documentary History" (full citation given in the preceding note). On Vergilio's possible relationship to Pope Clement, see Cummings, "Gian Maria Giudeo" (full citation given in n. 33).

38. Figure 32 is of the front panel of a mid-fifteenth-century wedding *cassone*, traditionally said to represent a scene from the wedding of Boccaccio Adimari. Of the extensive literature on the dance, see especially Daniel Heartz, "Hoftanz and Basse Dance," in *Journal of the American Musicological Society* 19 (1966): 13–36, especially p. 18; Manfred Bukofzer, "A Polyphonic Basse Dance of the Renaissance," in *Studies in Medieval and Renaissance Music* (New York, 1950), pp. 190–216, where the piece published here as example 5 was first identified as a polyphonic setting of a dance tune (various details in my transcription are borrowed from Bukofzer's; for a transcription that differs from his in several respects, see Allan Atlas, *Music at the Aragonese Court of Naples* [Cambridge, 1985], example 18 [pp. 230–31] and the accompanying notes and discussion [pp. 153–54, 238]); Ingrid Brainard, "Dance 3.2: Early Renaissance," *The New Grove Dictionary of Music and*

Musicians, ed. Stanley Sadie, 20 vols. (London, 1980), vol. 5, pp. 183–87, especially p. 184, for the quotation from Cornazano; and *Trattato dell'arte del ballo di Guglielmo Ebreo*, Scelta di curiosità letterarie inedite e rare, CXXXI (Bologna, 1873), pp. 65–69, for the dances choreographed by Lorenzo "il Magnifico."

39. Sherr, "Lorenzo de' Medici" (full citation given in n. 25), especially p. 634 nn. 8 and 11, and p. 635 nn. 12 and 14.

40. Ibid., p. 636 nn. 21–23 and 25–26.

41. See Alessandro Luzio, "Isabella d'Este nei primordi del papato di Leone X e il suo viaggio a Roma nel 1514–1515," in *Archivio storico lombardo*, 4th ser., 6 (1906): 99–180 and 454–89, especially p. 159, for a letter of Isabella d'Este's: "Heri per dar principio a stare in feste et vivere allegramente questo carnevale andai a cena col S. M.ᶜᵒ Lorenzo. . . . si fece una bella caza de tori. . . . La caza durò circa tre hore. Dopoi cominciandosi a far sera si ballò fin 4. hore di notte. Il pasto fu molto bello et sumptuoso, durò circa II hore, dopo si tornò a ballare et ballosi fin le VIII hore."

42. See, for example, the text quoted in n. 2 to my chapter 6, concerning a "grandissima festa" in Rome in 1514 at which Isabella d'Este, Cardinals Luigi d'Aragona, Marco Cornelius, and Innocenzo Cibo, and Giuliano and Lorenzo de' Medici, among others, engaged in "canti et suoni de varie sorte."

43. D'Accone, "Alessandro Coppini and Bartolomeo degli Organi" (full citation given in n. 30), especially p. 76, and idem, "The Musical Chapels at the Florentine Cathedral and Baptistery during the First Half of the Sixteenth Century," in *Journal of the American Musicological Society* 24 (1971): 1–50, especially p. 16 n. 34.

44. G. L. Moncallero, *Epistolario di Bernardo Dovizi da Bibbiena*, 2 vols., Biblioteca dell'"Archivum Romanicum," vols. 44 and 81 (Florence, 1955 and 1965), vol. 2, p. 127.

45. Frank D'Accone, "Heinrich Isaac in Florence," in *Musical Quarterly* 49 (1963): 464–83, especially p. 481; and F. Ghisi, *I canti carnascialecschi nelle fonti musicali del XV e XVI secoli* (Florence, 1937), p. 43 and corresponding n. 4, and p. 44.

46. Sherr, "Verdelot in Florence, Coppini in Rome, and the Singer 'La Fiore,'" in *Journal of the American Musicological Society* 37 (1984): 402–11, especially pp. 409–10.

47. For the texts of the letters documenting the exchanges of music between Florence and Rome, see Sherr, "Lorenzo de' Medici" (full citation given in n. 25), p. 637 n. 36; my article "Medici Musical Patronage in the Early Sixteenth Century: New Perspectives," in *Studi musicali* 10 (1981): 197–216, especially p. 207; and Howard M. Brown, "Chansons for the Pleasure of a Florentine Patrician," in *Aspects of Medieval and Renaissance Music: A Birthday Offering to Gustave Reese*, ed. Jan LaRue (New York, 1966), pp. 56–66, especially p. 64 n. 22; and for the works by Genet, see Elziarii Geneti, *Opera omnia*, ed. Albert Seay, 5 vols., Corpus mensurabilis musicae, no. 58 (n.p., 1972–73).

48. D'Accone, "Alessandro Coppini and Bartolomeo degli Organi" (full citation given in n. 30), p. 75. On p. 51 of the same study is an archival reference from Lorenzo II's accounts documenting a payment made at Baccio's command to have music books bound.

49. On the "succession" from Lorenzo's de facto rule to Cardinal Giulio's "regency," see J. R. Hale, *Florence and the Medici: The Pattern of Control* (London, 1977), pp. 100 and 106–8.

CHAPTER 10

1. On Cardinal Giulio's "stewardship" of the regime, see, for example, J. R. Hale, *Florence and the Medici: The Pattern of Control* (London, 1977), pp. 106–8; and J. N. Stephens, *The Fall of the Florentine Republic, 1512–1530* (Oxford, 1983), pp. 108–23.

2. On Giulio as art patron, see, above all, Sheryl Reiss, "Cardinal Giulio de' Medici as a Patron of Art, 1515–1523" (Ph.D. dissertation, Princeton University, forthcoming), especially chapters 10 and 11. I am grateful to Ms. Reiss for allowing me to read her work prior to publication and for many profitable and enjoyable discussions about Medici patronage of the arts.

3. See Richard Sherr, "Verdelot in Florence, Coppini in Rome, and the Singer 'La Fiore,'" *Journal of the American Musicological Society* 37 (1984): 402–11, especially p. 409, for the text of a document (Florence, Archivio di Stato, M. A. P., LXVII, 43) that suggests a relationship between Verdelot and Cardinal Giulio.

4. See Pietro Canal, "Della musica in Mantova," in *Memorie del R. Istituto Veneto di Scienze, Lettere ed Arti* 21 (1879): 665–774, especially p. 677; and, on three unpublished letters from Giulio's agent Agnolo Marzi concerning Gian Maria, my article "Gian Maria Giudeo, Sonatore del Liuto, and the Medici," in *Fontes Arts Musicae* 38 (1991).

5. See Frank D'Accone, "The Musical Chapels at the Florentine Cathedral and Baptistery during the First Half of the Sixteenth Century," in *Journal of the American Musicological Society* 24 (1971): 1–50, especially p. 41.

6. On the Cortona-Paris manuscript and its music-historical importance as a document of the "protomadrigal," see now my article "Giulio de' Medici's Music Books," in *Early Music History* 10 (1991): 65–122.

7. On Giulio's agents during the period of his "regency," see Hale, *Florence and the Medici* (full citation given in n. 1), p. 114, and Stephens, *The Fall of the Florentine Republic* (full citation given in n. 1), pp. 63–120.

8. Adriano Prosperi, "Clemente VII," in *Dizionario biografico degli italiani*, 32 vols. (Rome, 1960–), vol. 26, pp. 237–59, discusses Giulio's movements between Florence and Rome in the period 1519–23.

9. Hale, *Florence and the Medici* (full citation given in n. 1), p. 114. Ippolito inherited his father's cultural and intellectual interests; on him, see, above all, Giuseppe E. Moretti, "Il cardinale Ippolito de' Medici dal trattato di Barcelona alla morte," in *Archivio storico italiano* 98 (1940): 137–78; J. N. Stephens, "Giovanbattista Cibo's Confession," in *Essays Presented to Myron P. Gilmore*, 2 vols. (Florence, 1978), vol. 1, pp. 255–69; and, on some aspects of his cultural patronage, H. Colin Slim, "Un coro della 'Tullia' di Lodovico Martelli messo in musica e attribuito a Philippe Verdelot," in *Firenze e la Toscana dei Medici nell'Europa del '500*, 3 vols. (Florence, 1983), vol. 1, pp. 487–511. Most of the available references pertaining to Ippolito's musical patronage were collected and analyzed by Slim in "The Keyboard Ricercar and Fantasia in Italy c. 1500–1550" (Ph.D. dissertation,

Harvard University, 1960), pp. 170–73. A sixteenth-century manuscript chronicle of the Medici family (Paris, Bibliothèque nationale, Fonds italiens, no. 342, fol. 102ᵛ) records that "la Sua Corte era ripiena di Letterati; di musici e di uomini eccellenti, e famosi." Hieronimo Garimberto, *La prima parte delle vite, overo fatti memorabili d'alcuni papi, et di tutti i cardinali passati* (Venice, 1567), p. 515, recorded that "questo raro giovane . . . fosse bene instituto nelle lettere humane, e nell arti liberali, si come fù; & in tanta brevità di tempo, che fece stupire ogn'uno . . . con quella facilità e facilità di candore, che ancor si vede; come si vendono ancora delle sue compositioni musicali, nelle quali in tutte le qualità de' stromenti da sonare riuscì singolare." Paolo Giovio's eulogy, written to be placed under Titian's famous portrait of Ippolito (see figure 35), reads as follows (*GLI ELOGI: VITE BREVEMENTE SCRITTE D'HVOMINI ILLVSTRI DI GVERRA, ANTICHI ET MODERNI . . .* [Venice: Apresso Giouanni de' Rossi, M. D. LVII.], fols. 280–280ᵛ): "tradusse il secondo libro dell'Eneide di Virgilio, in lingua Thoscana, & . . . trasportò ancora i proloqui d'Hippocrate dall'arte della medicina, nell'uso della disciplina di guerra. Ma non molto dapoi si riuolse dalle lettere a diligente studio di tutta la musica, intrattenendo ogni eccellentissimo artefice & sonator di stormenti [*sic*], & col medesimo desiderio d'ardente ingegno, s'essercitò tanto sottilmente in ogni qualità d'armonia, che ne riuscì dolcissimo sonator di liuto, artificoso ne' uiolini, eccellente ne' flauti, & incomparabile ne' cornetti; tocaua ancora gentilissimamente il manacordo, & facendo diuersissimi concenti d'armonia, con marauigliosa imitatione sonaua cosi i nostri tamburi, & le trombe, come le nacchere, & gli altri stormenti Barbareschi, i quali sogliono risuegliare gli animi alla guerra." (I have checked Slim's transcription against the copy of Giovio's book in the Chapin Library at Williams College.) In the *Ragionamenti* of Cosimo Bartoli (on which see now James Haar, "Cosimo Bartoli on Music," in *Early Music History* 8 [1988]: 37–79, especially p. 62), two instrumentalists—the famous lutenist Francesco da Milano and the violist "il Siciliano"—are said to have been in Ippolito's employ: "havete voi mai sentito sonare il Siciliano di Viola? O Francesco da Milano di liuto o di viola ancora? . . . [Q]uando la buona memoria del Cardinale Hippolito de Medici era viva, erano amenduoi al servizio di quel Signore." Haar identified "il Siciliano" (correctly, certainly) with the "Messer Joa[n]battista Cicilian" cited in Silvestro Ganassi's *Lettione seconda pur della prattica di sonare il violone d'arco da tasti* (Venice, 1543), fol. G4ᵛ, where "il Siciliano" and Alfonso "dalla Viola" da Ferrara are called "[t]he most expert" players of the instrument "called del Violon"; see H. Colin Slim, "Francesco da Milano (1497–1543/44). A Bio-Bibliographical Study," in *Musica disciplina* 18–19 (1964–65): vol. 18, p. 76 (Slim cited the passage from Ganassi from E. Vogel, *Die Handschriften nebst den älteren Druckwerken der Musikabtheilung der Herzoglichen Bibliothek zu Wolfenbüttel* [Wolfenbüttel, 1890], p. 135; the translation is Slim's). Ganassi's reference in turn permits us to identify Ippolito's "il Siciliano" with Giovanni Battista Sansone *detto* "il Siciliano," who was in the employ of Pope Paul III; see Nino Pirrotta, "Rom," in *Die Musik in Geschichte und Gegenwart*, vol. 11 (1963), col. 705; and Léon Dorez, *La cour du Pape Paul III*, 2 vols. (Paris, 1932), entries in the index to Sansone, especially vol. 1, p. 232. "Il Siciliano" is also mentioned in Luigi Dentice's *Duo dialoghi della musica* (Naples, 1552), fol. 28ʳ: at the beginning of the second dialogue, Dentice described "una bella musica" performed by "M. Battista

Siciliano," among others; see Donna Cardamone, *The "canzone villanesca alla napolitana" and Related Forms, 1537–1570*, 2 vols. (Ann Arbor, 1981), vol. 1, p. 254 n. 17. Sansone's service as Ippolito's employee is confirmed by Giovanni Andrea Gilio da Fabriano in *Due Dialogi* (Camerino, 1564), fol. 7^r, where it is stated further that the famous clavicembalist Lorenzo da Gaeta was also in Ippolito's employ. Although Lorenzo da Gaeta, Francesco da Milano, and Giovanni Battista Sansone are, to my knowledge, the only musicians known thus far to have been in Ippolito's service, there are a few other references pertaining to his musical patronage and documenting his musical experiences. Another passage in Bartoli's *Ragionamenti* (see Haar, "Cosimo Bartoli on Music," p. 65) specifies that Ippolito was among those present in Rome on a famous occasion when Giulio Segni's harpsichord playing silenced a discussion: "una sera essendo il Marchese del Vasto arrivato in poste in Roma, e subito con gli sproni ancora in piede andato da Papa Clemente; e trovatolo a tavola, e intrato dopo la cena in discorso con il Papa e con il Sanga di cose importantissime, il detto Julio essendo comparso in una parte della sala con uno instrumento, cominciò di lontano a sonare di maniera, che quei duoi Principi, insieme con il Cardinale de Medici, e con il Sanga che havevano a risolvere cose importantissime, pretermessono per alquanto tali ragionamenti; e andarono ad udirlo sonare con una attentione maravigliosa." One might also note that Elzear Genet, who had been Leo X's *maestro di cappella*, dedicated his *Liber hymnorum usus Romanae ecclesiae . . .* (Avignon: Jean de Channay, n.d.) to Ippolito; see the dedication in Elziarii Geneti, *Opera omnia*, ed. Albert Seay, 5 vols., Corpus mensurabilis musicae, no. 58 (n.p., 1972–73), vol. 3, pp. 9–12. Finally, that Ippolito's mistress, Giulia Gonzaga, may herself have had musical interests is suggested by two of her letters to her cousin Federigo in which she enclosed newly composed motets—one by Sebastiano Festa, then in the employ of her uncle Ottobono Fieschi, the nonresident bishop of Mondovì from 1519 to 1522, who resided in Rome as protonotary, then assistant to Leo; see Edward Lowinsky, ed., *The Medici Codex of 1518*, 3 vols., Monuments of Renaissance Music, vols. 3–5 (Chicago, 1968), vol. 1, pp. 59–60 and corresponding nn. 18–20.

10. Hale, *Florence and the Medici* (full citation given in n. 1), p. 111.

11. Stephens, *The Fall of the Florentine Republic* (full citation given in n. 1), pp. 191–202.

12. Ibid., and Hale, *Florence and the Medici* (full citation given in n. 1), p. 112.

13. Stephens, *The Fall of the Florentine Republic* (full citation given in n. 1), pp. 195–96.

14. Hale, *Florence and the Medici* (full citation given in n. 1), p. 112.

15. For an evocative and stimulating study of the effects of the sack, see André Chastel, *The Sack of Rome, 1527* (Princeton, 1983).

16. Randolph Starn, *Donato Giannotti and His "Epistolae":* Biblioteca Universitaria Alessandrina, Rome, MS. *107* (Geneva, 1968), p. 51.

17. Professor Gilbert offered this and other suggestions in private conversation.

18. Giannotti, "Della republica fiorentina," in *Opere politiche e letterarie*, 2 vols. (Florence, 1850), vol. 1, p. 228; Nerli in Machiavelli, *Opere*, ed. Franco Gaeta (Turin, 1984), pp. 540–41, and Vasari, *Vita* of Aristotile *detto* Bastiano da San Gallo, *Lives of the Most Eminent Painters, Sculptors, and Architects*, 3 vols., trans.

Gaston Du. C. de Vere (New York, 1979). On the performance, see also Roberto
Ridolfi, *The Life of Niccolò Machiavelli*, trans. Cecil Grayson (London, 1963), pp.
207–10, and the accompanying notes; Ridolfi cited the principal texts attesting the
performance.

19. On Falconetti and the circumstances surrounding the performance, see especially Oreste Tommasini, *La vita e gli scritti di Niccolò Machiavelli*, 2 vols. (Turin
and Rome, 1883–1911), vol. 2, pp. 414–15 n. 1. The reference to the attendees is in
Giannotti, "Della republica fiorentina" (full citation given in n. 18): "al quale convito venneno tutti i primi cittadini della Città, ed i più onorati dello stato che
allora reggeva."

20. Vasari, *Vita* (full citation given in n. 18). On the *Compagnia della Cazzuola*,
which according to Vasari was responsible for the earlier performance of *Mandragola*, see n. 22 to my chapter 1.

21. Nerli, *Opere* (full citation given in n. 18): "Il Fornaciaio e voi, e voi e il
Fornaciaio, avete fatto in modo che non solo per tutta Toscana, ma ancora per la
Lombardia è corsa e corre la fama della vostre magnificenzie. Io so dell'orto rap-
pianato per farne il parato della vostra commedia; io so de' conviti non solo alli
primi e più nobili patrizii della Città, ma ancora a' mezzani e dipoi alla plebe; cose
solite farsi solo per i principi. La fama della vostra commedia è volata per tutto;
e non crediate che io abbia avuto queste cose per lettere di amici, ma l'ho avuto
da viandanti che per tutto la strada vanno predicando 'le gloriose pompe e' fieri
ludi' della porta a San Friano. . . . vorrei che voi mi mandassi, quando primo po-
trete, questa comedia che u[l]timamente avete fatta recitare."

22. Nino Pirrotta, *Music and Theater from Poliziano to Monteverdi* (Cambridge,
1982), p. 122.

23. Ibid., pp. 122 and 124. A performance of *Mandragola* planned for Faenza in
1526 was to have included *intermedii* of the type Machiavelli had earlier used in *La
Clizia*, but the performance never took place; the newly written prologue contains a gesture toward Clement VII, as Pirrotta observed (*Music and Theater*,
ibid., 141–44): "Per tal grazia superna, / Per sì felice stato, / Potete lieti stare, /
Godere e ringraziare— / chi [Clement] ve lo [Francesco Guicciardini, papal representative in Romagna] ha dato."

24. Ibid., p. 154.

CHAPTER 11

1. Ludwig Pastor, *History of the Popes from the Close of the Middle Ages*, ed. Ralph
Francis Kerr, vol. 10 (St. Louis, 1912), pp. 78 and 80.

2. Marino Sanuto, *I diarii*, 59 volumes (Venice, 1879–1903), vol. 52, cols. 184–
85, 189–90, 194, 264–66, and 268–69.

3. "Le trombe de l'imperador con suoi piferi, in tuto numero 8. Le trombete de
l'imperador numero 12, tuti a cavallo." Ibid., cols. 268–69.

4. "Quanti fussero li strepiti di voce, trombe, tamburi et artigliarie, che pareva
apunto che Bologna andasse tutta soto sopra." Ibid., cols. 264–66. See also col.
184.

5. On the ceremonies in front of S. Petronio, see Pastor, *History of the Popes*
(full citation given in n. 1), p. 82. The reference to the singing of the *Te Deum* by

the papal chapel is in Sanuto, *I diarii*, vol. 52 (full citation given in n. 2), cols. 270–71: "Sua Maestà intrò in chiesia de San Petronio a far oration acompagnato . . . da . . . cardinali, dove era la cappella del papa che cantava el *Te Deum laudamus*, et sopra l'altare erano poste tutte le prencipale reliquie che sono in Bologna."

6. Pastor, *History of the Popes* (full citation given in n. 1), pp. 82–83.

7. Ibid., pp. 83–89.

8. "Audict Boulongne fut conclud faire Alexandre de Médicis duc de Florence." Jean de Vandenesse, "Journal des voyages de Charles-Quint de 1514 à 1551," in Louis Prosper Gachard, ed., *Collection des voyages des souverains des Pays-Bas*, 4 vols. (Brussels, 1874–82), vol. 2, p. 94.

9. Gaetano Giordani, *Della venuta e dimora in Bologna del Sommo Pontefice Clemente VII. per la coronazione di Carlo V. imperatore* (Bologna, 1842), pp. 44 and 46.

10. For this observation, I am indebted to Dr. Jeffrey Dean; see his "The Scribes of the Sistine Chapel, 1501–1527" (Ph.D. dissertation, University of Chicago, 1984).

11. See my chapter 5.

12. On the performance of February 14, see Giordani, *Della venuta e dimora* (full citation given in n. 9), p. 91. On the membership of the papal chapel at the time of the imperial coronation, see Fr. X. Haberl, "Die römische 'Schola Cantorum' und die päpstlichen Kapellsänger bis zur Mitte des 16. Jahrhunderts," in *Bausteine für Musikgeschichte* (reprint; Hildesheim, 1971), p. 74, where the membership list for December 1529, is printed; on p. 73 n. 1, payments are listed to the "custos librorum," Orpheo Franc., and the "scriptores" Jo. de occhon and Aloysio Cassanen, who would presumably have been responsible for copying any works procured from members of the imperial chapel. For a list of members of the imperial chapel for July 1, 1528, see Hellmut Federhofer, "États de la chapelle musicale de Charles-Quint (1528) et de Maximilien (1554)," in *Revue belge de musicologie* 4 (1950): 176–83, especially p. 178; on Pickart as master of the chapel, see, for example, Joseph Schmidt-Görg, *Nicolas Gombert* (reprint; Tutzing, 1971), p. 279, where "M[aistr]e adrian th[iebau]lt" is listed as "maistre de la chapelle." Albert Dunning, *Die Staatsmotette 1480–1555* (Utrecht, 1970), pp. 279–81, relates Maistre Jhan's motet *Mundi Christo Redemptori* to the meetings between Charles and Clement, following Edward E. Lowinsky, "A Newly Discovered Sixteenth-Century Motet Manuscript at the Biblioteca Vallicelliana in Rome," in *Journal of the American Musicological Society* 3 (1950): 173–232. George Nugent, "The Jacquet Motets and Their Authors," 2 vols. (Ph.D. dissertation, Princeton University, 1973), vol. 1, p. 233, suggests that Jacquet of Mantua's motet *Repleatur os meum* may have been written for the imperial coronation ceremony. On manuscript Cappella Sistina 55, see Jeffrey Dean, "The Scribes of the Sistine Chapel" (full citation given in n. 10).

13. Pastor, *History of the Popes* (full citation given in n. 1), p. 88.

14. Ibid.

15. "Adì primo di Gennaio in Bologna fu cantata una messa solenne alla presenza del Papa e dello Imp[erato]re e di tutti gli Imbasciadori che si trovavano in quella Città." Florence, BNC, MS II. I. 313 (Magl. XXV. 17), "La Città di Firenze," fol. 142ʳ.

16. Pastor, *History of the Popes* (full citation given in n. 1), p. 92.

17. Ibid.

18. "Le 22ᶜ de febvrier, de bien matin, Sa Majesté se disposa de prendre la couronne de Lombardie, que se dit de fer. . . . Sa Majesté, . . . accompaigné . . . du duc Alexandre de Médicis, . . . vint vers la chappelle du palays." Jean de Vandenesse, "Journal des voyages de Charles-Quint" (full citation given in n. 8), pp. 86–87. Alessandro is identified as duke because he became duke of Penne in southern Italy on September 25, 1522 (see G. de Caesaris, "Alessandro de' Medici e Margherita d'Austria, Duchi di Penne [1522–86]," in *Bullettino della R. Deputazione abruzzese di storia patria*, 3d ser., 20–21 [1929–30]: 165–265, especially p. 169); he was not formally accorded the title of duke of the Florentine Republic until April of 1532.

I feel compelled to say that here again, as in the case of the 1513 Capitoline Investiture, my account is a patchwork, based as it is on a kind of digest of references from the principal sources. The imperial coronation ceremonies are attested by a large number of unusually detailed accounts, which, inevitably, are not entirely consistent among themselves, especially with respect to the identity of some of the individuals who were responsible for executing the various liturgical elements of the ceremonies. Moreover, I have eliminated much detail in order to highlight the references to the musical element. A complete reconstruction based on all of the available sources and on an analysis of their interrelationships ought to be undertaken.

19. Sanuto, *I diarii*, vol. 52 (full citation given in n. 2), cols. 606–9: "Et dite alcune . . . oratione, [the papal singers] cantorono poi le litanie." On the singing of the litanies, see also the important source "Prima et seconda Coronatione di Carlo Quinto sacratissimo Imperatore Re de Romani, fatta in Bologna," in Giordani, *Della venuta e dimora* (full citation given in n. 9), documents, pp. 59–68, which offers the information (pp. 60–61) that "li cantori cantarono le letanie; il Revᵐᵒ [Cardinal Wilhelm Enckenvoirt, on whom see n. 25 to this chapter] et tutti li altri prelati genuflessi legevano le medesime letanie; il reverendiss. poi in piede col pastorale canto: Vt hunc presentem etc. con certi altri versicoli et orationi"; and the detailed account in Cesare Baronio and Oderico Rinaldi, *Annales ecclesiastici ab anno MCXCVII*, 21 vols. (Antwerp, 1611–77), vol. 20, entry no. 10 for 1530 (text unpaginated), where the text of the Litanies is given: "Quibus sic dispositis duo cantores coeperunt in cantu laetanias genuflexi super uno scabello, & chorus aliorum cantorum capellae responderunt. Post versiculum, videlicet: Vt obsequium seruitutis nostrae, &c. surrexit celebrans, adhuc aliis omnibus procumbentibus, & manu sua sinistra tenes baculum benedixit dicens: Vt hunc electum in Regem coronandum benedicere digneris. Respond. Te rogamus audi nos. Vt hunc electum in Regem benedicere & conseruare digneris. Respond. Te rogamus audi nos. Rursum recumbens super faldistorio una cum aliis praelatis assistentibus, & similia dicentibus voce submissa fecerunt super electum Regem signum crucis. Cantores vero reassumpserunt laetanias. Quibus finitis celebrans solus consurrexit sine mithra, aliis tamen recumbentibus sine mithris, dixit super Regem versic., ut infra, adhuc prostratum. Pater noster, alta voce. Respond. per cantores. Sed libera. Vers. Saluum fac seruum tuum Domine. Respond. Deus meus sperantem in te. Versic. Esto ei Domine turris fortitudinis. Respond. A facie inimici.

Versic. Domine exaudi orationem meam. Respond. Et clamor meus ad te veniat. Versic. Dominus vobiscum. Respond. Et cum spiritu tuo. Oremus. Praetende Domine huic famulo tuo dexteram coelestis auxilii, ut te toto corde perquirat, & quae digne, postulat assequi mereatur. Actiones nostras quaesumus, &c."

20. Sanuto, *I diarii*, vol. 52 (full citation given in n. 2), cols. 606–9: "si principiò l'introito de la messa in canto."

21. Ibid., cols. 613–18: "la messa andò seguendo per insino a la epistola la qual per uno deputato di [the papal] capella fu cantata; et in quel mezo la si cantava el reverendissimo arcivescovo di Zara [in Dalmatia] [Francesco] da chà da Pexaro prese il libro et il sacrista prese la candela accesa in mano, et andò dinanzi al papa come assistenti, et il papa disse la epistola al solito." On the identity of the archbishop of Zara, see Conrad Eubel et al., *Hierarchia Catholica Medii Aevi*, 7 vols. (reprint; Padua, 1952–63), especially vol. 3, p. 231; he was named archbishop of Zara on April 18, 1505.

22. Sanuto, *I diarii*, vol. 52 (full citation given in n. 2), cols. 606–9: "Poi cantandosi el graduale, posto un cuscino d'oro ai piedi del pontefice, Cesare vi andò ad ingienochiarsi condoto da i due reverendissimi assistenti [Girolamo Doria and Ippolito de' Medici]." On Cardinal Girolamo Doria (d. 1558), see Eubel, *Hierarchia Catholica* (full citation given in n. 21), p. 22; he was raised to the cardinalate in 1529 in the fifth promotion of Clement VII's pontificate; Clement's cousin Ippolito (d. 1535), the illegitimate son of his first cousin Giuliano di Lorenzo, was named cardinal in the sixth promotion, on January 10, 1529. On him, and on his cultural and intellectual interests, see n. 9 of the preceding chapter. On the singing of the Epistle and Gradual, see also Baronio and Rinaldi, *Annales ecclesiastici* (full citation given in n. 19), entry no. 11, and "Prima et seconda Coronatione di Carlo Quinto" (full citation given in n. 19), pp. 60–61: "et cantata la epistola cole solite ceremonie lo Imperatore ando nanti al Papa genuflesso. . . . gli diede la corona . . . : et si canto il resto sin alloffertorio."

23. Giordani, *Della venuta e dimora* (full citation given in n. 9), pp. 102ff.

24. Vandenesse, "Journal des voyages de Charles-Quint" (full citation given in n. 8), p. 88: "Apres celle coronation, Sa Saincteté se meit en oraison . . . , disant: *Sta et retine locum*, et entonna *Te Deum laudamus*, que les chantres achevèrent." On the singing of the *Te Deum*, see also Baronio and Rinaldi, *Annales ecclesiastici* (full citation given in n. 19), entry no. 14.

25. Sanuto, *I diarii*, vol. 52 (full citation given in n. 2), cols. 613–18: "il papa et l'imperator stando sempre in piedi. . . . Hor quando li cantori furono al verso che dice *Te ergo quaesumus famulis tuis subveni*, il papa et lo imperator, li reverendissimi et tutti, erano in capela, se ingenochiorno. Et . . . il reverendissimo [Cardinal] Hincvorth [Wilhelm Enckenvoirt], qual cantava la messa, dete lo incenso a l'altar." On Cardinal Enckenvoirt (d. 1534), see Eubel, *Hierarchia Catholica* (full citation given in n. 21), p. 19. Enckenvoirt's participation may perhaps be interpreted as a gesture toward the emperor: Enckenvoirt was the only cardinal whom his countryman Pope Adrian VI created (he was raised to the cardinalate on September 9, 1523), and Adrian had been Charles's tutor; see Karl Brandi, *The Emperor Charles V*, trans. C. V. Wedgwood (London, 1939), p. 47.

26. Sanuto, *I diarii*, vol. 52 (full citation given in n. 2), cols. 606–9: "Et finite certe oratione, che per la capella si cantavano, . . ."

27. Ibid., cols. 613–18: "il diacono prese il messal et andò un poco discosto da l'altar et cantò il vangelio."

28. Ibid., cols. 606–9.

29. Ibid., cols. 613–18: "Finito, lo reverendo maistro di le cerimonie [Biagio da Cesena] dete a basar il libro a Nostro Signor, et il reverendissimo episcopo di Rogias dete a basar a Cesare." Marco Allegri, Nicolò Barozzi, and Guglielmo Berchet, the editors of vol. 52 of Sanuto's *Diarii*, identify the "episcopo di Rogias" with Ferdinando de Valdés (p. 787). Valdés (d. 1568) was successively bishop of Elne in France (1529–30), and of Orense (1530–32), Oviedo (1532–39), Leon (1539), Siguenza (1539–46), and Sevilla (1546–68) in Spain; see Eubel, *Hierarchia Cathol-ica* (full citation given in n. 21), especially pp. 138, 208, 228, 238, 283, and 315. At the time of his participation in the imperial coronation ceremonies, he had only recently become bishop of Orense, on January 12, 1530; see Eubel, ibid., p. 138.

30. Sanuto, *I diarii*, vol. 52 (full citation given in n. 2), cols. 613–18: "Et poi li cantori cominziorno a cantar et far una bela musica. . . . mentre che li cantori cantavano la soa musica, il reverendissimo [Cardinal] Hincvorth si voltò con le spale a l'altar . . . , et pigliò la patena in mano. Alhora Cesare . . . andò a l'altar. . . . Gionto che fu Sua Maestà dinanzi il reverendissimo Hincvorth si in-genochiò. . . . Alhora sua reverendissima signoria dete a basciar la patena a Ce-sare. . . . Sua Maestà andò . . . al suo locho. . . . Finita che fu la messa, il papa si levò in piedi, et disse: *Adiutorium nostrum in nomine Domini*, et dete la benedi-tion. Et . . . li reverendissimi cominciorno ad ussir di capela; et cussì [also] il papa et imperator. . . . et il papa andò a le sue stantie et l'imperator a le sue."

31. Pastor, *History of the Popes* (full citation given in n. 1), p. 93.

32. On the location of the papal and imperial singers, see the texts from Vasari and Sanuto in nn. 53 and 56 to this chapter.

33. Pastor, *History of the Popes* (full citation given in n. 1), p. 93.

34. Ibid., pp. 93–94. In Tiziana Bernardi, "Analisi di una cerimonia pubblica. L'incoronazione di Carlo V a Bologna," in *Quaderni storici*, n.s., 61 (1986): 171–99, in particular p. 179, there is a plan of the Church of San Petronio that greatly facilitates one's visualization of the various stages in the coronation's ceremonial action.

35. Pastor, *History of the Popes* (full citation given in n. 1), p. 93.

36. Vicomte Terlinden, "La politique italienne de Charles Quint et le 'Triomphe' de Bologne," in Jean Jacquot, ed., *Les Fêtes de la Renaissance*, vol. 2: *Fêtes et cérémonies au temps de Charles-Quint* (Paris, 1960), pp. 29–43, especially pp. 38–39. On the reference to the attendees in the choir of the Church, see Sanuto, *I diarii*, vol. 52 (full citation given in n. 2), cols. 629–38: "entrarono in capela, over choro, qual era così pieno di gente et persone da conto, che'l pontefice hebbe fatica andare al suo loco."

37. Sanuto, *I diarii*, vol. 52, cols. 625–26: "seguivano li provisionati del papa, et lui portato in pontifical *cum* il regno suo. Et entrato in capela, subito si cominciò a cantar nona secondo il solito."

38. Terlinden, "La politique italienne" (full citation given in n. 36).

39. Pastor, *History of the Popes* (full citation given in n. 1), p. 93.

40. Terlinden, "La politique italienne," and "Prima et seconda Coronatione" (full citation given in n. 19), p. 62.

41. Sanuto, *I diarii*, vol. 52 (full citation given in n. 2), cols. 629–38: "poi andando prima il clero cantando certo responso qual dice: «*Petre, amas me?—Domine tu scis quia amo te.—Pasce oves meas*», vene a la porta grande, dove andorono doi vescovi cardinali zioè [Alessandro] Farnese et [Lorenzo] Campeggio *cum* le mitrie et piviali." See also Baronio and Rinaldi, *Annales ecclesiastici*, vol. 20 (full citation given in n. 19), entry no. 18, on the singing of the response "Petre amas me?" On Cardinal Farnese (d. 1549), see Eubel, *Hierarchia Catholica* (full citation given in n. 21), p. 5. Farnese was raised to the cardinalate by Pope Alexander VI on September 20, 1493; he himself was elected Pope Paul III on October 13, 1534. On Cardinal Campeggio (d. 1539), see Eubel, *Hierarchia Catholica*, p. 17; Campeggio was named to the cardinalate in the famous promotion of July 1, 1517, when Pope Leo X created thirty-one cardinals.

42. Sanuto, *I diarii*, vol. 52 (full citation given in n. 2), cols. 629–38: "[Cardinals Farnese and Campeggio and the emperor] veneno a l'altar grande, abasso del quale era fata certa stangata per assimiliarlo a la soto confessione di San Pietro a Roma, dove Sua Maestà si inzinochiò et li due vescovi cardinali disceseno a lui, . . . inginochiati cantorno le litanie dicendo «*ora pro eo*». For assistance with the translation and interpretation of this passage, I am grateful to Nino Pirrotta. On the "confessio" and column screen of Old St. Peter's, see J. B. Ward Perkins, "The Shrine of St. Peter and its Twelve Spiral Columns," in *Journal of Roman Studies* 42 (1952): 21–33 and plates 1–7; for this reference and for useful advice I am grateful to John Shearman. The "Prima et seconda Coronatione," cited in n. 19, adds the following interesting details concerning the singing of the Litanies, although as one sees it identifies the two cardinals as Campeggio and Innocenzo Cibo rather than Campeggio and Farnese (p. 63): "Altri dui Rev. venero cioè il priore de diaconi che [was] il Rev. Cibo et il priore de preti che fu il Rev. Campeggio parati con piviali e mitre[;] il prior de Diaconi[,] ambidue genuflessi[,] comincio le Letanie e li suddiaconi, secretarii e capellani imperiali con li cantori imperiali replicava con alta voce." The account in Baronio and Rinaldi, *Annales ecclesiastici* (full citation given in n. 19), (entries nos. 21–22), similarly identifies the cardinals responsible for performing the Litanies as Campeggio and Cibo: "Interea reuerendissimus dominus Innocentius Cibo prior diaconorum dalmatica et mithra indutus, super uno cussino ante se super uno scabello librum laetaniarum habens; a sinistris electi Imperatoris et a dextris, super humili cussino reuerendissimus dominus Laurentius Campegius prior Cardinalium presbyterorum, ante se habens aliud scabellum commoniti superueuerunt et genuflexi sunt. Tum Cardinalis Cibo laetanias inchoauit alta voce cantando, et sibi respondentibus cantoribus: quas cum primum incoepit, electus Imperator prostrauit se super humili scabello panno aureo cooperto, et duobus cussinis deauratis sub brachiis, et duobus aliis sub genibus: duo Cardinales diaconi associantes, ac principes et proceres alii omnes retro Caesarem omnes genuflexi. Cantatis laetaniis per praefatum priorem diaconorum mox reuerendissimus Campegius prior presbyterorum et alii omnes Cardinales, praelati et principes sine mithris, et detectis capitibus super electum Caesarem adhuc prostratum alta voce dixit versiculos et orationes infrascriptas, videlicet"; and the account goes on to specify the texts that were sung.

43. Vasari, "Incoronatione successa in Bologna jnel 29 di Carlo quinto per mano di papa Cle[mente] VII alli 24 di feb[rai]o giorno di s[an]to Mathia," in *Lo*

Zibaldone di Giorgio Vasari, ed. Alessandro del Vita (Rome, 1938), pp. 91–107: "Fu poi lo Imperatore accompagnato da [Cardinal] Farnese per esser più vecchio et Decano del Collegio de Cardinali nella Cappella di San Mauritio dove disfibbiatoli la [emperor's] dalmatica li fu unta la spalla, et il braccio destro de olio sacro, fatte queste cose, subito fu cominciato la messa solenne con mirabil musica a coro doppio, la qual messa era celebrata dal Papa et lo Imperatore in habito sacro lo serviva all'altare." Vasari's account has been characterized, correctly, as little more than a translation of the relevant passages from Paolo Giovio's *Historiarum sui temporis* (Florence, 1552); see Del Vita's introductory note on p. 91 of the *Zibaldone*, and T.S.R. Boase, *Giorgio Vasari: The Man and the Book* (Princeton, 1979), p. 16. An answer to Nino Pirrotta's question as to the meaning of Giovio's reference to "alternantibus choris" in his description of the musical performance ("Die Erwähnung von Musik '*alternantibus choris*' in der Beschreibung des P. Giovio [1530] kann ebenso auf den Wechsel von ein- und mehrst. Ausführung wie auf Mitw. eines zweiten Chores [wie 1515 die frz. Hofkapelle] bezogen werden," "Rom, C. Spätmittelalter und Renaissance, II. Die Zeit der Hochrenaissance [1513–1550]," in *Die Musik in Geschichte und Gegenwart*, 17 vols. [Kassel and Basel, 1949–86], vol. 11, cols. 702–7, especially col. 703) is suggested by Vasari's account of the event and his reference to a *coro doppio*; see also Giordani, *Della venuta e dimora* (full citation given in n. 9), pp. 124 ff., and Ghiselin Danckerts's reference in his *Trattato*, as cited in Edmond Vander Straeten, *La musique aux pays-bas avant le XIXᵉ siècle*, 8 vols. (Brussels, 1867–88), vol. 6, p. 384: "più volte [the papal chapel] è stato visto ai tempi nostri, et tra le altre in Bologna, ove al tempo che Papa Clemente settimo donò la corona imperiale à Carlo Quinto, cantavano loro capelle ricetto." Joseph Schmidt-Görg has suggested (Nicolai Gombert, *Opera Omnia*, 11 vols. [Rome, 1951–75], vol. 2, p. 1) that Gombert's mass based on Richafort's chanson *Sur tous regretz*, which is entitled "A la Incoronation" in the first edition (Venice: Hieronymus Scotus, 1542), may have been the one sung at the coronation ceremonies.

44. Sanuto, *I diarii*, vol. 52 (full citation given in n. 2), cols. 629–38: "Et di poi, per il maestro di le cerimonie, disposte tutte queste insegne sopra l'altar, se ne tornorono sue signorie a li soi deputati lochi . . . , cantandosi . . . il *Kyrie* et la *Gloria*: et per il pontifice da la sede sua fu cantata l'oration del giorno et una per lo imperator." See also "Prima et seconda Coronatione di Carlo Quinto" (full citation given in n. 19), p. 64: "il Marchese di Monferrato, il Duca di Urbino, il Duca di Baviera, et il Duca di Savoia andaro al altare et in mano del sacrista e maestro de le cerimonie disposero il Scettro, la spada con la vagina e cingolo, il Pomo e la Corona, mentre il choro cantava lo Introito et il Kirie," and Baronio and Rinaldi, *Annales ecclesiastici* (full citation given in n. 19), entry no. 26: "tum Gloria in excelsis, etc. per Papam intonata cantores prosecuti sunt. . . . Finita Gloria, &c. Surgens Pontifex sine mithra versus populum dixit cantando: Pax uobis; et respon. &c. Et cum spiritu tuo, per cantores, dua orationes primam de die et alteram pro electo sub una conclusione: quibus expletis sedit Papa reassumpta mithra."

45. Sanuto, *I diarii*, vol. 52, cols. 645–51: "fu cantata la epistola per lo [Giovanni] Alberino subdiacono, et per missier Brazo Martelli camerier del papa . . . un'altra epistola in greco." On the subdeacon Alberino's participation in the cere-

monies, see also Baronio and Rinaldi, *Annales ecclesiastici* (full citation given in n. 19), entry no. 27: "Dominus Ioannes Alberinus subdiaconus apostolicus indutus paramentis subdiaconatus epistolam Latinam cantauit cum caeremoniis solitis, Graecam vero epistolam N. Florentinus [i.e., Braccio Martelli] camerarius Papae." Alberino may be identical with the "Joh. Bapt. de Alberinis," listed as one of Clement VII's "scriptores s. penitentiariae" by Walther von Hofmann, *Forschungen zur Geschichte der kurialen Behörden*, 2 vols. (Rome, 1914), vol. 2, p. 194.

46. Giorgio Vasari, *Le opere*, ed. Gaetano Milanesi, 9 vols. (Florence, 1878–85), vol. 8, pp. 167–73. However, as Professor Hale suggested to me, one has to regard Vasari's identifications in the *Ragionamenti* of the individuals portrayed in his frescoes with caution, since in some instances they are ex post facto fabrications. I am grateful to Professor Hale for his observation.

47. Ibid., p. 172.

48. Ibid., p. 171.

49. Ibid.

50. Ibid.

51. Michael Baxandall, *Painting and Experience in Fifteenth Century Italy* (Oxford, 1972), p. 72.

52. Vasari, *Le opere* (full citation given in n. 46), p. 169.

53. Ibid., p. 170; Vasari wrote: "In questa prospettiva delle colonne vi ho accomodato in alto il pergamo della cappella, dove fu la musica doppia del papa e di sua maestà, i quali cantarono solennissimamente quella messa, e risposono all'altre orazioni."

54. On Thiebault, see n. 12 to this chapter.

55. On the representation of the trumpeters, see Vasari, *Le opere* (full citation given in n. 46), p. 169, and on their playing at the moment of Investiture, see Giordani, *Della venuta e dimora* (full citation given in n. 9). pp. 124ff. On the ephemeral decoration of the Church, see Vasari, *Le opere*, p. 168; Vasari, however, does not mention the various representations of Clement's coat of arms.

56. Sanuto, *I diarii*, vol. 52 (full citation given in n. 2), cols. 629–38: "vene . . . il primo de li subdiaconi apostolici con altri subdiaconi e con i capelani suoi al luoco de le letanie, dove cantorono le laudi a lo imperator dicendo: «*Exaudi Christe*» et respondergli alcuni [others] che erano sopra il choro con li cantori: «*Domino Carolo invictissimo imperatori et semper augusto salus et victoria*». La qual laude replicata tre fiate, il primo dei diaconi disse: «*Salvator mundi*»; et lor risposeno: «*Tu illum adiuva*»; et poi disseno: «*Sancta Maria . . . tu illum adiuva*». Et in questa forma cantorono le litanie, rispondendo sempre: «*Tu illum adiuva*». See also Baronio and Rinaldi, *Annales ecclesiastici* (full citation given in n. 19), entry no. 30.

57. Sanuto, *I diarii*, vol. 52 (full citation given in n. 2), cols. 645–51: "Et poi comparse il maestro di le cerimonie a meza capela con il reverendissimo [Alessandro] Cesarino, et fate le debite reverentie, sua signoria reverendissima cantò lo evangelio come è solito cantarsi. Et finito, un altra volta comparse el mastro de le cerimonie con lo arzivescovo de Rodi [Marcus, *Ordinis Praedicatorum*], qual fato ancor lui le debite reverentie cantò lo evangelio in greco. Finito lo evangelio lo

imperator se mise a seder perfino che fu cantato el *Credo* in canto figurato. . . .
Finito che fu le secrete il papa disse el prefatio et molto bene, per haver bona voce,
et esser perfeto musico. . . . al *Pax tecum*, lo imperator si levò di l'altare, et basciò
in boca il papa et ritornassi ad inzenochiar al loco suo. Et . . . il papa se levò di
l'altar, et ritornsene a la sedia, come è costume, et l'imperator ancor lui a la sua.
Et in questo mezo se cantava lo *Agnus Dei*." See also "Prima et seconda Coronatione" (full citation given in n. 19), p. 64: "si canto il tratto et levangelio Latino
dal Rev. Cesarini, Greco dal Arcivescovo di Rodi," and Baronio and Rinaldi, *Annales ecclesiastici* (full citation given in n. 19), entry no. 30: "& reuerendissimus
Cardinalis Caesarinus diaconus euangelii capiens librum euangeliorum ante pec-
tus, factis Papae & altari debitis inclinationibus, posuit illum super altari, & inde
praecedente socio meo accedens ad Pontificem osculatus est manum sub auri-
phrigio. Rediens ad altare cum inclinationibus solitis genuflexus ante altare dixit:
Munda cor meum, &c. tum recipiens librum, thuriferario & ceroferariis
praecedentibus, ante Papam inclinatus petiit benedictionem dicens. Iube domne
benedicere; & Pontifex respondit: Dominus sit in corde tuo, &c. Tum descendens
ad locum euangelii paratum cum caeremoniis & solemnitatibus solitis cantauit
euangelium Latinum. Mox episcopus Scaliensis Hispanus assumens librum
euangelii Graecum factis reuerentiis debitis, & seruatis caeremoniis cum suo
diacono Graeco cantauit euangelium Graecum. . . . Mox Papa intonauit: Credo,
&c. & cantoribus continuantibus." On Cardinal Cesarini (d. 1542), see Eubel, *Hierarchia Catholica* (full citation given in n. 21), p. 18; he was raised to the cardinalate in the promotion of July 1, 1517, on which see n. 41 to this chapter. On the
identity of the archbishop of Rhodes, see Eubel, *Hierarchia Catholica*, p. 303; he,
like the bishop of Orense (see n. 29 to this chapter), had only recently been named
to his position (January 24, 1530). It is understandable, of course, that the archbishop of Rhodes in particular should have been selected to chant the Gospel in
Greek. For evidence that Clement maintained "chantori dello evangelio in
linghua greca," see A.-M. Bragard, "Détails nouveaux sur les musiciens de la cour
du Pape Clément VII," in *Revue Belge de Musicologie* 12 (1958): 5–18, especially
p. 12.

58. Terlinden, "La politique italienne" (full citation given in n. 36), p. 40.

59. Vasari, "Incoronatione successa" (full citation given in n. 43), p. 100: "si
udirno la gran grida et il suono delle trombe, et lo strepito de tamburi."

60. Pastor, *History of the Popes* (full citation given in n. 1), p. 95.

61. Sanuto, *I diarii*, vol. 52 (full citation given in n. 2), cols. 629–38: "lo imperador . . . fece molti cavalieri, fra li quali . . . molti gentilhomeni todeschi et di ogni
sorte moltissimi. . . . [V]eneno . . . li canonici lateranensi incontro a Sua Maestà
a la porta principal di la chiesa, dove . . . da loro fu honorevolmente receputo, et
da poi che l'hebbe basciata la croce et le reliquie . . . gli andorono inanti cantando:
Te Deum laudamus. Et a l'altar grande, . . . Sua Maestà fece oration, et . . . levatosi
basciò l'altar et si pose la corona et fu riceputo in canonico et fratelo de la chiesa
lateranense. . . . Et poi Sua Maestà vene con la sua compagnia per la più breve al
palazo. La via . . . era coperta de pani; le case tute fornite di arme et verdure." See
also Baronio and Rinaldi, *Annales ecclesiastici* (full citation given in n. 19), entry
no. 45: "Caesar cum suis proceribus et comitiua nobilium et praelatorum progre-

diens ad ecclesiam S. Dominici ibi a Laurentio episcopo Signino et episcopo An-
agnino uicario una cum nonnullis aliis canonicis S. Ioannis Lateranensis, qui Bo-
noniam uenerant, et ad haec uti procuratores aliorum canonicorum S. Ioannis de
urbe, in porta ecclesiae existentibus processionaliter cum cruce et aliis reliquiis
obuiam uenientes, crucem Caesari osculandam obtulerunt, et receperunt pro-
cedentes ante eum, Te Deum laudamus, intonantes et cantantes usque ad capel-
lam magnam a manu sinistra in introitu."

62. Pastor, *History of the Popes* (full citation given in n. 1), p. 95.

63. Vasari, "Incoronatione successa" (full citation given in n. 43), p. 106: "Era
una grandissima sala dove s'haveva a mangiare, tutta apparata de arazzi,
congiunta la camera del Card. [Ippolito] De Medici: nella quale l'Imperatore . . .
familiarmente si ritirò, havendo mandato fuora quasi tutti i servitori et quivi si
trasse il manto . . . et messesi una vesta di broccato d'oro, lunga fino a piedi. . . .
[A] suon di pifferi et trombe s'incominciò a portare le vivande in tavola con
meraviglioso ordine."

64. Sanuto, *I diarii*, vol. 52 (full citation given in n. 2), cols. 645–51: "finì el
pranzo, qual fu molto lauto, con diversi soni et musiche."

65. [Fol. Ai^r:] *COMEDIA DI AGOSTINO RICCHI DA LVCCA, INTITTOLATA I TRE
TIRANNI Recitata in Bologna a N. Signore, et a Cesare, Il giorno de la Commemora-
tione de la Corona di sua Maestà. Con Priuilegio Apostolico, et Venitiano.* M. D.
XXXIII. [Fol. Aii^r:] A lo Illustriss. et Reuerendiss. Signore Hippolito Il Cardinal
de Medici. . . . [Fol. qiv^r:] Stampata in Vinegia per Bernardino de Vitali, Adi xiiii
di Sette[m]bre del *MDXXXIII.* [Fol. Aiii^r:] "fu la presente Comedia . . . com-
posta, per apparentarsi in Bologna davanti al a S. di N. S. *CLEMENTE* VII. et a
CARLO Quinto [in a hall in the Palazzo Comunale] . . . nel giorno de la Commem-
oratione de la Corona di sua Maiesta." I have used the copy of the print in the
Chapin Library at Williams College. The assumption that the performance of *I tre
tiranni* occurred in early March of 1530 rests on a passage in the seventeenth-cen-
tury history of Bologna of Giovan Francesco Negri, *Annali di Bologna*: "La sera
di questo giorno, nel quale Sua Maestà haveva fatto una solenissimo convito a
tutti i Principi per celebrare l'ottavo giorno della sua coronatione fece recittar in
Palazzo una comedia piacevole e ridicula intitolata i tre Tiranni . . . con l'assis-
tenza del Papa, e di tutte le corte." See Michel Plaisance, "*I tre tiranni*, comédie
d'Agostino Ricchi représentée a Bologne devant Clément VII et Charles Quint.
En 1530 ou en 1533?" in *La fête et l'écriture: Théâtre de Cour, Cour-Théâtre en Espagne et en Italie, 1450–1530*, Colloque International, France-Espagne-Italie, Aix-en-
Provence, 6.7.8 Décembre 1985, Etudes Hispano-Italiennes N° 1 (Aix-en-Provence, 1987), pp. 321–33, especially p. 322. The Forni reprint of the 1533 edition of
Ricchi's text, with its "très documentée" introduction by Roberto Trovato where
Negri's text was published for the first time, was not available to me. Plaisance, "I
tre tiranni," reviews the whole question of the date of the performance and offers
an argument for a revision of the traditional dating. I do not feel qualified to offer
an opinion concerning his thesis, however, and I refer the reader to his article.

66. Nino Pirrotta, *Music and Theater from Poliziano to Monteverdi* (Cambridge,
1982), p. 78.

67. Ibid.

68. [Fol. fiii^v:] *"PHILE.[NO]* Prendi questo leuto, & per uscire di tanto duolo; fa che suoni, & canti qualche Canzone allegra. *CHR.[ISAULO]* Altro non posso cantar, se non di quel, che dentro il core mi muoverà. *PHIL.* Sù non star più, ch'io senta. *MADRIGALE. CHR.* Non vedrà mai queste mie luci asciutte / In alcun tempo il Cielo. . . . [Fol. fiv^r:] *PHIL.* Ah, tu sei pur di bello in su la grossa O che Canzone è quella, da cantare il di de morti."

69. Pirrotta, *Music and Theater* (full citation given in n. 66), p. 84 n. 25.

70. [Fol. kiv^v:] "Philócrate cognosciuto il suo errore esce uestito di sacco predicando; Et in penitenza del suo fallo delibera andare a san Iacopo di Galitia. . . . [Fol. lii^r:] *PHIL.* Apparecchiate la strada al Signore, / Diceva il gran Battista nel diserto. . . . [Fol. miv^v:] Philócrate ritornato di Spagna . . . uiene in habito di Pelegrino."

CHAPTER 12

1. On the events of the "restoration" of 1530–31, see Rudolf von Albertini, *Firenze dalla repubblica al principato* (Turin, 1970), pp. 179–201. Albert Dunning, *Die Staatsmotette 1480–1555* (Utrecht, 1970), pp. 298–302, relates Francesco Corteccia's motet *Laetare et exsulta* to Alessandro's return to Florence in 1531.

2. Starn, *Donato Giannotti and His "Epistolae": Biblioteca Universitaria Alessandrina, Rome, MS. 107* (Geneva, 1968), p. 42.

3. Von Albertini, *Firenze dalla repubblica al principato* (full citation given in n. 1), p. 200.

4. See, on *Giovanetta regal*, Thomas W. Bridges, "The Publishing of Arcadelt's First Book of Madrigals" (Ph.D. dissertation, Harvard University, 1982), pp. 42–43. In addition, Howard Brown has suggested that the reference to "margherita" ("daisy") in Corteccia's *Nuovo fior'è apparso al nostro cielo* may be to Margaret, although he does not relate the madrigal to a particular historical event; see "A Typology of Francesco Corteccia's Madrigals," in *The Well Enchanting Skill: Essays in Honour of F. W. Sternfeld*, ed. John Caldwell et al. (Oxford, 1990), pp. 3–28, especially pp. 20–21 and corresponding n. 45.

5. "Addì 16. daprile 1533. la figliuola di Carlo Imperadore non legittima d'età danni 9. e donna del signore Alexandro del Ducha Lorenzo de' Medici non legittima entrò in Firenze." Cambi, "Istorie," ed. Fr. Ildefonso di San Luigi, 4 vols., *Delizie degli eruditi toscani*, vols. 20–23 (Florence, 1786), vol. 4, p. 127–29.

6. *Il luogo teatrale di Firenze*, ed. Mario Fabbri et al. (Milan, 1975), pp. 67–68, catalog entry no. 1.36. On the *festa di San Felice* generally and its allegorical significance for the Medici, see Françoise Decroisette, "Fêtes religieuses, fêtes princières au XVIe siècle: Les Médicis et la fête de l'Annonciation à Florence," in *Culture et religion en Espagne et en Italie aux XVe et XVIe siècles*, Université de Paris-Vincennes, Documents et travaux de l'équipe de recherche culture et société au XVIe siècle, no. 4 (Abbeville, 1980), pp. 11–41.

7. Florence, BNC, MS N. A. 982, fols. 161^r–173^r, "Ragionamento di Niccolò di Stefano Fabbrini. . . . Dove si tratta delle Feste e magnificenze fatte alla Duchessa del mese d'Aprile 1533"; the reference to the "festaiuoli" is on fol. 163^v; Niccolò's explanation of the title of the *festa* ("festa di san Felice vuol dire la festa della

Annuntiatione della Vergine Maria, ma chiamasi di san Felice perché la si rappresenta in detta chiesa") occurs on fol. 164ʳ; the brief reference to the musical element ("melodie, suoni, musica et altri diletti") occurs on fol. 164ᵛ; the synopsis of the plot ("viene un Angelo e Annuntia la festa, esortando ciascuno a stare attento; dipoi chiama a uno a uno molti Profeti e sibille, comandando a ciascuno che dica quello che sa della Incarnatione del figl[i]o di Dio; e quali venuti alla presentia di detto Ang[e]lo, p[er] una sola stanza, dice cantando quello che gl'ha profetato del Nasc[e]re del Messia. . . . Al fine de quali profeti, s'apre il Cielo co[n] balli, suoni e feste, et v'è l'angelo Gabriello in mezzo di sei Angeli esultando e ballando, e Dio Padre l'impone l'ambasciata che gl'ha a dire alla Vergine Maria, la quale, scendendo dalla Nugola, saluta la vergine e dicegli le parole del Vangelo di Santa Luca, che comincia Missus est, e quivi rispondendo la Vergine Maria e l'angelo, alfine la Vergine dice: Ecce ancilla D[omi]ne, et l'Angelo si ritorna in Cielo; la Vergine impone il Cantico Magnificat, et li angioli sequitandolo, e con altri suoni e canti tornati in Cielo, si chiude el Cielo, et è finita") occurs on fols. 165ʳ⁻ᵛ. I should note that my transcription differs in some details from that which appears in Fabbri, *Il luogo teatrale* (full citation given in n. 6), pp. 67–68, catalog entry no. 1.36.

8. Michael Baxandall, *Painting and Experience in Fifteenth-Century Italy* (Oxford, 1972), p. 71.

9. Scipione Ammirato, *Istorie fiorentine*, quoted in Fabbri, *Il luogo teatrale* (full citation given in n. 6), pp. 65–66, catalog entry no. 1.29: "In S. Felice l'Annunciazione della Vergine, nel Carmine l'Ascensione di Cristo in Cielo; [and] in Santo Spirito quando egli manda lo Spirito Santo à gli Apostoli."

10. Jacopo Nardi, *Istorie della Città di Firenze*, quoted in Fabbri, *Il luogo teatrale* (full citation given in n. 6), p. 66, catalog entry no. 1.29: "Vergine Annunziata, che si rappresentò con ingegnoso e maraviglioso artifizio nella chiesa di San Felice in piazza."

11. Fabbri, *Il luogo teatrale* (full citation given in n. 6), pp. 63–64, catalog entry no. 1.25. On the use of the stage machinery, see Decroisette, "Fêtes religieuses" (full citation given in n. 6), pp. 17–18. On its design, see Pirrotta, *Music and Theater from Poliziano to Monteverdi* (Cambridge, 1982), p. 294 and corresponding n. 21. Photographs of a hypothetical reconstruction of the stage machinery, which assists in attempts to visualize the performance of 1533, may be found in Elvira Garbero Zorzi, "Le 'nozze' medicee del 1533 e le forme teatrali del principato," in *La fête et l'écriture: Théâtre de Cour, Cour-Théâtre en Espagne et en Italie, 1450–1530*, Colloque International, France-Espagne-Italie, Aix-en-Provence, 6.7.8 Décembre 1985, Études Hispano-Italiennes Nᵒ 1 (Aix-en-Provence, 1987), pp. 277–91, especially p. 287, and, less accessibly, in the "Itinerario" written for the exhibition, which resulted in the catalog *Il luogo teatrale di Firenze*, cited in n. 6. The frontispiece to the print Florence, BNC, E.6.7.53.¹⁶, reproduced here as figure 44, seems to be a kind of representation of Brunelleschi's stage machinery, since various details appear to correspond to elements of Brunelleschi's design; it too, therefore, assists in our attempts to imagine the artistic elements of the 1533 performance.

12. Pirrotta, *Music and Theater*, p. 20 and corresponding n. 46.

13. Becherini, "La musica nelle 'Sacre rappresentazioni' Fiorentine," in *Rivista musicale italiana* 53 (1951): 193–241, especially pp. 200–201; Becherini suggests, not implausibly, that Gabriel's *lauda Da cielo io sono mandato* was also sung. Belcari's text is published in Alessandro d'Ancona, ed., *Sacre rappresentazioni dei secoli XIV, XV e XVI*, 3 vols. (Florence, 1872), vol. 1, pp. 167–89.

14. See the text of *Laudate el sommo Dio* as edited by G. C. Galletti in *Lavde spiritvali di Feo Belcari, di Lorenzo de' Medici, di Francesco d'Albizzo, di Castellano Castellani e di altri* (Florence, 1863), p. 85; and, on the print containing it, p. IV. The *lauda* is also contained in the manuscript Venice, Biblioteca Marciana, Ital., classe IX, 78 (6453), fol. 88ʳ; see A. Feist, "Mitteilungen aus älteren Sammlungen italienischer geistlicher Lieder," in *Zeitschrift für romanische Philologie* 13 (1889): 115–85, especially p. 147, no. 601. I am grateful to Professor Jonathan Glixon for examining the manuscript and reporting on the entry in question. On the "cantasi come" rubrics that accompany many *lauda* texts, see, for example, Giulio Cattin, "I 'Cantasi come' in una stampa di laude della Biblioteca Riccardiana (Ed. r. 196)," in *Quadrivium* 19 (1978): 5–52.

15. On the *lauda Cristo, ver uomo e Dio*, see Galletti, *Lavde spiritvali*, p. 35, and, on the print containing it, p. IV.

16. *Cristo, ver uomo e Dio* is contained on fols. 47ᵛ–48ᵛ of Razzi's collection, *Libro Primo DELLE LAVDI SPIRITVALI DA DIVERSI ECCELL. E DIVOTI AVTORI, ANTICHI E MODERNI COMPOSTE. Raccolte dal R. P. Fra Serafino Razzi Fiorentino, . . .* (Venice, 1563).

17. I have taken the text of *Cristo, ver uomo e Dio* directly from Razzi's print; the text of *Laudate el sommo Dio* is taken directly from d'Ancona's edition of Belcari's text, *Sacre rappresentazioni* (full citation given in n. 13), pp. 178–79. For observations concerning the texts of the two *laude*, I am grateful to Professor Pirrotta.

18. Feist's index (see n. 14 to this chapter) contains entries that correspond closely, but not exactly, to the incipits of other portions of Belcari's text that may have been sung: the text of Gabriel's *lauda, Da cielo io sono mandato / Da Dio Padre verace / Annunziar la pace*, is similar to Feist's entry no. 295, *Da ciel mandato a salutar Maria*, which in the manuscript Venice, Biblioteca Marciana, Ital., classe IX, 77 is entitled *Di c[iel] m[andato] assaluatore M[aria], / Fu langielo ghabriello*; and the *terza rima* text corresponds closely to entries 1339–40 and 1347–48. On the Church of San Felice in Piazza, see Fabbri, *Il luogo teatrale* (full citation given in n. 6), p. 62, catalog entry no. 1.24.

19. Cambi, "Istorie" (full citation given in n. 5), pp. 127–29: "Addì 23. daprile 1533. il dì di S. Giorgio, el Ducha Alexandro . . . fece un magno, et gran convito, . . . e fecevisi commedie, e moresche." On the *moresca*, see Ingrid Brainard, "An Exotic Court Dance and Dance Spectacle of the Renaissance," in International Musicological Society, *Report of the Twelfth Congress, Berkeley 1977*, ed. Daniel Heartz and Bonnie Wade (Basel, Kassel, and London, 1981), pp. 715–29.

20. Niccolò di Stefano Fabbrini, "Ragionamento" (full citation given in n. 7), fols. 170ʳ–ᵛ: "In testa di detto cortile nella loggia verso borgo sa[n] Lorenzo era un parato d'una commedia con una bella prospettiva. . . . [I]n giovedì addì 24 d'Ap[ri]le si fece un convito nelle loggie del Cortile. . . . Et di poi [dinner] venne varie sorte di Maschere, e danzossi; per la sera una Comedia che fu finita a ore

quattro." The account seems to suggest that the stage set was constructed under the *loggia* that formed the south wall of the garden of Palazzo Medici (the "loggia verso borgo sa[n] Lorenzo"). The *convito*, on the other hand, seems to have taken place in the main *cortile*. In "Le 'nozze' medicee" (full citation given in n. 11) and in "L'hortus conclusus' tra gli archetipi del luogo teatrale," in *Firenze e la Toscana dei Medici nell'Europa del '500*, 3 vols., Biblioteca di storia toscana moderna e contemporanea, Studi e documenti, 26, vols. 1–3 (Florence, 1983), vol. 2, pp. 575–83, Elvira Garbero Zorzi has argued that the performance of the comedy on the twenty-fourth was the first to make use of the garden as a site for a theatrical performance; see "Le 'nozze' medicee," pp. 285–86, and "L'hortus conclusus,'" p. 576. However, as argued in my chapter 9, Cerretani's description of the decorations of Palazzo Medici for the wedding of Lorenzo and Madeleine suggests that the garden *loggia* was so used. Garbero Zorzi's article "Le 'nozze' medicee" contains much information about other festivities organized on the occasion of Margaret's 1533 visit; because they are incidental to my principal purpose here, however, I have not described them, and refer the reader instead to Zorzi's article.

21. For the remarks of Vettori, see von Albertini, *Firenze dalla repubblica al principato* (full citation given in n. 1), p. 357.

22. On the Fortezza, see J. R. Hale's characteristically stimulating article "The End of Florentine Liberty: The Fortezza da Basso," in *Florentine Studies*, ed. Nicolai Rubinstein (London, 1968), pp. 501–32, especially p. 501.

23. Ibid., pp. 509 and 512.

24. Ibid., pp. 509–10.

25. Ibid., p. 512.

26. Ibid., p. 513.

27. Archivio di Stato, Florence, Carte strozziane, ser. I, LXI, no. 51, as printed in *Le carte Strozziane del R. Archivio di Stato in Firenze, Inventario* (Florence, 1884–91), p. 317: "stamatina ad hore XIII et minuti 25 se è dato principio a fondare la Forteza."

28. Archivio di Stato, Florence, Carte strozziane, ser. I, XCV, fol. 20^r, as published in Luigi Dami, "La costruzione della Fortezza da Basso," in *Arte e storia*, 6th ser., 34 (1915): 162–66, especially pp. 164–65: "a lato al fosso si fece un apparato con uno altare in testa [of the platform], dove ci andò el Duca Alessandro el Sig. Alessandro Vitelli [the commander of the duke's guard] et altri gentilomini con tutta la sua corte e guardia; e con il reverendissimo M. Agniolo Marzi vescovo di Scesci, il quale disse la messa a detto altare." Camaiani, *Le carte Strozziane* (full citation given in n. 27): "Arrivato che fu Sua E.^{ta}, se dede principio a cantare la messa solenne." Carte strozziane, ser. I, XCV, fol. 20^r, as published in Dami: "e detto la messa detto Vescovo venne parato nel fosso dove si ordinava il fondamento di detta cittadella, cantando inni et altro; e finalmente la benedisse." Agniolo Marzi had long been a trusted Medici agent; on him, and on letters of recommendation he wrote on Cardinal Giulio de' Medici's behalf in 1522 for the lutenist Gian Maria Giudeo, see my article "Gian Maria Giudeo, Sonatore del Liuto, and the Medici," in *Fontes Artis Musicae* 38 (1991).

29. Vasari, in K. Frey, *Der literarische Nachlass Giorgio Vasaris* (Munich, 1923), pp. 40–41: "Messer Pietro [Aretino] Diuinissimo Venuto il Reuerendissimo [Agniolo] Marzi, postosi à sedere . . . fù spogliato dell'abito ordinario, sempre

salmeggiando con antifone et responsi et altri salmi. Appresso fù cominciato a uestire dell'abito pontificale con grandissime cerimonie; et poi uno stuolo di uoci con alcuni contrapunti cominciorno 'Spiritus Domini super orbem terrarum,' dando odoriferi incensi con profumi all'altare in particulare et di poi alle bandiere, che per detto castello doueuano seruire. Udi un' Chirie, che pareua fussi cantato da uoci celesti, et la terra pareua che si facessi lieta della 'Gloria,' ch'io senti intonare dal Reuerendissimo; alla quale fù risposto da una moltitudine di tromboni, cornetti et uoci, che certo si inchinaua per la dolcezza la testa, come quando si ha sonno intorno al fuoco. . . . [The oration] finito, fù da concenti di tromboni cominciato 'Veni, Sancte Spiritus'; et poi si seguito il uangelio, doppo il quale intonando il 'Credo,' gli fù risposto con assai più rumore [of the sort] che non si ode la quaresima al ponte uecchio intorno à una cesta di tinche. Finiro i cantori et ricominciaro, risposati, il uerso, che uà doppo, tal che ci riducemo al 'Prefatio' con tante cirimonie."

30. Ibid., p. 41: "armati di alcune arme diuinissime, che rassembraua il trionfo di Scipione nella seconda guerra Punica. Fù finita la Messa con una benedittione, che pareva che uenessi di cielo. . . . gli fù dato bandiera et bastone à ore diciannoue et minuti tre. . . . si senti un' rumore d'artiglierie et di trombe et archibusi [et] grida, [such] che pareua chel cielo et la terra et tutto 'l mondo rouinassi, et tanti caualli, che anitriuano con furia di paura et di rumore, [such] che si ste un'ora, innanzi che i uolti si uedessin' chiari per la quantita del fumo."

31. On the consultation of the astrologers, see Hale, "The End of Florentine Liberty" (full citation given in n̄. 22), p. 525; on the liturgical associations of the texts sung for the installation ceremony, see Carl Marbach, *Carmina scripturarum* (Hildesheim, 1963), pp. 278–79; and Willi Apel, *Gregorian Chant* (Bloomington, Ind., 1958), pp. 31 and 463–64; and on the masses sung during the Capitoline ceremonies and on the occasion of the conquest of Urbino, see my chapters 4 and 8.

CHAPTER 13

1. On Ippolito's biography, see Giuseppe E. Moretti, "Il cardinale Ippolito de' Medici dal trattato di Barcelona alla morte," in *Archivio storico italiano* 98 (1940): 137–78; and on the rumors concerning the circumstances of his death, J. R. Hale, *Florence and the Medici: The Pattern of Control* (London, 1977), p. 122.

2. J. R. Hale, "The End of Florentine Liberty: The Fortezza da Basso," in *Florentine Studies*, ed. Nicolai Rubinstein (London, 1968), pp. 501–32, especially p. 503.

3. Giuseppe Coniglio, "Note sulla società napoletana ai tempi di Don Pietro da Toledo," in *Studi in onore di Riccardo Filangieri*, 3 vols. (Naples, 1959), vol. 2, pp. 345–65, especially p. 345.

4. "Relation de l'entrée de Charles-Quint dans la ville de Naples," in Louis Prosper Gachard, ed., *Collection des voyages des souverains des Pays-Bas*, 4 vols. (Brussels, 1874–82), vol. 2, pp. 578–79: "Au sixiesme estoit une Joye couronnée de fleurs, avecs plusieurs nymphes qui chantoient." Among the participants in the imperial procession were trumpeters and *pifferi*, according to Gregorio Rosso, *Istoria delle cose di Napoli sotto l'imperio di Carlo V. cominciando dall'anno 1526. per insino all'anno 1537* (Naples, 1770), p. 62.

5. Rosso, *Istoria*, pp. 62–63: "andò lo Imperatore dalla Porta Capuana all'Arcivescovato, dove gionto, il Vicario, che veniva con esso, le dette l'acqua benedetta, e volendo inginocchiarsi, a me Eletto del Popolo toccò darle il coscino; e fatta orazione, mentre si cantava il *Te Deum laudamus* con musica solennissima, Antonio Mormile Eletto di Portanova li appresentò il Messale aperto, tenendo io li capitoli della Città in mano, & Ettorre Minutolo Eletto di Capuana le deze il giuramento, dicendoli, che tutti li Re & Imperatori soleno giurare in simili occasioni di allegrezza, di osservare li privilegj e grazie concesse da suoi antepassati a suoi vassalli . . . ; il che sentendo lo Imperatore se alzò in piedi, e posta la mano sopra lo messale, giurò di osservare, e far osservare ogni cosa inviolabilmente: il che in segno di allegrezza sonorno le trombette, e sparorno pezzi di artegliaria." Rosso remarked (p. 65) that his account was written some two years after the events he described. On Charles's *entrata*, and on the ceremony recounted here in particular, see also *Dell'istoria di notar Antonino Castaldo, libri quattro. Ne' quali si descrivono gli avvenimenti più memorabili succeduti nel Regno di Napoli sotto il Governo del Vicerè D. Pietro di Toledo* (Naples, 1769), pp. 49–55, especially p. 53.

6. Charles "sopra il suo grande e bel cavallo [paused] in mezzo la strada . . . (tra) tanti gridi, Imperio, Imperio; e le trombette, cornette, bifferi, e cantanti a ballo. Una dolce e grande melodia era sopra la Reale porta Capuana; erano molte altre trombette sopra le alte torri, e di donne ed uomini tutti li muri forniti e pieni." See "Racconti di Storia Napoletana," in *Archivio storico per le province napoletane* 33 (1908): 474–544 and 663–719, and 34 (1909): 78–117, especially p. 117.

7. Rosso, *Istoria* (full citation given in n. 4), p. 64: "La Città in tutto quello tempo, che ci stette l'Imperatore, comparse bellissima, e piena di . . . personaggi: oltre li Spagnoli, . . . ce vennero il Duca di Ferrara, il Duca di Urbino, il Duca di Fiorenza, e Don Ferrante Gonsaga Prencipe di Molsetti, e se ritrovava ancora in Napoli in quello tempo Don Francesco da Este Marchese della Padula."

8. Vincenzo Saletta, "Il viaggio in Italia di Carlo V (1535–36)," in *Studi Meridionali* 9 (1976): 286–327 and 452–79, 10 (1977): 78–114, 268–92, 420–42, and 11 (1978): 329–41, especially 10 (1977): 106–7.

9. Paolo Giovio, *Epistularum*, 2 vols. (Rome, 1956), vol. 1, p. 172, as cited in Saletta, "Il viaggio" (vol. 10), p. 106 n. 33: "cinquecento eletti archibugieri a cavallo e cinquanta celate borgognone con la lance alla coscia; aveva oltre di ciò 500 altri cavalli."

10. Rosso, *Istoria* (full citation given in n. 4), p. 64: "il Duca di Fiorenza era venuto per lo matrimonio promessoli, quale procuravano disturbarcelo alcuni Fiorentini, e li Cardinali Salviati & Ridolfi, pregando con umili supplicazioni l'Imperatore a volere restituire a Fiorenza la libertà, e con larghe promesse ancora accompagnavano le loro preghiere: ma non fecero niente, perchè l'Imperatore aveva proprio mala volontà con li Fiorentini, come genti de tutto core inclinati alla fazione Franzesa."

11. Ibid., pp. 65–66 and 68: "Tutto quello inverno, . . . non parse inverno, ma una continua primavera senza freddo, senza pioggia, senza vento, il cielo sereno sempre, che pareva che giosse con l'animo de Napoletani. Alli 19. di Dicembre . . . il Vicerè [Don Pietro da] Toledo fece all'Imperatore uno solennissimo banchetto allo giardino de Poggioreale; dove se pigliò l'Imperatore grandissima recreazione, e particolarmente da una Egloga o Farza pastorale, che ci fu molta ridicola. Alli 6.

di Gennaro nella ... piazza Carbonara si fece una bellissima giostra. . . . Nello Castello de Capuana la sera ce furono balli, e così seguitorno per parecchi giorni con la occasione delle nozze di Madama Margherita de Austria figlia delo Imperatore, benchè picciolissima di età, con lo Duca di Fiorenza. . . . Mentre il Sindico, e li Deputati ogni giorno se univano a Santo Lorenzo per le cose publiche, lo Imperatore se tratteneva in conviti & in feste per tutto quello Carnevale, convitato dalla Prencipe de Salerno, dallo Prencipe de Bisignano ... e dallo Vicerè Toledo, il quale un giorno apparecchiò una bella mascara, & una bella festa, dove chiamò tutte le belle donne, e Signore di Napoli, in casa dello Tesoriero Alonso Sances suo confidentissimo." On the joust in the Piazza di S. Giovanni a Carbonara and the *convito* at Sanchez's home, see also *Dell'istoria di notar Antonino Castaldo* (full citation given in n. 5), pp. 56–58.

12. Falco, *Antichità di Napoli e del suo amenissimo distretto*, 6th ed. (Naples, 1679), p. 42, as quoted in Donna Cardamone, *The "canzone villanesca alla napolitana" and Related Forms, 1537–1570*, 2 vols. (Ann Arbor, 1981), vol. 1, pp. 252–53 n. 1. My translation borrows from Cardamone, *The "canzone villansca alla napolitana,"* p. 105, and Karen Eales's translation of Nino Pirrotta, *Music and Theater from Poliziano to Monteverdi* (Cambridge, 1982), p. 108.

13. The quotations from Maffei's dispatch are taken from Coniglio, "Note sulla società napoletana" (full citation given in n. 3), especially p. 360. The translations are from Donna Cardamone's excellent article "The Debut of the *Canzone Villanesca alla Napolitana*," in *Studi musicali* 4 (1975): 65–130, especially p. 62 n. 2; and Nino Pirrotta, "Willaert and the *Canzone Villanesca*," in *Music and Culture in Italy from the Middle Ages to the Baroque* (Cambridge, Mass., 1984), pp. 175–97, especially pp. 175–76. Both Cardamone and Pirrotta relate the appearance of the print entitled *Canzone villanesche alla napolitana* (Naples, 1537) to Charles's visit. Maffei also reported on other musical performances he witnessed during his stay in Naples. On January 22, he and the Mantuan singer Pozino, who was in Maffei's company, were at the home of the princess of Salerno, who gave a reception that included a musical program in which a Catalan woman sang "nella viola maravigliosamente." Further, at the home of Artalo and Maria de Cardona, the count and countess of Culisano, Maffei and Pozino heard the count's and countess's daughter Antonia sing, and Maffei reported that "Prometto a V. Ex.a che mai il Pozino puoté cenare, tanto restò confuso et giurò di non toccare mai più viola, dicendo ch'el sa certo che gli Angeli et Arcangeli non cantano si suavemente e dolcemente. . . . io per me confesso non haver mai udito tal harmonia, né credo ch'ella habbi pari al mondo, et cosa da far stupire a terra et cielo, poi più lo tengo per certo, quando ho visto ch'el Pozino ha perso il manzar di dolcezza." On Maria di Cardona, an important patroness, see Carol MacClintock, *Giaches de Wert (1535–1596)*, Life and Works, Musicological Studies and Documents, no. 17 (n.p., 1966), p. 21 n. 11. The texts of Maffei's letters are not published in full, and the available excerpts (see Coniglio, "Note sulla società napoletana," p. 362) do not permit us to conclude that either the emperor or Alessandro were present; they do, nonetheless, demonstrate that the Carnival season in Naples in 1536 indeed passed in musical performances of various kinds, and they document once more how extraordinarily widespread was the practice of improvisatory singing. On the Mantuan ducal singer Pozino, the son of a Lorenzo da Pozo, see Iain Fenlon, *Music*

and Patronage in Sixteenth-Century Mantua, 2 vols. (Cambridge, 1980), vol. 1, p. 17 n. 18, p. 53, p. 68 n. 59, and pp. 171–72 doc. 2, and the references he cites.

14. Rosso, *Istoria* (full citation given in n. 4), p. 69: "Alli 2. di Febraro . . . l'Imperatore andò a Monte Oliveto, dove concorse tutta la Nobiltà, e Signoria Napolitana e forastera, che era in Napoli. Lo Imperatore magnò quella mattina in casa de [Ferrante Sanseverino] lo Prencipe di Salerno, dove la sera ci vennero tutte le Signore e gentildonne de Napoli, e si fece una bellissima Comedia." It has been argued that the comedy was the famous "farsa cavaiola" entitled *Ricevuta dell'Imperatore alla Cava*, but see Bonner Mitchell, *The Majesty of the State* (Florence, 1986), pp. 155–56, who expressed a reservation based on the inappropriateness of the text to an occasion when the emperor was present.

15. Pirrotta, *Music and Theater* (full citation given in n. 12), pp. 38 and 39, p. 40 and corresponding n. 9, and p. 106, and Giuseppe Ceci, "Il palazzo dei Sanseverino, principi di Salerno," in *Napoli nobilissima, Rivista di topographia ed arte napoletana* 7 (1898): 81–85, especially p. 83.

16. Saletta, "Il viaggio" (vol. 10) (full citation given in n. 8), p. 107 n. 36, following *Dell'istoria di notar Antonino Castaldo* (full citation given in n. 5), pp. 55–56.

17. Modesto Rastrelli, *Storia d'Alessandro de' Medici, Primo Duca di Firenze, Scritta, e corredata di inediti Documenti*, 2 vols. (Florence, 1781), vol. 2, p. 184.

18. "Nelle nozze fece fare lo Imp[erato]re una giostra nella quale ancor egli corse armato alla Moresca et immascheratosi danzò"; Florence, BNC, MS II. I. 313 (*olim* Magl. XXV. 17), fol. 153ᵛ, "La città di Firenze."

19. Rosso, *Istoria* (full citation given in n. 4), p. 70: "Il resto dello Carnevale finì in continue maschere, festi, banchetti, musiche, commedie, farze, & altre recreazioni, mascarandosi spesso Sua Maestà per la Città, quando in compagnia dello Vicerè Toledo, e quando con lo Marchese dello Vasto." See also *Dell'istoria di notar Antonino Castaldo* (full citation given in n. 5), p. 58.

20. Florence, BNC, MS II. I. 313 (full citation given in n. 18).

21. Saletta, "Il viaggio" (vol. 10) (full citation given in n. 8), pp. 114 and 430.

22. Ibid., p. 432.

23. The principal source for Margaret's *entrata* is Vasari's letter to Aretino of June 3; see *Opere*, ed. Gaetano Milanesi, 9 vols. (Florence, 1875–85), vol. 8, pp. 262–65, especially pp. 263 and 264–65: "giunse a' vent'otto [of May] . . . al Poggio a Caiano; la quale, vedendo tale edificio, stupì. . . . Era adorno moltissime stanze di sete d'oro ed altri drappi e corami, per la vergogna nol dico, senza lo esservi tanto grand'impeto di musica, e di che sorte maestri da insegnar cantare agli angioli le note celesti, senza i cornetti, tromboni, flauti, storte, violini, chitarre, liuti, che nel sonar loro si vedea che veniano da quella vera letizia che dalle barbe del cuore si suol partire." "E così entrata in Santa Maria del Fiore. . .e così detto una orazione, avuta la benedizione, cantato il *Veni Sancte Spiritus*, si partì."

24. Varchi, *Storia fiorentina*, ed. Lelio Arbib, 3 vols. (Florence, 1838–41), vol. 3, p. 223: "e addì tredici di giugno [1536] [Margaret] udì in san Lorenzo la messa del congiunto insieme col duca suo marito, la qual fu cantata da messer Antonio Pucci cardinale di Santi Quattro . . . ; e di poi . . . se ne vennero . . . al palagio de' Medici, là dove era apprestato un bellissimo convito . . . e dopo desinare si ballò alquanto, di poi si recitò una commedia." That Pucci celebrated the nuptial mass is also attested by the anonymous "Diario Di tutti i Casi Seguiti in Firenze . . ."

(Florence, BNC, MS Conventi C, 7, 2614, fol. 65). However, the date is given there as June 20. On contemporary nuptial rites, see Klapisch-Zuber, "Zacharias, or the Ousted Father: Nuptial Rites in Tuscany between Giotto and the Council of Trent," in *Women, Family, and Ritual in Renaissance Italy,* trans. Lydia G. Cochrane (Chicago, 1985), pp. 178–212, especially pp. 186–87.

25. I have borrowed liberally from the translation of Vasari's *Vita* of San Gallo in *Lives of the Most Eminent Painters, Sculptors, and Architects,* 3 vols., trans. Gaston Du. C. de Vere (New York, 1979). On the reconstruction of the *loggia,* see also Elena Povoledo's discussion in Pirrotta, *Music and Theater* (full citation given in n. 12), p. 342 n. 16. In its references to a single, two-tiered structure at the back of the stage that was apparently visible to the audience, Vasari's description suggests that the reconstruction in several respects evidently did not conform to Nicolò Sabbatini's recommendations in *Pratica di fabricar scene e machine ne' teatri* (Ravenna, 1638) that there be constructed "due palchi, cioè uno per ciascheduno dei lati della scena" and that "così si sarà accomodato il luogo di dentro per li musici, mentre non si siano veduti di fuori, secondo che l'esperienza persuade essere più sano consiglio." In other respects, however, it does seem to have conformed: because the structure was separate from the stage proper, there was no danger that the movements of the actors "sconcertarebbono gl'organi, et altri instromenti"; moreover, the structure left the entrances onto the stage clear, a feature of its design that may have appealed to San Gallo, as Vasari's account suggests. For Sabbatini's treatise, see Elena Povoledo's edition (Rome, 1955), p. 50, and Nino Pirrotta's discussion in "The Orchestra and Stage in Renaissance *Intermedi* and Early Opera," in *Music and Culture* (full citation given in n. 13), pp. 210–16, especially p. 212 and corresponding nn. 5–6.

26. See my chapter 10.

27. Hale, *Florence and the Medici* (full citation given in n. 1), p. 125.

28. Vasari, *Vita* of San Gallo (full citation given in n. 25).

29. For an account of Alessandro's assassination, see, for example, Eric Cochrane, *Florence in the Forgotten Centuries, 1527–1800* (Chicago, 1973), pp. 15–18.

30. See Hill, review of Pirrotta, *Music and Theater,* in *Journal of the American Musicological Society* 36 (1983): 519–26, especially p. 521 n. 2; and Pirrotta, *Music and Theater* (full citation given in n. 12), pp. 124–25. Hill and Pirrotta advance somewhat differing hypotheses about the order in which the madrigals might have been sung and their texts' possible relationship to the action of the comedy; I should note, however, that Pirrotta's thesis was offered in the abstract, without reference specifically to the text of Lorenzino's play. Howard M. Brown, "A Typology of Francesco Corteccia's Madrigals," in *The Well Enchanting Skill: Essays in Honour of F. W. Sternfeld,* ed. John Caldwell et al. (Oxford, 1990), pp. 3–28, especially pp. 27–28, speculates that Corteccia may have composed madrigals to serve as *intermedii* for *Aridosia;* he seems unaware of Hill's thesis concerning the Arcadelt cycle. I should add that Hill's thesis entails some minor difficulties. First, as we have seen, Vasari's description of the reconstruction of the *loggia* suggests in its reference to a second stage for the instrumentalists that the performance included other musical elements besides the vocal *intermedii;* second, the reference to a stage having been constructed specifically for the vocalists may imply that they were to be permanently stationed there, whereas the text of the first

madrigal in the cycle clearly suggests that they were fully visible to the audience and therefore presumably on stage when they performed (however, the careful distinction Vasari draws between the purposes to be served by the first and second platforms—the first at stage level, for the vocalists, and the second above, for "instruments that cannot be moved or changed with ease"—may imply on the contrary that the vocalists' platform was constructed at stage level precisely so that they could be clearly seen by the audience or, alternatively, so that they could move readily onto the stage at the appropriate moments). The *loggia* dei Tessitori has been restored and from its present state it is difficult to visualize the setting for the performance of *Aridosia*, as it was in June of 1536.

31. The document in question, Carte strozziane, serie I, 13, 3, fol. 12ʳ, "Nota delle boche di chasa di Sua Ex.ᵗⁱᵃ, levata questo dì VIII di luglio MDXXXV," was located in the Archivio di Stato by John Walter Hill and James Chater.

32. The references to Antonio da Lucca in Bartoli, Parabosco, and Lenzoni may be found in Andrew Minor and Bonner Mitchell, *A Renaissance Entertainment: Festivities for the Marriage of Cosimo I, Duke of Florence, in 1539* (Columbia, Mo., 1968), pp. 50 and 52–53; and in Bartoli and Lenzoni also in James Haar, "Cosimo Bartoli on Music," in *Early Music History* 8 (1988): 37–79, especially p. 70; the reference in Vasari is in *Opere*, vol. 6 (full citation given in n. 23), pp. 5–16, especially p. 7: "perciocchè essendo questo prete galantuomo e dilettandosi di pittura, di musica, e d'altri trattenimenti, praticavano nelle sue stanze che aveva in San Lorenzo molte persone virtuose, e fra gli altri messer Antonio da Lucca, musico e sonator di liuto eccellentissimo, che allora era giovinetto, dal quale imparò Giovann'Antonio a sonar di liuto." For this reference I am grateful to Sheryl Reiss. There is documentary evidence that Antonio continued in Medici service after Alessandro's murder; see Frank D'Accone, "The Florentine Fra Mauros. A Dynasty of Musical Friars," in *Musica disciplina* 33 (1979): 77–137, especially p. 137 doc. 88, a list of musicians in Duke Cosimo's service in 1543, which includes the name "Maestro Antonio da lLuccha musico." Contrary to what Haar argued, I think it unlikely that Bartoli's Antonio da Lucca is to be identified with the Antonio "dal Cornetto" who was in Ferrarese service in 1535 and then in the service of Cardinal Madruzzo of Trent; Bartoli's Antonio is likelier to have been someone with specifically Florentine associations, and the Antonio mentioned in the Medici documents and Vasari's life of Lappoli is a more plausible candidate. The documents D'Accone published reveal that several of the other musicians listed as Alessandro's employees in 1535 continued in Medici service: the 1543 document (doc. 88, p. 137) lists Giovanni da lLuccha and Mattio tronbone, among others; a 1559 document (doc. 87, pp. 136–37) lists Mathio di Giovanni trombone, Pietro Greco trombetto, and Santi di Francesco trombetto, among others; and later documents (docs. 83, 84, and 85, pp. 134, 135, and 135–36 respectively) again list Matteo Trombone (in one instance called Mattio di Giovanni Tronbone). Another instrumentalist known to have been in Alessandro's service who is *not* listed in the 1535 document is Lorenzo da Lucca trombone; see Marino Berengo, *Nobili e mercanti nella Lucca del cinquecento* (Turin, 1965), p. 151 and corresponding n. 1, on his service as Alessandro's employee. That he achieved some measure of renown is suggested by the fact that Bartoli mentioned him (see Haar, "Cosimo Bartoli," p.

72), as did Cellini in the autobiography (see *The Life of Benvenuto Cellini*, trans. J. A. Symonds [New York, 1920], pp. 36–37). And that he, too, continued in Medici service after Alessandro's death is suggested by the dedication "Al magnifico e Virtuoso messer Lorenzo da Lucca musico eccellentissimo dell'illustrissimo et eccellentissimo Duca di Fiorenza e di Siena" of Bartolomeo di Poggio's "Vita manoscritta di Vincenzo di Poggio nobile lucchese" (Lucca, Biblioteca governativa, MS 101; see Gabriella Biagi-Ravenni, "I Dorati, musicisti lucchesi, alla luce di nuovi documenti d'archivio," in *Rivista italiana di musicologia* 7 [1972]: 39–81, especially p. 68 n. 133); the fact that the duke of Florence is also called the duke of Siena indicates that the "Vita" was written after 1559—i.e., during Cosimo's time as duke—at the earliest. The documents published by D'Accone confirm that Lorenzo was indeed in Cosimo's service: he is listed in 1543 (p. 137, Lorenzo tronbone), in 1559 (pp. 136–37, Messer Lorenzo da Lucca trombone), and in 1564 (p. 134, Messer Lorenzo da Lucha Musicho).

33. Hale, *Florence and the Medici* (full citation given in n. 1), p. 7.

34. Cochrane, *Florence in the Forgotten Centuries* (full citation given in n. 29), book 1.

CONCLUSION

1. Hale, *Florence and the Medici: The Pattern of Control* (New York, 1977), pp. 83–84.

2. Ibid., p. 87.

3. The phrase is borrowed from Kenneth Levy, "On Gregorian Orality," in *Journal of the American Musicological Society* 43 (1990): 185–227, especially p. 187.

4. See Donna Cardamone, *The "canzone villanesca alla napolitana" and Related Forms, 1537–1570*, 2 vols. (Ann Arbor, 1975 and 1981). The rustic pieces sung by the Neapolitan minstrels are, of course, very different in kind from the "free, ecstatic deliveries" of the amateur instrumentalists, since they were preexistent works, performed presumably after some rehearsal.

5. *Music and Theatre from Poliziano to Monteverdi*, trans. Karen Eales (Cambridge, 1982).

6. Ibid., chapter 3.

7. Procacci, *History of the Italian People*, trans. Anthony Paul (New York, 1973), pp. 164–65.

8. Ibid., p. 164.

9. Cochrane, *Florence in the Forgotten Centuries, 1527–1800* (Chicago, 1973), p. xiv.

10. Cochrane, *Historians and Historiography in the Italian Renaissance* (Chicago, 1981), p. x.

11. Pirrotta has characterized the style of Verdelot's theatrical madrigals thus: "Chordal texture, a prevailing feature in many of the early madrigals, is also predominant in the music for Machiavelli's comedies, where it was doubly important because words spoken on stage needed to be especially clearly enunciated." See *Music and Theater* (full citation given in n. 5), p. 145. James Haar has similarly described the style of the early madrigal as "syllabically declaimed, completely

vocal chordal polyphony with a gently imitative coloration." See "The Early Madrigal," in *Music in Medieval and Early Modern Europe*, ed. Iain Fenlon (Cambridge, 1981), pp. 163–92, especially pp. 189–90.

12. On humanistic attitudes about music, see especially Pirrotta, "Music and Cultural Tendencies in Fifteenth-Century Italy" and "Novelty and Renewal in Italy: 1300–1600," now available in *Music and Culture in Italy from the Middle Ages to the Baroque* (Cambridge, Mass., 1984), pp. 80–112 and 159–74. The quotation is from *Music and Theater* (full citation given in n. 5), p. 248.

13. Brown, "A Cook's Tour of Ferrara in 1529," in *Rivista italiana di musicologia* 10 (1975): 216–41, especially p. 216.

INDEX